Death awaits . . .

Harry G. Plover had dumped his armload of trimmed twigs and other rubbish well back into the dark recesses of the jungle edge. Turning, his eye caught by a hint of motion—he checked—over *there*, in deep gloom. He peered into near-darkness, then scrambled back. His legs seemed to be trapped in an invisible syrup. He fought the rising panic.

"Oh, sure," Harry said to himself. "I'm having a nightmare—it'll be over in a moment." But the moment passed . . .

STAR COLONY

KEITH LAUMER

ACE SCIENCE FICTION BOOKS
NEW YORK

This Ace Science Fiction Book contains the complete
text of the original hardcover edition.

STAR COLONY

An Ace Science Fiction Book/published by arrangement with
St. Martin's Press

PRINTING HISTORY
St. Martin's edition / 1981
Ace edition / March 1983
Ninth printing / November 1986

ISBN: 0-441-78042-3

Ace Science Fiction Books are published by The Berkley Publishing Group,
200 Madison Avenue, New York, New York 10016.
PRINTED IN THE UNITED STATES OF AMERICA

INTRODUCTION

THE HISTORY OF COLMAR IN THREE VOLUMES
VOLUME ONE: STAR COLONY

Being a short history of the founding of humanity's
first extraterrestrial colony

by
Keith Laumer

This history is based on official Terran archives only recently released to scholars, as well as on letters and diaries of early settlers, supplemented by material from the Oral History Project initiated in honor of independent Colmar's Centennial celebration in CY 325 (AD 2437). For the first time, the authentic course of events has been extracted and separated from its overlay of myth and folklore. Prepared by a distinguished board of editors under the leadership of our world's preeminent chronicler, the present history, designed especially for use in the schools through post-doctorate levels, will lay to rest for all time, it is earnestly hoped, the maze of conflicting legendary and mythical accounts of Early Times, which have heretofore clogged scholarly avenues of inquiry into Colmar's settlement, the origin of the curious dichotomy that has existed between our East and North Continents, and the events leading to Unification and at last to Independence itself.

In a work of such scope, it would of course be quite impractical to recount every detail of those turbulent times. Instead the editors have chosen an anecdotal approach, at once livelier reading and most effective in communicating the spirit of long-gone times, as well as clarifying at last the early events which contributed importantly to Colmar's present global society.

It is felt that existing standard histories of the period beginning with Unification present an adequate account of Colmar's more recent years; accordingly, the present work is limited to the era prior thereto, an era in which our great Founding Families came to Omega from far-off Terra, a world toward which Omegan patriotism once seemed to require an attitude of implacable hostility, and not without reason. Latterly our relations with the mother planet have vastly improved, based on the genuine achievements of our common humanity.

The original picket vessel ordered into orbit by Captain Brill and supplied for an extended cruise was able to maintain its surveillance post for over eighty years (eighty-one years, three months, and nine days, (Standard)) without incident, before its crew of two, Commander S. Takai and Chief Yeoman Betty Pate were forced by severe shortages of food and repair parts, exacerbated by a minor meteorite strike, to make planetfall. The small scout-type boat was immediately repaired and resupplied, and returned to orbit, this time with a single man aboard, a volunteer: Ensign (later Vice Admiral) Jerry von Shimo. It was von Shimo who detected the approach of ACV *Galahad,* Commander (later Rear Admiral) Greylorn commanding.

PREFATORY NOTE

For some time the need for a definitive and authoritative account of Colmar's earliest days has been evident to the lay public as well as to specialists.

Only now, with the release of key documents from Terran Naval files, has it become possible to reconstruct such a history.

While doubtless there are many who will mourn the deficitionalization of these events and the loss of credulity of such tales in the Colmarian mythos as *Oliver and the Space Beast, The Fallen Evil One, The Nine Deeds of Grall,* and others, all should instead take pride in the reality of the nuggets of fact round which these old tales were woven.

SPECIAL NOTE

Be it noted that, while the History has not yet been accorded the Imprimature of the Church of the Revealed, neither has it been placed on the Index, a fact sure to comfort the pious with an interest in their world's past. His Complexity has stated: "It is not the policy of the Church to attempt to suppress fact."

READER'S FOREWORD

For the present generation of Colmarians—no less than for visitors from Terra—it is difficult, if not impossible, to imagine the planet as it was a scant century and a half ago, at the time Independence was demanded and peacefully though reluctantly granted, due more to growing Colmarian military power than to enlightened Terran policy.

Where broad grain fields now glow in the greenish light of our sun, drab gray tundras once spread across a continent. It seems impossible to grasp that our great forests of oak, ash, beech, pine, and walnut are not indeed indigenous to Colmar or that the abundant wildlife—from the great elk to the timid field mouse—are all descendents of fertilized ova transported across space a few centuries ago. Where our mighty cities rise, rude huts sheltered the frightened, starving, half-frozen men and women who had left the comparative comforts of home (meaning Terra) to make new lives on an unknown and alien world.

It requires an effort of will to realize that those men and women, for all their heroism and hardiness, were no more nor less human than we and that the encounters and struggles by which they mastered the manifold hostilities of their new home were to them no more than the events of the day, rather than grand epics in which the voices of strange gods were heard off-stage, directing events.

Nonetheless, it is worthwhile to make that effort and to see in these pioneers the distant reflections of ourselves as we, no less than they, contribute to the Colmar of the future, to whose citizens we of our era will in turn seem remote and historical.

Reluctant though we, your editors as well as other Colmarians, are to abandon treasured fables like *How Oliver Defied the Giant* and *When Grall Fought the Many-Headed Beast,* we will nonetheless find it rewarding to contemplate our true history, stripped of embellishment, and to discover again our closeness to those mighty Founders, no less deserving of honor for their mere humanity. Once, they lived and breathed as we do, and in these pages they live again for those who seek them.

ACKNOWLEDGMENTS

The editors express their gratitude for the assistance of each of the surviving descendents of Our Founders, especially that of Miss Olivia Brill-Smythe, widow of the first man born on Colmar subsequent to Independence, and that of Colonel Harry Halland III, CAF (ret.), both of whom contributed not only extensive collections of family documents, but their own early reminiscences of their grandparents.

When—last year (CY 331) the last recollection of Colmar's pioneer days passed from living memory with the death of Miss Brill-Smythe at the advanced age of 107 years, Miss Brill-Smythe having been the companion-nurse to Vice Admiral Jerry von Shimo (ret.) during the last five years of his astonishing life—it became apparent to all that the task of organizing and collating all extant genuine data regarding Colmar's early years could no longer be deferred. Accordingly, the present Panel for the Authentication of the Historical Record was formed by the Tey-Grall Foundation and assigned appropriate authority and responsibility for the task.

Somewhat to the surprise—and greatly to the satisfaction—of the scholars thus empowered, it was found that in addition to the several various official records, including bridge logs of *Galahad, Princeton,* and *Special Hull 731* and other documents extant in various archives—including those of the Planetary Museum—there was also in existence a wealth of unpublished personal memoirs, journals, and letters, which amplified and completed the highly fragmentary accounts provided by the official sources.

With the availability of long-suppressed material from Terran archives, the Panel was at last able to assemble all data into a single, coherent narrative—one not without its surprises, for the actual roles of many hitherto neglected individuals were revealed, while actions traditionally ascribed to certain well-known figures were found to have been mistakenly accredited during the long era of word-of-mouth transmission. A number of well-loved traditional heroes were discovered to be either less admirable than believed, or nonexistent, while to the acknowledged delight of the Panelists, more than a few who had long been discounted as mythical were found to be, if not entirely as legend had preserved their memories, at least substantially real people.

Now, at last, the Panel can publicly acknowledge and express its gratitude for the generous assistance of the many unselfish citizens who contributed treasured family papers, informal voice-recordings, and personal recollections, if not of personally experienced pioneer days, then of long-ago conversations with relatives and others who participated in the events herein narrated. Chief among these is perhaps Miss Brill-Smythe, who had devoted many decades of her long life to the organization and clarification of just such oral history sources, including, in her youth, such pivotal figures as her grandfather, Captain A.J.R. Brill-Smythe and a number of his contemporaries, then surviving. It would be impractical to attempt to mention here all the persons whose assistance was invaluable, but we must express our debt especially to Mr. Tome Yosho, subarchivist for formerly classified documents at the Planetary Museum; Miss Kelly Jaxon, chief of the Documentary Section of the Cultural Board; and Mrs. Deane Fetrow, who typed the initial manuscript and pointed out many apparent discrepancies and inconsistencies which we were then able, in most instances, by intensive research and computer analysis, to resolve. For any such flaws which may still mar the text, the Panel alone accepts full responsibility.

It should also be mentioned that no liberties have been taken with fact. All conversation attributed to individuals can be fully authenticated in the record, although to have footnoted all such entries would, we felt, have rendered the book inacceptably cumbersome for the general reader, while the serious scholar is well aware of the avenues for authentication of such quotations. It is indeed fortunate for the present generations of Colmarians that our ancestors, well aware of the historical importance of their bold ventures, took care to make records of their times. Almost without exception, every early immigrant kept a journal or composed an after-the-fact account of events. And not only do these documents exhibit a gratifying degree of agreement and internal consistency, but in many instances, archaeological investigation has served to substantiate the recorded data. Thus, it is with confidence that the Panel offers its reconstruction of those stirring days. Let us go back, then, to those not-so-long-distant times when Terra was still "home" in the minds of Colmarians. Where they ventured with their bodies and their lives, can we be so timid as to refrain from reaching out with our minds?

Edison Colmar for the Panel at East City
Ma 23, CY 332

FINAL PREFATORY NOTE

Difficult it is for Colmarians of the present generation, nurtured in our present highly sophisticated society and having enjoyed all the amenities of modern culture for all their lives, to envision a day when bare tundra and treacherous boglands represented the typical Colmarian landscape, a time when green foliage was unknown to our garden world, an era in which total ignorance of this great planet was leavened only by superstitious conjecture regarding its vast unexplored areas. Harder still, to imagine life on distant Terra during this period of population crisis, the Terra where our Founders were born and from which they voluntarily departed to venture into the unknown. Still, difficult though it is to grasp in its reality the concept of actually participating in the establishment of the first extraterrestrial human colony, the effort is rewarding, and the compilers and editors of the History would encourage all Colmarians to make that effort. We must turn our thoughts back to the beginning —or before the beginning.

The Editor-in-Chief

STAR
COLONY

ONE

Before the Beginning

Think first of a man: middle-aged, round-shouldered, his face weather-beaten and creased from his years as a stockbreeder and farmer; uncouth, ambitious; his name is Jake Colmar and he was Special Rank aboard the great colonizing vessel *Omega*, thirty-seven months out of Terra with a full complement of fifty-four, and two hundred and six passenger-colonists, on a live run. During the entire three-year voyage out, Colmar had been, quite properly, the most inconspicuous man aboard. Now, in a precontact orbit about the big planet selected by the Destination Committee consisting of Captain Brill, Sub-Captain Ohara and Superchief Dan Nolan, plus the colonists' representative, D.B. Halland, and Colmar himself, Colmar's hour had come. From now until all instruments read AT REST, he was absolute dictator aboard Brill's beloved *Omega*, and Jake wasn't the man to slight his duty. He ordered a Senior Officers Call as soon as the first faint whisperings of atmospheric contact were audible.

"Get this straight, gentlemen," he said in a voice quite transformed from the patient and submissive tone which they had all become accustomed to hearing—and to ignoring. "There's only two tough guys aboard this tub," he stated, "and I'm both of 'em. Dismissed." He waved a weary hand and returned his attention to the high-resolution table over which he had been poring for the past ten hours.

"Brill," he called just as the tight-lipped group was crowding into the lift. Not looking up to see if his once and future captain had responded, he touched a light-scribe to the glassy photo map.

"Here," he said. "I've narrowed it down to a hundred-mile-deep stretch along the coast. Looks like fine country. Albedo says some chlorophyll; level ground, too. Chilly, but temperature readings for the whole hemisphere are well within limits. But I've got this coastal range to contend with. Young mountains, peaks over forty thousand. Someday there'll be damn fools trying to get their name in the news by climbing 'em. Right now, we have to ease in past them."

Brill listened silently, not asking the Special Rank why he didn't set up an approach from the east, thereby avoiding the troublesome range altogether.

"Can't risk a shortfall," Colmar said, as if reading the other's mind. "Desert, bogland, and a major active fault. As you can see, to the west, we have open sea; due south, this island, low ground but firm enough."

At this moment Captain R. N. Brill, FSA, OBE, CMH, felt only relief that the responsibility was not his. Colmar, he knew, was the only man who had successfully completed the five-year course of special study designed to qualify a man to conn a deep-space vessel in to a safe touchdown on unprepared ground —or open sea if need be—an unprecedented task for which no computer could be programmed due to lack of data. Brill felt a brief but profound satisfaction that *he* was not faced with responsibility for the task.

"Sir," he muttered, "I have, of course, perfect confidence that you will see us safely through."

"All right, Brill," Colmar replied brusquely. "I want all personnel confined to basic areas, as of—" he glanced at the master chronometer, "now," he finished. "That includes crew as well as supercargo, with the exception of my active list, which you were handed an hour ago. Execute."

· 2 ·

An observer on the ground noticed first a distant roll of thunder, followed almost at once by a brilliant lightning discharge which bathed the forest clearing in a blue-white glare that flickered and was gone. Lesser rumblings followed, accompanied by intermittent bursts of yellow light which glared sickly through the high cloud cover, slowly traversing south-north. Then for an hour the immemorial stillness reigned again, to be terminated this time by the shocking intrusion of a vast, moving body which broke through the low overcast and hung, impossible but real, in the misty sky.

It was not quite stationary, the observer noticed, but rotated on its long axis while sliding slowly forward beneath the opaque ceiling which had hidden it till now. It watched in total absorption as the phenomenon crawled across the sky, to disappear at last in the haze which also hid the High Places. For an instant the observer knew terror at the concept of the strange thing actually invading the sacred precincts, but that, of course, was absurd. Still, it was time now to alert the Supreme that the unthinkable had happened at last: *Nestworld has been invaded!*

· 3 ·

On the bridge of *Omega*, Special Rank Jake Colmar lay exhausted in the conn chair. Captain Brill stood over him, watching him anxiously.

"Sir," he said stiffly, "I believe that under the circumstances of your indisposition at this crucial moment, it is my duty to reassume command and attempt to salvage what I can."

"Try it and I'll shoot you myself, Brill," Colmar said in a crisp tone at variance with his slack posture. "Sit down," he added. "I'm not just being dictatorial for the fun of it, nor am I napping." He opened his eyes as he continued: "The task of matching velocity with the surface, so as to come to rest in contact therewith, properly oriented and at zero velocity relative, is one which cannot be reduced to formulae," Colmar said coldly. "It requires all my attention, plus total cooperation. This conversation is accordingly going to be both very brief and our last until I release command. Dismissed." He closed his eyes again.

"But this is no aerodynamic body; it's a deep-space hull," Brill muttered, but he knew he was talking to himself. "We're bleeding off velocity at a rate . . ."; his eyes went to the instrument array, and he fell silent and turned away.

"Well, I don't know," Brill muttered, frankly addressing himself. "I have my orders—crazy as they are. But I'm no doctrinaire robot to watch this mission—and two hundred and sixty human lives—go smash on a mountain while I stand by and do nothing. Still . . . if he's right . . . Well, FIIGMO!" He paused at the lift and raised a hand in ironic salutation to the dozen picked crewmen and women of the active list, who, intent on their microsecond timing, ignored him.

"FIIGMO, ladies and gentlemen," he said cheerily, "FIIGMO, and I hope we meet again."

· 4 ·

This time there was no sound at all to herald the reappearance of the strange phenomenon so aloofly crossing the gray sky of Nestworld. Unhurried, it moved, majestic and unheeding, toward the gray mass of the High Places. The thing, whatever it was—the observer groped for a term to describe the immense body—seemed, perhaps, to be descending with infinite sloth. Surely its course would intercept the high barrier of rocky peaks dead ahead—unless by chance it slipped through between the twin spires known as the Great Ones. The observer waited, wondering at the cataclysm in the making before its eyes. The thing moved on, deep into the mists of distance, definitely descending; surely at any moment now, a great explosion would mark its end against the unyielding rocks of the High Places.

Professor Dr: D.B. Halland, PhD, CD, ORS, OM, SR(F), once Dean of Phillips University of Enid, Oklahoma, now elected representative of the colonists aboard *Omega*—stepped grimly into the long and narrow passage which ran the length of passenger country. He looked both ways, saw no one, heard nothing but the pervasive hiss of atmosphere sliding over the long hull, with the almost subsonic rumble of the ship's systems providing a monotonous counterpoint. He was a short man, of stocky physique, with dark hair going gray over the slightly jugged ears. He was dressed in the well-fitted issue shipsuit of dark brown, without so much as a button to ornament its drabness. He put his head down, as one challenging a powerful foe, and started doggedly aft. He had covered ten feet when a firm voice spoke from the nearest grill: "Out of order. All passengers are to remain within assigned quarters, in prescribed impact harness until the down-and-clear signal is sounded. ETI, one hundred and forty-three seconds. Mark, including automatic hold at minus five seconds. There are no exceptions, and . . ." the stern voice hesitated, "I must tell you that I am astonished that you, Professor, would be the one to violate ship regulations in this overt manner. You set a poor example for your people, Doctor. If you return at once to quarters, no record will be made of this incident."

"Don't kid me, Jake," Halland said, not pausing. "You're forgetting I was only .02 points into the flunk zone at the institute. I know we're on collision course with that damned coastal range, and we've got about two seconds to do something about it."

"That's precisely the difference between you and me, D.B.," Colmar's voice came back. "You were in the flunk zone. I was one position higher—and I graduated. Now, disappear."

Halland was turning back to his cubicle when a door slid open a few feet along the passage. A pert feminine face, framed by rust-red hair, popped out.

"Hi, Perfesser," the girl said in a tone of pleased surprise. "Never thought I'd see *you* sneaking out on the curfew."

"Why not, Connie?" Halland came back. "You think I'm too timid to try to preserve this expedition from disaster?"

"Well—" Connie oozed into the passage, clad in a nonissue and nearly nonexistent wisp of a garment. "—you always seemed like a pretty quiet fella, you know."

"Look here, girl," Halland said tautly. "In one sense it's commendable that the passengers have accepted the decisions of the Captain and the Special Rank without question, but there comes a time—" he paused as if listening. The faintest of tremors caused the deck underfoot to vibrate for an instant. Halland took a step toward the girl. "Did you feel that?" he demanded in a voice suddenly grown hoarse. "That—" he paused for effect. "That was our death knell. We struck a mountain peak a glancing blow." He broke off as the voice of Jake Colmar boomed from wall speakers:

"Some of you may have noticed a slight vibration just now. I've jettisoned a superfluous cargo pod. Continue as you were. Static contact minus eighty-nine seconds."

"Come on," Halland said, seizing Connie's arm with a roughness that caused her to draw back—but Halland's grip merely tightened as he pulled her to him. "Look, we're in trouble. We'll hit again any moment now—and that's the end." The girl moaned and slumped against him.

"Hell," he muttered thickly. "I'm not thinking of romance at a time like this. We've got a minute and a half, according to Jake —he's a good enough intuit that I'll trust him on that—and if we hurry we can still stop him before he kills us all. We have to add power—and in the right places."

Connie began to whine, bracing her feet in an attempt to break free of this old coot's astonishingly powerful clutch. Halland released her with a curse, turned and ran at his best speed toward the OFF LIMITS sign fifty feet ahead. Connie slumped against the cold polystyrene-coated bulkhead and watched him go, a faint feeling of alarm rising in her as he dashed past the sacrosanct OFF LIMITS barrier and disappeared around a bend in the passage, head down, legs pumping hard. She whimpered and followed. A second shock rocked the deck underfoot; she fell headlong.

On the command deck Special Rank Jake Colmar roused from his near-trance of concentration to wait for the brief but sharp shock of the contact between the ship's ablative hull and an up-reaching rockspire, which he had intuited and accepted as a calculated risk in order to slow the vessel while remaining on the course he had chosen among the high peaks. An instant's survey both of instrument readings and of his own somatic sense told him that *Omega* had dumped the necessary kinetic energy and was holding steadily on course. No harm done. The picked crew manning controls under this supervision looked toward him with shocked expressions, but were instantly reassured by his calm voice announcing static contact in seventy-seven seconds.

Once clear of the mountain barrier, Colmar planned to touch down almost at once, since each ten seconds of delay would place the colony another 3.1 miles from the sea. He gave the necessary orders; the emergency retrorockets ringing the vessel's blunt prow fired an explosive thrust of energy that braked the ship hard, throwing personnel against their restraining harness with painful force.

Jake Colmar watched two large indicator dials with total concentration. Altitude dropped dramatically from 900 to zero; velocity fell off as swiftly. There were small jolts and vibrations; the heavy inertial drag of major deceleration; then both dials showed AT REST. Jake smiled gently while the duty crew cheered him enthusiastically. Then the strictly CAPTAIN ONLY, one-man lift from the navigation deck announced its arrival with a red light and a single tone from the alarm system. Its door slid aside, and Halland, bruised and bleeding from a cut on his jaw, carrying in his arms an unconscious young woman, stepped out, dumped the girl on the nearest standby bench, and advanced toward Colmar.

"Fun's all over, Jake," he said loudly. "You're under arrest. Get away from that console fast. I'm taking over."

"You're out of your mind, D.B.," Colmar said lazily, moving

closer to an inconspicuous length of small-diameter dull-black wire projecting from an adjacent auxiliary console. The duty crew, with grim expressions replacing the grins of a moment before, in an instant reached silent accord, and all but a basic few began to converge on Halland, while one woman went to Connie. Colmar waved them back. Facing Halland, he folded his arms and frowned at the intruder as one would at a curious animal washed up on the beach.

"Just what in the nine hells is eating you, D.B.? What do you think you're doing marching in here and spouting nonsense?"

"You'll soon see how nonsensible it is, Jake," D.B. replied confidently. "You seem to forget that not everyone aboard this vessel is slack-jawed with awe of you. I was at the institute just as long as you were; I know how you do your tricks."

"That's right, D.B., you were there," Colmar replied calmly. "But *I* was number one. Remember that little detail. You were ranked two, I believe."

"Not hard to remember, Jake, considering only the two of us qualified for the final series."

"Better beat it, D.B., before this fiasco gets into the record. Now. Move. And you'd better take your friend with you. She's slept it off, it seems."

"Slept off the crack on the head she got when you blundered into a mountainside," Halland retorted. "What now? I see you've gimmicked your idiot-clocks to show an at rest condition. That's so you can hand over to Brill and duck responsibility for your blundering, I suppose."

"You don't suppose anything of the sort, you damned fool," Colmar cut him off. "Now, move." He brushed past the black rod and paused to look at Connie, now unsteadily on her feet, supported by the aide woman.

"Gosh, Perfesser," she whined, "I thought you said—" she broke off, as if suddenly aware of all the eyes upon her fine and lightly clad figure.

"Doubtless he said many things, Miss," Colmar said comfortingly. "Disregard them. Poor D.B. has just a touch of paranoia; that's why they flunked him."

"You're a damned liar, Jake," Halland yelled. "You're also just plain old Jake Colmar—now that we're 'at rest' as you claim. You outsmarted yourself, Mister Number One. You're relieved and you're under arrest. Crew arrest. That's IAW SAM 202-4b, you know."

"So you're running interference for Brill now, Deeby. An errand boy. You can tell Brill, next time he admits you to the Presence, that I'm relieved when *I* say so."

"Crap," Connie said. "We're all waiting for the second bounce, and you two big brains are scrapping over a few game points like two fairies quarreling over a piece of lace."

Jake turned to her in a mock-gracious gesture. "Right, my dear," he said suavely. "Except for one minor point. We actually *are* at rest. The voyage is safely ended." Again a cheer went up from the duty crew, Connie joining in faintly.

". . . really think it could be true?" her voice emerged from the hubbub as it faded. She was clutching Halland's arm, shaking the harassed man. "Could it?" she repeated. "If we're on the ground, all bets are off! That means we're not going to die, and I take back a lot of things I said when I thought doomsday was here."

Jake sighed and lightly brushed the almost invisible black rod as if accidentally. At once, red lights glowed against dark panels all around the small room, the words RED ALERT in dazzling white against the red. All personnel froze in position. Even Connie stopped whimpering and stood erect, shaking off the solicitous aide woman.

"All right, D.B.," Jake said in a tone of reluctance, "You're forcing the issue, so from now on it's all going into the sealed record."

At that moment a metallic *clack!* from behind Colmar caused all eyes to turn that way. They beheld the short, stout figure of Captain Brill stepping from behind a pivoted panel.

"Fun's over, Mr. Colmar," he said crisply. "You've damaged my ship, you damned incompetent. Now, step down from there and get out—you and this pair with you. Legitimate crew stand by."

"Yes, but it was a calculated braking maneuver," Colmar said defensively, his aura of total command gone without a trace.

"And now what?" Captain Brill demanded and, without awaiting a reply, continued. "So you've lodged us on a mountainside. How do we disembark passengers? How long will the keel take the G-load? And to top it off you've already got dissention among the passengers." Brill stared with hostility at Halland, who stood dejectedly, uncertain now. "But, Captain—" he started.

"But me no buts," Brill snapped.

Connie stepped forward. "That's not fair!" she blurted. "Deeby was just trying to save your old ship for you, Capting Brill, and all our lives too." She moved to Halland's side, he turned to her gratefully, and they moved uncertainly toward the lift door.

"The weak point in the whole concept of the special rank," Brill said, "is that it calls on a man like you to exercise supreme authority when you've never experienced the discipline. It takes a lifetime of active service with the fleet to give a man the true spirit of leadership. You can't give orders until you've learned to take 'em. Now, let's end this farce. Mr. Colmar, ladies and gentlemen, I now formally reassume command of this vessel. Dismissed."

·7·

The observer had watched in awe as the intruder, unswerving, had brushed the base of the Lofty One itself, pressing irresistibly on through a great cloud of ice-chips, stone shards, and snow, to settle without visible impact onto the snow-slope beyond, while the spire itself unhurriedly disassociated into a series of great stone blocks hanging momentarily in place only to drop, with new explosions of ice and snow, into the roil left by the violent, though brief, encounter of the intruder with the slim peak. Slowly, the ice-storm subsided. The invader lay at rest in a shallow groove in the ice, its nose buried in a great bank of snow pushed up by its advance. Hazy daylight glittered briefly on the last of the falling ice crystals. Then all was still.

Patiently, the observer waited, coiled at the base of a clump of dense vegetation, far up the forbidden slope, closer to the High Places than any had ever before approached. Still the newcomer lay unmoving. Perhaps it was dead, killed by the brief, violent encounter with the holy spire. *Very likely,* the observer decided. But just as he was about to turn away, an astonishing thing happened. From a tiny orifice on the curve of the stranger's belly, small creatures began to issue, quickly forming a dense cluster of moving dark points against the ice. No wonder the alien being had come to ground so precipitately, the observer thought with relief; it was a gravid female, desperate for a spawning ground. The larvae were astonishingly small for a mother of such bulk, but "to each kind its own ways," as Bordup the Blessed had admonished so long ago. There was no danger after all; merely a brooding female with her young. The observer turned away, the sense of urgency gone; still, the news must be relayed. The observer hurried downslope and entered the great thicket, forcing a path through dense growth which yielded reluctantly to its advance, groping ahead for contact with the hive.

· 8 ·

On the ice Jake Colmar strode across the glacier on which the ship had come to rest to the edge of the great fissure, and paused to rally a group about him.

"Now, folks," he said, grinning so as to disarm any resentment of authority, "what we got to do, we got to get off this iceberg, which it's likely to slide the rest of the way down the mountain any time." Bad grammar, being folksy, cemented the relationship, of course.

Captain Brill approached, a short, almost comical figure picking his way with care across the slippery snow-dusted ice. He began his prepared speech while still some distance away:

"You people are, of course, quite free to do as you choose,

now that we come to planetfall," he began.

To Jake's resentment, some of his small flock turned and began to move toward this new center of interest.

"Looky here," he barked, immediately regretting the note of harsh command he had allowed to harden his voice. "Mustn't stir up no resentment, Captain. These folks had a bellyful of big shots giving orders back home. That's why they volunteered for this hare-brained expedition."

"Now, folks," Colmar tried again—mustn't wheedle, neither, he cautioned himself—"it's purty plain we got to get organized here. Can't have everybody just goin off on his own. Got to pull together."

The small group, which had responded to Brill's voice, hovered, undecided whom to follow.

"People," Brill said in a reasonable tone, "of course my actual authority does not extend beyond the hull—except for my crew, of course." He paused, belatedly regretting that he had not disembarked the crew first and posted them to shape up this mob. Dangerous situation: Damn fools go wandering off, no manpower to shift the vessel into emergency lift mode. "So just form up here, into two columns by the numbers as you've been taught."

"Crap," a tall, lean man said and turned his back. Others, nodding, followed suit.

". . . none of that old jazz, now we're here," another voice rose above the murmur.

". . . think he is, anyways?" another queried.

"At ease!" Brill snapped. "Fall in!" He realized at once his tactical error. These weren't Navy personnel, deeply conditioned to respond to boot camp drill. They were drifting back, some edging toward the larger bunch around that damned fool Jake Colmar.

". . . over here, folks." Jake was winding up his harangue.

Brill caught the eye of a plump little woman in the front rank. "Now, madam," he began.

"I ain't no madam!" she retorted.

"All right, you, then—the big chap in the blue alls . . ."

"I ain't no chap," the tall fellow stated defiantly and advanced to face the self-important little man who had been such a remote authority figure aboard ship for the last three years. Not much *to* him, up close. Just an ordinary middle-aged storekeeper type, looking plenty nervous. Why, he's scared of *us!* the man realized with amazement. With sudden urgency, he turned to the mob of his fellow passengers.

"Listen here!" he yelled. "We got to look out for ourselfs. These hot-shots have got us in a hell of a tight. Clobbered us in on a mountainside. They don't know what to do, any better'n we do. Maybe not as good. What we got to do, we got to salvage what we can, so's to stay alive until a relief ship can get in here. Got to get off this here glacier before we all freeze . . . and start doin' somethin' about gettin' some shacks built an' all . . ."

His voice was drowned by a chorus of agreement.

"You tell 'em, Slammer!"

". . . something about some eats!"

"Who's in charge . . . ?"

A heavily built man with a sneer on his knuckle-scarred face shouldered through to confront Slammer.

"Who elected *you*, Bub?" he started, but was cut off by a stiff left hook to the belly, followed by a casual right cross to the jaw which put him on his back, pawing for a grip on the ice. Slammer stepped past him, fixed his eye on a man in the crowd with an expression of distaste on his narrow features. "How about you, Harry?" Slammer called. "What do *you* think? Come on up here and let's hear from you."

The man hunched his shoulders as if attempting to squeeze himself so thin as to be invisible. Then he stepped up, sudden confidence on his face, and turned to address the crowd from which he had so unexpectedly emerged.

"Elections," Harry said in a thin but penetrating voice. "It's the democratic way. We need to choose candidates for leadership and then vote."

A plump woman pressed forward waving a dimpled arm in a vague way.

"We got no call to go nominatin' nobody," she declared hotly.

"We already got volunteers: Capting Brill and Mr. Jake, and—and this here feller Slammer, too."

"Not me, lady," Slammer's big voice boomed out. "*I* don't know how to get us out of the fix we're in. We need somebody knows what he's doin' to be boss."

"Guess that means Cap'n," someone said. "Or maybe Mr. Colmar. Both of 'em had all kinds of fancy schooling." Voices rose in agreement or protest.

Halland chose this moment to push through to the speaker's circle. "I can tell you what we need to do," he cried. The babble faded, permitting him to be heard. "First we need to get the crew out here and establish that *we*'re running things now. Get them to off-load some basic supplies, food, and maybe—"

"We don't need to camp here on the ice, Deeby," someone yelled. "We can see green land down below. We got to get down there, where a man can live."

"Sure," Halland countered. "But how we going to get there? Damn slick ice sheet . . . and a cliff at the end of it. And we got to unload and pack our supplies down too. In fact that's number-one priority. I need . . . Let's see . . ."

"You will not interfere in any way with my ship," Captain Brill yelled, coming toward Halland with a scowl on his square, red face. There were a few catcalls. Brill looked around belligerently. "And I am prepared to enforce that," he said in a conversational tone. "*Omega* was entrusted to me by the duly constituted authorities and the naval high command. No one touches her without a direct order from me." Unseen by the crowd, he touched the appropriate button on the remote command unit in his pocket. At once the first of the crewmen, who had been standing by aboard ship awaiting orders, jumped down from the open port into the shallow drift of snow. He was a powerman, and over his shoulder a Mark XX was slung. Eyeing the restless mob apprehensively, he slipped the weapon into his hands, casually covering those directly before him, and took his place in the line quickly formed up by his fellow crew as they poured out into the bright, cold light of day, blinking but alert.

Half an hour later fifty battle-trained men stood ready, the great vessel looming above them all deserted except for the standby crew of three under Ohara, who monitored the proceedings via closed circuit. Brill took up his post at the center of the line.

"As you see," he shouted, "there's to be no disorder here, no irresponsible foolishness, no waste of vital supplies. Now . . ." he paused, frowning as if in concentration. "Naval regulations specify procedures applicable to this—and to all situations—as I carefully explained to you in my pre-debarcation briefing. Our first responsibility is to my, er, *our* vessel, our sole lifeline to civilization. Accordingly, my cadre will form all personnel into work teams of ten, without respect of personality."

· 9 ·

On a high spur of rock among the towering trees, the observer experienced dawning comprehension. After the curiously tiny spawn had formed up around three nuclei, it had appeared for a moment that the intruder was not, after all, so alien. Now, it seemed apparent, each nuclear body would coalesce, and the strongest would eliminate the others, genedoomed to extinction. But instead, a new order, encompassing the now quickly disintegrating nuclei, was swiftly taking shape: an evolutionary innovation of great refinement, it was clear. To make use of the extraneous spawn—which, after all, represented a considerable investment of vitality—to integrate them all into a single, far more viable larva was clearly a survival strategy of great potential effectiveness. It would be most interesting, not only for the Supreme, but for the whole of Mancji, to see how it fared.

And still the parent lay inert on its harsh bed of rock and ice, the observer noted with empathy. How dreadful it would be to spawn far from a prepared spawning ground, without the comforting presence of the attendants and the knowledge that the spawn brought forth from dissolution and death would enjoy the care and support of a chosen one. . . .

Turning with difficulty from these compassionate ruminations, the observer again determined to take the shattering news to the hive at once—and perhaps a way could be found to ease the agony of the unfortunate mother on the ice.

· 10 ·

"Looky here, Brill," Colmar started, sauntering along the line of grim-faced crewmen to confront the former commander, who ignored him, "you got no call to start threatening to kill folks. Reckon even the navy brass'd sort of disapprove if your private army here was to murder all us colonists. And if the shooting starts, that's what'd happen—unless maybe four, five to one is too much odds for these boys."

"There is no question of murdering passengers, Mr. Colmar," Brill returned without heat. "I simply want it understood that we will proceed in an organized manner. The first item is to discover a practical route to the valley, after which all supplies provided for the colonization effort will be off-loaded."

"Damn right," Jake Colmar barked. "I guess you ain't forgot, Brill, them supplies was paid for by the Colonization Committee, including these folks right here."

"I am well aware of the status, funding-wise, of every paper clip aboard my command, Mr. Colmar," Brill commented stiffly. "Now, you can be of assistance, if you wish, by selecting three able-bodied men from among the passengers to assay a descent."

"Reckon the democratic thing'd be to call for volunteers, Brill," Jake rebuked the officer. "Even some of your gun-boys here might want to help out."

"Only a fool would volunteer for such an attempt, Mr. Colmar," Brill stated flatly. "And a foothold so fragile as yours—ours—is no place for fools. Democracy be damned. It's ability that counts now."

Jake Colmar muttered, but in assent, not dispute. "Anyways, we got to wait till morning," he said. "No use letting 'em get overtook by dark halfway down—or getting down and just setting until daylight."

As a bleary, pinkish dawn at last illuminated the long snow-slope below the initial vertical ice-cliff, a team of two men and a woman at the cliff edge readied their gear, preparing to set pitons and rappel down the north face of the giant cake of ice. Slammer, in charge of the detail, yawned and, without ceremony, laid out his lines, set an ice-piton deep into hard ice, and went over the edge. An hour later, the crowd clustered about the damaged ship in neat groups of ten raised a cheer as Colmar released the news that the three tiny figures far below had waved a white signal-flag to indicate all's well.

"Okey-doke," Colmar said, "I reckon you got no objection, Brill, to letting your Navy boys off-load our stuff now, so's we can get this here colony under way."

"Mr. Ohara already has his instructions, Mr. Colmar," Brill replied in a tone of patience abused.

"Too bad we can't use the cargo-flat," Jake muttered. "Hell of a stiff climb down there, even without carrying a load."

"I propose to carry my share, Mr. Colmar," Brill said. "What of yourself?"

"Me? I got too much to think about without being no pack-mule, Brill, and if you got your smarts, you won't haul no cargo neither. We got our dignity to think about. Folks don't want to take orders from somebody no better'n they are. And anyways," he went on, "that there VIP car you got stashed in the stern could get down there; she's some kind of flying car, ain't she?"

"An air-cushion vehicle is hardly capable of flight, Mr. Colmar," Brill replied. "However, it may be possible, by blasting a short ramp from the ice there at the edge, to maneuver her down."

"That's it, then!" Colmar blurted. "We'll load her to the gun'ales with cargo and leave the folks to climb. Just good for the one trip, I reckon, cause we'd never get her back up."

"In the interest of the mission, I concur," Brill said formally.

"Though knowingly to condemn Navy property will not be easy to justify before a court of inquiry."

"Court of my old Aunt Mabel," Jake sneered. "Unless we do a lot o' things jest right, we'll all be dead, and not worrying about no promotion."

"Don't be a fool, Mr. Colmar," Brill said urgently. "There's nothing here for anyone except a miserable death—for nothing. Cooperate with me in man-handling *Omega* into a favorable position for liftoff and you can yet be saved."

"I told you no, and no it is, Brill. That's crazy. We got a colony to establish here—and that's what we're a-doing. Course you got no reason to stay. Lift her if you can—and rots o' ruck!"

· 12 ·

When the chain saw bit into the gray-green husk of the first "tree," Jake Colmar watched with apprehension. The prefab hutments, which had been carried down with such labor from the heights—heaped on the stripped VIP car's chassis—were grossly insufficient for the housing of over two hundred men and women plus fifteen small children born on the voyage out, to say nothing of storage space for the supplies yet to be brought down. Of course, the Logistical Planning Committee had expected the Site Selection Committee to pick a site in a more salubrious climate, nor had it provided adequate space-per-person even then. Too late now to protest. If these over-sized gray dandelions would provide lumber, well and good; if not, there was still the possibility of stone or mud-brick, or even sod—though in this rain-jungle the last didn't look promising.

The man on the saw gave a yell of satisfaction.

"We got timber, Jake," he reported. "It's a hollow stem, but the rind's six inches thick, and we can rip it into two-by-sixes fifty feet long, and tougher'n peavy."

Colmar congratulated the man and moved on to a cluster of prefabs which had been erected quickly, if not well, in the curiously artificial-looking clearing they had stumbled upon.

Looked like maybe some natives had cleared it out with power equipment, maybe for planting, but it was carrying a good stand of weeds and saplings, and no sign of the farmers, except a few scraps of some kind of tough plastic—probably used containers —lying about. This, Colmar had decided, thrusting aside caution, was as good a place as any to set up, and better than most. No telling how far this darn weed-patch of a jungle ran—time enough later to explore, after they got the big air-car down from the ship—and they could always move on, if it worked out that way. Meantime, they needed to get everybody in out of this raw wet and mud, and get some hot food into them. Maybe Brill and his boys would have a power cable laid down here by then. Then we'd see some progress!

Jake turned with an angry reprimand ready as someone called his name as he bent to study the cut in the native tree, then checked his objection as he saw it was ex-Captain Brill who had come up, looking solemn as usual, and attended by a straggle of colonists.

"People," Brill began, turning to address the cluster of gaping colonists, "it's time now we begin to face the realities of our situation. Ah, through no fault of our own, we seem to have committed ourselves to a singularly inappropriate site on an unsuitable world. Accordingly we must adapt plans to match reality. First, of course, we must accept the fact that if we continue to draw on ship's stores for food as well as equipment, we will soon be in the position of having no stores remaining— neither for subsistence while awaiting a support mission, nor for a return voyage, should I be successful in my attempts to relift *Omega* for a return voyage."

Over a rising chorus of muttered resentment from the audience, Jake said close to Brill's ear:

"That's one where we agree, Brill," he said, his voice being amplified, unknown to him, by the inobtrusive command mike on Brill's lapel. "The part about not trying to live off the ship, I mean. We got to find ways to support ourselves off the land —like using native timber to build and all. And we got plenty seeds aboard—we got a right to use *them*. They can grow in this soil, all right. Minerals is the same everyplace. And yonder, where I had the fellers dig down two foot, you can see this here is jest about the richest soil you could want.

"So we got to build a storage shed first and stock her with the seeds and cuttings so we can start to farm soon as the cool weather lifts. Got about sixty days, ship time, I figger. More like fifty, local. We got enough grub off-loaded to make it that long, if we ration careful."

"You may as well understand once and for all, Mr. Colmar," Brill said, without visible patience, "so far as I am concerned, this entire venture is an irresponsible, not to say criminal, waste of time, effort, material, and human lives. None of these poor, deluded dupes will ever see home again."

"They're home right now, I tell ya, Brill," Jake snarled in reply. "And you don't need to go worrying none about wasted money. These folks sold everything they ever owned and put the cash in the kitty. They got nothing to go back to. They're goin' to make it right here."

"That's as may be, Mr. Colmar," Brill returned icily. "But wishful thinking won't transform this sub-Arctic desert clothed in poisonous growths into a livable habitat for human beings."

"No, wishing won't, but these here humern beans like you call 'em, will! Jest give us a little time, Brill. And seein's you're stuck here with the rest of us, you might's well pitch in and stop thinkin' negative and all."

"The quality of my thinking, Mr. Colmar, is unlikely to solve your problems," Brill said flatly. "As for 'pitching in,' my men have worked as diligently as anyone, and more so than most."

"But if you keep spreading these ideas about 'goin' home,' you gonna get folks restless."

"I don't think, Mr. Colmar, that you actually believe that I have attempted to sow dissention. On the contrary, I have advised one and all to work together, under your direction."

"Well, just see you don't," Jake muttered. "Now let's get back to business. Them ten crates full of windmill need to be set up."

"I'd appreciate it, Mr. Colmar," Brill said rather stiffly, "if you'd assemble the passengers in orderly fashion to hear a few words I have to say to them."

"You would, would you, Brill?" Jake replied belligerently, knowing even as he did so that it was incorrect tactics. Still, even taking away the old boy's title had neither taken the ramrod from his back nor lessened his former passengers' tendency to go to him for confirmation of orders.

"Indeed so," Brill said. "And in a perfectly amicable manner. Open dispute between you and me at this point would benefit no one."

"There sure-bob ain't going to be no dispute, Brill," Colmar growled. "Me and my colonists aim to plant a colony here, with your help or without it."

"It is precisely the welfare of the passengers with which I am concerned, Mr. Colmar," Brill stated. "Their only hope is to assist me and my crew in reorienting *Omega* by careful blasting and melting of ice so as to make liftoff possible."

"That's crazy talk, Brill," Colmar cut in roughly. "That tub lays right were she's at, and as time goes by we can dismantle her bit by bit and get some use out of her power plant and systems. Lot's o' good raw material there."

"—do no such thing!" Brill's amplified voice cut across Jake Colmar's complacent statement. "Anyone who so much as touches my command without a direct order from me is guilty of high treason and will be dealt with accordingly. Be sensible, Mr. Colmar. Have all your passengers pitch in while there's still time, and they can yet see home again."

"This *here* is home," Colmar's voice roared out across the clearing as he leaned close to Brill's lapel mike. "Some folks got to get their thinking straight on that! We come here to build a colony where a man can breathe free, and by Gemini, that's what we're gonna do!"

A ragged cheer, not unmixed with catcalls, rose from the dumfounded colonists, who had downed tools to listen as the two big shots began, unwittingly, airing their disagreement.

"There comes a time, Mr. Colmar," Brill went on heavily, "when one who is entrusted with authority must exercise it for his people's benefit, even though they resent it, not understanding the reasons."

"I hope you got no complaints, Brill," Jake said. "I been babying these colonists along like they was my own kin."

"As they are," Brill said firmly. "Aside from ship's complement, there is no organism as closely related to you as a bacterium, within four light-years. In fact, that is a part of what I intend to point out to the passengers."

"Calling us colonists 'passengers' won't change nothing, Brill," Jake pointed out. "OK, I'll speak to Slammer, and you can tell your cadre boys to shape 'em up."

"Quite right, Mr. Colmar," Brill replied crisply. "I readily authorize an issue of seeds and cuttings, which in any case are not Navy property, but nonappropriated fund items earmarked for use by the passengers—colonists, if you insist it's an important distinction."

"Damn right," Jake said. "Let's get at it."

· 13 ·

Nestled in a vegetation-lined crevasse as near the mysterious activities of the alien grubs as it deemed prudent, the observer monitored the falling air pressure impinging on its barometric membranes, scanning the heavy, dark sky for the to-be-expected electrical discharges, so satisfying, yet so dangerous. Soon hail would sweep across the peaks, hammering the exposed and helpless alien female stranded on the high slope and pounding the defenseless grubs as they struggled to erect their pods. There was nothing to be done alone, the observer reflected sadly; and haste was needed now if it were to report to the hive and urge immediate action in time to be of any avail. Reluctantly it left its cozy shelter and set off at its best crawl; then, impatient, it assumed the Posture and levitated, an energy-intensive strategy, but it was momentarily vastly pleasant to be relieved of the gross weight of its rapidly maturing body and the drag of the steep slope. On impulse it swerved, then turned, and went directly to the nearest edge of the nesting-site of the alien grubs.

· 14 ·

Harry G. Plover had dumped his armload of trimmed twigs and other rubbish well back into the dark recesses of the jungle edge and, dusting his hands, was about to head back, feeling a cleansing sense of self-righteousness that he, Harry Plover, CPA, had so nobly pitched in with the manual labor to help the bosses get everybody out of this mess they'd gotten them into. Turning, his eye caught by a hint of motion—he checked—over *there,* in deep gloom. He peered into near-darkness, then scrambled back. His legs seemed to be trapped in an invisible syrup. He fought the rising panic.

Oh, sure, he thought. *I'm having a nightmare—it'll be over in a moment.* But the moment passed and still he saw the dull-glistening hulk, like some obscene giant intestine, writhing slowly toward him. *"Go away! Death waits!"* a silent voice yelled inside his head. At last he broke loose, quite unaware of the ululating scream of pure horror he was uttering until it had exhausted all the air in his lungs. He struggled to draw another breath, and ran, full-tilt, into a tree.

· 15 ·

Groping outward for mental contact, merely from long habit, the observer was startled at the alien flavor of the mentational field it encountered—no, *fields,* it corrected. And fields of such intensity! Tiny, but sharp as the peaks of the High Places. It settled down in the shelter of dense plant growth more closely to study this unexpected phenomenon.

Imagine larvae—even phase-one compound grubs—capable of such sharply focused mentation:

. . . *get these——shacks up and rack out.* . . .

. . . *wish I'd stayed home—old Braunstein—no I don't.*

. . . *better to tell them now.*

. . . *me, a professional man, hauling loads like a contract coolie.*

This last, cutting clear above the background babble, was close. The observer noticed the grub, then a small wizened creature with fuzz at one end among the external sense organs, like an aborted fetus. And manipulative members as well as ambulatory ones.

The observer spasmed in shock at the realization that struck it: These spawn were fully equipped for *independent* existence! The concept was almost impossible to hold in the mind. Imagine a tiny, helpless grub, brought forth abruptly, to its own astonishment, into the harshness of the exocosm, abandoned to its own devices, to make its way on its own, not even the simplest rules of life to be taught to it by endless, gentle repetition. Overcome with emotion at the dreadful picture, the observer offered what comfort it could, holding the supportive concepts clearly before the curiously blunt-edged alien mentational field:

Get away quickly, or you shall be destroyed. (The poor things would be smashed flat by hail stones before they realized that destruction was upon them.)

Tell the others . . . little time is left—run! Make all haste! Be gone at once! Hide yourselves—there! The observer indicated the direction of the Sacred Caves; then, shocked at its own sacrilege, countermanded the concept:

No! Stay away! Only the Exalted may safely penetrate there. Hurry! Death approaches!

An orifice opened amid the fetal fuzz of the alien grub, and it set up an unbeamed atmospheric vibration at 10,971.02 cycles per second. Interested in this new manifestation, the observer spontaneously edged closer, only to watch, frustrated, as the grub spun and hurled itself against a rough-barked qwill tree. Then it entered a dormant phase. Incomprehensible!

· 16 ·

As Plover's yell ripped through the rustling silence of the clearing, Jake Colmar dropped the short, thick length of heavy wood he had selected as his badge (and, if need be, weapon) of authority and hurried toward the point of origin of the screech, which seemed still to echo in his ears. He was bucking the outward-streaming tide of colonists, who as one had turned to flee the sound. Only Brill was standing his ground, with two of his top crew beside him. Jake slowed and joined the group.

"You coming?" he asked.

"Not yet, Mr. Colmar," Brill replied evenly. "Let's get an idea of what's going on over there before we dash in. These people need leadership, you know."

"So we better not all suicide at once, eh?" Jake assented thoughtfully.

"I was just about to speak to you, Mr. Colmar," Brill said. "I'm sending two men up to my ship to prepare the courier boat for launch. I'm putting her in a DSO to guide in the support mission when it comes."

"DSO, that's Navy for distant surveillance orbit; waste of time, Brill. You know there'll be no support mission well's I do."

"Nevertheless, we mustn't lose hope. And it will help passenger morale to feel we're doing something constructive."

"Most constructive thing we can do is get settled into our new home quick as we can," Colmar countered. "Steada throwing that little bum-boat away, be better to use it to do a recon of the local area, locate us some flowing water for a power plant and all that; we can't draw on ship's reserve forever—or even for more'n a few months."

"As for that, I am discontinuing energy service as of sunset tomorrow," Brill said stolidly.

"Huh?" Jake recoiled in only partly feigned shock. "You can't do that to us, Brill. We got—" he broke off as Plover jostled between him and Brill. The man was staggering. *Wonder where he got the stuff,* Jake thought, truly shocked by the *lese majeste. Could use a snort myself. Blood on his face.*

". . . get out of here, fast, Cap'n!" Plover was babbling. "God-awful thing— Bushes are full of 'em— Said they'd pound us all to bits if we didn't get out fast!" He paused, swaying on his feet.

"This man is injured," Brill said and turned to one of his aides. "See to his wound."

"You've got to listen," Plover persisted, pulling his arm away from the grasp of the concerned crewman, who was eyeing the cut across his forehead.

"Superficial, but scalp wounds always bleed like hell. Have to stitch it," the aide said.

"We've got no time to waste, dammit!" Plover's voice grew louder—and more demanding than appealing: "I'm telling you fellers we're surrounded by critters like a pile of guts! Horrible! And they give us no time at all to get out! We've got to move out now!"

"Be calm, Harry," the crewman said, almost wrestling now to steer Plover away from the captain. "I know you as a good, steady passenger, Harry, a responsible man. You're a little dazed just now from that blow on the head; be reasonable, calm down and let me bandage it. How did it happen?"

"Didn't just *happen*," Plover said. "It was DID! I tried to get away and they jumped me. Horrible-looking things: like maybe a big oyster without no shell." Plover subsided suddenly, with a final shudder. Then his knees folded.

Jake Colmar looked down at the man with a frown. "Brill," he said, "Plover was always a nice quiet feller—done what he was told. Reckon he just went crazy, hey?"

"Perhaps he actually saw something, Mr. Colmar," Brill replied gravely. "I'm going to take a look over there."

· 17 ·

Fleeing, the observer wondered what mistake it had made. Clearly the warning, timely and lucid though it had been, had not had the effect of alerting the grubs—imagine communicating with grubs!—who were standing fast, though apparently somewhat agitated. Still, he had done all he could. And there was still time to help the stricken mother. . . .

Hurrying now, it set off toward the hive.

The first hail-stones, lumpy ice-balls as big as a fist, came with a powerful gust from the east, crashing through foliage, sending a burst of ragged leaves and shattered twigs ahead into the clearing. As everyone froze at the explosive *crash!*, the ice-balls swept almost horizontally across the camp area, knocking men down, ripping stretched tarpaulins, thudding against the rude half-constructed log-built shed, knocking it askew.

"They're a-firing on us," Jake Colmar yelled, reeling from a solid impact on his forehead. "Take cover! No! In the woods there, you damn fools! Can't you see they're knocking that shed apart?"

"As you were!" Brill's amplified voice boomed across the scene. Having penetrated some yards into the dense undergrowth when the storm struck, he had been reached by only a few spent hail-stones which dropped through the leaves about him. He picked one up and stamped back toward the clearing. Jake Colmar and a few others were still on their feet. "Only a hailstorm," Brill's voice boomed. "No cause for panic." He stepped behind a tree as, in the thinner fringe of the timber, hail-stones began to reach him, administering slight bruises before falling off harmlessly.

"Got to take shelter anyways!" Colmar was yelling. "Let's go, folks!"

"Belay that!" Brill's amplified voice overrode all else. "Can't have these people getting scattered in the woods! Be over in a minute!"

Harry Plover, supported by the crewman, stood shakily in the lee of the battered shed.

"Said about some caves," he said. "Better tell the big shots, George. I'll be OK here for a little. Said . . . stay out of the caves —but to heck with that; we got to get under cover. Over that way."

"What language did this monster talk in, Harry?" George inquired.

"Standard, of course," Plover replied. "Only language I know. Funny, I guess. Didn't think about it at the time."

George was examining the contusion on Plover's forehead. "Bits of bark," he muttered. "He skulled you with a tree branch, looks like."

"Better hurry, George. Some of those folks out there are out cold and getting pounded bad."

George hurried away; Harry watched as he made it to Jake Colmar's side. The storm was definitely weaker now, he saw. Still no fun, but not like that first gust.

George was pointing, Jake nodding; while across the clearing, Cap Brill was staggering. A large stone, falling almost vertically, had hit him on the head and knocked him down, but he had come doggedly to all fours, shaking his head, then stood.

"Back to the ship!" he bellowed. "Got to get out of this!" Former First Officer Tate hurried to his side.

"Don't nobody move!" Colmar yelled, shaking off George's restraining hand. "Form up in a column of bunches, right here!" he added, with a vague impulse toward military precision. The colonists, confused, merely milled about, each one trying to address another, who was equally intent on haranguing someone else. Only Brill's crew rallied to him, as Plover confronted Colmar, talking excitedly.

Two men, dispatched by Jake Colmar to make a search for the monster described by Harry Plover, poked half-heartedly about in the underbrush, noting Plover's bootprints in the humus, but no monsters.

"All right," Colmar responded to their report. "But dang sure *something* put that knot on Harry's skull!"

The wind having died, the final small hail-stones dropped in normal hail-stone-fashion, hardly noticeable now, though the ground was littered thickly with the ice-balls. Jake kicked one and made his decision:

"No damn reason to go running off back to the ship!" he called. "Trip's over, folks. Thing now's to get settled in." He glanced at the ever-looming ice-slope topped by the bare rocky peaks, one now truncated, which had flawed the precision of his landing—then halted in his tracks and whirled. The broad white snow-slope was bare—the ship was gone! Jake yelled:

"Brill! I got to see you right now!"

"I'm right here, Mr. Colmar," Brill said almost at the civilian's elbow. Jake turned on him.

"Better switch off that damn pickup of yours," he barked. "What I got to say I don't want broadcasted. You won't get away with this one, by God! Where is it? Snuck off up there while I was tied up with this hail storm, did ya?" His face was six inches from the rigid features of the former captain.

"That's asinine," Brill said quietly. "And your bombast doesn't cover the fact that you've gone altogether too far this time. What did you do, blast the ice from under her port side to let her slip into the ravine?"

"I never did such a thing!" Jake yelled. "I guess you fellers used a few tricks you been keeping up your sleeve to kind of nudge her over to that northeast slope, eh? Let her slide down outa sight and figger to sneak off and lift her later." Jake paused, breathing hard, glaring at Brill like an animal at bay. "I been up to here," he stated, "doing all I could for these folks—and whilst I wasn't lookin', you and your boys give us this here stab in the back!"

"I," Brill said, "and my 'boys' have pitched in unreservedly to lend all the help we could. In fact, without the organizational experience of a trained cadre, you'd not yet have so much as backpacked your first load of modulars down here, to say nothing of erecting them." He looked scornfully at the excited Jake.

"All right," Colmar snarled. "I got to admit your boys have held up their end—But that don't change nothing now!" He pointed a finger quivering with rage toward the former site of the downed vessel. "We got our rights!" he yelled.

"Indeed you have, Mr. Colmar," Brill replied, "and you've been diligent to secure full advantage of them. But they do not include tampering with naval property. All of your possessions have been off-loaded, with the full cooperation of myself and crew, including the unauthorized use of a Mark IX class A car; ground, flag officers, for the use of—"

"You can skip all the fancy talk." Jake spat, missing Brill's shoe. "Fact is, we got no place to take shelter, 'cept the ship.

You know well as I do, the next hail storm's gonna kill somebody. Still got Fred and poor little Jeannie down with all those bruises, not to say nothing about Harry Plover, which he prolly won't ever be right again."

"So you took action to ensure I wouldn't lift *Omega,*" Brill countered. "I remind you, Mr. Colmar, ship's complement did *not* volunteer for a one-way voyage. They have every right to expect to return to their homes."

"Including you, hey, Brill?" Jake sneered. "In fact, *especially* you."

"You're quite aware that I have remained clearly in your field of view throughout the storm under cover of which you claim I scaled the slope and moved my ship," Brill stated firmly.

"Oh, sure, reckon you sent that sharpie Ohara up, with a few picked men . . ."

"That's idiotic, Mr. Colmar. I will brook no accusations against my crew, who have, throughout, conducted themselves in exemplary fashion. It appears to me that in view of your attitude, the time has come for me to withdraw their service, and organize an investigation into the whereabouts of my command, as well as to search out the natural caves I heard mentioned."

"Sure, take yer dolls and go home," Jake said, in a tone of syrupy sarcasm. "Like you said, we trusted 'em to get things organized, and if they pull out now—" he looked sadly toward the mob churning aimlessly now, while tan-uniformed crewmen struggled to restore order.

"Mr. Colmar," Brill said in a no-nonsense tone, "if at this point you will inform me, in precise detail, just how you moved *Omega,* I shall consider the entire incident expunged from the record, even though you may well have damaged her beyond repair, to say nothing of placing her in an impossible situation for launch."

"A real kidder, ain't you, Brill?" Jake said with a yellow-toothed grin. "You tell me sumpin: If you admit you and yer crew'd have the Devil's own time shifting her, how'd *I* do it—in the middle of a bombardment?"

"If you choose stubbornly to maintain your untenable attitude of shocked innocence," Brill said unyieldingly, "you doom your passengers to an agonizing demise here in this alien place you have chosen for your own suicide. I counsel you to revise your thinking."

"Way I remember, Brill, you was on that there committee same as me. Anyways, here we are and here we stay—so you better get used to calling it home." As the last word echoed back in Colmar's ears, he realized that Brill had not, as requested, switched off his lapel microphone, and that the entire conversation had been broadcast to one and all.

· 19 ·

The small groups being shaped up by Brill and his crew were responding distractedly to the cadre's orders. Those in the fringe were drifting away, losing themselves in the mob. Among them was D.B. Halland.

"Come on, Connie," he said carelessly to the girl who, with an ankle twisted in her fall aboard ship, had gratefully accepted his help in the long trek down from the mountainside, and had since stayed close to him.

"Jake's right," Halland added. "Let's go give him a hand getting this straightened out."

"Sure, Deeby," Connie agreed readily, catching Halland's hand, staying close to his side. Colmar glanced up as the two came up to him.

"All right, D.B.," he said almost eagerly. "You got sense enough to know we had to cut loose from that crutch of a ship up there, anyways."

"That's right, Jake. What you got in mind?"

"Old Harry Plover says there's caves yonder." He jerked his head vaguely. "Pretty good shelter till we can get something better set up here. We got to get over there and find 'em. I need a couple volunteers to go take a look. Not you," he added quickly as he noticed the expression hardening Halland's face.

"Connie still ain't strong," Halland said, "and I'm staying with her till I got her fixed up nice and cosy with a shack of her own, and something to eat."

"Durn shame," Jake muttered. "A hard-workin' gal like Conn hadda be the first one to go and git herself knocked up. Where at is that Slammer feller?" Jake made a show of rising onto tiptoe and stretching his neck to scan the clearing.

"See can you find him, DB," he said. "I'll see to Connie while—"

"See to me nothing, Jake Colmar," Connie said spiritedly. "I'll have that sucker Slammer over here before you two big-domes have got a speech ready to give him," and she was gone.

Jake looked at Halland with an expression as near arch as his meaty features could manage. "You got yourself quite a gal there, DB—if you can handle her."

"Handle, hell, Jake," Halland replied. "Nobody can move Connie one inch in any direction she don't want to go." He smiled complacently.

The man called Slammer appeared abruptly, almost colliding with Halland.

"That little Connie gal said—" he began, but Jake Colmar cut him off.

"I need a man, Slammer. There's caves south o' here, get the folks in outa the weather." He slanted a knowing look at the sky. "She's let up for now, but there'll be more. We got off easy this time, nobody kilt." Colmar's gaze returned to the tall, husky man, who was still breathing hard.

"Need you to go take a look, Slammer," Colmar stated matter-of-factly. "Pick us out the best route and all. Better get Corky to issue ya a big feed first." He turned away casually as if the matter were concluded.

"Looky here, Jake," Slammer said. "You got to give me more directions than that. And . . ." He paused to peer past Colmar at the brooding forest fringe. "No tellin' what a feller could run inta out there," he concluded.

Colmar turned and looked at him with an expression carefully compounded of heartiness and contempt. "You ain't been listening to old Harry Plover . . . ?"

Ten minutes later, as Slammer was wolfing down his oversized ration of hot stew, former Captain Brill came up and engaged in conversation with Colmar, who had come along to authorize the off-schedule food issue.

'Bout outa ship's rations, Brill," Colmar said casually.

"Then, presumably you'll agree with me that it's time to set in motion some constructive measures toward finding local food sources, Mr. Colmar," the ex-Captain said coldly.

"Sure we will, Brill," Colmar replied. "But first we got to stay alive long enough to do it. That's why I'm sending this here feller out to scout them caves."

"It's not a good idea to send a man alone on a mission potentially of great importance, not to mention hazard." All across the clearing, people were busy, some attempting hastily to erect more of the panels as temporary shelter, some merely pressing through the crowd as if bent on an errand of import. At the edge of the clearing, the two leaders stood talking quietly, like bystanders at a carnival.

"Plover's crazy story's got you spooked, hey, Brill?" Colmar cackled.

"The man saw *something*, Mr. Colmar," the former commanding officer replied doggedly. "I have a certain responsibility to my passengers even now, Mr. Colmar. I haven't yet talked to the man, but I intend to do so at once—and by the way, Mr. Colmar, I hope that in your planning, you are keeping in mind that my crew did not volunteer for a one-way voyage."

"What's that 'pose to mean, Brill?" Colmar growled.

"Simply that I intend to ready my command for lift-off, immediately I find her. Any plans you may have for further exploitation of my ship's stores will have to be cancelled."

"Just like that, eh, Brill? Well, I'll tell you, my colonists got rights, too—and we got you outnumbered. So you just stand pat, boy, and don't do nothing to aggravate me, and we get along fine. I don't aim to dismantle the wreck right off, jest off-load the supplies we need is all."

To this, the once and future captain offered no objection, except to point out:

"That's still a considerable climb, Mr. Colmar—and after

these days of mild weather, that ice slab may break up any moment. I suggest we come to an agreement, as to proper use of naval stores."

"Sure, Brill, plan to," Jake grunted. "Slammer," he went on, addressing the tall, lean man who, finished with his meal, was standing by with signs of impatience. "You go on now, do your job, and get back soon's you can. I may need you on the next supply run." Colmar strolled away like a man without a care in the world. Slammer looked after him without visible admiration.

"If I may comment, ah, Mr. Slammer—" Brill began.

"Call me Max, Cap'n," the passenger-colonist suggested. "Ain't slammed nobody in a while—not since that smart-alec paper-pusher back at Denver tried to shove me."

"Very well, Mr.—ah, Max," Brill said awkwardly. "Not my business any longer, of course, but I strongly suggest you do not undertake your mission alone. A single man is under a grave disadvantage. He can find himself in a disastrous situation which, had he a partner, would be trivial: in rough country, a foot wedged in a rock cleft, say, or being pinned by a rock-slide."

"I get the idea, Cap'n," Max replied. "Friendly of you to mention it, but Jake said go. I was for electin' him, and I'll back him up."

"I don't suggest you refuse the mission, Max, only that you set about it correctly. First, you'll need iron rations, at the least." He turned to the open-mouthed cook, Corky, a former bartender, and said briskly: "Two B ration-packs for Mr.—"

"Sure, Cap'n, fyew say so, but Jake—"

"I'm sure that on mature consideration, Mr. Colmar would approve. I'll take full responsibility, of course."

"Sayin' you're right, Cap'n—" Max said, "—and I'm not sayin' otherwise—who'd I get to go along?" He turned his head to glance across the busy crowd filling the clearing. "Them folks is all busy enough as it is, unpacking stuff and calcalating how ta miss the next dirty detail."

"Quite simple, Max," Captain Brill said. "I'm going with you."

"Well, Cap'n," Max said. "Reckon I can't complain none."

"Ahh, sir," Corky murmured. He handed over two of the

boxed B rations; then with a grin, two more. Brill accepted them with an answering grin. Emboldened by the comradery, the cook cleared his throat and asked, "Cap'n, ah, what's all this stuff about some caves and all?"

"Mr. Colmar feels we should seek shelter, in the event of more hail storms," Brill replied affably.

"We could jest take to the woods, like I was saying—" Corky persisted. Brill shook his head. "It's best not to let ourselves become scattered," he explained. "Once in the jungle, a man would be unable to find his way to a rendezvous." He turned to Max, "We'd best strike straight for the coast, to get in the clear as soon as possible; then east along the shore. No doubt the caves will be found to be in the cliff face there."

Max nodded. "If they're anywhere," he agreed doubtfully.

"Let's go find out," Brill said, as if making a suggestion. As he started off across the crowded clearing, Jake Colmar appeared, intercepting him as if by accident.

"Well, Brill," he greeted his former superior. "I see Max has got hisself a partner. Well, reckon I ain't going to say no." The man always assumed his folksiest manner when baiting him, Brill had long been aware, just as he always swaggered when approaching and sauntered away. Poor fellow, Brill reflected, carrying that huge ego problem as well as all the substantive responsibilities he had so casually assumed.

"Now," Jake Colmar went on, "whilst you're off on this here expedition—" he paused and looked vague, as if doubtful of the wisdom of some curious undertaking insisted upon by the officer, "reckon I'll get your boy Tate to take charge of a bunch of volunteers to make that supply run yonder." He tilted his head toward the bare high slope where *Omega* had for so long lain in full view.

"Very well, Mr. Colmar. I have a return request to make: While there, kindly permit your men to dig out her aft-starboard trim-tube orifices. Jammed with packed ice, you know. They'd explode in rather spectacular fashion if ignited in that condition."

"Sure, why not?" Jake Colmar acceded casually. "By the way, where is she?"

– 35

"Not far away, doubtless," Brill replied, "though perhaps difficult of access."

"Access or no," Jake said, "you'd orter forget this idea of lifting that tub again. She ain't going nowheres. I know about you boys not planning on being colonists and all, but they'll be better off pitching in to help get our new home ready than to get blowed into little bitty specks trying to run."

"Your repeated references to this hostile wilderness as 'home' does little to diminish one's desire to return to one's real home, Mr. Colmar," Brill stated in a mild voice. "And now we really must be off, to take advantage of the remaining hours of light."

· 20 ·

From a point of vantage high on a promontory above the restless sea a thousand meters below, the observer paused to scan, for one last impression, the spawning nest of the strange creatures of whose presence he would, in a few minutes, be giving report to the Supreme. Still they churned, apparently aimlessly, in the old place of hatching, seemingly unaffected by the brief storm. Perhaps they employed personal force shields (imagine a grub with adult capabilities), thus their failure to respond to warnings of the impending hail. But—the observer checked just as it was about to turn away—there was a tenuous wisp of mind field *there*, separate from the rest. It focused its attention, and quickly realized that a portion of the swarm had indeed detached itself from the main body and was now moving steadily closer, quite apparently a survival gambit of irreproachable logic: to divide and establish a secondary swarm was a reproductive strategy which established that these curious embryos were capable of rational planning —a breathtaking concept. Now the observer realized that the detached group comprised only two individuals (individual grubs, indeed!). It would be best to attend and observe the location of the about-to-be-established secondary nest before reporting, it decided.

Half a mile, and half an hour into their trek, the two men had penetrated to the beach, a narrow, scum-clogged strip of coarse, gray sand, littered with leathery molluskoid shells of utterly alien form and color, reeking of iodine.

At this point the jungle ran almost to the water's edge, while to the east, their left, the trees gave way to a rise of ground which split the narrow beach, showing a low, striated rock face dropping vertically to the beach. After a few hundred meters it had risen to form a majestic cliff, falling sheer to the gray-white line of the surf below, rimmed at the top with clustered, bushy-topped trees. The stone face was riddled with the black mouths of caves, most with tongues of discoloration marking the cliff-face below, a few with the water that had formed them still trickling in meandering patterns down the dry stone. By common consent they started east along the cliff-face.

It was an easy climb up the crumbling rock to the lowest tier of caverns. Brill, in the lead, entered one and re-emerged a moment later with an expression of disgust on his usually urbane features.

"Stinks," he muttered to Max before gagging dryly. The younger and taller man reached out to steady him on the narrow ledge, until he shook his head and, still muttering, said, "I'm all right; it just got to me for a moment there."

"Sure, Cap'n," Max said, and climbed past Brill to thrust his head and shoulders into the opening. In the deep gloom of the nearly cylindrical tunnel, he could distinguish what appeared to be heaps of building panels, half-inch thick formed plates of curious shape and complex contour, plus other, puckered forms, like unfinished pots. Then, cautiously, he sniffed, and without conscious intention, was back out on the ledge, snorting the indescribable vileness from his nostrils.

"Next to that, a ripe skunk would be perfume," he commented with an attempt at nonchalance, spoiled by retching.

More cautiously, they investigated two more caves, speculating on the probable nature of the pots and slabs with which each was littered, before returning to the beach.

"Looks like some kind of supply depot," Max suggested. "Maybe bench stock for repairs to their ships, if they've got any."

"In any event it will require more than a few ice-balls to drive anyone inside these foul dens," Brill pointed out. "What's that?" he inquired cooly, as a movement above caught his eye. Max followed his glance. Something bulky and slow was creeping along a ledge twenty feet above. It halted, rested immobile as a boulder.

"Was it really moving?" Max inquired vaguely. "I thought at first it was, but now it's not—and looks like it never did."

"It was moving, Max. Emerged from the cave up there."

· 22 ·

As the observer backed respectfully from the cave it had entered only long enough to make the five ritual obeisances, it saw that the two bold grubs had begun to scale the sacred cliff-face. Observing the creatures for the first time at close range, it noted at once their clumsy method of locomotion, using—fantastic concept!—what appeared to be semipermanently extruded pseudopodia. Resting, the observer monitored the busy exchange of almost unbearably loud mentational impulses between them, accompanied by atmospheric vibrations in the lower thousands-of-cycles-per-second range. Anxiously it hoped they would not emit any painful pulses like those uttered by the first grub it had encountered.

". . . sure about that, Cap'n?"

"Quite, Max . . ." [Here was another startling concept: a thought-form clearly assigned as a designation for a single entity —and a grub at that!] "I happened to be considering that particular cave for our next investigation and saw it quite clearly."

No! the observer instinctively thought. *You must not profane the sacred places. Go elsewhere!*

"Ye gods," Max commented, shaking his head. "Did *you* get that too?" His intended statement changed to the question when he saw the expression of shock on Brill's face.

"Like a voice inside my skull," Brill said thoughtfully. "No, more like a subvocalization: 'Go away! Don't disturb the exalted places!' "

"Close," Max agreed. " 'You must not profane the Sacred Places. Go elsewhere!' Are we losing our marbles, Cap'n?"

"No," Brill replied steadily. "That fellow Plover—the one who became hysterical—he spoke of something of the sort. " 'Right inside my head,' he kept repeating. I had assumed he'd simply cracked. Now it seems there *is* some sort of entity here which is, shall we say, telepathic, for want of a better term."

"Sure," Max said. "Does that mean it can listen in, too?"

"Presumably," Brill answered Max, then called out: "Entity, if you hear me—nonsense, if you don't hear me, an admonition is superfluous—we don't mean you—or your sacred places—any harm. We need shelter from the weather until we can erect appropriate structures."

The fleeting mental image the observer had caught, associated with the thought-form "suitable structures," was so astounding that for a moment it was lost in the wonderment of all that was implied by the outré concept; then it rallied and replied:

To approach the Sacred Places is forbidden, save only for those who feel Exaltation coming on them. No grub, even of the Hive, has ever entered here. I myself will likely be held culpable, though my violation of the beloved tabu was entirely in the interest of protection of the sacred from profanation. What are you, strange grubs?

Brill and Max instinctively moved closer together as the alien thoughts formed in their minds, as clear-cut as if carved in granite.

"Just like I was talking to myself," Max said. "Funny, I never thought telepathy would be like that."

"Presumably," Brill said, "the thought impulses are detected by our own word-forming equipment, and are processed just as are thoughts originating in our own minds, and are thus articulated, subvocally, as words."

"You're ahead of me, Cap'n," Max said. "I'm just glad I'm not hearing things all alone. With two of us, the chances we both fused our main panels at the same time are a lot less, I think."

Brill nodded. "You may safely accept the experience as substantive, Max. We're on an alien world—it's to be expected we'll encounter alien experiences."

An alien world? the observer's query came unexpectedly weakly. In fact the creature was somewhat dazed by the impact of one astonishing concept after another. How could the world be alien? But perhaps it had misunderstood . . .

"Not at all," Brill said aloud, which, he had already discovered, was the natural way to project thought-images. "To us this world is alien, though of course to you it is not."

The observer pondered that. Brill and Max caught only nebulous suggestions of dimly conceived astral planes.

"Not like that," Brill corrected. "This planet is a captive satellite of your sun, a star we call RGC 9079, epsilon, whereas we originate on a planet of the star Sol, some light-years distant, out-galaxy. As I said, we are quite peaceable unless attacked, and mean you no harm."

But, the observer objected, *the stars are such tiny things— mere points of light. How could creatures as large as yourselves live on such a dust mote?*

As Brill explained the anomaly, assisted by interjections from Max, the observer appeared gradually to accept the idea of the existence of novelty—of that which lay outside its previous existence.

Of course, I am but young, it pointed out. *No doubt all these matters are well known to the Supreme.*

"You live in these caves, I suppose," Brill proposed, eliciting another shocked blank. This critter, he reflected, is easy to shake up, if the conversation strays outside its paradigm. . . .

There can be only the one, true paradigm, the observer returned, dazedly. *One does not carry on mundane activities here in the Sacred Portals to Exaltation.*

"Looks like we're into superstition, or religion, Cap'n," Max commented to Brill, then directing his thought at the alien creature: "I guess that's why there's no steps, or a ladder. But how *do* you get up and down this here rock face?"

To the astonishment of both men, the inert-appearing heap of glistening organic matter with which they were conversing stirred, assuming a nearly spherical form, and rose, as lightly as a soap bubble, to drift down and come to rest, draped like a burst bladder, over a rock fragment half a meter from Brill's toe. He stepped back in instinctive recoil from such alienness.

It appears, both Max and Brill received with perfect clarity, *that we are not alone in being "easy to shake up" if I have interpreted the simile correctly.*

"Teleportation!" Brill said at last. "Unless you're using some sort of antigravity device."

Device? Again the alien creature seemed to reel mentally in shock. Then, when it had brought under control the kaleidoscopic whirl of dizzied impressions, a query emerged, a nonverbalized yet imperative request for information regarding the concept: . . . *article created to perform a stated function by organic manipulation of the exocosm. An artifact!* The alien's mind reeled, unable actually to grasp the concept with sufficient clarity to inquire rationally.

"Sure, we make all kinds of things," Max offered in reply to the stunned and stunning response of the friendly alien to the simple idea.

. . . *and coupled with those fantastic, permanently extruded pseudopods, these beings represent an alienness impossible to describe. A hive communion is clearly necessary. But now I see that they employ the lower pair for movement across horizontal surfaces, employing the upper only for vertical ascents, which leaves them free to—manipulate! external objects* . . . Its thought trailed off in vagueness.

"If you don't make things," Brill inquired, "how do you manage for tools and weapons and utensils? How do you *do* anything?"

If I might investigate your persons a trifle more closely, the alien's thought, now calm, came, ignoring Brill's question. *Perhaps it will assist me to grasp these wonders.*

"Go ahead, as far as I'm concerned," Max agreed affably. At once, the quality of the touch in his mind changed to a more palpable, more tactile sensation, which probed, poked, and once again dissolved into unfocused confusion.

Specialized cells! the alien's mind echoed its fantastic discovery. *A multicellular being of incalculable complexity, each cell derived by replication from a single coded pattern—yet with infinite variations on the lone theme.*

The two men monitored the alien's confused mental emanations, unable to voice a response.

An incredible skill, the alien mused on. Then, deducing the reproductive mechanism, apparently by extrapolation, its thoughts once again shattered into incoherence: . . . *incredible complexity—yet so simple—and to consider that each individual grub possesses this capacity. Yet to continue to conceive these remarkable creatures as grubs is clearly invalid: each, in effect, is a mature hive, possessing all the attributes of the Supreme itself! Astounding!*

Shaking his head as if to clear it of the confusion transmitted by the shocked creature, Brill addressed Max: "It's hard to believe an organism could evolve so complex a mind, without artifacts or the ability to manipulate objects. But it can't be lying —one of the drawbacks of mind-to-mind communication, I suppose. . . ."

"I agree," Max said. "According to O'Reilly's book, *The Evolution of the Intellect,* or whatever—yeah, I read a book now and then—it can't happen. Like a stone lying in a streambed doesn't need any brain because it doesn't *do* anything. But as soon as an organism starts to interact with its surroundings, it has to start controlling what it does, instead of just responding to natural forces like a leaf blowing in the wind. So even a clam has some brains, so it can squirt water or open and close at the right time. And here this critter even has consciousness— Well, you know all that."

Brill noticed that the usually inarticulate fellow expressed himself now with unaccustomed clarity and precision; then, with a slight sense of shock, he realized he had been monitoring Max's thought-pattern, amplifying his verbalization.

I must interrupt, the alien came in clearly,—*in order to cor-*

rect a false impression: Of course we interact with the material exocosm, handle materials, and form artifacts—but not by means of pseudopods, as you do. Our method is simpler, more natural.

"Telekenesis?" Brill inquired dubiously.

No—though the concept is a pretty one, the monstrous alien replied—calmly, Brill reflected, and for once not going ape at the human's idea.

We proceed in the direct fashion which one would have assumed any rational creature would employ, the alien went on, rather didactically. *Alas, I cannot offer a proper demonstration, since we are but young, and our cuticle is not yet sufficiently developed.*

The men let this one ride, except that Max queried: "You call yourself 'we,' or are you speaking for others?"

Among the Mancji (people) the concept "I" applies to the Supreme, when attained. As for oneself, the plural form seems best to express one's—at this stage—dual nature.

"You call yourselves Mancji?" Brill persued the point at once.

Seldom, since we have little reason to refer to the hive to other than hive fellows. However, you may employ the term, for convenience.

"But what's *your* name?" Max persisted. "What do we call you?"

There was no reply, only a sense of stunned shock at the impact of a concept so strange. *A "name": a nonunique designation attached to a unique suborganism.*

"OK, so you're anonymous," Max commented. "How about 'Nonnie' for short?"

The alien projected numb agreement, musing over the curious thought-form which was now so oddly attached to itself. . . . There was, it seemed, no end to the strangeness of these supergrubs.

"Yeah," Max broke in on the ruminations, "but you were telling us how ya make those pots—like we saw in the cave."

To be sure, the alien responded calmly, withdrawing its thoughts from the bizarre world-view of the alien larvae, if such they were, to the humdrum, mundane matter of pot-budding.

Attending closely, Brill was at first unsure of the alien concept; then as the creature swiftly visualized the steps in the controlled production of artifacts, he grasped it and blurted: "You just grow things on your shell; you have adventitious buds you can start growing at will—and you control the shape of the growth—even its internal structure."

"Sure," Max chimed in, "that's what I get, too. Pretty neat trick."

"But energy intensive, I'd think," Brill countered. "What do you eat?"

For half a minute Brill and Max rode out the most turbulent amazement-response yet, until the alien recovered control and enunciated carefully, as though handling a fragile concept:

"Eat": to place a foreign object within the actual person, it ruminated. *Then to disassemble its constituent molecules, make use of the fragments to construct new tissues, employing the released binding forces as well. Fantastic! But why do you employ so complex a method, rather than simply gathering in the needed quanta?*

Max spoke up: "Cap'n, I get the idea it lives on pure energy —something like that. What do you get?"

"The same," Brill confirmed, then to the alien: "Where do you get these quanta?"

They are all about, somewhat sparsely at this point in space-time . . . The latter concept was a dizzying flash of the endocosm-exocosm, evolving serially along a convoluted path of least demand.

"It means sunlight, maybe, Cap'n," Max offered.

"Lightning, too," Brill put in. The alien's prompt mind-images confirmed that static electricity was the staple of its diet.

Brill thought of the great generators aboard *Omega* and was almost overwhelmed by the alien's instant, eager response. Mentally reeling from the input of the alien's thought, Brill fought to clear his own mind, visualizing his own identity and needs, struggling to impose his own world-view on the chaos dimming his senses.

"Cap'n!" Max's voice cut through the fog. At once, Brill was the competent commanding officer again, aware of the needs and problems of his ship, his people. . . . And perhaps if he could work something out with the alien . . .

Come, alien spawn, the creature's restrained thought came, carefully conforming to the contours of the human mind. *This is a matter for the hive. I perceive that we must come to an agreement.*

To Brill, it seemed that a gentle breeze, of which he had been only subliminally aware, grew somewhat in force, became a strong wind enveloping him, then a hurricane which curled about him, pushing, PUSHING, PUSHING until he felt his equilibrium go and he was falling—and still falling. Instead of the impact of the rock on which he had been standing, there was only the endless fall. He opened his eyes. Twenty feet away, Max lay sprawled in empty air. Below, a strip of jungle treetops thinned, became open parkland, with bare tundra beyond, stretching to a range of hills. The sea, he observed, was a narrow strait, embracing a large, roughly triangular island which reflected late daylight from myriad lakes and ponds.

Max turned his head lazily and smiled a remarkably boyish smile.

"Don't wake me up, Cap'n," he said, and yawned. "Dreamed I could fly lotsa times, but this is the first time I woke up and I was still airborne."

"Wrong word, Max," Brill said soberly. "We are not flying—we are being teleported."

"That's where some guy moves things around with his brains, right?"

"Approximately, Max. In this case, the 'guy' would appear to be our new friend, Mr. Anonymous."

"But how—and where the devil is that critter?"

"I have no idea, but, Max, I think I'm beginning to enjoy this."

"Sure," Max said. "Me, too. If this is my dying delirium, it's a swell way to go."

"You're not dying, Max. We're on our way to meet the hive!" Or—he reflected, confused—have we already?

· 23 ·

The silence was broken by the babble of Nonnie's voice mingled with many others: some shrill, others deeply resonant. A curious conceit, Brill reflected, attempting to cope with the clamor, since no sound is involved. Still, the silent mental voices seemed to have all the characteristics of vocal speech. Then the deeper, more commanding voice of the Supreme cut through clearly, quelling the clamor.

. . . strange being, pause, all, and permit the thing's feeble voice to prevail.

"That's better," Brill said aloud. "I think possibly we can come to a mutually beneficial agreement. But first, tell me about yourselves—yourself," he corrected at a quick mind-nudge from Nonnie.

The Supreme is all, the observer's familiar voice touched Brill in an instantaneous gestalt: *You may address us directly, being-to-being.*

Very well, Brill thought he had said aloud, but realized he was unsure, so accustomed had he become to communicating directly. He moved his tongue rather awkwardly, testing, and felt that he had in fact not vocalized. At the same moment, he became aware that he was, somehow, simultaneously in transit and stationary in a dark, cold cavernlike space. "Max!" he blurted, this time aloud, and tried to penetrate the darkness to catch a glimpse of his partner, but to no avail.

Have no fear, the Supreme's bass tones reassured him. *Your "Max" unit is safe and will be reassociated with you very soon.*

Fine—but where in Tophet am I? Brill demanded.

The locus Tophet is inapplicable to your present spatial-temporal coordinates, the Supreme replied shortly, then added: *You may, without excessive damage to your paradigm, consider yourself to "be" at the cavern of the Supreme.* Behind the concept Brill sensed a gigantic, multicelled mass of living tissue, grown to conform to the contours of a maze of deep natural caverns.

Very well, he communicated, holding a tight rein on his latent claustrophobia, *why am I here?*

You are "here," because our unit designated "Anonymous," or, alternatively, "Nonnie," transferred you in such a fashion as to bring to pass this juxtaposition.

Sure, sure, Brill came back. *Let's not engage in semantic quibbles. I have an important duty to perform—to find shelter for my passengers before the weather kills them.*

This time, Brill's consciousness nearly collapsed before the tornado of shock and bewilderment emanating from the Supreme himself, a mind-chaos of which Nonnie's confusion had been the merest hint. Out of the whirling of dislodged, deformed, and contradictory mind-forms, clear words emerged at last:

I (we) perceive that our (my) initial impression was quite correct: You clever grubs do indeed precociously carry out all those complex activities which we had imagined could be performed only by a mature hive, such as extracting useful molecules from the foreign objects which you place in your bodily cavities and, at the same time, forcing other foreign bodies into configurations useful to yourself(s), such as pots, arrowheads, television sets, and so on. I concede that we (I) find these "physiological" chores most demanding of both time and attention. Remarkable! Perhaps you will consent to explain to me (us) just how you are capable of such virtuosity. . . .

Actually, Brill replied, *it's not difficult. In fact we leave it to our nervous systems entirely. On the other hand, I found a number of Nonnie's statements almost unbelievable: that you manufacture your artifacts biologically, without external tools or materials, for example.*

That is correct, and pathetically simple, compared, for example, with your own practice of manufacturing counter-bodies against invading organisms.

May I see a demonstration? Brill requested humbly.

Of course, the Supreme agreed at once, after only momentary difficulty with the concept of a material manifestation to confirm a phenomenon already clearly visualized. *Would you care to specify just what "demonstration" you desire?* it queried.

What about this? Brill extended his hand, with the heavy, gold Academy ring on the third finger. Then quickly, he pulled off the ring and placed it in the palm of his hand.

Ah, that's much simpler, the Supreme commented. *Still, the material is rather dense—but no matter; it will require merely a few moments longer than some simpler substance.* The Supreme went on to explain that artifact production was a task usually assigned to the chitin of a nearly mature unit, somewhat more fully formed than Nonnie, for example, but which had not yet fully developed its cuticle, and not, of course, fully integrated. Thus it was necessary for the Supreme to isolate an appropriate member and assign the task to it. *Nothing so sophisticated as your own clever division of labor, of course, but still something of a challenge,* it concluded.

Well, Brill began, *I don't mean to be hard to get along with, so let's make it something simpler.*

By no means. The Supreme rejected the suggestion with a trace of pique. *Your request is perfectly legitimate. Kindly excuse me (us) a few moments,* and abruptly its mental presence was withdrawn.

· 24 ·

With no detectable transition, Brill felt pressure, the drag of gravity, sensations to the absence of which he had adapted without effort. Then the darkness lightened minutely, and Brill was startled to hear Max's voice abruptly vibrating against his tympanic membranes:

"—must be the end o' the line. But I'm going to get Nonnie to teach me that trick. Cap'n, you all right?"

"Certainly I'm all right, Max," Brill blurted, shocked anew by the harsh vibrations of his own voice in his skull. "Just a bit disoriented for the moment." He sat up and looked around. Max sat on the smooth floor a few feet away, grinning lazily.

"I was about to get worried about you, Cap'n," he said. "Glad to see you're back with the group."

"I should think you'd hardly have had time to develop any serious concern," Brill said. "I sat up the instant I sensed I was no longer in motion."

"Cap'n," Max said earnestly, "you been laying there having nightmares for about three hours, I'd guess."

"Here?" Brill echoed meaninglessly. "But I've had a fantastic experience: I met the Supreme and we had a nice chat. Splendid fellow, actually."

"Whoa, Cap'n. I think you lost me on that one," Max responded, less lazily; then: "Hey—there's *something*—I mean, uh, look over there, Cap'n." Max pointed and at the same time instinctively moved closer to Brill, who stared into the deep gloom and suddenly recognized the contours of the cavern wall about him. He was in the same underground chamber in which his interview with the Supreme had been conducted—but now the space which had been filled by the alien's bulk, was empty —or almost so. Something, as Max had said, moved there. Then Brill relaxed.

"It's only Nonnie," he told Max; then, to the alien: "Come on out and be friendly, Nonnie. We're waiting for the demonstration."

We (I) have undergone assimilation, the alien's familiar mental "voice" responded. *No more can we (I) function aloof from the hive. As for "demonstration"—another bizarre concept— the task has been allotted to us (me). May I proceed?*

"Pray do," Brill urged, wondering just what sort of trickery this curious creature was about to foist on them.

"What's happenin'?" Max cut in, as an amoeboid body, iodine-colored and dull-glistering like a heap of viscera, emerged from the tunnel's mouth to rest inert before the two men. The last portion to appear bore a roughly circular fragment of what seemed to be a thin husk.

As you see, the former Nonnie informed them, *cuticula formation has been initiated. It is indeed the circumstance that the protochitin is at its most protean stage that occasions the selection of this specific unit to produce the artifact you desire.*

"Don't forget the engraving on the inside," Brill cautioned, tongue-in-cheek. Nonnie's response was an impression of confusion.

Kindly observe the cuticle, the suggestion came clearly, as the formless mass shifted to present the thin plate, front and center. Brill watched it. He saw a faint change of color, which rippled across the shiny surface, leaving a yellowish patch near the center. The patch seemed to vibrate, then to bulge, rising as if pushed from below. It assumed a roughly spherical shape, developed a dimple which deepened until a cup form was attained. Opposite edges of the cup curled inward and merged. The short, thick tube, thus produced, shortened, refining quickly into a narrow, circular band, all the while deepening in color to a brassy sheen. Now a hump appeared on the upper curve of the ring, evolving swiftly into a broad bezel, the flat upper surface of which blurred and rose to form the embossed griffin and lettering.

"Ye gods," Max muttered. "That's a regular finger-ring; looks something like the one you wear, Cap'n." He looked at Brill's hand, noted the absence of the familiar sigil, and grinned.

"Neat trick," he commented, "but what's the point in conning *me?*"

"Not you, Max," Brill said in a tight voice. "I'm the one who's being conned—"

The term "con" is inappropriate, the alien voice cut in on his thoughts.

As the newly budded ring spontaneously broke free of its growth site and fell to the floor, Brill raised his hand, on the third finger of which his ring was in its accustomed place.

Max picked up the duplicate, examining it closely. He weighed it in his hand, eyeing Brill quizzically. "Heavy," he commented. "Feels like brass-painted lead." He peered closely at the ring. "Something scratched on the inside," he said. "Lousy spelling: 'I saye and I doe.' " He glanced at Brill, who took the replica ring and held it uncertainly. "Fleet property," he explained. "Or is it?"

"My God, Cap'n," Max said urgently, "did that thing really—?"

Brill nodded. "The dream of the alchemists," he said. "The synthesis of gold from base material."

"Sure," Max said, "but can it make anything useful?"

"Very likely," Brill replied, and at once offered the alien a clear visualization of a steel hammer, a self-energized crosscut saw, a three-point intercom system, a holographic projector with audio attachment, a fully programmed silicon chip, a fertile hen's egg, and a living mouse, which were quickly produced, in correct order, each from a distinct point on the cuticle, which had warped into a shallow saucer shape so that each item remained in place, including the mouse, which kicked its right hind leg twice, and died.

Sorry about that last item, the alien said. *I see that a number of dynamic processes, which I of necessity halted for replication, are vital to the full function. I hope this doesn't destroy my credibility in your esteem.*

"Not at all," Brill said urbanely, then went on: "By the way, would you be agreeable to supplying various substances in bulk, in return for appropriate consideration?"

A delightful and most novel proposal, the answer came at once. *I presume you are not unwilling to show us (me) the trick of carrying out all those clever metabolic processes simultaneously.*

"I'd be quite willing, my dear Supreme," Brill acceded. "But, alas, I have no conscious awareness of these processes, to say nothing of the method of initiating them."

All the more remarkable. Perhaps you'd kindly permit me, then, to rummage a bit in your suppressed minds? Fantastic structure: so many layers, rigidly held down by the ruling conscious. If I might . . . ?

Brill agreed, and at once experienced a sensation as if tendrils of palpable smoke were caressing his skull—not his scalp, he realized with a considerable shock, but the surface of the brain itself—carefully tracing its contours, exploring the patterns of convolutions, poking deep into the great fissures—at which he felt ghostly pin-pricks in his hands and feet, and fleeting sensations of heat and cold.

"Hey!" Max's baritone voice broke through the cloud of strange impressions. "What's happening? Cap'n, you all right? I don't like this. Hey, lay off, you! Get out!"

- 51

It appears my proposal is impractical, the Supreme stated calmly. *Your sensitivity is too great. A pity. An exchange would have been of incalculable interest—and value—to us both (all).*

"Wait a moment," Brill cut in on the fading impression of reluctance and regret as the Supreme withdrew contact. "I have a better idea! Something you *need* to have!"

The Supreme turned back, registering interest, not unmixed with skepticism.

Max spoke up: "This is no time to fake, Cap'n," he said tensely. "Having these critters—or this critter—on our side could make all the difference."

"But don't you see, my dear Supreme?" Brill inquired. "What I propose to offer to you is not some trick contrary to your nature, but is instead the gift of your true destiny."

"That's fancy talk, Cap'n," Max spoke up. "But does it mean anything?" Then, after a pause, he added, "Oh, sure, I guess it's like a lot of other things: pretty clear once it's pointed out."

"Do you know, Max," Brill commented, "I believe we've unconsciously adopted a practice of picking up each other's subvocalizations."

"Could be," Max grunted. "I guess you haven't really said it aloud yet."

Pray proceed with the explication, the Supreme urged gently. *As you are aware, I find it impractical to "read" those visualizations not specifically directed at us (me). Of course, I (we) will make appropriate recompense for data with which you endow us (me).*

"Think about it, Soup," Max said. "You live on raw energy, you can ignore gravity, and you're capable of endowing that versatile cuticle of yours with whatever properties you specify, including shielding against hard radiation. There's a name for it: preadaptation. What this means is: Your natural habitat is space. You don't need a ship—you can just go. You don't need to inhabit this honeycomb in the rock; you can pick your spot, with a whole universe to choose from."

There was a momentary impression of astonishment and exultation that burst like a silent, forceless bomb in the men's minds. There was silence. The Supreme was gone.

· 25 ·

Max looked across at Brill. "Well, Cap'n," he said lazily, "Here we are—but where in hell are we?" He stared around the eroded cavern walls, pocked with mouths of tunnels large and small. "What did you get out of that last blast from old Soup, Cap?" he inquired harshly. "You think he just blew his top and pulled out?"

"I hardly think so, Max. Be calm."

"You know what, Cap?" Max went on relentlessly. "There's no way out of this place. We're stuck. Old Soup just comes and goes, so I guess he didn't think about us needing a way to crawl out on our pseudopods."

"Perhaps," Brill assented. "But surely Nonnie would be aware—"

"Old Nonnie ain't no more," Max cut him off. "He's just one of the boys now. No more independent than one of our kidney cells, say."

In theory you are quite correct, Max-unit, the observer's familiar "voice" came clearly to them. *But the long habits of my duties as observer seem to have conferred on me an individuality of sorts. Curious.*

"Hey, don't hang up!" Max blurted. "I mean, dammit, tell us how to get out of this dead end you boys dumped us in. Where are we, anyway? How far from the camp?"

Not far. As for your mode of egress, I suggest you follow me, the alien thought-form responded, as, simultaneously, the men saw a flicker of movement at the mouth of one of the tunnels, otherwise identical with a hundred others. Without discussion, both men started toward it. Max, being closer, reached it first, and paused as if to urge Brill ahead.

"After you, Max," Brill said severely, then experienced a moment of amusement at his own residual insistence on protocol: the captain debarks first, but boards last. Max went in head first, accepting a boost from Brill, who followed at once, finding it a tight squeeze but negotiable.

"He's laid out like a rope for us to follow, Cap," Max reported.

"But we'll have to hump right along to keep it in sight."

Unfortunately, their Cicerone's voice came reassuringly, *there is no path to the outer surface of sufficient diameter to permit you to employ your clever limbs in their most effective mode.*

"That's OK," Max replied for both. "Just hang in there and don't forget about us; we'll manage as long as we can."

It was a tortuous progress, hour (or week) after hour, pressing on, on bleeding knees and gashed hands, while the ache of cramped muscles rose to a crescendo and began to fade. There was no energy for conversation, though at one partial respite in a cavern all of five feet in height, Max suggested they use the last of their meager food packs.

"You know what?" Max said. "We don't need to talk, because we're keeping in touch mind-to-mind, without even trying. It's an easy habit to get into."

Brill agreed. "But with the Supreme, or even Nonnie, it's easier," he added. "And better vocalized. I suppose that's because an alien has to identify our verbalizations in order to match concepts, like using sign language with savages."

Max nodded. "Old Soup just went off and left us sealed in—but not quite, because *he*'s never sealed in—or rather that's his natural state; he and his environment are coterminous. He fills the cavern complex and can 'be' anywhere in it—or everywhere, at once."

The living "rope," an extension of the substance of Nonnie, itself now a component of the Supreme, anxious at the delay, touched Max, eliciting from him a curse of startlement, then: "Sorry, Nonn; go ahead, we're OK. Don't jump, Cap, if somebody starts feelin' up your leg. It's just old Nonnie."

Half an hour, or half of eternity later, they saw the faint, grayish glow of light ahead and, at the same time, caught the scent of iodine-tainted ocean air. Then they emerged on a shallow ledge high on the cliff-face above the narrow, tideless beach where they had met the alien, an eon ago it seemed.

"Looks like the same spot," Brill said. "No visible differences —but there's miles of beach down there, and it all looks alike. I wonder how long we *were* inside."

"Beats me," Max said indifferently. He looked down dubiously. "That's a hell of a climb to have to make right now," he commented. "But let's get going. Looking at it won't make it any easier."

"Hey, Nonnie," Max said softly, aloud, addressing the tip of the living rope, which, having emerged onto the ledge, was groping uncertainly for continued support, and finding only the void.

Ah, there you are, the disembodied voice came, with a distinct undertone of relief. *How strange that any living intelligence, even such unlikely ones as yours, Max and Brill, could actually enjoy this naked exposure to emptiness.*

"We sure do," Max confirmed heartily. "I guess you like being outside about the way we enjoyed being buried alive, but you'll have to get over that. Space is *really* empty." He was lying face-down now, his head projecting over the cliff-edge, studying the near-vertical surface that fell sheer, fifty feet to the rock-littered sands below.

"Reckon a feller could make it," he grunted. "Ain't makin' no money laying here, so wish me luck, Cap." Before Brill could respond, the lanky man had squirmed around to lower his legs and grope for purchase. He paused for a moment before lowering himself to hang by his hands. Brill said, "Wait," but Max was gone.

Looking over the edge, Brill saw him ten feet down, feeling in vain for new footholds.

"Take it easy, Max," Brill said. "Don't do anything desperate."

At that moment he felt a touch on his arm. He turned to see the ropelike pseudopod of Nonnie, no longer with the opalescent bluish membrane surface, but now having a leathery, pistol-grip texture instead—and coiled, ready for use.

I (we) overheard your cogitations, Brill and Max. It appears that one of the concomitants to independent existence which I had considered in fancy is indeed one you curious beings are prepared to experience: to have one's person actually broken. But no matter. Shall I (we) assist him up, or down?

"Down," Brill said as the tough cable paid out over the edge.

Almost at once Brill caught a blast of near-mortal shock. He looked down. Max lay at the foot of the cliff, sprawled among rock fragments, unmoving, the dangling rope undulating indecisively above him.

"Nonnie, get me down there quick!" Brill ordered. At once, the living rope took a turn around his ankle and dragged him over the edge.

"All in one piece! I'm fragile!" Brill amended his hasty command. His fall was caught up short, with no more than a painful richochet off a projecting shelf. Then Nonnie lowered him gently to the beach beside Max.

"The Goddamned brainless bastard pried my grip loose," the injured man snarled. "His idea of helpin' me down—well, I got down in a hurry. I think my leg's busted."

After a swift examination, Brill determined that Max, had, in addition to cuts, scrapes, and bruises, sustained a sprained ankle and possibly a broken arm. The painful leg, except for a gash, was sound. With Brill's help—Max rejected that of the solicitous Nonnie—the tall, lanky man got to his feet and found that he could hobble, painfully. After Brill bound the ankle with the traditional strips torn from his shirt, the injured member held his weight well enough for him to walk, limping, but well enough. With no more ceremony, they set out up the beach, Max leaning on Brill's arm.

After an hour, by Brill's estimate, he proposed a rest stop. Max, impatient, avowed his willingness to continue without a break, but Brill over-ruled him.

"At the rate we're going," he said, "it will take us days to cover the distance we made in a few hours coming out, so let's pace ourselves."

"Sure, Cap, I guess you're right," Max conceded. "Shape we're in, and with no eats, it's not going to be any picnic. In fact —" he added, "maybe you best go ahead, and bring a stretcher party back for me. Don't want to starve *you* to death, too, stayin' back to help me."

"I suppose you had to get that off your chest," Brill said. "But we're sticking together."

"Too bad we can't eat these oysters or whatever you want to

call 'em," Max said, eyeing the life forms thickly clustered on
the rocky shingle washed by the surf. "I guess we'll eventually
work out a way—maybe grind 'em up to make fertilizer for our
own crops."

"I suppose that the Supreme evolved from some such mollusk," Brill commented. Max agreed. They discussed the matter
in a desultory way until Max broke it off with: "Well, Cap, it
looks to me like it's starting to get dark on us. We better get
moving." He got to his feet unassisted, then aided Brill in rising.
"Sat there too long," the older man commented. "Stiffened up
some."

They resumed their painful progress, skirting fallen rock-
masses, but avoiding the dense jungle growth pressing on their
right.

"Somewhere along here we've got to head inland," Brill said
with unaccustomed indecision.

"I've been watchin' for the spot where we cut our way out,"
Max commented. "We haven't passed it yet. But it can't be a
whole lot farther."

· 26 ·

Two rest stops and three falls each later, with the gray daylight faded to a murky dusk, they agreed it would be best to
sleep out the hours of darkness.

"My meteorology lieutenant said the local day was thirty-one
hours," Brill told Max. "So we've got fifteen hours to use those
clever metabolic mechanisms the Supreme admired, to rebuild
the old bodies a bit."

· 27 ·

They awoke to an icy mist, not quite a rain, that had soaked
them and the leaf pallets they had scraped together. Visibility
was close to zero. With little conversation, they started on,
keeping the beach on their left. It was wider now, and the cliff

lower, as Max discovered by groping his way to it, to find that he could reach the top with his fingertips. "We've got a way to go yet," he declared disgustedly. "Where we broke out of the woods, all we had was about a six-inch drop."

"Or perhaps we've passed it, and the upper level has risen again," Brill suggested.

"So which way do we go, Cap?"

"When this mist lifts, we can orient ourselves on the peaks on the other side." *Where my ship was,* he added silently.

"You really think old Jake swiped it, Cap? What for?" Max responded casually.

"Just to prove something," Brill replied. "The poor fellow has a serious ego problem."

"I think that ankle's taking my weight better, Cap'n," Max said, hobbling across the beach. "I can manage OK now without you having to hold me up. So let's get going."

"Which way do you propose, Max?"

"Inland. By the time the mist clears, we'll be maybe a mile or two in. Then we can see the mountains, and we'll know which way to go. Bettern' sitting here, waiting it out."

"Still, so long as we're on the beach, we can maintain our orientation—and if a search party is out, this is where they'll be looking for us."

"Right—except I don't reckon old Jake is going to be worrying too much about us. He's got his hands full."

"Still, Mr. Colmar is in need of the information he dispatched us to obtain. I suggest we continue as we have, until we can see better."

After that, hunger became prominent in their thoughts and conversation. Once, Max plucked a gray leaf from a low bush, crushed it, and sniffed it. "Smells kind of like mud," he commented, offering the wad to Brill for his opinion.

"Max, even if it smelled like *chateaubriand avec pommes frites,* we couldn't risk tasting it," Brill said. "Later, my dietician will conduct an orderly study, and will perhaps discover some edible materials. Meanwhile, we simply must not be so irresponsible as to kill ourselves merely from impatience."

On a rock-strewn stretch where the breaking waves washed completely across the beach to splash against the low cliff-face, Max lost his footing and fell, twisting his injured ankle severely, after which he again required Brill's aid in walking. Their pace was slowed, by Max's estimate, to twenty feet per hour. "Cap," he said, "it makes no sense for both of us to die out here, when you could make it on your own—and maybe bring help back. I'll get up above the high-water mark and get comfortable; go ahead."

· 28 ·

Jake Colmar was engaged in fussily rechecking the dimensions of the foundation layouts for the last two hutments in the east row. It was the lunch hour, and everyone else was gathered at the VIP dining salon, or chow-hall. He looked back down the rigidly surveyed street of close-cut grass, neatly defined by its rows of dwellings on either side and terminating at the imposing ten-foot-high facade of the Governor's Palace-cum-warehouse, all built of slabs of the pea-green timber of the cigar tree —as the commonest local tree had been named by common usage—with windows and doors salvaged from otherwise unused prefabs. Beyond the warehouse—Palace, he caught himself—the woodshop was turning out furniture machined from the almost gold-colored twenty-dollar tree—also an abundant species—by windpower. The whine of the saws was an ever-present background to the activities of the colonists, who were seemingly quite content now that their time was occupied in the constructive labor of tending garden plots, making fences for the pastures of alfalfa being prepared for the rapidly developing embryos of horses, pigs, sheep, and kine, all of which appeared to be thriving in the stock-brooders so laboriously carried down from the ship.

At a faint sound from somewhere behind him, Jake Colmar turned to see a curious scarecrow figure with spindly limbs draped in black rags totter from the undergrowth at the end of the roughed-in street. A second grotesque, Jake realized, was being dragged by the first via a grip on one preternaturally long, lean arm.

"Good God!" Jake said with feeling, and took a step toward the weird pair.

At twenty feet from the incredibly shabby and emaciated intruders, recognition struck Jake like a ten-foot drop. He hesitated, his mouth open.

"Captain Brill, welcome, sir!" he gasped. "And Slammer— How is he?" Max groaned.

"By God, Jake," Brill replied, "it's good to be home."

TWO

The Beginning

Think next of a man who lies sleeping on a narrow cot, one of several thousand identical cots, each in its half-walled cubicle, the cubicles ranked in rows under the dim-glowing ceiling of the Granyauck Municipal Dormitory. The man does not sleep peacefully. He fights his dream. His lips are drawn back and his jaw is clamped hard as he struggles against the nets that close around him. His fists are clenched, but even in his dream he is disciplined. He does not lash out, does not shout and curse his enemies. Within him the tension is not resolved. He sweats, but in a gentlemanly way, a light beading on his forehead. His breathing is harsh between his teeth. Now he turns on his back, and for a moment the agony of doubt shows in the rictus of his cheek muscles, in the harsh line of his mouth. His name is Taliaferro Tey, and he is a cashiered naval officer.

Abruptly his eyes are open. He lies on his back, looking up at the ceiling, at the firefly-green glow of the glare panels. There is no confusion on his face, no puzzlement. He knows precisely where he is, what has happened to him; he remembers yesterday, he understands the nature of the new day which will begin now in a few seconds.

The ceiling grows suddenly brighter. He narrows his eyes against the glare. A recorded voice rasps from the small grill in the wall beside him:

"Shift ends. Shift ends. Ten-minute alert. Ten-minute alert."

Ex-Captain Tey sits on the edge of the cot. He flexes his shoulders, which are wide, well-muscled, but stiff from lack of recent exercise. He feels the small aches and pains in his body, fits himself into their pattern, resuming the flesh. All around, voices mutter, groan; feet shuffle. A laugh, a curse. In the next cubicle, there is the soft hiss of the U-for spray. Tey looks at the blue button beside the inhaler mask clamped to the wall beside the PA speaker. He reaches out, touches its smoothness. But he does not press it. *Not yet,* he thinks. *I don't know why. But not yet. It has been twenty-nine days now, and I have fallen a long way, but not yet that far.*

He rises, feeling the coolness of the floor under his feet, drops his issue garment, and steps into the precipitator stall; at once there is a high-pitched hum, and his skin tingles as the high-frequency sonospray washes his body. He uses the depilator, pulls a fresh one-piece issue garment from the dispenser and dons it, puts his head under the comber. The flying mechanical fingers massage his scalp briefly, dress his short-cut black hair. All around now, the big room hums and sighs as other men activate baths and combers and dispensers. But not all. Many sleep on, and others feel no need of cleanliness.

There is a click from the bunk, and a new section of endless-belt bedding rotates into position. Cries ring out as late risers are dumped from sleep. There is laughter, a catcall. Steel-capped heels clack, and a gray-clad dorm monitor stalks past the open end of the cubicle, showing the flag, reminding all present of the relentless authority that watches every move.

A surly-looking man appears in the cubicle entry, rumpled, unshaven, his day-old issue coverall threadbare and fraying at the elbows and collar. He eyes the public bed impatiently. He has a face that reminds Taliaferro of the business end of a stake mallet. He smiles at the analogy, but he does not feel light-hearted. There is a faint sensation in his body as unused emotions stir tentatively, reflexively. His mind flashes again over the closed loop of cause, effect, which has led him here, now. But the memories no longer have the power to move him. The emotional machinery clicks off, like an empty drink dispenser clucking over an empty cup. After twenty-nine days his responses have become numb.

He moves past the waiting man, catches a sour whiff, which merges with that of the crowd shuffling toward a wide doorway at the far end of the long room. There is no jostling, no crowding. The monitors stand at intervals, with impersonally wary eyes, armed, invulnerable. They watch no one and everyone. For an instant Tey feels the quick touch of pity for them, for their innocent faith in the system which employs them; but it is only the ghost of an emotion. Empathy requires a framework of involvement against which to operate, and this man is not involved. Not any longer. Not ever again. He repeats the words to himself and finds his thoughts jumping back, flicking over remembered scenes like photographs in an album. Not ever again. Not ever. Again. Not. Ever again. But he halts this train of thought decisively, focuses his attention on the immediacy of the moment.

Most of the men are moving off to the right, toward the downramp which leads to the municipal kitchens; but he joins the favored group whose possession of jobs or friends or small, carefully hoarded funds allows them the privilege of dining elsewhere. Not that he has a job or a friend or money, Tey reminds himself, keeping the record straight. But at this particular moment hunger pangs seem preferable to processed kelp, even with liver flavoring added.

He emerges on the walkaway into keen night air under a midnight sky filled with flashing glare-signs celebrating the attractions of the megalopolis. Far away across the city the four-hundred-foot pink arrows which indicate the entrance to the Recpark quiver in a way which suggests mingled agony and ecstasy. Directly overhead, the stars gleam pale and lusterless, chaste and remote. For an instant, staring up at them, Tey feels devastating emptiness sweep over him, but he has felt this before, too. He presses back against the feelings that press in on him. After a moment the sensation fades. At that moment the light flashes on over the down car. The door opens, and a man emerges and hurries away. The bright-lit car waits, empty. Tey steps in.

He leaves the car at Level Five. The lights of luxury restaurants are soft; music is in the air. The walkaway is wide, curving gently past the gleaming entrances of tower hotels, shops with displays of costly merchandise. People pass him with quick glances at his issue garments. One man pauses, looks surprised, almost speaks; but Tey turns his head away and walks on toward a fire-fountain dazzling against the black sky.

For an hour he walks, paying no attention to where he is going. He follows the winding avenue, walking steadily, head up, shoulders back. He fixes his attention on the lights, on the facades, on the small, glittering two-man vehicles that sweep along the wide pavement or flit overhead with a sharp chopping of stubby rotors. He does not look at the people. He does not think, does not plan. He walks, only vaguely aware of the emptiness of his stomach. He does not tire. He has no destination. He does not hurry.

Later, he is on a downramp. A section of glare-strip has peeled away from its contacts, leaving a cave of darkness. There are bits of rubbish here, and foul odors waft from the shadows. A man separates from the wall and steps out as if to wait for Tey. Tey does not slow his pace or deviate from his course. As he comes closer, he is able to see that it is a young man, rangy, big-handed, hard-faced, dressed in extravagantly cut clothes which are limp and grimy, sweated-in, slept-in. The waiting man shifts his weight.

"Let's see what you got on you, palsy," he whispers. Tey walks straight at him. He feels a mild curiosity as to whether the young man will move from his path. He knows that his body will automatically act to deal with any obstruction in his way, and he is aware of wondering briefly whether he will strike first with the edge of his hand or with a doubled, knuckle-projecting blow, down low. But at the last moment the youth jumps away with a curse. His voice follows Tey, swearing loudly, but Tey is not listening.

Just ahead the point of a giant arrow of pink light jabs down from the sky toward the light-encrusted arch beyond which fanciful spires and turrets loom, bathed in lights of changing colors. A big glare-sign says EVERYTHING FREE TONITE. It is the

Recpark; Tey realizes with surprise that he has walked straight to it, across the city. For the first time, he hesitates. Then he walks slowly up to the gate. There are people there, crowding through the turnstile. As from a distance, he observes himself as he takes his place in line, places his wrist disc against the recognition plate of the mechanical gatekeeper. There is no credit balance encoded against his ID, he knows, but the park is free to all. The turnstile palms him through the sound-screen into the blare of noise and light.

· 2 ·

At the same moment on the other side of the city, a man was entering an opulent salon. He was slim, quick-moving, elegant in silver-appointed black. His face was narrow, pointed; his bushy, silver-white hair was long and brushed straight back. His features were sharp, regularly chiseled; but his appearance was dominated by the scar which ran from his hairline down across the corner of his right eye, nipped the nostril, raised his upper lip in a faint sneer, and continued across his chin. It was not an old scar; it looked pink and tender.

A tall woman in silver greeted him. Her hair was as white as his own, and she was wearing a silver gown that glittered with sprinkled jewel chips.

"Oliver . . . how good of you to come." Her voice faltered only for an instant as she caught a full view of his face. "I was deeply shocked when I heard of your . . . accident."

"It was not an accident, my dear Cudelia," he said, his voice a crackling whisper projected by a throat amplifier. He inclined his head and offered his arm. In a small open space under a vast chandelier at the center of the room, a pretty girl in a blue gown looked up as they approached. The two men to whom she had been talking fell silent, and eyed Oliver Jaxon impassively.

The girl smiled nicely as the introductions were made, her eyes not quite meeting Jaxon's. The two men—one small, elderly; the other massive, red-faced—offered little more than grunts.

"I wonder, m'lady, if you'd care for a pop?" The larger of the two men brushed Jaxon with his elbow as he extended a jeweled dopestick case to the girl.

"No thank you, m'lord. I don't smoke."

"Come, now, you must try one. I insist!" The big man thrust the case toward the girl, easing his weight against Jaxon as he did so. There were creases in his neck where it bulged over his pleated collar. He was holding the case almost in the girl's face, and as she leaned away, he followed, thrusting heavily against Jaxon. Jaxon felt the man's foot touch his shoe; he shifted his weight, moved his foot an inch—far enough to avoid being trodden on—and delivered a short, sharp kick to the other's ankle. The big man uttered a bark of pain and whirled on Jaxon.

"You—" he started, and broke off as bystanders' eyes swung, staring.

The elderly man plucked at his sleeve and hissed, "Lord Banshire," but the big man shook him off to confront Jaxon:

"I believe, sir," he said in a controlled voice, "that your foot struck me."

"Indeed?" Jaxon allowed a slight smile to twist his face. "What with the crowding, I daresay I was scrambling for footing."

Lord Banshire's eyes lingered on the scar crossing Jaxon's face. "Perhaps your injuries have made you clumsy, sir. Too clumsy for polite society."

Half of Jaxon's face was smiling. The scar across his features was like a fresh wound.

"Perhaps your lordship will join me in a breath of fresh air," Jaxon whispered.

"Paugh! I suggest you descend to the port and roister among the stevedores," the big man rumbled. "Fit company for a blackguard of your stripe, sir!" He nodded stiffly to the girl and pushed away through the circle of wide-eyed listeners, the old man doddering behind him. A moment later Jaxon made his excuses and followed.

On the roof he waited until the older man's machine had lifted off, then thumbed the recall button which summoned his own car, which was waiting in a parking fix a thousand feet above.

"Where to, sir?" his driver asked as they climbed away from the pooled light below.

"Just cruise, Arno. And keep an eye open for reckless drivers."

"Did you see him, sir?" Arno asked quietly.

"I saw him."

"What do you think?"

"Just what I thought before."

"Let it lie, sir. You can't go up against a Starlord. Not and go on living."

"You may be right. It might be interesting to find out for sure."

"I don't get it, sir! You're a rich man, you've got everything going for you! Why risk it all, just for . . ." The man fell silent.

"For a whim, Arno? Maybe it's more than a whim. Maybe it's something rotten at the bottom of the barrel that's spreading a faint, unlovely odor over this entire planned Utopia of ours."

"Sure, there's things that happen, questions that don't get answered. But most people are living better than they ever did —except for Prekes, of course. Everybody's got money, and places to spend it—"

"Is that what it's all for, Arno?"

"You know what I mean, sir. It's not perfect, but it could be worse—lots worse."

"So . . . I shouldn't rock the boat. That's Lord Banshire's feeling in the matter, too."

"Don't pair me with that octopus," Arno grunted. "All I say is, why smash yourself against something you can't beat?" The driver broke off as the helicar swerved violently. Air buffeted as another machine swept past mere yards above. Arno swore with feeling, fighting the controls.

"Drop her!" Jaxon rapped. "Douse your lights and take her down!"

"That maniac tried to ram us!"

"Not quite; he was trailing cables to foul our rotors." Jaxon held on as the lightless machine fell like a stone. The altimeter clocked backward—fifteen hundred feet, twelve hundred, nine, six . . .

"Flatten her out," Jaxon ordered. Ahead, colored lights swept toward them, dazzling against the night.

"Set her down there—by the park."

The machine settled in on a cabflat cantilevered from the curving wheelway that swung under the towering pink arrows above the Recpark gate. Jaxon jumped out.

"Light up and take her home, Arno," he said.

"What are you going to do?"

"Give my impulsive friend a chance to think it over."

"You think that was intentional?"

"Don't you?"

"Not even Banshire can get away with that!"

"Can't he? Show plenty of lights, Arno. Let them see you're alone."

"What about you, sir? What if he puts a man on you?"

"Not in the Recpark. Too many people."

"I don't like it."

"Better on the ground than up there."

"Why not advise the police?"

"And then tell them what? Relax, Arno. I'll be home in an hour. But stand by, just in case something comes up."

Jaxon turned and walked briskly toward the queue filing through the lighted archway.

· 3 ·

Less than a mile from the park, deep within the cubic-mile steel and plastic mass of Gradapt Twelve, a man named Nat Grall sat alone at a table in a small room. A large sheet of yellow paper was spread on the table, and on the paper were laid out dozens of intricately machined metal parts, distinct under the brilliant light of a drop-lamp. Painstakingly, Grall was engaged in cleaning each part with a fine-pointed air-core brush. His fingers were thick, powerful, not clumsy. He handled the small objects deftly, surely, examining each through a magnifying loupe before laying it aside.

He completed the cleaning, began assembling the parts inside the housing shell, without haste, but without waste motion, using a variety of delicately fashioned tools. In a matter of minutes, the completed assembly lay on the table before him. It was a simple cylinder, tapering slightly at each end, ten centimeters long, three centimeters in diameter at its widest point, a dull gray in color. Few would have recognized it for what it was: a modified and disguised Mark IX rup-gun. The penalty for its possession was transportation for life.

Grall put away the cleaning materials, disposed of the paper, switched off the powerful light, and retracted it. He left the gun in the center of the table as he stripped off his clothes and stepped into the sonospray stall. He was a big man, almost two meters tall, massively muscled. His blunt-featured head was set on a short, thick neck which rose from sloping shoulder muscles, like an oak rooted amid boulders. Thick black hair matted his barrel chest. Only a slight thickening around the waist and a glint of gray in his short-cropped, sandy hair indicated that he was past his prime. Those, and the fine lines around his small pale blue eyes.

He punched dispenser keys, selecting his clothes: underwear, a well-cut plain gray coverall, a short jacket of deep red, a black cap with a curling, scarlet plume. He dressed carefully, adjusting his cuffs and collar, smoothing back his hair. He slipped a ring with a large red stone onto the middle finger of his left hand; it nestled among curling black hairs. The gun fitted into a small pocket stitched under his left arm without making a bulge. Grall switched on the mirror light and examined himself closely, then left the apartment.

It was a ten-minute ride via slidecar to the northside departure ramp, set high in the featureless side of the Gradapt. There, Grall fitted himself into a seat in a beltcar, sat stolidly, without impatience, until the buzzer sounded and the car surged off along its rail. Five minutes later, he left it at the bright-lit Two Level concourse, made his way among the hurrying crowds toward the railed walkaway spanning across to the lighted gate of the Recpark.

People in carnival attire thronged the gate. The great glowing arrows hung pulsating above them, like aimed weapons singling out victims. Grall's tongue touched his lips. His palms were damp. His hand trembled minutely as he pressed his ID against the turnstile plate. Then he was through, moving down the ramp toward light and sound, trees, colors, hucksters' shouts. Grall was not hurrying now. He walked slowly, almost heavily along the curving, stall-lined promenade, hardly aware of the noise around him, oblivious of the smells, the electric feeling in the air that was human tension aching for release. A wild-eyed girl in orange skintights and with blue-painted breasts ran out of a doorway shaped like a mouth and threw herself at a gibbonlike man wearing a wig of stiff green hair. He knocked her away and darted to a booth where robot arms strapped him into a canvas chair and tripped a lever that sent him whirling away at the end of a cable. An immensely fat man waded past, half-floating in a liftbelt, popping scented air-balls into a pursed mouth like an empty eye-socket. There was a shriek like a falling bomb, and a wire-car racketed overhead, scattering confetti that people scrambled for. One bit fell at Grall's feet; he saw that it was a low-denomination lux-chip, before a spider-lean girl, naked and painted with green stripes, snatched it up and darted away, screeching.

A band rolled past, playing light-music that hurt the eyes to look at. Fireworks burst overhead, trailing down the sky. A perfume projector jetted scented water high over a pool where naked swimmers splashed, screaming. A small man with an over-large head leaned from a booth and thrust an iridescent balloon in Grall's face. He brushed it away absently. His eyes were fixed on a wide, spot-lit open-air stage ahead, where a line of long-legged girls in glittering diablo costumes moved in intricate patterns against a backdrop of leaping flames. He joined the watching throng, working his way forward along one edge. A narrow walk led back beside the structure, shielded by flowering bushes with dusty leaves. At the rear corner the walk turned, leading to a short flight of steps and a red-painted door lettered in white: NO ADMITTANCE. He climbed the steps and tried the handle. The door opened into a dim-lit passage. The sound of the music from the stage was loud here. Grall followed the corridor to a turn, and was facing a row of narrow dressing room doors. A small, effeminate-looking man in a loose pastel violet shirt and tight yellow pants darted forward.

"Here! Who are you? You can't come in here!" He halted, then swayed back at the look Nat Grall gave him.

"Where do I find Tulina?" Grall's voice had a harsh, rasping edge, as if his vocal cords had been damaged. He spoke slowly, with little change of inflection.

"Are you a friend? A relative? What do you want with her? I've told you, you can't—"

Grall brushed the small man aside with an economical movement of his hand. He tried the nearest door, found it locked. The little man squeaked and fluttered around him. Abruptly the music stopped, and in the near-silence feet clattered. A stream of costumed girls came pouring back past Grall, darting him glances from painted eyes. He stared at each one as they passed. When a slim-waisted, long-legged redhead appeared, Grall thrust through to her; she whirled on him.

"Tulina," Grall said, and stopped, looking into her face.

"What do you want?" she hissed, looking around as if to see who had observed the interception.

"Tulina—I had to see you."

"I told you I was busy!"

"You can't be busy all the time, Tulina."

"To you, I am!" She stared at him with furious eyes, her painted mouth twisted. "Keep away from me! I want nothing to do with you, you . . . you ape!"

Grall's eyes changed; a light came and went behind them like a signal from a smuggler's cave. The girl backed a step.

"Don't touch me," she whispered. "Don't ever touch me!"

"Tulina, I only—"

"I hate you! The sight of you, the sound of you, the smell of you! Go somewhere and die! Leave me alone, alone, alone!" She spun and disappeared through a door which slammed behind her.

Grall stood like a man frozen. The other girls were gone. The little man hovered.

"You can't stay here," he piped.

Grall turned, and walked past him and back along the corridor the way he had come. Outside, he went up the walk and pushed through the crowd like a sleepwalker. The people he thrust from his path looked at his face and choked back their protests.

Ex-Captain Taliaferro Tey walked along a curving path, jostled by hurrying pleasure seekers, only dimly aware of the flashing lights, the cacophony of voices and musics and noise-makers. He halted on a narrow bridge that spanned a gurgling stream, the surface of which was clotted with floating rubbish. Leaning on the rail, he looked down into the black water, watching an empty cup whirl in an eddy before bumping away downstream. Reflected lights glinted and wavered, broke apart, shimmered together again. A stream of brightly glowing sparks boiled upward from below, red, green, yellow, blue.

A thin scream cut through the mindless background noises like a hot wire cutting styrofoam. This was no yelp of brainless excitement, Tey knew at once; this was naked fear. He turned and saw the swooping track of the ride called the Deathcar, for which no fee was charged, but rather five steel credits were paid to anyone rash enough to ride it. Tey bucked the crowd, which flowed on, ignoring the repeated scream. He pushed through to the heavy railing which edged the abyss crossed by the Deathcar track. At the point where the track, after dropping steeply, made an abrupt left turn, a car was wedged, canted with its aft wheels off the track; under it its guide trolley hung free. A child, a girl no more than ten years old, in a yellow dress, hung half-in, half-out of the car, clinging with both hands to the shiny handrail. She did not hang inertly, awaiting the moment when her grip would fail; she swung one leg up, groped, almost found purchase on the sill of the car, slipped back, lost the grip of one hand, and hung now by the other. She screamed again. Only Tey seemed to notice, though a park cop stood just a few feet away, idly twirling his prod, gazing across the crowd with a stern expression on his meaty face.

Tey's glance swept the shadowy spaces above, at a glance taking in the configuration of girders and cables through which the Deathcar track twisted. At once he spotted the broken cable which had allowed the track to deflect under the weight of the car, thus prying the trolley from its guide. The frayed end of the cable swung in a slow arc, to and fro, passing two yards from the track just above the car. A red light on a column blinked, indicating another car on the way. An emergency maintenance beeper chirped, unheeded far above. Tey's eyes followed the path a repair crew would follow from the nearest open and lighted utility accessway. There was, Tey realized, barely time if they appeared there now.

Without conscious decision, he moved off along the rail, thrusting past the still-flowing crowd, among whom not one face had turned toward the source of the child's screams. Tey realized that only a man who had known violence, agony, and death at close range would be able to distinguish a cry of mortal terror among so many other sounds. And had they heard, the clever thing to do was to ignore it, avoiding involvement.

Tey's glance flicked again toward the jammed car. When the next one arrived at high speed, loaded to overflowing with thrill seekers, there would be an impact that not even this blasé crowd would ignore. Tey winced at the thought; then motion caught his eye. A man dressed in black was sliding down the Deathcar track, squatted low and riding the rails on his hands and feet. Here was a fellow, Tey reflected, whose death wish wouldn't wait for the next car—or perhaps he was merely a celebrant, high on the pink stuff, taking a dare. He'd meet a rude surprise at the bottom of the long, twisting descent. . . .

With the agility of a howler monkey, the speeding madman rose to his feet, continued his breathless slide toward the wedged car in a half-crouch. Then, incredibly, he threw himself backward, caught the rail with both hands, and braked to a halt just as the track entered the sharp turn. With casual grace he stood up on one rail, crossed the three steps to the car, hopped lightly onto the seat, and caught the child up into his arms. He held her close, patting and soothing her. Her arms went around his neck as he sat holding her in his lap.

Tey had a momentary thought that he had misjudged the maintenance crews; then his attention was on the silver piping on the black clothing. No crewman's coverall this, he realized, but a tailored garment of the highest fashion.

An overweight fellow in bile green pushed against Tey and wheezed, his round face puckered and sweaty. Tey eased him aside with an elbow and resumed his progress along the rail.

So far, so good, Blackie, he thought, *but what do you do for an encore?*

The broken cable dangled above the car, swaying slightly. *Too far,* Tey thought. *And even if the man in black could reach it, no one could climb that greasy rope, even unburdened.* The cable trembled, twitched, and swung now in a slower, wider, arc. Tey traced its length up into the gloom high above. Something clung there: a gray lump—*a man,* Tey realized, *sliding down the stranded wire.* He would reach the car, it seemed. Then what?

Tey bucked the crowd, ramming his way through with sudden urgency. He reached the shelter of a mighty steel-plate column, vaulted the rail to a catwalk, went along to the lighted archway through which a utility cart and the foot of a flight of narrow iron steps were visible. A lighted panel above it read: OFF LIMITS. WARNING: AUTOMATIC SENTENCE FOR TRESPASS. PENAL CODE NINE. Tey was through it and had leaped up the steps halfway to the next landing before he recalled that Penal Code Nine was the one which applied to the Star Court, whose minimum sentence was death.

At the landing he saw a square iron door, which, he calculated by dead reckoning, should open onto the catwalk he had seen from below. It was a standard navy-model latch, Tey saw. He drew a six-inch wire from his lapel, inserted it in the tiny hole next to the heavy latch, and something *snick!*ed inside the thick panel. Now the latch yielded easily. Tey opened it a few inches and squeezed through. The cable hung quivering, ten feet away. The big man in gray had reached the car, a few feet below Tey's level, and he and the man in black were engaged in tense conversation. The latter was shaking his head as the big man's blunt, close-cropped head loomed over him by nearly a foot. He stooped slightly, scooped up the man in black, still holding the little girl, and looked around—and up. His pale blue eyes met Tey's. The black-clad man appeared to be expostulating vigorously, his voice inaudible. Tey frowned in inquiry. The big man shook his head, shifted the weight of his burden slightly, stepped up on the seat of the gaily painted car, reached with one hand, and took a grip on the cable hanging above, almost out of reach. Only a few inches of frayed cable extended below the big man's grip. Tey gripped the handrail before him and muttered, "No. You can't do it, big boy. Nobody could."

The big man braced his feet and shook the cable, sending a ripple up into the shadowy heights, where only vague shapes were visible. As the ripple returned, the cable jumped, causing the big man to shift his footing; then the cable shifted away from Tey. The man in grease-stained gray kicked off suddenly, swung out another six feet, then back, toward the catwalk. Tey stepped close to the rail, braced his feet, and reached—too far—but as the human pendulum slowed, the big man swung his legs forward and, releasing his grip at the last possible instant, slammed hard against Tey and the railing. Tey grabbed the child as the big man, with the man in black still slung over his shoulder, hooked the rail with a desperately outthrust foot. Tey lifted the girl over the rail, put her down with a soothing word, and turned back in time to catch the big man's leg as his toe slipped, and haul hard. A moment later hard hands were lifting him to his feet. They were on the catwalk—all four of them, Tey saw at a glance. The child clung to the smaller man's black-clad arm and smiled tentatively up at Tey.

"Welcome to our group, gentlemen and lady," Tey said. "If you're willing to associate with a certified enemy of the state, that is."

"An honor, sir," Grall aped Tey's pseudoformal manner.

"You're him," Jaxon said. "The fellow—the big brass they court-martialed and fired. It seems you called Lord Banshire a crook and a liar. True, of course, but foolish of you."

"Calling the guy a liar was bad enough," Grall contributed in his bass rumble. "Proving it was going too far."

"I was naive," Tey agreed. "A quality I've now lost, I trust."

"You've lost plenty, Captain," Grall said. "But there's still your life to lose—so let's get out of here."

As Tey nodded, Grall stooped to the girl. "What's your name, sugar?" His voice was gentle. She looked up brightly. "Philomene," she said. "But I like 'Sugar' better."

"Very well," Grall said. "We'll call you Sugar. How did you get out there all alone, Sugar?"

For a moment it seemed she would burst into tears; instead she spoke calmly—*too* calmly, Tey thought. "Alice—she's my m-mother—told me to sit there. She was looking for her friend, but he was late. Then some grown-ups came along, and they started to make fun of the man who takes the tickets, and they said they'd give me a free ride and at first it was fun and then there was a big bump and I hit my knee." She touched a developing bruise above her kneecap and began to weep silently.

"But you're all right now," Grall said. "We'll find Alice for you."

She shook her head solemnly. "I don't think Alice likes me," Sugar said. "I want to stay with Oliver. He told me his name. He likes me."

· 4 ·

As the three men emerged from the service entry, Jaxon carrying Sugar, a park cop lounging nearby gave them a sour look, pushed away from the wall, and sauntered into their path, unlimbering his prod as he came. He halted when the men were ten feet from him, turned lazily, and remarked in a nasal whine that penetrated the background: "Didn't see the sign, eh, boys?"

"We saw it, your honor," Grall volunteered. "And we said to hell with it. So what?" He had continued his advance and, when the cop failed to yield right-of-way, rammed him with his shoulder in what seemed an almost gentle contact, yet the cop slammed against the floor, full-length, his head striking concrete with an audible *bonk!* muffled only slightly by his immense, frizzy head of hair.

"Tsk," Grall said, heard only by Tey, who was at his side. "Did I jostle you, sir?" He took two steps, leaned to take a grip on the cop's two-foot-wide hair bush, and lifted him casually until his feet were clear of the floor. The man groped for footing, both hands going to Grall's arm.

"Oh, your lordship want me to let go?" Grall inquired solicitously, and released his grip. The man collapsed, again striking the floor a sharp rap with his skull.

Grall went on, Tey and Jaxon on either side. A second cop appeared from behind a massive column and headed determinedly toward Grall, who appeared not to notice. Jaxon spoke quickly to Tey, who took Sugar from his arms as the smaller man forged ahead a few inches. Just as he was about to pass the cop, who kept his gaze unwaveringly on Grall, the cop said, "Get back, you." Jaxon half-turned away, hooked the cop's ankle with his foot, and continued offside to the rail edging the Deathcar pad. The cop fell against Grall, who made a swift motion, caught him, and eased him upright. The cop's legs wobbled; he shook his head.

"What did you slug me with, you bum!" he barked.

Grall showed him a clump of scarred knuckles smaller than a cabbage. "Seems like someways you bumped me on the fist with your jaw, copper," he explained.

"Hey," the cop said, "it was that other bum. He tripped me up!"

"Gracious," Grall said, turning to glance toward Jaxon, who was watching a belated maintenance crew at work freeing the Deathcar. The cop went toward him, prod in hand. As he came within reach, Jaxon plucked the weapon from him with a swift, complicated motion, and tossed it over the rail. The cop grabbed the rail with both hands and stared after it. As he turned back toward Jaxon, with his mouth open, Grall came up, scooped up the cop's ankles and pushed him to a vertical handstand position, then stepped back to gaze at him admiringly.

"That's really some balance, Governor," he said. "And dangerous, too. Do you give autographs?" He smiled at the twisted face, not reassuringly. The cop made sputtering noises and began to lean outward, slowly toppling toward the abyss. Frantically he kicked his legs, but his precarious balance was gone.

"Gosh, I must of distracted you, Chief," Grall said, taking a firm grip on the man's hair, a Max-Bush, which was apparently a part of the uniform as well as an effective skull protector.

As the toppling man's tumble accelerated, Grall carefully set himself and received the shock as the man's full weight came upon his arm, which he had lowered to contact the rail for support. The cop screeched as Grall held him suspended above thirty yards of empty air over a rough pavement barely visible in the gloom below.

Tey came to Grall's side. "You'll be out of luck, my friend," he said, "if you ever meet a baldheaded cop."

"Purely a matter of convenience, Captain," Grall replied. "Then, too, the necks one gets hold of nowadays seem to snap so easily." He lifted the terrified man back over the rail and held him at face-to-face level.

"I wouldn't want this cop to come to harm while he's in my possession," he said. "That's all for today, cop," he added, and dropped the man, who fell the eighteen inches to the floor and scuttled away to rejoin the passing throng beyond the barrier-rail which ignored him completely.

"I don't like cops," Grall said, and wiped his right hand on the seat of his garment.

· 5 ·

"I seen that puss before," the cop at the gate commented, eyeing Grall bleakly. "A troublemaker. For what? Maybe this world ain't perfect, Mac, but it's the one you're stuck with." Wearily he waved them through. Jaxon, still carrying Sugar, made a show of ostentatiously examining Grall's face.

"It's definitely not pretty," he said at last, as if solving a problem. "But I was glad to see it, Nat."

Grall nodded. "When I saw you go over the rail, I kept an eye on you. That monkey routine on the track was all right. I saw the broken cable was too far offside, so I got up on the pipes up there, and hooked it over as far as I could."

"You fellows work well together," Tey commented. "Quite a team."

"The three of us," Jaxon said. "Let's drink to that. I know a place. And there's a girl—Renee; she'll love Sugar."

Jaxon seemed at home in the narrow ways of Deuce Level, leading the way with assurance along a complex route through cramped alleys, up trash-cluttered steps squeezed between age-blackened walls, past a glare-sign with an arrow lettered THREEVEE MALL (7). Only when he kneed open an inconspicuous, low gate that opened onto the unshielded racketcar line did Tey comment:

"Perhaps it would be better if we went to Westrat, after all. Sugar looks tired."

"With respect, Captain," Jaxon replied, "I know this looks like Forkwaters, but it isn't—not quite yet. Solar Corona's on the line, and we'll be there in a minute. Renee will be there."

In the sour, brown gloom, the blinking, antique gas-tube sign —SOLA   RON —looked almost cheery with its missing letters. The haggard Treys hanging around the entrance gave way grudgingly, with darting looks at Tey. When Grall spoke suddenly, asking Jaxon if he were encountering any difficulty in cutting through the scum, all eyes went to him, and abruptly the path was clear. A badly-fitting and warped panel, which appeared to Tey to be of genuine reconstituted wood, swung back to reveal an ocher-lit interior, where vague shapes moved in a slow, churning motion. Without pausing, Jaxon plunged in, Grall beside him, opening a path across a floor of chipped red tile to a sagging booth, where a small man in red-and-green livery sat alone. He greeted Jaxon briefly, then scuttled away.

Jaxon waved Tey and Grall in, hostlike, and placed Sugar beside himself.

"I think I've heard of this dive," Grall said in a low tone that seemed to slide under the background surf-roar, which was less loud than that at the Recpark. "Nothing good," Grall added.

Jaxon nodded. "The *Corona*'s not without reputation," he acknowledged. "Still, the food is nontoxic, and as for the drinks —"

A cadaverous fellow with a missing nostril leaned up against the table. Jaxon spoke to him inaudibly, and he went away, studiedly not looking at Tey.

"I ordered beer-and-a-half all around and cinnapple for

Sugar," Jaxon said. "Then, Stag says, we can have the stew, or the casserole, Chinese-Italian style."

Stag returned with four tall mugs, three green and one deep red, which he deposited on the table by holding the rimless tray an inch above it and jerking it away suddenly. Each glass dropped, then slid on a film of moisture to come to rest before its intended user. Sugar watched with delight as hers almost slid past, spinning slowly and at the last moment seeming to swerve —but then coasted to a spot directly before her and came to rest.

Tey glanced up. Stag was gone, and a slender girl stood there, the collar of her brown suede jacket which seemed to be genuine leather turned up to meet her short-cut coppery hair. She smiled at Tey uncertainly.

"I followed the trial, Captain," she said in a pleasantly breathless voice. "It was a farce. I'm *so* sorry."

"That was twenty-nine days ago, Miss," Tey said. "Ancient history."

Then Jaxon greeted her, knowing her well, and made introductions. By pulling Sugar into his lap, where she at once slept, he was able to make room for Renee. Grall watched her, fascinated.

"I hope you won't be offended, Miss," he said, "if I tell you that you are a truly beautiful woman."

Renee smiled. "Offended?" she repeated in an incredulous tone. "No fear. The Thunderbroad Law hasn't changed human nature. And may I say that you look very manly." Her eyes went to Sugar, half-awake and moving restlessly, seeking a comfortable position in Jaxon's arms. Renee took her, and in a moment the child was sleeping again. Briefly Jaxon explained how they had met the child. Renee listened bright-eyed. "Poor baby," she murmured, clearly addressing Jaxon as well as the child. Jaxon picked up his glass, studied it as though hoping to find one more swallow in it.

"Don't drink any more, Oliver, all of you," Renee pled. "The Organization—"

"To hell with the Organization," Jaxon cut in.

"Oliver—you don't really mean that." Renee looked hurt.

"You really came for the meeting didn't you?"

"I'd forgotten," Jaxon said. He glanced at Tey. "Maybe we'd best be going," he suggested.

Tey shook his head. "Not yet."

"Captain," Jaxon said hesitantly, "you've not—I mean, I've heard—"

"I was contacted," Tey said. "Right after the trial started, when I was still expecting someone to stand up and say, 'Fellows, there's been a dreadful mistake . . .' I deferred judgment."

"Forget it," Jaxon said. "The Organization might have been something once, but now it's no better than Banshire and his gang—it's just working a different angle." He paused. "You're right, Renee. I've had too much. I'm starting to tell the truth."

"Let's all go to my place," Renee said. "I have my whole week's issue. You don't want to eat stewed gerbil-culture. I'll fix something."

Tey smiled at Renee as her eyes caught his. "Nat's right," he said. "You're beautiful, Renee," he added with finality, then eagerly: "Let's get out of this—the whole thing—go someplace."

"Don't make a joke of it, please," the girl replied appealingly. "It's a serious thing: a man like you—all of you—reduced to this."

"Who's joking?" Tey said. "Somebody said I was stuck with this world; maybe I am . . . and maybe I'm not."

"But there's no place to go," she argued. "There hasn't been since the Lost War. Senator Skorn from Jersey is no better than Banshire. The Organization is the only thing—"

"Too late," Jaxon said as he leaned forward and slapped the table, but not too loudly. "We should have hit them years ago. While we waited, Skorn found our caches one by one—and picked up our best men, while we held meetings."

"Oliver, don't talk so loudly—"

"Nobody's listening," he said. "Not even us. We fight among ourselves, scrambling for top position." Jaxon grumbled on: "And meanwhile Banshire's consolidated his hold on twenty thousand square miles and built an organized police force of three thousand men."

"But we can't just—give up," Renee offered.

"I just want out." Jaxon lowered his voice. "There's something I'll tell you about. If I only had—"

"Oliver"—Renee took Jaxon's hand, held it tightly—"don't confide in me if you've set yourself against the Organization . . ."

"You still believe in it, I know. In a way I envy you."

Renee shook her head. "This is my world. I have to do what I can for it."

"Organizations have no emotions, Renee. Your love is unrequited."

"Please . . . stay with us." She looked appealingly at Tey for support.

"Sorry, I've had enough." Tey finished his drink in one swallow.

"That's quite a wrist action you got there, Captain," someone said.

Tey turned, and looked into pale blue eyes in a seamed face.

"I need the practice," Tey said. "I'm way behind on my dissipation."

"Let's talk a minute, Tey," the blue-eyed man said.

Across the table Renee caught Tey's eyes and nodded pleadingly.

"All right," he said. "But make it fast. I have my career to think of."

The man hooked a chair, dragged it over, and sat. He took a tiny square of polished metal from an inner pocket, propped it against an empty glass, and looked toward the door.

"Expecting somebody, General?" Tey asked him.

"Call me Jack." The man leaned across the table. "I followed your so-called trial, ex-Captain. Now I guess you can see sticking with the Legits wasn't such a good idea, after all. Now maybe you can see the point of working with the Organization."

Tey shook his head. "The Organization's gotten old," he said. "It died a virgin."

"Still kidding yourself you're somebody, eh, Captain?" The blue-eyed man glanced at the polished metal square, then said, "Oh-oh, the situation is deteriorating . . . The takeout squad must've missed."

Tey glanced toward the door. A sallow man wearing a mustard-colored beret stood by it, looking over the crowd.

"Listen carefully, Tey," the blue-eyed man said, his face close to Tey's ear. "I don't like it, but I'll have to rely on you—"

"Forget it. I'm not playing secret agent."

"I'm not playing, either." Jack took a flat metal box from his breast pocket and held it in his hand.

"This is hot—lethal, top-secret information passed to me just ten minutes ago by a man who's dead now." He glanced at Jaxon. "This has to get to Claude fast, Ollie. He'll know what to do with it."

Tey looked at the bold red L on the box. "Count me out, General."

The man glanced again into the metal square, then looked at Tey. "Time's run out," he said softly. "It's you—or nobody. That's thirty-minute paper in the box. Now get out fast." He rose. Someone staggered against the man in the mustard beret; he reeled back, uttering a yell drowned in the din. His hand darted into his shirt, snaked out. Two rapid shots snapped, muted by a silencer. The blue-eyed man stumbled. A whiskery man sitting at the bar dropped his glass, fell off the stool. The crowd closed in around him. The bartender whirled, reached for a panel. As the lights dimmed, Jack lurched against Tey, thrusting the box into his hand as he fell. The lights came up. Jaxon was on his feet, Renee at his side, still holding Sugar. Tey rose and jammed the box into his side pocket. "Our best bet is to stay put," he said, his eyes on Renee's. She glanced at Jaxon as he resumed his seat. The room was almost quiet again. No one seemed to notice the unconscious man at Tey's feet. The man in the beret was gone.

"Stay here," Tey said, and rose and went to the bar.

In the booth he had left, Renee was speaking earnestly to Sugar, who listened wide-eyed. Neither Grall nor Jaxon was in view. At the barman's querulous inquiry, he ordered whiskey, dropped a brass coin on the bar, turned to look over the crowd. A small man with a loose mouth and red eyes eased onto the next stool.

"Looking for me, Mac?" he said.

Tey looked at him. "Would I be?"

"I can spot 'em." The red-eyed man looked at the drink in Tey's hand. "You better lay off that stuff—if you want to work for the senator."

"You hiring for Skorn?"

"Could be." The loose mouth worked, the red eyes on the glass.

Tey put the drink on the bar. "I'm through with it," he said.

The small man picked it up, gulped the liquor. He smacked his loose lips, blinked his red eyes. "Come on," he said. "In the back. I got a partner." He slid off the stool, headed for the rear of the room.

Tey followed down a short corridor, stopped before a scarred door.

"You can slip me a ten now if you want to," the small man said.

"Suppose I don't?"

The red eyes darted a glance at Tey.

"I got a bad memory," he said. "What was it you wanted?"

"On second thought, nothing. Maybe later."

Tey felt the small man's sneer on his back as he returned to the booth, where Renee sat alone with Sugar, the corpse at her feet. When he looked back, the small man was nowhere to be seen, but Jaxon was making his way through the crowd toward him.

"I see you met Jitty," he commented as he stepped over the dead man on the floor and sat opposite Tey.

Jaxon slid over to allow Nat Grall to slide in beside him. Both he and Tey greeted the big man casually, as he stepped over the dead man on the floor.

"Went to the can," Grall said. "Seems someone assaulted a peaceful Greenback. Imagine. Tsk. Some fellows just have no respect for law and order."

"Now if you gentlemen don't object to a little old death penalty," Tey said easily, "this is as good a time as any to see what it was the late Buck General John H. Cassida got himself killed for."

THREE

The Greylorn Report

"**B**eing born carries a death penalty," Jaxon commented, his eyes keen.

Tey opened the flat tin, took out the sheaf of thin, much-folded papers, opened them to expose a scarlet overprinted classification block. At the top, in crisp print, was a letterhead: FLEET SPACE ARM OPERATIONS, HQ, GRANYAUCK.

Below was a date over a century past, followed by a note in hasty scribbling:

> This is a true copy of FSA LTS document No. 1. Copy No. 1, authorized S/ unreadable.

The print, apparently an old-fashioned dictyper typeface, resumed:

> This is a transcript of an informal conversation with Rear Admiral A.H.B. Greylorn, FSA (ret.)
>
> S/L. Wheeler, UIPiie October 5, 2238.

"Greylorn," Grall muttered aloud, craning for a better view. "I remember something about him from second school: some nut that cooked up a scheme to find the old colonizing ships that were sent out back in '21."

"Somehow, as I remember," Jaxon contributed, "he conned the council into giving him a long-range scout at the tax-payers' expense. Out about ten years and came back with a wild story about finding traces of one of those old colonies."

"But the crew gave him away," Grall added. "A reporter got to them, and they spilled their guts. Seems he was a regular Queeg; gave the men a hard time—shot some—and what they really ran into was a gigantic alien ship. And instead of negotiating some kind of diplomatic arrangement, the damn fool fired on it. It's a wonder they didn't trail him back home and clobber us."

"Quite a stink back then," Jaxon agreed. "But what makes this nut's big statement so hot now?"

The men read on:

Transcript of Informal Interview (Greylorn/Wheeler):

W: Sir, there are rumors that there's more to the story than what Williams and the other crew said. Would you care to comment?

G: We were five years out. I'd been hearing talk about turning back for some time. One watch-end, some of my officers laid for me in my quarters, armed.

W: Unauthorized entry, sir? Isn't that in itself a serious offense?

G: That was the least of it. But I ran a bluff on 'em. Or maybe I wasn't bluffing.

W: Does that mean you were prepared to kill, Captain?

G: Perhaps I had made a mistake in eliminating formal discipline as far as possible in shipboard routine, but it had seemed the best course for a long cruise under those conditions. But now I had a morale situation that could explode into mutiny at the first blunder on my part. And you can be damn sure I'd kill in defense of my ship.

W: A terrible responsibility.

G: I knew that Kramer was the focal point of the trouble. He was my senior staff officer and carried a great deal of weight in the officers' mess. As a medic he knew most of the crew better than I. I thought I knew Kramer's driving motive, too. When he volunteered for the mission, he had doubtless pictured himself as quite a romantic hero, off on a noble but hopeless quest. Now, after five years in deep space, he was beginning to realize that he was getting no younger, and that at best he would have spent a decade of his prime in monastic seclusion. He wanted to go back now, and salvage what he could.

W: A dismal prospect.

G: It was incredible to me that this movement could have gathered followers, but I had to face the fact—my crew, almost to a man, had given up the search before it was well begun. I had heard rumors, but the idea spread through the crew like wildfire. I couldn't afford drastic action or risk forcing a blowup by arresting ringleaders. I had to baby the situation along with an easy hand and hope for good news from the Survey Section. A likely find now would save us.

W: A forlorn hope, Captain?

G: There was still every reason to hope for success in our search. To date all had gone according to plan. We had followed the route of the colony ship *Omega* as far as it had been charted, and had then gone on, studying the stars ahead for evidence of planets.

We had made our first finds early in the fourth year of the voyage. It had been a long tedious time since then of study and observation, eliminating one world after another as too massive, too cold, too close to a blazing primary, too small to hold an atmosphere. In all we had discovered twelve planets of four minor suns. Only one had looked good enough for close observation. We had to move in to a category-three resolution range before realizing it was an all-sea world.

Now we had five new main-sequence suns ahead, within six months' range. I hoped for a confirmation on a planet at any time. To turn back then to a world that had pinned its last hopes on our success was unthinkable, yet this was Kramer's plan, and that of his followers. They would not prevail while I lived. Still, it was not my plan to be a party to our failure through martyrdom. I intended to stay alive and carry through to success. I dozed lightly and waited.

W: A truly unenviable situation, Captain. It's amazing you could sleep at such a time.

G: Insomnia wouldn't help anything. The attempted coup—abortive though it was—helped to let off some steam. The men would have, I calculated, something to talk about for a few precious days.

W: Of course, Captain. I only meant—

G: I heard a sound that brought me out of my reverie in a hurry; then I felt the tremor, followed a few seconds later by a heavy shuddering. Papers slid off my desk and scattered across the floor.

W: It must've been something serious to have shaken the whole vessel so.

G: I reached for the squawk box and called Duty Section for a report. There was a momentary delay before Lieutenant Taylor answered: "Captain, we've taken a meteor strike aft, apparently a metallic body. It must've hit us a tremendous wallop because it set up a rotation. I called Damage Control."

"Good work, Taylor," I said. Then I put in a call to Stores, to check on the damage there. I got a hum of background noise, then a too-close transmission:

"Uh, Cap'n, we got a hole in the aft bulkhead, and there's an ugly piece of iron laying on the deck here. I slapped a seal pad over the hole. Man, that coulda killed somebody."

W: A shocking event.

G: I flipped off the intercom and started aft at a run. In the passage men stood, milled, called out questions. I ordered all hands to emergency stations, and they cleared out fast.

Taylor appeared out of the fog with his Damage Control crew. "Sir," he reported, "it's punctured inner and outer shells in two places, and fragments have riddled the entire sector. Three men are dead, and two hurt."

"Taylor," I called, "Let's have another Damage Control team back here on the triple; and get the medics back here, too." Taylor and his men put on gas masks and moved off. I borrowed a mask from a man standing by and followed.

The large exit puncture was in the forward cargo lock. The space had already been sealed off to limit air loss. I told Clay to pass this up for the moment and get the entry puncture sealed. I put the extra crew in suits to handle this one.

W: That was a serious situation, Captain, calling for fast action.

G: Yeah. I moved back into clear air and called for reports from all sections. The worst of the damage was in the auxiliary-power control room, where communication and power lines were slashed and the panel cut up, but no serious damage to essential equipment. We had been lucky. This was the first instance I had ever heard of, of encountering an object at hyper light-speed.

W: A fantastic accident.

G: It was astonishing how the emergency cleared the air. The men went about their duties more cheerfully than they had in months, and when I returned Kramer to duty, he was conspicuous by his subdued air. The emergency had reestablished, at least for the time, normal discipline; the men still relied on the captain in time of trouble.

W: But, Captain, that didn't mean that you were out of danger. The ship, after all, was seriously damaged.

G: Damage Control crews worked steadily for the next seventy-two hours, replacing wiring, welding, and testing. Power Section jockeyed, correcting our motion. Meanwhile I checked hourly with Survey Section, hoping for good news to consolidate the improved morale.

W: And did something turn up? At that moment in particular, it was important.

G: It was on Sunday morning, just after dawn relief, that my lieutenant came up to the bridge looking sick.

"Sir," Taylor said, "we took more damage than we knew with that meteor strike."

"What have you got, Lieutenant?" I said.

"We missed a piece. It must've gone off on a tangent through Stores into the cooler. Clipped the coolant line, and let warm air in. All the fresh-frozen stuff is contaminated and rotten." He gagged. "I got a whiff of it, sir. Excuse me." He rushed away. This was calamity.

W: Captain, that meant your food supplies were lost.

G: We didn't carry much in the way of fresh natural food, but what we had was vital. We could get by fine for a time on vitamin tablets and concentrates, but there are nutritional elements that you couldn't get that way. Hydroponics didn't help; we had to have a few ounces of fresh meat and vegetables grown in sunlight every week, or start to die within months.

W: It was essential that something be done at once.

G: I knew Kramer wouldn't let this chance pass. As medical officer he would be well within his rights to call my attention to the fact that our health would soon begin to suffer. I felt certain he would do so loudly and publicly at the first opportunity.

W: And what reply could you make, Captain?

G: I wanted the crew to know where we stood. I gave it to them—short and to the point.

"Men, we've just suffered a serious loss. All the frozen stores are gone. That doesn't mean we'll be going on short rations; there are plenty of concentrates and vitamins aboard. But it does mean we'll be suffering from deficiencies in our diet.

"We didn't come out here on a pleasure cruise; we're on a mission that leaves no room for failure. This is just one more fact for us to face. Now let's get on with the job."

I walked into the wardroom, drew a cup of blackpot, and sat down. The screen showed a beach with booming surf, while the soundtrack picked up the crash and hiss of the breakers.

Mannion sat at a table across the room with Kirschenbaum, my two light commanders. They were hunched over their cups, not talking. I wondered where they stood. The question was whether they were smart enough to realize the stupidity of retreat now.

Kramer walked in, not wasting any time. When he saw the captain, he approached me and stopped a few feet from the table. "Captain," Kramer said loudly, "I'd like to know your plans, now that the possibility of continuing is out."

I sipped my blackpot and looked at the seascape. I didn't answer Kramer. *If I can get him mad*, I thought, *I can take him at his game.*

The two men at the other table were watching. Kramer didn't like being ignored.

"Captain," he said, obviously trying to keep in command of himself. "As medical officer I must know what measures you're taking to protect the health of the men."

W: Technically he was within his rights, at that point.

G: "I'll see you at 1700 in the chart room, Kramer," I told him. He wilted, then left without making his speech.

I went back up to the navigation deck then. Young Lt. Taylor, one of my dependable men, had reported he spotted a slight perturbation in the orbit of the sun we'd named Delta Three. I heard the lift open behind me. Kramer, Fine, and a half-dozen enlisted crew chiefs crowded out, all wearing needlers.

W: This was the showdown you expected would happen sooner or later?

G: Kramer tried to start his speech again.

"We're going on, Kramer," I said. "As long as we have even one man aboard still able to move—teeth or no teeth."

"Deficiency disease is no joke, Captain," Kramer said. "You can get all the symptoms of leprosy, cancer, and syphillis just by skipping a few necessary elements in your diet. And we're missing most of them."

"Giving me your opinions is one thing, Kramer," I said. "Mutiny is another."

W: A tense moment.

G: I decided I'd best take Kramer to his quarters and lock him up myself. We were about halfway there when the wall annunciator hummed and spoke.

"Captain Greylorn, please report to the bridge. Unidentified body on main scope." Every man in sight stopped in his tracks, listening. The annunciator continued: "Looks like it's decelerating, Captain."

W: A timely interruption.

G: I turned Kramer over to a couple of reliable men and got back to the bridge. Taylor was at the main screen, studying the blip.

W: The moment you'd been waiting for.

G: Maybe. I stepped over behind my radar officer, who was at the beam controls. "Take it a few mags at a time, Miller," I told him. I didn't want him to lose the fix.

I watched Miller's screen. A tiny point near the center of the screen swelled to a spec, then jumped nearly off the screen to the left. Miller centered it again and switched to a higher power. This time it jumped less, and resolved into two tiny dots.

Step by step the magnification was increased as ring after ring of the lens antenna was thrown into play. Each time the centering operation was more delicate. The image grew until it filled a quarter of the screen. We all stared at it.

W: A fantastic moment. First contact!

G: In the electronic light of the radarscope, it showed up in stark silhouette, two perfect discs, joined by a fine filament. As we watched, their relative positions shifted slowly, one moving across, half occluding the other.

W: Strange.

G: "It ain't got no orbit, Cap'n," Miller said. "I'm tracking it, but I don't understand it. That rock is on a closing curve with us. Averagin' about 1,000, relative, but slowin' down fast."

W: Clearly it was attempting rendezvous.

G: I ordered all hands to action stations for possible contact.

W: You were prepared for hostile action.

G: I ordered Number One Battery to arm and stand by, just in case. It clearly wasn't a natural body. Could have been anything from a torpedo on up.

I went back to the beam screen. The image was clear, but without detail. The two discs slowly drew apart, then closed again. It had to be two spheres, rotating around a common center.

W: Truly a strange phenomenon.

G: If this was—as I hoped—a contact with our colony, perhaps our troubles were over.

W: If only that were so.

G: I estimated the body would match speeds with us at about 200 miles. We had to hold everything we had on her and watch closely for anything that might be a missile.

W: You had to be on the alert.

G: Taylor reported a figure of over a hundred million tons mass, and calibrating the scope images yielded a length of nearly two miles.

W: A fantastic size.

G: I had a very strong and very empty feeling that this ship—if vessel it were—was not an envoy from any human colony. Pretty soon, Mannion checked in to report a short-wave transmission from a point off the starboard bow. I told him to tape it and get to work on deciphering it.

W: The suspense must've been terrific.

G: Mannion was our only language-and-code man. I hoped he was good. I told him to tune me in, and after a moment a high hum came from the speaker. Through it, I could hear harsh, chopping consonants and a whining intonation. I doubted that Mannion was capable of making anything of that gargle.

W: Imagine! A nonhuman language, more alien than ancient Sumerian.

G: Our bogie closed in steadily. At four hundred twenty-five miles she began trying to match our speed, moving closer to our course. There was no doubt she planned to parallel us. At that range we could see her in clear, stark definition. There were no visible surface features; the iodine-colored forms and their connecting shaft had an ancient and alien look.

I made a few rough calculations. The two spheres were about 800 yards in diameter, and at the rate the structure was rotating it was pulling about six gravities. That settled the question of human origin of the ship. No human crew would choose to work under six G's.

W: Truly an alien vessel.

G: At just over two hundred miles, the giant ship spun along, at rest relative to us. It was visible through the direct observation panel, without magnification, subtending an angle of about four degrees.

W: Must've been difficult to know what to do next, Captain.

G: I left Taylor in charge on the bridge and went down to Com Section. The compartment was filled with the keening staccato of the alien transmission.

Joyce, the communications officer, shook his head. "Nothing, Captain. I've checked the whole spectrum, and this is all I get. It's coming in on about a dozen different frequencies; no FM."

Mannion took off his headset. "It's just a short phrase, Cap'n, repeated over and over. I'd have better luck if they'd vary it a little."

I told him to try sending.

Joyce tuned down the clatter to a faint clicking, then switched his transmitter on. "You're on, Captain," he said.

"This is Captain Greylorn, ACV *Galahad;* kindly identify yourself." I repeated this slowly, half a dozen times, as it occurred to me that this was the first known time in history that a human being had addressed a nonhuman . . . intelligence. That was a guess, but I couldn't interpret their guest's purposeful maneuverings as other than intelligent.

I checked with the bridge; no change. Suddenly the clatter stopped, leaving only the carrier hum. Then the clatter started up again.

"This is different," Mannion said. "It's longer."

"Mannion," I said, "every half hour I want you to transmit a call identifying us, followed by a sample of our language. Give them English, Japanese, and Standard. Maybe they'll understand some of it."

"As you order, Captain."

W: It was a remote possibility.

G: I stayed on the bridge when the watch changed, had some food sent up, and slept a few hours on the OD's bunk. We had been at general quarters for twenty-one hours when word came through. "Captain, this is Mannion. I've busted it . . ."

W: An exciting moment.

G: I went directly to Com Section, where Mannion offered me a scribbled sheet of paper. "This is what I've got so far, Captain," he said. I read it silently: INVADER; THE MANCJI PRESENCE OPENS COMMUNICATION.

W: A cryptic message.

G: Mannion had determined that the language was a highly inflected version of early Standard. After he taped it he compensated it to take out the rise-and-fall tones, and then filtered out the static. There were a few sound substitutions to figure out, but he finally caught on. It still didn't make much sense, but that's what it said.

W: More and more alien, it seems.

G: They just repeated that over and over. They didn't respond to transmission. I told Mannion to try translating into Old Standard, adding their sound changes and then feeding their own rise-and-fall routine to it.

"Put plenty of horsepower behind it," I told him. "If their receivers are as shaky as their transmitters, they might not be hearing us."

They went for five minutes, then tuned them back in and waited. There was a long silence before the long, spluttering singsong came back.

Mannion worked over it for minutes. "They must've understood us," he said excitedly. "Here's what I get."

THAT WHICH SWIMS IN THE MANCJI SEA; WE ARE AWARE THAT YOU HAVE THIS TRADE TONGUE. YOU RANGE FAR. IT IS OUR WHIM TO INDULGE YOU; WE ARE AMUSED THAT YOU PRESUME HERE. WE ACKNOWLEDGE YOUR IN-SOLENT DEMANDS.

"Looks like we're in somebody's back yard," I said. "They acknowledge our insolent demands, but they don't answer them." I thought it over and made my decision: "Send this," I said. "We'll outstrut them."

THE MIGHTY WARSHIP GALAHAD REJECTS YOUR JURIS-DICTION. TELL US THE NATURE OF YOUR DISTRESS, AND WE MAY CHOOSE TO OFFER AID.

W: Wasn't that rather risky, Captain? Provocative, even?

G: That's what Mannion thought. I didn't agree. They were eager to talk to us, and that meant they wanted something.

"Why do you want to antagonize them, Captain?" Mannion asked. "That ship is over a thousand times the size of this can."

"Mannion, I suggest you let me handle this," I told him.

W: At first Mannion had seemed to be a ringleader with Kramer.

G: He had sense enough to change sides and follow or-ders. The Mancji whine was added to my message and was sent out.

W: The wait for their reply must've been trying, Cap-tain.

G: It came back in just a few seconds.

MANCJI HONOR DICTATES YOUR SAFE CONDUCT. TALK IS
WEARYING: WE FIND IT CONVENIENT TO SOLICIT A TRANS-
FER OF ELECTROSTATIC FORCE.

Mannion wrote out a straight query, and sent it.

W: Those were tense moments.

G: The answer came, in a long, windy paragraph stating
that the Mancji found electrostatic baths amusing and that
crystalization had drained their tanks. They wanted a flow
of electrons from us to replenish their supply.

"This sounds like simple electric current they're talking
about, Captain," Mannion said. "They want a battery
charge."

"They seem to have power to burn," I said. "Why don't
they generate their own juice? Ask them; and find out
where they learned Standard."

Mannion sent again, and their reply was slow in coming
back.

THE MANCJI DO NOT EMPLOY MASSIVE GENERATION-
PIECE WHERE ACCUMULATOR-PIECE IS SUFFICIENT. THIS
SIMPLE TRADE SPEECH IS OF OLD KNOWLEDGE. WE SE-
LECT IT FROM SYMBOLS WE ARE PLEASED TO SENSE EM-
PATTERNED ON YOUR HULL.

W: A stroke of luck.

G: I was intrigued by the reference to Standard as
a trade language. I wanted to know where they had
learned it, partly because they were using an antique
version of the language that dated back to Omega
times.

W: It appears the situation became steadily more puzzling.

G: I sent another query, but the reply was abrupt and
repeated that Standard was of old knowledge. Then
Mannion entered into a long technical exchange with the
aliens, getting details of the kind of electric energy they
wanted.

"We can give them what they want, no sweat, Captain,"
Mannion reported after half an hour's talk. "They want
DC; 100 volt, 50 amp will do."

"Ask them to describe themselves," I directed; I was beginning to get an idea.

Mannion sent, got his reply. "They're apparently molluscoid, Captain," he said. "They weigh about two tons each," he added, "if I understand—and I don't."

W: Rather shocking news, I imagine.

G: Not really. You see, I was on to something. I directed Mannion to ask them what kind of food they eat. Then I told Joyce to get Kramer, on the double. He reported to me five minutes later.

"I'm releasing you from arrest temporarily on your own parole, Kramer," I said. "I want you to study the reply to our last transmission and tell me what you can about it."

"Why me?" he said. "I don't know what's going on." I didn't answer him.

There was a long, tense half-hour wait before Mannion copied out the reply and handed it to me. The message was a recital of the indifference of the Mancji to the biological processes of ingestion.

I told Kramer to make up a list of our basic nutritional needs.

"What is this, a game?"

"It's an order, Kramer," I said.

The medical officer sat down—his manner was openly offensive—wrote quickly and handed me a list. "The symbols refer to common proteins, lipids, carbohydrates, vitamins, and biomins," he said.

"All right, Mannion," I said, "ask them if they have fresh sources of these substances aboard."

The reply was quick; they did.

"Tell them we'll exchange electric energy for a supply of these foods. Tell them we want samples of a half-dozen of the natural substances."

Again Mannion coded and sent, received and translated, sent again.

"They agree, Captain," he said at last. "They want us to fire a power lead out about a mile; they'll come in close and shoot us a specimen case with a flare on it. Then we can each check the other's merchandise."

"All right," I said. "We can use a ground-service cable. Rig a pilot light on it; then kick it out as soon as they get in close."

W: Wasn't that risky, Captain?

G: Yes . . . I told Mannion to send two of his men out to make the pickup. This wasn't a communications job, but I wanted a reliable man handling it. Then I called Bourdon and directed him to arm two penetration missiles, lock them onto the stranger, and switch over to my control. With the firing key in my hand, I watched for any sign of treachery. The ship moved in, then came to rest filling the screen.

W: Another tense moment, Captain.

G: Mannion's men reported out. I watched them, like flies against the side of the vast iodine-colored wall looming across the screen. Then the alien vessel signaled that their offering was ex-hull. It was a plain cannister that could have been Navy issue.

Nothing else emerged from the alien ship. Mannion reported six thousand feet of cable were out before the pilot light disappeared abruptly.

"Captain," Mannion reported, "they're drawing power."

"OK," I said, "let them have a sample; then shut down."

G: I waited, watching carefully, until Mannion reported the cannister inside. Then I told Kramer to run a fast check on the samples in the container.

W: The suspense must have been great.

G: Kramer was quickly recovering his usual swagger.

"You'll have to be a little more specific, Captain," the medical officer said. "Just what kind of analysis do you have in mind? Do you want a full . . ."

"I just want to know one thing, Kramer," I told him; "can we assimilate these substances, yes or no? If you don't feel like cooperating, I'll have you lashed to your bunk and injected with them. You claim you're a medical officer; let's see you act like one."

Mannion's call interrupted. "Captain, sir, they say the juice we fed them was 'amusing.' I guess that means it's OK."

"I'll let you know in a few minutes how their samples pan out," I told him.

Kramer took a half-hour before reporting back. "I ran a simple check such as I normally would in a routine mess inspection—" he began.

"Yes or no, Kramer," I cut him off.

"Yes, we can assimilate most of it," he answered angrily. "There were six samples. One was a very normal meaty specimen."

W: That must have been heartening news.

G: Right.

I called Mannion: "Tell them that in return for 1,000 kwh we require 6,000 pounds of sample six."

Mannion reported back: "They agreed in a hurry, Captain. They seem to feel pretty good about the deal. They want to chat, now that they've got a bargain. I'm still taping a long tirade."

"Good," I said, then ordered: "Send out six men with an auxiliary pusher to bring home the bacon, and start feeding them the juice again."

Kramer was staring at the video image. "Report yourself back to arrest in quarters, Kramer," I ordered him. "I'll take your services today into account at your court-martial."

Kramer looked up, with a nasty grin. "I don't know what kind of talking oysters you're trafficking with, but I'd laugh like hell if they vaporized your precious tub as soon as they're through with you." He walked out.

W: Insolence.

G: At least.

Mannion called in again from Com Section. "Here's

their last, Captain," he said. "They say we're lucky they had a good supply of this protein aboard. It's one of the most amusing foods. It's from a creature they discovered in the wild state, and it's very rare. The wild ones have died out, and only their domesticated herds exist."

"It better be good," I said, "or we'll step up the amperage and burn their plates for them."

W: A fortunate find.

G: We were lucky. I didn't like the delay, but it would take us about ten hours to deliver the juice to them at the trickle rate they wanted. So we settled down to wait.

W: Waiting under such circumstances must've been very trying.

G: Yes. I left Taylor in charge on the bridge and made a tour of the ship. The meeting with the alien had apparently driven the mood of mutiny into the background for the moment. The men were quiet and busy. I went to my cabin and slept for a few hours.

I was awakened by a call from Taylor telling me that the alien ship had released her cargo, and Mannion's crew was out making the pickup. But before *Galahad*'s delivery team could maneuver the bulky cylinder to the *Mancji* cargo hatch, the alien released the power lead.

I called Kramer and told him to meet the incoming crew, and open and inspect the cargo. *If it's the same as the sample,* I thought, *we've made a terrific trade. Discipline will recover if the men feel we still have our luck.*

Then Mannion called again. "Captain," he said, all excited, "I think there may be trouble coming. Will you come down, sir?"

"I'll go to the bridge, Mannion," I said. "Keep talking." I turned my talker down low and listened to Mannion as I ran for the bridge.

"They told us to watch for a display of Mancji power, sir. They ran out some kind of antenna . . . and now I'm getting a loud static at the top of my shortwave receptivity."

I stepped onto the bridge and spoke into the talker: "Stand by to fire."

W: You were prepared to attack that giant vessel.

G: As soon as the pickup crew was reported in, I keyed course corrections to curve the *Galahad* away from the alien. I didn't know what to expect next, but I liked the idea of putting space between them.

Mannion called. "Captain, they say our fright is amusing —and quite justified."

Suddenly the entire radar screen flashed white, then blanked. Miller, who had been at the scanner searching over the alien ship at close range, reeled out of his seat, clutching at his eyes. "My God, I'm blinded," he cried out.

Mannion called. "Captain, my receivers blew. I think every tube in the shack exploded."

W: So they *did* attack you!

G: I wached the screen as the alien ship turned away from us in a leisurely curve. There was no sign of whatever weapon had blown us off the air. I held my firing key pretty tight, but I didn't press it. I told Taylor to take Miller down to Med. He was suffering severe pain.

W: Unfortunate.

G: Apparently they were satisfied with one blast; they were dwindling away with no further sign of hostility. After an hour of red alert, I ordered the missiles disarmed, then spoke to the crew.

"Men, this is the Captain," I announced. "It looks as though our first contact with an alien race has been successfully completed. Their vessel is now at a distance of three hundred miles and moving off fast. Some of our screens are blown, but there's no real damage. And . . . we have a supply of fresh food aboard; now let's get back to business. That colony can't be far off."

W: Suddenly things looked quite different.

G: I may have been rushing it some, because if the food supply we'd gotten was a dud, we were finished. We watched the direct-view screen till the ship was lost, then followed on radar.

"It's moving right along, Captain," Joyce said, "accelerating at about two G's."

"Good riddance," Mannion said. "I don't like dealing with armed maniacs."

"They were screwballs all right," I said, "but they couldn't have happened along at a better time. I only wish we had been in a position to squeeze a few answers out of them."

W: Tantalizing, to meet an alien race and learn so little of them.

G: At that moment I was feeling too relieved to nitpick.

"Now that the whole thing's over," Taylor said, "I'm beginning to think of a lot of questions myself."

"Yes, indeed, Lieutenant," I agreed. "Their planet of origin, and so much more."

After a while, the talker hummed. It was the cargo-deck mike that was open. "If you have a report, Chilcote, go ahead," I said.

Suddenly someone was shouting into the mike, incoherently. I caught words, cursing, then Chilcote's voice: "Captain—" he said, "Captain, please come quick." There was a loud clatter, noise, then only the hum of the mike.

I told Taylor to take over, and started back to the cargo deck at a dead run. Men crowded the corridor. I forced my way through, and found Kramer surrounded by men, shouting.

"Break this up," I shouted. "Kramer, what's your report?" At that moment Chilcote walked up to me, pale as chalk. "Out of the way, men," he yelled. "Let the captain through."

When I was face to face with Kramer, I said, "Get hold of yourself, and make your report, Kramer."

"Yes sir, Captain," he said. "We got the delivery open and hauled the load out onto the floor. It was one big frozen mass, wrapped up in some kind of netting. Then we pulled the covering off and—"

"Go ahead, Kramer," I prompted him.

"That load of fresh meat your star-born pals gave us consists of about six families of human beings; men, women, and children." Kramer was talking for the crowd now, shouting. "They should be pretty tender when you ration out our ounce a week, Captain."

W: Shocking indeed, Captain.

G: The men were quiet, but wide-eyed and open-mouthed. I pushed through them to the cargo lock. The hatch stood ajar and wisps of white vapor curled out into the passage. It was bitter cold in the lock. Near the outer hatch the cannister, rimed with frost, lay in a pool of melting ice.

W: A terrible moment. After coming so far—to find men like this.

G: They were frozen together into one solid mass. I estimated twenty corpses. Kramer was right. They were as human as the rest of us. Human corpses, stripped, packed together, frozen. I pulled back the lightly frosted covering and studied the glazed bodies.

W: A horrifying experience, to be sure.

G: Kramer yelled to me from the door. "You found your colonists, Captain. Now that your curiosity is satisfied, we can go back where we belong. Out here man is a tame variety of cattle. We're lucky they didn't know we were the same variety, or we'd be in their food lockers now. Now let's get started back. The men won't take no for an answer."

I leaned closer to the mass to study the corpses. "Come here, Kramer," I called. "I want to show you something."

"I've seen all there is to see in there," Kramer said. "We don't want to waste time; we want to change course now, right away. I'm in charge now."

I said nothing; I walked back to the door, and as Kramer stepped back to let me out the door, I hit him in the mouth with all my strength and knocked him out into the passage.

"Pick this up and put it in the brig," I ordered the men standing by; I stepped over Kramer. The men in the corridor moved back, muttering. I walked through the throng and kept going. One wrong move on my part then, and all their misery and fear would've broken loose in a riot the first act of which would be to tear the cause of their unhappiness from limb to limb.

W: A perilous moment.

G: I traveled ahead of the shock, but I heard the sound of gathering violence growing behind me. On the bridge I got a quick response from Bourdon. The panic hadn't penetrated Missile Section yet.

W: Then, there was still a chance to restore discipline.

G: Right. I ordered him to arm all batteries and lock onto that Mancji ship; then I altered course to intercept our late companion at two and one-half G's.

W: A daring move, Captain.

G: I could tell that's what Bourdon thought, but he obeyed my order.

I made a general announcement. "This is the captain. All hands at action stations—in loose acceleration harness. We're going after Big Brother. You're in action against the enemy now, men, and from this point on, I'm remembering for the record. You men have been letting off a lot of steam lately; that's over now. All sections report."

W: That made the situation plain enough.

G: One by one the sections reported in, all except Med and Admin, but I could spare them for the present.

I ordered Joyce to lock his radar on target and switch over to autosteer. Then I called Power Section. "I'm taking over all power control from the bridge," I said. "All personnel report out of power deck and control deck at once."

W: Rather a heavy responsibility for a single individual, Captain, no matter how well qualified.

G: The men were still under control, but that might not

last long. I had to have the entire disposition of the ship's power, control, and armament under my personal direction for a few hours at least. But first I had one more errand to run.

I was braced for violence as I opened the lift door, but I was lucky. There was no one in the corridor. I could hear shouts in the distance. It was hard to stand against the acceleration G forces. I dragged myself along to Power Section and pushed inside. A quick check of control settings showed everything as I had ordered it. I reset the locks.

Back in the passage, I slammed the leaded vault door and threw in the combination lock. Now only I could open it without blasting.

W: So far, so good.

G: Control Section was next. I locked it, then started back for Missile Section. Two men appeared at the end of the passage, having as hard a time as I was in the high G. I got into the cross corridor just in time to escape a volley of needles.

W: It was mutiny, out in the open now, for sure.

G: I had cut it a bit fine. They were crawling, frantically striving against the multi-G field to reach Missile Section before me.

W: A race for life against dreadful odds.

G: I had a slight lead. It was too late to make a check inside before locking up. The best I could hope for was to lock the hatch before they reached it.

W: You were fully exposed to their fire.

G: I had my Browning in my hand. One man stopped and reached for his needler. "Don't try it," I called to him. I concentrated on the hatch, reached it; and as I threw in the lock, a needler cracked. I whirled and fired. The man in the rear folded. The other two kept coming.

W: Tragic, but necessary.

G: It would have been tragic if I'd missed. I was tired. I wanted a rest. "You're too late," I told them. "No one but the captain goes in there now." I had to rest. The two came on.

W: They were desperate now.

G: So was I. Two men on a maintenance shuttlecart whirled around the corner a hundred feet aft, laying down a hail of needler fire. One of the tiny slugs stung through my calf and ricocheted down the passage. I returned fire and held them back. Then I called to the two I had raced, "Tell your boys if they ever want to open that door, just see the captain." .

I hesitated, considering whether or not to make a general statement.

But I decided what the hell. By then they all knew there'd been a mutiny. Wouldn't hurt to get in a little life insurance.

W: Good thinking.

G: I keyed my talker for a general announcement. "Hear this. This is the captain" I said. "This vessel is now in a state of mutiny. I call on all loyal Fleet men to resist the mutineers actively and to support their commander. Your ship is in action against an armed enemy. I assure you this mutiny will fail, and those who take part in it will be dealt with as traitors to their Service, their homes, and their own families, who now rely on them.

"We are accelerating at two and one-half gravities, locked on a collision course with the Mancji ship. The mutineers cannot enter the bridge, Power, Control, or Missile Sections since only I have the combination. Thus they're doomed to failure.

"I am now returning to the bridge to direct the attack and destruction of the enemy. If I fail to reach the bridge, we will collide with the enemy in less than three hours, and our batteries will blow."

W: That must've impressed them.

G: Now my problem was to make good my remark about returning to the bridge. I took a chance and crossed back to Corridor A at my best speed, sent a hail of needles down the corridor behind me, and heard a yelp from around the corner. Those needles have a fantastic velocity. They bounce around a long time before coming to rest.

I was getting pretty tired; without the extra stamina and wind my daily calisthenics in a high-G field had given me, I would've collapsed before then; but I was almost ready to drop. With only a few feet to go, my knees gave. I went down on all fours, but managed to reach the cross-passage, and a locked hatch. Three, five, two, five . . . I had trouble remembering it, though I'd used it daily for years.

W: A terrible ordeal.

G: I pushed; nothing. I had lost count. I started again.

W: A desperate race against time.

G: No one was shooting now. They realized that if I were killed, there would be no way to enter the vital control areas of the ship; they had to take me alive. On that thought I passed out.

W: Truly a desperate situation. If they found you helpless . . .

G: I came to lying on my back, and men were sitting on the floor around me.

A blow from somewhere made my head ring. I tried to sit up. I couldn't make it. Then Kramer was beside me, slipping a needle into my arm. He looked pretty bad himself. His face was bandaged heavily, and one eye was purple. He spoke in a muffled voice through stiff jaws. His tone was deliberate.

"This will keep you conscious enough to answer a few questions," he said. "Now you're going to give me the combinations to the locks so we can call off this suicide run; then maybe I'll doctor you up."

Kramer took a large scalpel from his medical kit. "I'll start operating on your face, make you into a museum freak. But maybe, Greylorn, just maybe if you start talking I'll change my mind."

W: A fantastic threat.

G: But he meant it. I could see the watch on his wrist. We would intercept in one hour and ten minutes. I had to get back to the bridge before we hit. "Kramer," I said, "we have only an hour."

Kramer lost control and jabbed the knife at my face, screeching through gritted teeth. I jerked my head aside far enough so that the scalpel grated along my cheekbone instead of slashing my mouth. I hardly felt it.

"We're not dying because you're a fool," Kramer yelled. "I've taken over and relieved you as unfit for command. Now open up this ship or I'll slice you to ribbons." He held the scalpel under my nose. The chrome plating had a thin film of pink on it.

W: It was a terrible nightmare.

G: Except I couldn't wake up. I was lying on my face now, with my head almost against the bulkhead. The grogginess cleared a bit, and I saw Kramer standing a few feet away with half a dozen others, all talking at once. Apparently Kramer's display of uncontrolled temper had the others worried. They wanted me alive. Kramer didn't like anyone criticizing him. The argument was pretty violent.

I saw that I lay about twenty feet from the lift; too far. The hatch in front of me led to a utility locker; it was small and contained nothing but a waste-disposal hopper. But it did have a bolt on the inside, like every other compartment on the ship. I concentrated on getting my hands under me, to push up. Then I heard a shout, turned my head, and saw Kramer swinging at someone. I went on with my project.

W: Against great odds.

G: I got my hands under my chest, raised myself a little, and got a knee up. I felt broken rib ends grating and a pressure like a padded claw holding me. Then I was weaving on all fours. I looked up, spotted the combo, and put everything I had into lunging at it. My finger hit the latch, the door swung in, and I fell on my face; it hadn't been locked. Another lunge and I was inside. I kicked the hatch shut and reached for the lock control; just as I flipped it, someone hit the hatch from outside, a split second too late.

It was dark, and I lay on my back on the deck and felt strange short-circuited stabs of what would have been agonizing pain running through my chest and arm. I had a few minutes to rest now, before they blasted the hatch open.

I hated to lose like this, not because we were beaten, but because we were giving up. My poor world, no longer fair and green, had found the strength to send us out as her last hope. But somewhere out here in the loneliness and distance, we had lost our courage.

W: It's clear that *you* hadn't.

G: Success was at our fingertips, if we could've found it; instead, in panic and madness, we were destroying ourselves.

W: Tragic.

G: I sensed that someone was standing beside me, and opened my eyes. A crewman wearing greasy overalls grinned down at me. I wondered why he'd abandoned his action station to hide here. He must've been there all along, but I'd been too busy to notice him when I came in.

The man's hand went up; he straightened, and held a fairly snappy salute. "Sir," he said, "Spaceman First Class Thomas."

"At ease, Thomas," I managed to say. "Why aren't you at your duty station?"

Thomas squatted down beside me then. "Cap'n, you're hurt, ain't you? I was wonderin' why you were laying down in my 'sposal station."

"Yes, I'm hurt," I conceded.

I was only about half conscious, but I remember those minutes. Thomas was doing something about my chest. This was Thomas's disposal station. Thomas owned it. I wondered if a fellow could make a living with such a small place way out here, with just an occasional tourist coming by. I wondered why I didn't send one of them for help; I needed help for some reason.

W: You were delirious.

G: I realized Thomas was talking. "How long you been in here, Cap'n?" Thomas was worried about something. I tried hard to think. I hadn't been there very long; just a few minutes. I'd come there to rest. . . . Then suddenly I was thinking clearly again. Whatever Thomas was, he was apparently on my side, or at least neutral. He didn't seem to be aware of the mutiny. I realized that he had bound my chest tightly with strips of shirt; it felt better.

"What are you doing in here, Thomas?" I asked. "Don't you know we're in action against a hostile vessel?"

"This here's my action station, Cap'n. I'm a waste recovery technician, first class. I keep the recovery system operatin'."

"You stay just in here?" I asked.

"No sir," Thomas said. "I check through the whole system. We got three main disposal points and lots a little ones, an' I got to keep everything operatin'. Otherwise this here ship would be in a bad way, Cap'n."

"How did you get in here?" I asked. I looked around the compartment. There was only one hatch, and the gray bulk of the converter unit, which breaks down wastes into their component elements for reuse, nearly filled the tiny space.

"I came in throught the duct, Cap'n," Thomas said. "I check the ducts every watch. You know, Cap'n," he said, shaking his head, "there's some bad laid-out ducting in this system. If I didn't keep after it, you'd be gettin' clogged ducts all the time. So I just go through the system and keep her clear."

"Where does it run, Thomas?"

"Well, sir, one leads from the mess; that's the big one. One leads from the wardroom; and the other one leads down from the bridge."

"How big are the ducts?" I asked. "Could I get through them?"

"Oh, sure, Cap'n," Thomas said. "You can get through

'em easy. But are you sure you feel like inspectin' with them busted ribs?"

"I can make it," I told him.

"Cap'n," Thomas began, "it ain't none of my business, but don't you think maybe I better get the doctor for you?"

"Thomas," I said, "maybe you don't know, but there's a mutiny under way aboard this ship. The doctor is leading it. I must get to the bridge. Let's get started."

Thomas looked shocked. "Cap'n, you mean you was hurt *by* somebody? I mean you didn't have a fall or nothin'? You was beat up?"

"That's right" I said, and Thomas jumped forward to help me to my feet; I saw then that Thomas was crying.

"You can count on me, Cap'n," he said. "Just let me know who did it, an' I'll feed 'em into my converter."*

I leaned against the wall, waiting for my head to stop spinning.

"I *thought* something was wrong, Cap'n," Thomas said. "Otherwise you'd never put a two-and-a-half G spin on her." Thomas opened a panel on the side of the converter unit. "It's okay to go in, Cap'n," he said. "She ain't operatin'."

Thomas boosted me into the plenum chamber of the converter and pointed to an opening about twelve by twenty-four inches near the top.

W: In your condition, were you ready to attempt it?

G: What choice did I have?

W: Anyone else would have given up.

G: I'm afraid I'm being too long-winded when all you want is the basic facts. I've been indulging in reminiscences, I think.

---

*Readers will recognize in this curious incident the factual basis for the beloved legend of *Greylorn and the Genie*. Doubtless it will come as a surprise to many that the founder of the great clan Thomas was not, as commonly believed, a stowaway political refugee and physicist. The account, quoted word for word from surviving documents, is presented here in the interest of historical accuracy, without fear or favor.

W: By no means, sir. It's the little human touches, the details that make the story. Please continue as you were.

G: "That one there is from the bridge, Cap'n," Thomas said. "If you start in there, sir, I'll follow up."

I got head and shoulders into the opening. Inside it was smooth metal, with no handholds.

"Cap'n, they're workin' on the hatch," Thomas reported. "They've already been at it for a while. We better get goin'."

G: Thomas crowded into the chamber behind me then, lifting my legs and pushing. I eased into the duct. The pain wasn't so bad now.

W: You were near death.

G: Aren't we all?

The heat in the duct was terrific. Above I could see light from the utility locker leaking around the edge of the hatch cover. The disposal slot on the bridge had been installed in a small compartment containing a bunk and a tiny galley for the use of the Duty Officer during long watches on the bridge.

I reached the top of the duct and pushed against the slot cover; it opened easily. Suddenly the light from below went out. I heard a muffled clank; then a hum began, echoing up the duct. Air started whistling past my head.

"She's closed and started cyclin' the air out, Cap'n," Thomas said calmly. "We got maybe half a minute."

G: The slot cover slammed, sucked shut by the air pressure. I got it open again. Below me Thomas waited quietly. He knew I wasn't wasting any time, and he couldn't help me now. The air was whistling around my face, blowing dust in my eyes. Papers began to swirl off the chart table. I had to fight like hell to get clear. Then I was on the bridge.

W: A triumph, sir.

G: Thomas had one hand through. The metal edge cut into it and blood started, but the cover was held open half an inch. I grabbed a short permalloy rod that was within reach and levered the cover up. Thomas got his arms through and heaved himself a little higher. I grabbed his arm and pulled. He scrambled through and was sprawled on the bridge deck beside me, looking up at the unfamiliar screens, indicator dials, controls.

From where I lay I could see the direct-vision screen. I wasn't sure, but I thought I saw a small bright object in the center of it that would be our target.

Thomas looked at the dead radar screen, then said, "Cap'n, that radarscope is out of action?"

"It sure is, Thomas," I said. "Our unknown friends blew the works before they left us." I was surprised he recognized a radarscope.

"Mind if I take a look at it, Cap'n?" he said.

I told him to go ahead.

Thomas had the cover off the radar panel and was probing around. He pulled a blackened card out of the interior of the panel.

"Looks like they overloaded the fuse," Thomas said. "Got any spares, Cap'n?"

"How do you know your way around a radar set, Thomas?"

Thomas grinned. "I used to be a radar technician third class before I got into waste disposal," he said. "I had to change specialties to sign on for this cruise."

W: This Thomas was an astonishing fellow.

G: I had an idea there'd be an opening for Thomas a little higher up when this was over. Later, I wrote him up for the Distinguished Service Order and the Navy Cross.

I told Thomas to let me know when we were twenty miles from target. I wanted to tell him more, but I could feel consciousness draining away. Then I managed to tell him to get the first-aid kit and give me a B-3 shot.

I wavered in and out of consciousness. It was just as well; I needed the sleep. Then I heard Thomas calling me.

"We're closin', Cap'n," he said. "Wake up, Cap'n, only twenty-three miles now."

I felt the needle in my arm. It helped. It was time to use the talker.

"This is the captain," I said, trying not to let my voice shake. "We are now at a distance of twenty-one miles from the enemy. Stand by for missile launching and possible evasive action. Damage Control crews on the alert. We're going to take out the Mancji ship, men. All two miles of it."

Thomas handed me the firing key. "Cap'n," he said, "I notice you got the selector set for chemical warheads. Want me to set up pluto heads for you?"

"No, Thomas," I said. "Chemical is what I want. Stand by to observe." I pressed the firing key.

W: Surprising, Captain, that faced with such an enemy, you didn't use your potent N-weapons.

G: I was hoping for a prisoner to interrogate. Of course, if I had known . . .

Thomas was at the radarscope.

"Missiles away, Cap'n. We're trackin' now."

I used the talker again. "Missiles homing on target," I announced. "Strike in thirty-five seconds. You'll be interested to know we're employing chemical warheads. So far there is no further sign of offense or defense from the enemy." I figured the news would shock a few mutineers. David wasn't even using his slingshot on Goliath. He was going after him barehanded. I needed a few clues as to what was going on below and wanted to scare a response out of them.

Joyce's voice came from the wall annunciator. "Captain, this is Joyce reporting. Sir, the mutiny has been suppressed by the loyal members of the crew. Major Kramer is under arrest. Unfortunately he injured himself. He apparently tried to eat his left arm.

"We're prepared to go on with the search for the Omega colony. But sir—" he paused, gulping, "we ask you

to change course now before launching an attack. We still
have a chance. Maybe they won't bother with us when
those firecrackers go off."

W: One can understand the lieutenant's desperation.
Yet you pressed on.

G: I watched the direct-vision screen. Zero second
closed in. And on the screen the face of the left hand disc
of the Mancji ship was lit momentarily by a brilliant spark
of yellow, then another. A discoloration showed dimly
against the dark metallic surface. It spread, and a faint
vapor formed over it. Tiny specs could be seen moving
away from the ship as the disc elongated, with infinite
leisure, and widened.

"What's happenin' Cap'n?" Thomas asked. He was staring at the scope in fascination. "Are they launchin' scouts,
or what?"

"Take a look here, Thomas," I said. "The ship is breaking up."

The disc was an impossibly long ellipse now, surrounded
by a vast array of smaller bodies, fragments, and contents
of the ship. Now the stricken globe moved completely free
of its companion. It rotated, presenting a crescent toward
Galahad, then wheeled farther as it receded from its twin,
showing its elongation. The sphere had split wide open.
Now the shattered half itself separated into two halves,
and these in turn broke down, apparently along a regular
pattern of juncture lines, strewing debris in a widening
spiral, mostly in regular five-sided units.

"My God, Cap'n," Thomas said in awe. "That's the
greatest display I've ever seen. And all it took to set her
off was 400 pounds of PBL. Now that's somethin'."

I keyed the mike again. "This is the captain," I said. "I
want ten four-man patrols ready to go ex-hull in fifteen
minutes. The enemy has been put out of action and is now
in a derelict condition. I want only one thing from her: one
live prisoner. All section chiefs report to me on the bridge,
on the triple.

"Thomas," I said, "go down in the lift and open up for

the chiefs. Here's the release key for the combination; you know how to operate it?"

"Sure, Cap'n, but are you sure you want to let them boys in here after the way they jumped you an' all?"

I opened my mouth to answer, but Thomas beat me to it. "Forget I asked you that, Cap'n, please sir. It ain't my place to question my orders."

"It's OK, Thomas," I said. "There won't be any more trouble." And there wasn't. The chiefs looked sheepish, but they got businesslike as soon as they saw the screens.

Later that watch I scheduled an Officers' Call and found that except for poor ex-Major Kramer, all officers were ready to be rehabilitated and get back to work. Kramer had gone right off his rocker and had to be restrained.

W: After quashing the mutiny, sir, how could you rely on these officers?

G: Simple self-interest. We had to find that colony—and they knew there was only one way to do it. They needed me.

W: Still, sir—after the near lethal attack on yourself, it seems—

G: And I needed them. We declared peace, then got on with the job. It was different then, knowing we were so close.

Your next question is: how did I know I could take the Mancji ship? After all, it was big, vast. It loomed over us like a mountain. The Mancji themselves weighed almost two tons each; one to a pentagon. They liked six-G gravity. They blasted our communications off the air, just for practice. They talked big, too. We were invaders in their territory. They were amused by us. So where did I get the notion that our attack would be anything more than a joke to them?

W: That's precisely the question.

G: The answer is quite simple. In the first place they were pulling six G's by using a primitive dumbbell configuration. The only reason for that type of layout, as students of early space-vessel design can tell you, is to simplify setting up a G-field effect using centrifugal force. So they obviously had no gravity field generators.

Then their transmission was crude. All they had was simple old-fashioned short-wave radio, and even that was noisy and erratic. And their reception was just as bad. We had to use a kilowatt before they could pick it up at 200 miles. We didn't know then it was all organically generated, that they had no equipment.

W: Astoundingly alien life forms, to be sure. Yet you were not intimidated.

G: I was pretty sure they were bluffing when I changed course and started after them. I had to hold our acceleration down to two and a half G's because I had to be able to move around the ship. And at that acceleration, we gained on them. They couldn't beat us.

W: You saw that.

G: The evidence was there to see, but there's something about giant size that gets people rattled. Size alone doesn't mean a thing. It's rather like the bluff the Soviets ran on the rest of the world for a couple of decades back in the war era, just because they sprawled across half the globe. They were a giant, though it was mostly frozen desert. When the showdown came, they didn't have it. They were a pushover.

W: An apt analogy. But even then, you still had to restore order aboard ship.

G: The, ah, confusion below evaporated as soon as the section chiefs got a look at the screens and realized that we had actually knocked out the Mancji. We matched speeds with the wreckage and the patrols went out to look for a piece of ship with a survivor. If we'd had no luck, we would've tackled the other half of the ship, which was still intact and moving off fast. But we got quite a shock when we found the nature of the wreckage.

Pretty puzzling, at first. But it became clear once we learned about the Mancji hive intelligence and their evolutionary history. We were startled to find that the only wreckage consisted of the Mancji themselves, each two-ton slug in its own hard chitin shell. Of course a few of the cells were ruptured by the explosions, but most of them had simply disassociated from the hive mass as it broke up. So there was no ship, just a cluster of cells like a giant bee hive, and mixed up among the slugs was the damnedest collection of loot you can imagine. The odds and ends they'd stolen and tucked away in the hive during years of camp following. The corpses, it turned out, were accident victims found floating at sea on the planet the Mancji called Hive World. We know it as Omega, or New Terra; and the colonists call it Colmar.

The patrols brought a couple of cells alongside, and Mannion went out to try to establish contact. Sure enough, he got a very faint transmission, on the same bands as before. The cells were talking to each other in their own language. They ignored Mannion, even though his transmission must have blanketed everything within several hundred miles. We eventually brought one of them into the cargo lock and tried different wave lengths on it. Then Mannion had the idea of planting a couple of electrodes and shooting a little juice to it. Of course it loved the DC, but as soon as we tried AC, it gave up. So we had a long talk with it and found out everything we needed to know.

W: At last!

G: They gave us the position of New Terra, a planet of the system we had already spotted. It was only a few days' run. We didn't land, but established voice contact with a picket vessel and got all the information we needed. They wouldn't give me clearance to make planetfall. New Terra, they told us, is a thriving world and needed nothing from Old Terra, and though they seemed friendly enough —at least not openly hostile—they had no desire to establish close relations.* Still, they offered us whatever technical assistance we might require and told us the location of

---

*Clearly, Captain Greylorn had no way of knowing what an accomplished liar Jerry von Shimo was. In a good cause, of course.

two more inhabitable planets* we were welcome to settle if we so desired. I thanked them for that, and accepted the specs of their new torsion-drive unit, which, as you know, has become the basis for our own new space drive. It is far more efficient than the primitive, unstressed space drive I had in *Galahad*.

W: So you didn't actually meet these people face to face.

G: No, it's just as I've told you: They were a bit standoffish, and I felt it would be very poor diplomacy to be pushy.

W: And how did you, in the end, solve the food problem?

G: A Colonel Chan in Com Section turned out to be a moonlighting biochemist. He and Thomas, who was full of surprises, worked out a modification of the disposal units which enabled us to break down any organic matter into basic molecular units and recombine these into perfectly wholesome, impersonal nutrients that contained the vitamins, and so on, that we needed. We had plenty of bulk food, you know. This was just a supplement. That technology too, as you know, has been developed here on Terra to good advantage. The long age of systematically robbing the planetary crust of vital elements by sealing them away in lead-lined coffins is over. The converter returns every molecule, purified, to reuse.

W: Then we're already indebted to the voyage of *Galahad* and to New Terra for a number of vital developments.

G: Exactly.

W: There's still the one question, sir, that naturally occurs: how was it that you rejected what seemed to be *prima facie* proof of the story the Mancji told: that they were the lords of creation out there and that humanity was nothing but a tame food animal to them?

G: I guess it's a good question, but there was nothing supernatural about my figuring that one. I didn't suspect the full truth, of course.†

---

*These, of course, were Aldo Cerise and Farhome.
†We must remember that at that time on Terra nothing had yet been reported on the now well-known but still inexplicable sense of humor of the Mancji.

Well, when this hive spotted us coming in, they knew enough about New Terra to realize at once that we were strangers, coming from outside the area. It appealed to their sense of humor to have the gall to strut right out in front of us and try to put over a swindle. What a laugh for the oyster kingdom if they could sell Terrans on the idea that they were the master race. It never occurred to them we might be anything but Terrans—Terrans who didn't know the Mancji. And they were canny enough to use an old form of Standard.

Then we needed food. They knew what we ate, and that was where they went too far. They had, among the flotsam in their hive, those human bodies they had picked up; they had them stashed away like everything else they could lay a pseudopod on. So they stacked them the way they'd seen New Terran frozen foods shipped in the past, and sent them over. Another of their little jokes.

W: They were taking a chance—which should have worked.

G: I suppose if you're already overwrought and eager to quit, and you've been badly scared by the size of an alien ship, it's pretty understandable that the sight of human bodies, along with the story that they're just a convenient food supply, might seem pretty convincing. But I was already pretty dubious about the genuineness of our pals, and when I saw those bodies, it was pretty plain that we were hot on the trail of Omega colony. There was no other place humans could have come from out there. We had to find out the location from the Mancji.

W: True enough the corpses were human, and presumably had some connection with the colony, but they were naked corpses stacked like cordwood. The Mancji had stated that these were slaves, or rather domesticated animals; they couldn't have done you any good.

G: Well, you see, I didn't believe that, because it was an obvious lie. I tried to show some of the officers, but I'm afraid they weren't being too rational just then.

I went into the locker and examined those bodies; if Kramer had looked closely, he would've seen what I did.

These were no tame animals. They were civilized human beings.

W: How could you be sure, Captain? They had no clothing, no identifying marks, nothing. Why didn't you believe they were cattle?

G: Because they all had neatly trimmed fingernails.

W: This is fantastic news, sir. Your report—that is, the official report, Captain—said merely that traces of dead humans had been found and that contact had been established with a sentient species. Nothing to indicate the existence of a thriving human colony out there on Omega.

G: My statement was doctored. At that time, as it was explained to me, the public wasn't ready for such news.

W: It seems incredible, Captain—the most welcome development the world could know, and it was suppressed.

G: You said it; I didn't. By the way, have you noticed the two fellows dressed in inconspicuous clothes, over by the check-in counter?

W: Why, no, I hadn't Captain. What—I think they're coming over . . . As to the matter of the precise locations of Omega colony, sir, I think if you could—

TRANSCRIPT ENDS.

FOUR

Escape from Terra

As Jaxon read the last words, he leaned back with a slight smile. "Nobody could accuse the admiral of overwhelming modesty," he commented. "But I wonder why the security blanket for this wild stuff?"

"Funny," Grall said, "I thought this was going to be the hot scoop on a torsion-drive breakthrough, or something."

Tey restacked the flimsy sheets, folded them, and replaced them in the metal box, noting as he did some scribbled numbers on the back of one sheet. Jaxon noticed his glance, craned for a better view. "Stellar coordinates," he muttered.

"Yes," Tey agreed, then said quietly, "Gentlemen, I submit that the reason this was never made public is that it's close enough to the truth to have turned this planet inside out, if it had been generally known."

"This Wheeler," Jaxon said, "that's the big-shot media man who signed this—before he was a big shot."

"Maybe passing this directly to DCS/Security instead of his own copy desk had something to do with his big career," Tey suggested. "If this was all nonsense, why the heavy classification?"

"And could this be the same Greylorn whose statue is collecting guano in the plaza right now—our first hero lost in space in the line of duty?" Grall mused.

"My God," Jaxon put in. "Do you realize what this means?

For the last century, while we stewed in our own juice, Fleet Command has had a colony world on tap that could relieve the population squeeze, and they kept it under their scrambled eggs."

Tey nodded. "Turning the economy inside out, as you can well imagine, would have been the last thing First Lord Banshire would have wanted. His boys were in complete control. Planet Earth was their private property—and still is. News of habitable worlds—to say nothing of a going colony—would have smashed that arrangement flat. Could still smash it flat. How many of us would go on in their treadmill if we knew there was a way out?"

"Not many," Grall agreed. "If the docile mob knew what the Banshire group has been sitting on for a century, the riots would make the Boston-Bombay Bread Battles look like a Girl Scout picnic."

"At your court-martial, Captain," Jaxon commented, "they called you a traitor—a lot of stuff about 'security violations.' "

Tey nodded. "I was researching an old exercise coded 'Snowfall,' and I got a little too close, it seems."

"The dirty, lousy, stinking, bad-word scum," Jaxon said dreamily. "Just to protect their own playhouse, they suppressed the biggest breakthrough in human history."

"If there's anything in it," Grall corrected.

"There's something in it," Tey said with assurance. "It explains a number of rather strange NSA regs regarding penetration of trans-Plutonian space among other things. And they *did* give us the torsion drive. Snowfall was a cover for the supposed breakthrough."

"No wonder Enguerrand Banshire One, plus his next six descendents in the direct male line, sat on it," Jaxon commented. "Think about what the world would be like today if we had a live colony out there—instead of the dreary picture of dead space we're taught in first school and from there on."

"It seems we've accepted Greylorn's deposition as the real thing," Jaxon said. "Very well. What are we going to do about it?"

"I don't know about you fellows," Tey said, "but *I'm* going to steal a ship of the line."

"My word, Captain," Grall said, "isn't that a rather ambitious way to embark upon a life of crime?"

"How do we do it?" Jaxon asked quietly, leaning forward intently. "I understand that security measures at Kennedy-La Guardia Base are, to say the least, vigorous."

Tey nodded. "We need a hundred-thousand tonner, minimum, fully stocked for the T-P cruise. There are two, plus *Pas d'Encore,* at K-L. Ergo, we penetrate the base."

"Simple enough," Grall said as if in agreement. "All we have to do is go over all the electronic spookstoppers they've thought up since the teller's floor button, plus nine layers of elite Greenbacks, backed up with armor and emplacements, and we're in. Then we can at least stand and look at a Fleet ship. But where do we go from there?"

"The security ring around K-L can't be penetrated, short of a full nuclear strike," Tey agreed.

"That was fun," Jaxon said lightly. "What'll we play now?"

"That Jikky," Tey said. "Is he still here?"

A moment later the little man was beside the table. "Any time you mention my name, I hear it," he said. "Just me and the Devil can do that. The two of us."

"Skip the comedy," Jaxon said. "I pushed the button and gave you the high sign."

"Don't hurt none to let a fellow kind of beef up the old mystique," Jikky muttered. Tey put a brass ten-C coin on the table.

The shill pocketed it, led the way down the service corridor to a door, keyed it open. Tey went past him into the room.

A heavily built man with a bald radiation-scarred scalp sat in a chair tilted against the far wall. A dozen other men stood around the room, not talking. They eyed Tey silently.

The man in the chair brought the front legs down with a thump.

"Ok, we got enough here now," he said. "You farmers line up and show your cards."

Tey fell in at the end of a loose line; the man ahead turned. "Well, Cap'n," he said softly. "Welcome to the brotherhood."

"I'm not hired yet," Tey said.

"If you're lucky, you won't be."

"I'm not looking for a pleasure cruise."

"I heard you didn't like the senator—"

"So what? There's prize money in it."

"Yeah. That's what I tell 'em, too."

The line advanced, men moving off, expressions unreadable. Tey's turn came up. He took a card from an inner pocket, handed it to the bald man, who squinted at it, looked up at Tey.

"Well, well," he said. "I guess I'll have to disappoint you, mister. I'm fresh out of fancy plush-lined equipment. All I've got to offer is just some kind of beat-up JAZ 93's, so I guess you wouldn't be interested." He offered the card negligently, half of his mouth smiling.

"I've got eight hundred hours in JAZ 93's," Tey said expressionlessly.

The bald man stood up.

"This is all work, mister," he grated. "Just the old Sweepstakes grind."

"You've sold me," Tey said. "When do I start?"

"Start by calling me 'sir,' farmer." He tossed the card to Tey. "Some people claim our equipment don't get maintenance," he said. "It's up to you farmers to put on a show, even if maybe there's a few safety hazards involved. Any time you don't feel like another run, you can quit—all you lose is the pay for your last two runs, to cover overhead—like running this office."

The bald man sat down, took papers from a coat pocket. "These are your passes to the Senators' Line area," he said. "Don't lose 'em. Show up—sober—at, oh, six hundred hours. Any questions?"

Two armed men in green uniforms stood by the gate in the high wire fence under a sign lettered AUTHORIZED PERSONNEL ONLY. As Tey approached, one of them took a step forward, worked the action of a short-barreled scattergun.

"Tell it from there," he said.

"Relax, boys," Tey said. "I've had a rough day myself." He put a hand carefully inside his jacket, pulled out his line pass.

"Stay put, pal," the guard growled. "I heard sirens here awhile back."

"I'm racing one of Senator Skorn's boats; take off in ten minutes—"

"You ain't going no place, pal."

Tey came closer. "You want to be the cause of a scratched boat sitting on the ramp costing the senator money?"

"Cripes, five minutes don't—"

"I might make it, if I don't waste any more time here."

The guard motioned, took the paper, looked it over. The other man watched, scattergun ready.

"A new guy, huh?" he said. "You guys don't last long, do you?"

"No sweat," Tey said. "I've got Blue Cross."

"Oh, a funny guy." The guard tossed Tey's pass back, motioning him through the gate. Tey crossed the ramp to the equipment shed. Inside, he rapped on the counter for service. A fat man with a wart on his jaw came out from between the storage bins.

"I'm racing for Skorn," Tey said. "I want to draw—"

"We don't issue nothing for speed merchants."

"Where do I draw my gear?"

"You don't need nothing; them boats are all cocooned."

"That's only an emergency rig."

The fat man gazed at a corner of the room. "That's good tough plastic. It'll last as long as the rest o' them cans."

Tey looked at the rows of neatly racked oxygen equipment, communications gear, pressure suits.

"Who uses this?"

"VIP crews, like when the big shots decide to hold an orbit party or watch the races—if it's any of your business."

"Pretty fancy."

"You want the senator should suffer hardships?"

"Not me—I'm true blue." Tey looked solemnly at the fat man.

The fat man thumbed his wart, turned away. "Speed merchants," he muttered. "They're all alike."

"Hold it," Tey said. The clerk turned, eyes wary.

Tey took his left hand from his pocket, showed the pistol. "Sit down right there," he said. "Use that wire to tie your ankles together . . ."

Tey went along the bins, selected a pressure suit, pulled it over his street clothes. He added a power pack, a Fleet band communicator, emergency rations, a recycler.

He stopped beside the chair where the fat man eyed him silently.

"It might take you fifteen minutes to work your way back to that wire cutter on the bench," Tey said. "If you're lucky, nobody will find out you've been hijacked. And if you're smart, you won't mention it—unless you like making alibis to the senator.*

Beyond the inner barrier fence, the shabby shuttles squatted in an irregular row, crews working over them by floodlight. Nearby, half a dozen of People's Senator Skorn's private racing stable were ranged, their peeling decorative paint giving them a raffish air. Far to the right, three VIP craft glistened in pristine elegance under the lights.

Tey walked quickly to the VIP line; a uniformed cop eyed him from a guard post, said nothing. He passed the shuttle hardstands, went up to the gate in the fence surrounding the VIP area. A green uniform slouched near it.

"Let's go," Tey said impatiently. "I'm running late."

"All right, all right." The sentry looked him over. "Always something new with you guys. Now you're using the mechanics' gate."

"I told you I'm running late. I had to draw my gear and beat it up here the back way."

"Maybe I'd better check."

"You want to keep Senator Skorn waiting?"

---

*This man, one Charles P. Broat, later emigrated to Colmar (at that time still known on Terra as New Terra.) Admiral-in-Chief Tey encountered him on the still unpaved street at Prime City, recognized him at once, and acknowledging that Broat could have betrayed him, and did not, offered him a post on his personal staff, a position Broat fulfilled with distinction.

"OK, OK," the guard keyed the lock, and Tey pushed through. Ahead two tall shapes loomed against the pink sky. Tey headed for the nearest one. A line-cart stood by the gantry, half-a-dozen men working around it. Tey went up to the nearest man.

"All set?"

The man looked at him.

"Wise up, dummy," he said. He jerked a thumb toward the next ship. *"That's* your tub."

"Whoops," Tey said. "My mistake."

"Hey, Sam," the mechanic called. "Run this cowboy down to oh-nine-oh before he gets lost again." He turned away muttering. Tey climbed into the line-cart.

"You're kind of early, ain't you, pardner?" the driver said, wheeling the car around.

"I like to check in early."

"You got nothing to worry about. Old Skorn's tub gets all the best." He glanced at Tey. "No disrespect meant, of course."

"Let's watch those cracks," Tey said. "Some people might take it the wrong way."

"Me, I'm loyal, you bet," the driver said, indicating himself with a thumb. "I mean, I just got a kind of ha-ha informal way of talking—"

Five minutes later, Tey talked his way past another guard detail and inside the fast private vessel without an alarm. In the control compartment, he strapped in and flipped levers. A low rumble began, built rapidly. Tey reached out, scratched a fingernail across a daub of black paint on the panel. It flaked away, exposing the legend: NAVY 2956B. The command band light went on. Tey tuned it in.

"You in oh-nine-oh," the communicator barked. "What the devil are you doing?"

A red light glared on the panel. With a sound like Niagara, the main drive cut in. A giant weight crushed Tey back in his couch. Then the first alarm buzzer sounded, indicating cold feed lines. Tey dealt with it, and two others, then rested. He opened his eyes at a sudden blast from the tight-code communicator. He leaned forward to twist the speed control, pressed the replay.

"Five-six-bee, Blue Boy calling. Acknowledge, over."

Tey keyed the mike.

"Who are you, Blue Boy?"

"Tey—I had a hunch it might be you. There were rumors and then we picked up a blip heading out—but where you heading, man? You've—"

"I said who are you?" Tey cut in. "And how did you know my wavelength?"

"This is a friend of Jack."

"Jack's dead."

"Sure. I'll cover the epitaph later. Right now—what did you do with the box he gave you?"

"I'm looking after it."

"Those papers are vital documents, Tey—"

"Maybe you should have kept them when you had the chance, Jack-friend. But I guess you were pretty busy."

"You've stuck your nose into something big, ex-Cap'n. I don't like talking about it, even by tight beam. I can tell you this much —we were ready to hijack that boat ourselves—for a very special mission. Your play has knocked that out."

"Too bad. I saw my chance and I grabbed it."

"Now here are your orders—"

"I swiped this boat with no help from you, Bub. I have plans of my own."

"Where do you think you're going?"

"Don't worry about me, chum. I have a destination in mind."

"We're tracking you right into K-L. Short trip. Just across town. You could've taken a hack."

"Except the hack couldn't get past the gate. I'll go over it."

"This is no time for a suicide run, Tey. We need that boat."

"I have business of my own—"

"Skip it, Tey. This is—"

"Yeah, I know. War."

"You're carrying official documents of the Organization, Tey. I'm going to give you a set of coordinates—"

"I've plotted my course."

"That boat is Navy property. You'll bring it in or I'll see you shot for treason."

"You'll have to get in line, Blue Boy. There's a waiting list."

"You're a funny man, Tey. Here's one you won't find so amusing, maybe. The Greenbacks have Renee. We intend to get her back. I had an idea you might want to be in on it."

"Got her how?"

"Nobody knows. She was last seen with you."

"What are you planning?"

"We're hitting the citadel—in force."

"What force?"

"We have a few secrets in reserve."

"You've been sitting on them too long, Jack. You should have hit Skorn a long time ago."

"That's my decision to make. What about yours?"

"If I'm not there in thirty seconds, start without me," Tey said and without waiting for Blue Boy's retort, switched off the receiver, turned to the map screen, adjusted coordinates, refining the course he had given the ship's computers, so as to place him precisely in the spot he had selected, close to the outer wall of the well-guarded port area.

Tey stood in shadow. Abruptly the silence of the night was broken by the squeal of tires, an engine suddenly gunned. A beam of blue light lanced along the grim facades on the opposite side of the near-empty lot. Tey took three steps into the deeper shadow of a signboard. The glare of approaching headlights glinted on a parked car and pushed a black shadow behind it. Tey ran behind the parked car just as the oncoming vehicle screeched to a cruising speed, its red beam gyrating to the howl of its siren. Tey ducked down, flipped the pistol's beam control to narrow aperture, burned away the car's door lock. He pulled the door open, slid into the driver's seat, ducked under the dash, found the terminal box. With a gimmicked permatch, he welded the heavy conduits and wiring together. Instrument lights flickered and went on.

Tey sat up. Red light blinked through the glasteel top as the police car pulled alongside, the siren dying in a minor wail. Doors opened; two green-uniformed men jumped out, unlimbering guns.

"Climb out with your hands up," one cop called. "Don't try nothing."

"Make it fast!" another cop called. "I got a like nervous gun."

Tey tossed the pistol to the floor, took out the metal box, and slipped it behind the seat. He opened the door and stepped out onto gritty pavement, his hands raised.

"Kick a cop in the gut, will you?" a shrill voice cried excitedly.

"Yes, I'd love to, thanks," Tey said and saw a fist coming, rode with the blow. Somewhere a light dimmed, flared, dimmed . . .

"Don't kill him, you damned fool," one cop snarled.

"These kind are tough, like sewer rats; it takes more than a little tap or two—"

"Lay off. I got to see what he's got."

"Try the pockets."

Tey felt rough hands pulling at him, opened his eyes, and blinked at the raw light of an unshielded glare panel. He straightened, felt the bite of steel on his ankle. Blood trickled into his eye. He blinked it away. "You got nothing on me," he said huskily.

"You ain't going no place, Captain," one cop said.

"Hey," the other cop spoke up, "you in the Solar Corona earlier this evening?"

Tey looked at him. "Listen, boys," he said thickly, "you've got me all wrong. I just wandered into the place—"

"Skip it, Mr. Tey. We had an eye on you a long time."

"Then you know I don't mix in politics."

"Yeah?" The cop leaned over, showing bad teeth in a mirthless grin. "You birds are all alike. The Glory Boys, full of big ideas about how to change the world."

"Maybe it could stand one or two weensy improvements—"

"Save the lip, Tey. We got you cold." He fumbled in a shirt pocket, pulled out the metal box, waggled it under Tey's nose.

"Full of dust," he said. "They said thirty minute paper. What was on it? A lot of junk, maybe. But why hide it then? Maybe you can tell me what it's all about."

"You found it, huh?" Tey mumbled, more groggily than necessary.

"Too bad, Tey. The cops aren't as dumb as you figured, maybe."

"Look," Tey said—he licked his lips, tasted blood—"I'll make a deal."

The cop laughed. "He's good," he chuckled. "He'll make a deal."

"If I were you, copper," Nat Grall's deep voice growled, "I think I'd take that deal."

Both cops whirled at the unexpected intrusion; one fired, too late. The yellow-pink flame that stabbed from his crashgun licked harmlessly against cracked pavement as Grall's hand swept him aside, to rebound from the tarnished brick wall beside them, then slump on his side, still, except for a twitching leg. At the same instant, Jaxon slid over the roof of the cop car and struck down the second deputy.

"Gentlemen, well met by moonlight," Tey said. "I should've known better than to worry about you."

"We were keeping an eye on the Ward Six Dispatch Office," Grall explained. "When we saw these boys head out with everything hanging out, we trailed. And sure enough, you'd gotten into mischief again."

"That I did," Tey agreed. "But everything's on schedule. The boat is tucked away in the middle of the storage lot under the old bridge abutment, next to the outer security fence. I didn't have time to be clever."

"The Purloined Letter," Jaxon commented. "Let's see if it's still there."

"There's one other thing," Tey said. "They've got Renee and Sugar."

"How?" Jaxon demanded. Grall merely growled.

"I don't know the details," Tey said. "But the first order of business is to get them back."

"We have to use common sense," Jaxon said. "If we travel fast and light, we might have a chance; if we start on the knight-in-shining-armor routine, it's hopeless."

"There wasn't much common sense in the way you rode those rails," Grall said. "I'm with you, Captain."

"Never mind," a cool feminine voice said from the shadows,

and a slim figure emerged into the cold light of the corner polyarc.

"Thanks to Arno, they missed," Renee said quietly. "Missed *me*, that is, but they have Sugar."

"What happened?" Jaxon demanded. Tey went to the girl, gave her a comforting hug. "I suppose they jumped the car without waiting to see who was in it," he said. Renee nodded. "Arno saw them in time to ground the car. I didn't know what was happening. He slammed it down in the center of an intersection and told me to jump. Before I had time to say a word, he had the door open and practically threw me out—then he took off, and the Greenbacks didn't let him get half a block before they crowded him down. So they have Sugar—and Arno. I hoped I'd find you at the Rainbow."

"She'll be all right," Jaxon said. "Arno will see to that. And the Greenbacks have no reason to harass a child, anyway."

"That's what I've been telling myself," Renee said, sounding distressed.

"Just a minute," Jaxon said. "We're acting as if all was lost. But maybe . . ." he turned the signaling device which called his car. The suspense was shortlived. It was less than a minute later that Arno grounded the sleek vehicle in the street beside them.

"Sugar's with me," he said, without preliminaries. "Let's move out—Greenbacks in the area."

Jaxon spoke briefly to Arno, who departed in haste.

"Funny," Tey said, "Jack's friend, Blue Boy, knew all about the snatch before it happened—only it didn't happen—which kind of puts the Organization in a bad light."

Renee nodded. Jaxon said, "Good. Now we can forget the Organization."

·2·

The stolen racing boat stood almost invisible in the shadow of the high outer security wall of the Fleet base, precisely as Tey had left it.

"Seems the boys aren't on the ball tonight," Tey said, as they

looked across the deserted lot. They approached the racer war-
ily, but no waiting Greenbacks appeared. It was the work of a
moment to settle all personnel into crash gear.

"What do you plan to do, Captain?" Jaxon inquired after
everyone was settled.

"I'm going to strap on this tub and ease it over the wall," Tey
replied. "From there on we play it by ear."

Tey selected a hardstand close to a flood-lit crew working
over a Fleet courier boat close to the General Officers' Club
building. As he stepped out via the utility hatch, a young officer
in crisp whites with an artfully wilted collar strode briskly to
meet him.

"Here, you'll have to move that thing," he said wearily as he
came up. Tey stopped, turned to face the fellow. Subtly Tey's
stance changed: his back went stiffly erect, his expression grim.

"Better let me see your ID, Commander," he said to the
lieutenant, whose collar insignia was partly obscured by the curl
of the nylon to which it was pinned, a rather juvenile old gim-
mick still indulged in by junior officers who took pleasure in
being mistaken for bridge grade by their juniors. The lieutenant
came to attention and dutifully handed over a plastic-encased
card.

"Only a top secret clearance," Tey commented, keeping the
card. "If you're not cleared for GUTS, what are you doing bull-
ing into a CADO exercise, eh?"

"CADO, sir?" the young officer said in a strained voice. "I'm
line Staff Duty Officer, sir, and my briefing book—"

"At ease, son," Tey said more kindly. "Probably stuck in the
back of the book by your duty NCO, so you hadn't gotten to it
yet. No harm done, as long as you stick to your routine and don't
give your crew chief and his boys anything to gossip about. I'm
taking your Ready unit out. What kind of equipment do you
have on Ready for me?"

"Well, sir, there's the JAZ 105, the regular extra, and three
mediums, crewed and hot, and of course,"—the lieutenant
paused to offer a hollow chuckle—"*Princeton's* on the line, fueling."

"Cease fueling at once, and pull all maintenance personnel,"

Tey ordered crisply. "Clear the area. You'd better run your confirmation immediately. I have no time to waste—delayed by some kind of disturbance in the town just outside the outer ring." He waved in the general direction of the Rainbow. "No doubt you heard the sirens and firing."

"Yes sir, I did. Wondered about it, sir. As for the confirmation, sir, since you're pressed for time, I think I should dispense with the formality this time. Would you care to initial my sheet, sir, in case some nit-picker questions it? Since the senator assigned you his favorite go-boat to use as a shuttle, I guess there's not much doubt about the importance of the mission. Right, sir?" The boy extended his 'crap card', and Tey scribbled IOU on it. The lieutenant didn't glance at it as he tucked it away. "But, sir," he said in a troubled tone, "there's no crew on board, not even a standby team."

"Good. Just as I ordered," Tey said. "I have a special task team with me, operating under condition blue. Get me a line car, on the double."

The lieutenant hastened to comply, then stood by hoping to be ignored as Jaxon, Grall, and Renee with Sugar boarded the car which Tey then drove at an illegal speed across the dark ramp to the majestic bulk of the deep-space cruiser *Princeton*. To his surprise, no alarm siren cut the attempt short. Aboard, Tey briefed them.

"*Princeton*'s our most modern series, highly automated. Requires a base crew of only fifty-three specialist ratings. And she has the new emergency shortgear as it's called. The computer takes over all but the absolute minimum 'discretion-required' functions, allowing her to be handled on a reduced capability basis by a crew of six. The five of us are going to take her out."

He then proceeded to assign positions and duties, the others absorbing their hasty but crisp briefings with total concentration.

"That's it," Tey concluded. "Now for your final exam: only perfect scores will pass. The penalty for failure is death. Let's go."

·3·

The liftoff was uneventful. After clearing atmosphere Tey worked for some hours with relentless intensity over the NAV course-programming board. At last he was satisfied.

"I'm a little rusty, but fortunately the old IWD-2000 is a fairly rational sort of brain. It accepts all Stack Four languages up through Phi-19. We'll be feeling a course change in about ten minutes. I want to be well clear of the cluttersphere."

"How far— I mean, are we going to try directly for Omega?" Jaxon inquired diffidently.

"We've got the numbers," Tey said. "You saw 'em, Oliver; why not use 'em?"

"No reason. I only meant—that is, if they weren't what we thought—After all, it was just a hasty scribble, an afterthought. Anyway, since I'm not an astrogator, I can't memorize a twenty-six digit configuration in a single gestalt."

"Twenty-seven," Tey corrected.

"I'd hate to think what it must've taken, for Captain Greylorn to get his hands on that transcript and jot those coordinates down," he went on. "I suppose he was still hoping the full story would be made public—if not at once, then someday. And someday I'd like to find out how the Organization got its hands on a copy."

"How far *is* it?" Jaxon wanted to know. "How long will we be locked in this space-going solitary?"

"At full operational cruise, perhaps four years," Tey said. "A modern torsion drive can make about one and a half times the best speed a fast scout-boat could manage a century ago on the old flat-warp principle. So it's not so bad. Assuming, of course, that all is as well on Omega as the captain's brief report suggests."

"Captain Tey," Renee said gravely, "do you suppose we'll actually find a civilized world—out *there?*" She shuddered slightly.

"I feel pretty confident we'll find *something* worth the trip," Tey said. "Why don't you go back to your quarters and get some rest? You're going to be busy again soon."

"Yes," Renee said, rising. "I'll just look in on Sugar. I don't want her to wake up and find herself alone . . ." With another shiver, she departed.

"What are our chances, really?" Jaxon wanted to know. "What have we got, other than Greylorn's claim that he found New Terra—a very imaginative name, that. I still think of it as Omega."

"Considering how unpopular his find made him—and Greylorn was sophisticated enough to know Lord Banshire wouldn't welcome news of a rival world out there—I'd say Captain Greylorn's report can be relied on."

"Either way," Grall put in, "even if it's nothing but a collection of mud huts, it will be vastly preferable to what we left back there."

In the ensuing weeks, the four adults and the lone child developed a satisfactory accommodation to the schedule established by Captain Tey, and to the rigors inherent in life aboard a deep-space vessel. There was a moment of drama when Tey summoned all hands to catch a last glimpse of the faint star which was Sol, before he switched magnification on the direct-vision screens to the wider panoramic view demanded for astrogation. Only Sugar seemed disturbed by the idea of the end of actual sunlight, but her tears were soon dried, as other, more spectacular suns came into brilliant view. During the first five months, they sighted three planets, of two suns, none of which approached Earth-like conditions, to no one's surprise.

"It's Omega or bust," Grall commented. "At that, according to Grumblusky's hypothesis, it's some luck to find a habitable planet as soon as Greylorn found Omega."

They devised games, puzzles, exercise routines; and Tey, with the assistance of Jaxon—who, the captain soon realized, was a talented amateur computer programmer—devised teaching programs, both for Sugar, an astonishingly quick study, and for Grall and Renee and themselves. Soon all could converse intelligently on all aspects of the function and maintenance of the great vessel in which they traveled so monotonously. The ship's library contained, as did those in all capital ships of the Space Arm, extensive collections of literature, both fiction and nonfiction, and music, as well as a splendid sampling of the graphic and plastic arts of Earth. Sugar decided that her favorites were Sisley (whose name she loved and pronounced Sizzly) and Puccini. No one disagreed.

The ship's stores, stocked for a complement of two hundred for a nine-month cruise, provided an ample and varied diet. The culinary unit being programmed for hamburgers, hot dogs, subgum chow yok, as well as *cordon bleu* Parisien cuisine, there was no monotony in their diet. Tey established a nonvoluntary exercise schedule in the regulation one-point-six-G gymnasium. In this, as in other matters directly concerned with the well-being of the subskeleton crew and of the success of the mission, he made it clear that his title of captain was no mere formality and that orders would be obeyed.

Renee was the first to demur, tearfully, when Tey brushed aside her confident proposal that everyone take a week off from the more arduous tasks, including high-G calisthenics, ship status readout monitoring, log-keeping, and so on. At first she assumed he was merely assuming a stern facade in response to her deliberately, though playful, provocative initiative: coming across to his quarters clad only in a damp towel, which repeatedly slipped, and bumping him with her hip as she wheedled. She recoiled, hurt and astonished, when he ordered her back to her quarters.

"—and stay there, girl! We've got enough pressures on us without getting sex into the act. You're certainly aware that all three of us males have a yen for you—we'd be pretty sad sacks if we didn't—and as the only adult female within a few parsecs, you could stand this vessel on its ear, if you lifted a finger to get a little active rivalry going. God knows I want you, Renee, and you'll never know how close you came to having your bluff called—but get *out!* Go to *your* quarters, nowhere else! Nat and Oliver may not be able to take the gaff, so for the good of the mission—go!"

Renee nodded, solemnly adjusting her towel a hair's breadth from disaster.

"Now I see why they made you a captain," she said. "I'm sorry, you know I was only fooling around. And of course you're right. As for you poor deprivēd males, how about *me?* with three virile guys around and no competition—not for a few more years, though Sugar is coming along fast. In another six years she'll be of age—and you can feel assured, she'll be one sharp cookie—and a raving beauty. Good *night,* Captain."

The next day (Tey had established ship-board routine on a twenty-four-hour cycle) the first time Renee caught Tey's eye, she winked; thereafter the incident was ignored. Then, one silent night on the log watch, Jaxon came to Tey, explaining that he had a problem, and requested Tey's advice.

"As captain, of course, your word is law," he concluded. "I wouldn't want it any other way. God knows *I'd* hate to have the responsibility. But this is something that making a rule won't fix. It's Renee. You know I've known her for some time. We were never lovers, you understand. She had none. But we were close friends. Aside from her beauty, she was the only reasonable one in that whole nut-bunch they called the Organization. Now I'm demoted, in a sense, to being just one of three men, any one of which she could knock over with a come-hither look. Or—" he glanced at Tey's expression—"maybe she couldn't. What it boils down to is, I'm jealous. Every time I see her leaning on Nat's shoulder or crowded up against you, watching the NAV board —I want to yell at her, 'Hey, why don't you come over and rub up against *me* for a change!' But I realize that's unfair. She's just naturally an affectionate creature: she likes body contact. I get as much as anybody, but—"

"I understand completely, Oliver," Tey said. "And I appreciate your intelligence—and your courage—in bringing it out into the open. We're all jealous, and I confess I've watched her leaning over you, practically in your lap, and wondered why *I* didn't get more of her attentions. No doubt Nat feels the same way. And it *is* a problem we'll have to deal with before it blows up."

"We have four alternatives, as I see it," Renee said, some hours later, after Tey had made a dispassionate presentation of the situation as he saw it to all hands. Renee was first to respond. "One: I can pick one of you and settle down in domestic bliss —'with this ring I thee wed' and all that; two: you can draw straws; or three, I can rotate; or four: I can go out that airlock you showed us, Captain, and take a great, healing lungful of vacuum."

"Scratch three and four," Oliver said. "Four, at least. I suppose three has its points."

"Not for me," Nat said. "And no lottery, either."

"That seems to leave proposal number one," Tey said. "Unless someone has another suggestion."

"I propose that we call on Renee to decide," Jaxon said in a formal tone. Only Renee voted against the suggestion.

"The ayes have it, so ordered," Tey said firmly. "Meeting adjourned, Renee. Can you make your decision by first bell?"

"I've already made it," she replied. "I'll take all three of you to be my lawful wedded husbands."

"Back to where we started," Jaxon commented.

"Except now you have no reason to throw me out of your quarters," Renee countered. She looked at Tey with a serious expression and winked. "Can the captain perform the ceremony at once?" she inquired. "In accordance with FSA reg. 2097, paragraph 17, subsection nine. I looked it up a long time ago."

"But—" Jaxon blurted, "who gets—I mean, how do we decide . . . the first night," he finished lamely.

"Get out the straws," Renee said, laughing. "And why wait for tonight?"

Without further discussion Captain Tey read the marriage service, "By the authority vested in me as captain of a ship of the line . . ." only slightly amended to accommodate a triple bridegroom. Renee said, "I do," three times, with all due solemnity.

"I'm spending the next off-watch in Sugar's quarters," Renee said. "I promised her a long time ago." She smiled warmly at her three husbands, and left the chapel-card room which the captain had chosen for the ceremony. The three men looked at each other.

"Gentlemen," Tey said, "I'm speaking now as a husband among husbands, not as captain of this vessel. We can take this in the breezy way that our wife has so intelligently adopted, or we can go down to the gym and fight to the death with knives, or we can each concentrate on his good fortune in winning such a lovely bride for one day in three, and forget other men's wives the other two days. Have I left anything out?"

"Sure," Jaxon said. "We can each take a vow of celibacy, perhaps reinforced by a shot of Lust-no-more from the dispensary. I understand that last is highly effective, though it does have side-effects."

"Right," Nat Grall said. "After six months on LNM, you're a soprano for life."

"On a new world," Tey said thoughtfully, "we'll naturally have to evolve new customs, appropriate to the situation. This is Custom Number One. Now let's get back to work before the course monitor starts getting neurotic and decides we're all dead."

· 5 ·

On the thirteen hundred and fifty-third day Tey called all hands to the main forward display screen, on which was centered a bright yellow star, distinctly brighter than the background scatter, an isolated sun with no stellar neighbor within a light-year. A lone planet showed a crescent.

"Ladies and gentlemen," the captain said coolly. "Allow me to present New Sol—or the Omega Sun, or Greylorn's Star. We'll have an official name-giving ceremony later."

A spontaneous, though ragged cheer cut off the last few words. Sugar hugged Renee, and Renee hugged everybody. After the laughter and tears had subsided, Jaxon asked seriously:

"Have you looked her over at high mag, Captain?" What about other planets? That one looks cold."

"There's at least one other," Tey said. "I had already computed a perturbation, but I took only a quick look. I wanted to save the big moment of discovery for all of us together. Now let's go to the direct-vision screen and crank her up to max. That'll pick out anything big enough to be useful."

The direct-vision screen, being a ten-mirror periscope, naturally afforded none of the brilliance of the electronically enhanced navigation screens. Still, the sight of the great sun, a yellow diamond against the faint smear of the Milky Way of which it was a minor component, brought oohs and ahs from each viewer in turn as the view widened, dimming in response to the blaze of the sun. Then the center of view changed, shifting to a crescent at first nearly invisible until the screen readjusted and filtered out the star-glare in the background. Now it was a sharp-cut, white-glowing crescent against total blackness. A tiny blob of greenish white was visible near the edge of the screen.

"Make that at least four planets," Tey said, consulting a readout board. "The computer seems to think this is the most Earthlike, although it's closest to the star."

"It's even got a big moon," Renee said.

"We should look all of them over," Jaxon said. "This is too big a decision to leave to a discrimination circuit to make for us."

"What are the chances we could lift again if we put her down?" Grall asked.

"Not good," Tey replied coolly.

· 6 ·

After a full month of deceleration, the ship entered a seemingly endless period of orbiting Greylorn, as they had, with only semimock formality, named the planet, reserving Omega for the big yellow sun. At an altitude of fifty thousand miles, they scanned the cloud-streaked greenish-tan world at a velocity slightly less than that of the surface so far below, and at a slight angle to the planet's ecliptic plane, thus permitting the auto-cameras to record the entire planetary surface in a few hundred orbits.

"Not a sign of human works anywhere . . ." Jaxon voiced the despair that all were feeling. "No roads, no city glow, harbor dredging—nothing."

"Don't take it too hard," Grall said. "You know the only sign of intelligent life on Earth visible from geosynchronous orbit—only about half what we're holding—is the Great Wall of China. We're pretty small organisms, compared with even a minor world like Earth."

"I sort of had an idea we might be met by a welcoming committee," Jaxon grumbled. "After all, Greylorn reported they still had space-travel, including a planetary federation—and they gave him a big welcome. They've probably been wondering why his contact wasn't followed up a hundred years ago."

"I like that big island," Sugar said. "Or maybe it's a small continent—in between East Continent and North Continent. It's shaped like a dog's head."

"Over there on East," Jaxon commented, "just opposite the nearest point of the island, looks like it might be man-made. A rectangle—or is it? Maybe I'm imagining things."

"It's there," Tey said, "barely visible; no more than a kilometer long, and narrow."

"Really, Captain?" Jaxon said admiringly. "And what sort of structure is it? Does it have a sign out front?"

"No structure," Tey said. "Just a clearing, I'd say. But it'd make a good target for our landing."

"Risky," Jaxon commented. "That looks like a fairly impressive fissure just to the west of the shoreline. And I get a reading that matches bogland—and that dry tundra doesn't look too inviting, either."

"What would you like, Oliver," Tey inquired. "Swaying coconut palms and sugar-white beaches bordering turquoise lagoons?"

"I'll settle for something we can walk on," Jaxon said.

The ship's long-range planetary analysis unit reported a surface gravity of 1.3 Earth standard, an equatorial mean temperature of 25° Celsius, a daily rotation period of thirty-one hours, and a year 209 Earth-years in length. The moon, at a distance of half a million miles and only slightly larger than Luna, would appear puny in the night sky of Greylorn. The atmosphere was of the expected nitrogen-oxygen type. The seas were water.

"—otherwise the Omega people wouldn't have picked it, of course," Jaxon commented.

"How do we know they did?" Nat Grall inquired. "We just sort of arrived here, you remember, without more than a quick look at two, three, and four."

"We'll have to put her down to find out," Captain Tey pointed out. "And once down that's it, as we've already discussed. We can stay off here in orbit and wait for a contact, or we can hold our noses and jump in."

The vote was unanimous. Within hours the first near-supersonic squeak of contact with the outermost wisps of atmosphere broke the silence of nearly four years. There was an immediate change in the tempo of life aboard ship as long-unused equipment came to life, preparing the ship for the drastic transition from free-fall to normal G conditions.

· 7 ·

Underfoot, springy greyish turf; in the distance a hazy horizon, dead-flat all the way around; above, a high haze, slightly greenish as compared with the deep blue of Earth's sky. It seemed to Tey that the bitter wind blew through him unimpeded, chilling his bones. Oliver and Renee had closed in on either side of Sugar, while Nat Grall stood head up, facing the wind, providing a lee to shelter in.

"Maybe half an hour," Jaxon said, between teeth clenched against the tendency to chatter. He caught Tey's eye. "Before we're d-dead of exposure," he explained.

"Captain," he went on, "we're in no condition to set up a democracy. If you'll go on b-being in charge, we'll have a better chance. Custom Number Two."

Tey nodded. "We've had our 'breath of fresh air' that seemed so important a few minutes ago. By now the ship's air will have been exchanged and brought up to ship-normal temperature. We'll live aboard for the next few days, until we've analyzed all the data and taken stock."

Still huddled together, bundlesome in cold-weather gear, they moved awkwardly to the personnel hatch, which on command opened and deployed the short escalator. Inside, they began to move again, cautiously, like long-bedridden patients just released from hospital.

"Now we know what it feels like to be ninety years old," Jaxon said. "And this is Spring, near the equator. It appears that life on Greylorn won't be any luxury cruise."

"Half an hour ago," Grall commented, "if anybody had told me I'd be back aboard in ten minutes and glad of it, I'd have laughed at him."

"That's called adaptability," Jaxon said. "Be glad we've got it. On this God-forsaken tundra we'll need it."

"The first thing we'll need out there is shelter," Tey said.

"Perhaps we should stay here—use the ship as a base, I mean," Renee suggested. "And gradually explore until we find a more favorable site."

"If we're going to live aboard, we might as well not have landed," Jaxon pointed out. "We've got to meet this planet on its own terms—and beat it."

"Not 'beat' it," Sugar spoke up. "Make friends with it." The comment drew agreement from all hands.

"We have facilities here aboard ship that we can use to find out what we're up against," Tey said, "starting with the data our computer gathered while we were orbiting. So—first we'll have a good hot meal and then we'll go into conference and see what our next move is—as we should have done in the first place; only I was as eager as any to breathe fresh air."

FIVE

First Contact

"**W**e're parked on permafrost," Tey said, as he paced restlessly around the library table where the readouts were spread, and around which the others were seated. "So sod huts and dugouts are out of the question for the present. We have aboard—" he paused to glance at one of the papers on the table—"approximately one square kilometer of class-A heavy-duty durafilm, in thicknesses of from one-half millimeter to half a centimeter. There's sufficient 6029 tubing to maintain all ship's systems operational for the next five years—or to erect enough tents to house several hundred thousand people." He looked from one attentive face to another. "Any better ideas?"

"Maybe," Jaxon said. "You said sod huts are out, but we could set up heating equipment—or just use the main drive at idle—to thaw as much as we need. But I suppose that would just turn the area into a bog that would start to freeze again as soon as it melted. I withdraw the idea."

"I don't see anything wrong with the tents," Grall said, "except we don't need forty acres of 'em. And we can use Oliver's heating system to keep 'em warm."

"I agree with Nat," Renee said. "It's the simplest way—and best of all, we can get started on it at once."

"I demur," Sugar put in coolly. "We shouldn't think in terms of settling down right here, just because we happened to land on this spot because I said I liked the island because it's in the shape of a dog's head."

Tey spoke up to agree. "She's right, of course—and there *is* that rectangular whatever-it-is to investigate. We should explore first. We should carry out a recon at once, while we're still fresh and full of enthusiasm. If we build houses, later we'll be reluctant to leave them."

"I vote with Sugar," Grall said. Jaxon and Renee were quick to agree.

"I see no important objection," Tey commented thoughtfully. "But it will require some planning. We can't just off-load the crawler and drive off into the sunset."

"Of course," Jaxon said. "But—"

"We have three ground vehicles," Tey said. "The heavy crawler designed to haul cargo over any terrain we're likely to meet; a light recon-car, fast but with a limited range; and the protocol-car, a fast, armed luxury vehicle for two, intended for formal occasions and impressing people. All are class-one capability equipment; low-pressure, ground-effect type. We shouldn't all go. Two of us should stay with the ship, keeping in touch at all times, ready to act in any emergency that might arise. I vote for the crawler. There's plenty of room aboard; it's set up for a crew of ten. And of course it will carry all the supplies we could want for any reasonable length of time."

"In a way," Renee said, "it frightens me—a whole world, I mean, with all its oceans and rivers and lakes and mountains and forests and meadows and beaches and canyons and falls—everything Terra has in the way of landscapes, and maybe more. All ours, to do with as we choose. One day there'll be great cities and a network of highways—all that. And it's up to us to see that it all gets off to a good start, that we don't close off any options by foolish actions."

"Let's not think about it all at once, dear," Jaxon said. "Let's just take it a day and a mile at a time."

"Of course," Renee said, and placed a hand on Jaxon's.

"This spot will probably be preserved in its virgin state as a memorial," he said. "Funny, I don't feel like a historical figure; I just feel like a fellow who'd like to be secure and comfortable and have plenty of all the good things in life."

"We won't get 'em sitting here jawing," Nat said in a jocular tone.

There was no disagreement with Tey's proposal, and it was quickly decided that Jaxon, Renee, and Sugar would stay with the ship the first time.

· 2 ·

After a trip to the aft lazaret to inspect the vehicles (all three were in flawless condition), Tey called an informal meeting in the library, to summarize all the planetary data supplied by the computer.

"Our soil," he said, "is a light loam when it's not frozen, and it has all the elements we need for farming. It's also—" he added before conversation drowned his voice.

"Also?" Jaxon inquired, raising an eyebrow in exaggerated query. He motioned the others to silence.

"—full of seeds, spores, and dormant microorganisms," Tey continued. "No doubt when summer arrives and the soil thaws, a thick vegetation will spring up, including, we can assume, plants that will be useful, perhaps even edible. The present tundra seems to be an adaption to the long seasonal cycle. We're in the midst of a fifty-plus year Spring."

"What about animal life?" Sugar asked.

"No large animals, it appears," Tey said. "Unless they hibernate for very extreme periods. A wide variety of microscopic fauna, though."

"It *is* frightening, as Renee said," Jaxon commented. "A whole planet—bigger than Terra—and completely unknown." He feigned a melodramatic shiver. "When summer comes, anything could happen. Suppose there are deep caves full of dormant dinosaurs?"

"We'll have some twenty years to prepare," Tey said, "before Summer arrives and our sleeping beauties awake."

"My God, twenty years," Jaxon said. "That sounds like eternity, but it's only the bare beginning."

"But," Sugar said, "by that time . . ." she paused, looking uncertain.

"Yes, Shyug?" Grall encouraged her.

"Well, we *are* going to tell them, aren't we?" she blurted, looking from face to face for a hint of response.

"Tell who, Sugar?" Renee was first to ask.

"Everybody," Tey replied for her. "The people back home. They *need* Greylorn, and we can't possibly use all of it. The question is, how?"

"Right," Grall was saying.

"—to that later," Jaxon's words came next. "As for now . . ." he looked thoughtful.

"Think how happy they'll be," Sugar cried. "I'll bet they can't wait to get out of that awful world and come here."

"Don't be too sure," Renee said. "Most people dislike change. They won't want to give up a niche that's keeping them alive, even though just barely."

"But there'll be some," Tey put in. "It's up to us to be ready for them."

"Ready how?" Renee and Jaxon inquired together.

"Ready to help, if they want help. Ready to fight if they arrive shooting."

"Why would they want . . . want to be hostile?" Renee asked.

"Probably they won't," Tey said. "But if they do, we'll be ready. We've found a new chance for mankind here. We have an obligation to keep all the options open, just as Renee pointed out."

"But first," Jaxon reminded them, "we have to get that message back to Terra." He looked inquiringly at Tey.

"There are at least two possibilities," Tey said. "But you're the electronics expert, Mr. Jaxon."

Jaxon got to his feet. "I'm going into a huddle with the computer," he stated firmly. "The first order of business is to see just what I've got back in stores to work with—other than the stuff we've been using for the last forty-one months. It already seems more like twenty years." He nodded and left the library.

"What are the two possibilities?" Grall asked. "A tight enough beam with the ship's reactors behind it could punch through. What else?"

"We have aboard six ultra high-speed space-to-ground torpedoes," Tey told him. "We could rig one as a message torpedo. But let's see what Ollie comes up with."

· 3 ·

"We can put it in a parking orbit, and blanket all channels," Jaxon said the next day as he stood beside Tey, who was studying the other's sketches for modification of an Ali-class torpedo. "And we can arm her against ground-to-space attacks."

Tey nodded. "There's nothing here we can't handle, Jaxon; but once in Earth orbit, we have an option. As you pointed out, we can broadcast it, let the whole world know at once. Or—" he paused, "we can make contact with Fleet HQ, on the emergency UTS band, and give Banshire's mob a choice: initiate a colonization plan at once—or we spill the beans and it'll all come down around them like a house of cards in a hurricane."

"Umm . . ."—Jaxon looked thoughtful—"I don't like leaving Banshire's machine in charge," he said. "But if we let the secret out, there'll be economic chaos among other things, and it will take decades, if not centuries, to normalize sufficiently to mount a first-class colonial venture. So I suppose I must vote for alternate two."

"I concur," Tey said. "If the crowd has the word, it will mean, at best, duplicative effort and a flock of half-ready, inadequate amateur efforts, doomed to failure and massive loss of life and vital supplies. So—we'd best opt for a well-organized enterprise by the totalitarian—but qualified—government."

Only Sugar was inclined to demur, but when the others described for her the fate awaiting an ill-mounted effort produced by laymen with no qualification but enthusiasm, she reluctantly agreed.

"—how it was with us, for only three and a half years and with free run of a big vessel," Jaxon reminded the fourteen-year-old.

"—packed in like commuters on the late car," Grall was saying, his face reflecting the suffering he was depicting. Sugar wept, and was comforted, and voted for the "official" contact.

Then Jaxon, who had been frowning thoughtfully, spoke up. "I wonder," he said, "if it might be possible to give it to the Organization instead—a compromise," he added. "Those people at least have the nucleus of an orderly society, and they hate the Banshire machine as much as we do."

"How?" Tey and Grall said together. Jaxon shook his head impatiently. "I have no idea, but it's a possibility we shouldn't overlook."

"Meanwhile," Tey said, "I propose to take the scout-car and do a quick reccy as far as the rectangle, which I make to be about twenty miles east; that's enough for the first time out. I could be talked out of it, if someone comes up with a good reason . . ." He glanced inquiringly at each face in turn: Jaxon nodding; Grall frowning; Renee smiling, though a bit worriedly. Only Sugar spoke up:

"I ought to go with you, Captain," she said firmly. "In case of a disaster back here, there'd still be one woman alive, to found the colony."

The logic of this was irrefutable. "So ordered," Tey said.

· 4 ·

Tey set his course due east, keeping the lowering sun at his back. For the first hour there was no detectable change. The drab expanse of stunted, grayish tundra grass stretched as if without end to the hazy distances all around. Only the single tiny spire that was the great warship, now far behind, interrupted the monotony minutely. The car moved swiftly and smoothly across the turf on its air-cushion.

The ground-map screen, linked to the ship's data banks, showed the ragged coastline some twenty-one miles ahead.

"At idle speed, that's just over an hour's run," Tey said. "We may as well break out some rations and enjoy our first ex-ship meal on Greylorn."

As they consumed their leisurely meal, the car, on autodrive, had scaled a slight incline, too gradual to have been noticeable to most people, but Tey, with his pilot's habit of watching the dials, had noted the one-point-four degree angle of inclination and the gradual creep upward of the altimeter. Then, when the instrument indicated they had climbed one hundred and fifty meters, and just as he had decided to halt the machine, it stopped. Cautioning Sugar to remain inside, Tey climbed out through the hatch to look over the situation at first-hand.

The searching, steady wind seemed, if anything, colder than before. Tey heard his suit thermostats clatter almost at once, and immediately he felt the welcome warmth glowing at wrist and throat and ankle. A moment later, the big chest unit came on, suffusing his torso with welcome energy; meanwhile, he had walked a few steps away from the scant shelter of the recon-car, to pause at the edge of the steep declivity which his car's sensors had noted and responded to by halting. A slope of broken rock strata stretched down to an arc of tallus below. Something caught his eye—or was it but an effect of the watery sunlight? It was a faint double line, like a ground-car track, which, emerging from under the fallen rubble, ran out across the plain ahead in a dead-straight line as far as he could see. Still unsure, Tey changed position by a few feet; the illusion, if illusion it was, persisted. He went back to the car. Sugar greeted him calmly: "Oliver is trying to contact us on band Blue-three," she said. "I knew you'd want to take the call personally."

Stifling his eagerness to tell the girl of what he had seen—he no longer doubted that it was a road, or at least a trail—Tey activated channel Blue-three via his command talker, a tiny but effective device concealed in the gold braid on his collar, which drew power from a one-gram nuclear cell and which not only transmitted all sound above an adjustable threshold level to any of some two hundred code-designated listeners aboard ship, but also recorded both transmissions and receptions in a sealed capsule. In addition it monitored and recorded the passage of time and could use the PA system of any naval vehicle within five miles. The recordings constituted competent legal evidence. At once Jaxon's voice, sounding slightly hoarse, boomed in the car speaker:

". . . repeat: We have contact! So far all we have is a definitely local transmission on the general band—male voice, heavily accented, but speaking a dialect of standard. He seems to think we might leave before he can talk to us; pleading, if the word 'prease' means anything, for us to wait for him. Seems he's in a vehicle of some sort and has us in sight. Repeat: we have contact! So far—"

"All right, Jaxon," Tey cut in on the recording. "I read you twenty-five. How about cutting me in on the reception, and meanwhile stand fast."

"Roger, Captain!" Jaxon's voice revealed relief. "Thank God you answered. For all I know, this fellow may be fingering us for a sitting-duck air strike. But—" Jaxon's speech was cut off, and a strange voice, amid static, came in:

"—to assure your ners of our riabirity, on oar counts. Quest confirm confrence soonest. Kerner-Genaru von Shimo. End transmission prease. Hoping your ners proval prease."

Tey glanced tensely at Sugar, who met his eyes smilingly. "He has a very funny way of talking," she said, "but he seems eager to please us." Her smile faded. "I wouldn't trust him as far as Nat could throw him," she concluded, and smiled again. "What do you think, Captain?"

"Funny," Tey said, "I have the same hunch." He spoke again for the record: "Ollie, sit tight—and don't let your guard down. I assume you have your phase-one defenses armed and loaded."

"Roger, Captain," Jaxon replied at once. "Screens are in place, except for the one voice channel, of course, not counting your command link, naturally. I'm afraid I'm not very good at these terse, official, don't-waste-a-word transmissions. Anyway, I've told this clown to stay off at ten miles and I've got everything but the dishwasher zeroed in on him. I've maintained strict in-house silence naturally. The poor guy's been at it for over half an hour now, but it's probably a recording. I'll check. Right! A ten-point identity, static and all. So he *is* being tricky."

"Not necessarily," Tey replied. "If this is the Omega colony, they might still have a surface-based monitor system, even though we didn't find the off-planet picket Greylorn talked to. I'm on my way, estimating outer-screen contact in . . ." he glanced at a readout—"fourteen seconds, mark. Arano." At once, he gunned the light car in a sharp turn and set off at flank speed along his back-trail.

"Captain," Sugar said seriously, "do you really suppose it's possible, after over three hundred years, that they—their descendents, of course, are still waiting here in this bleak place, hoping for someone to come?" She shivered.

"I don't see any other possibility, Shyug," Tey replied. "Probably they explored and found a more favorable area than this to start with. They may well have thrived. Back home—on Terra, that is," he corrected himself, "people with no modern technology have lived in far harsher environments than anything we've seen so far."

"I don't know whether I hope it's true, or not," Sugar said quietly. "In a way I like the idea of having a world to ourselves."

"We'll soon know," Tey replied, as the car hesitated momentarily while its IFF gear examined and matched the outer energy screen that emanated from the ship three miles distant. Then, through the barrier, it hurried on. The vessel was in sight now, a needlepoint at extreme range.

"No use bothering Ollie," Tey said. "If this contact were located between us and him, he'd have said so."

· 5 ·

A quarter of an hour later, safely inside the ship and feeling a surprising degree of relief at being inside again, Tey and Sugar described the monotony of the landscape they had seen. Then Tey mentioned the trail he had discovered.

"Not a paved road, eh?" Grall commented. "Maybe that tells us something about how vigorous this Omega colony is. Or maybe not," he went on. "Now, if it had been a class-A autopike, *that* would have told us something."

Renee and Jaxon had met them at the entry port, and the party had hurried to the signal deck, where Grall was manning the board. As he rose to greet them, he threw switches, and at once a roar of static burst out, and over it a thin but clear voice:

". . . ners of our riabirity, on oar counts. Quest confrence soonest. Kerner-Genaru von Shimo. End transmission prease—"

"Maybe I'm wrong," Tey said as Grall reduced the volume, "—but I'd guess he's speaking a dialect that's influenced by Old Japanese."

"Quite possibly, Captain," Jaxon said. "It's an estabrished—ah —established fact that *Omega's* crew was made up with all major ethnic groups represented in ratio to their percentage of the general population. Considering the vigor and effectiveness of the Japanese, it wouldn't be surprising if they had managed to influence the common tongue to that extent, As the Academy had been complaining for years, we have examples of the same phenomenon back on Terra—in our own speech, in fact. I hadn't been conscious of my own tendency to substitute R for L untear I heard this fellow, and began introspecting. Did you notice—I caught myself once or twice just now. Actually 'estabrish' sounds just about as right as—and is easier to say than —'establish.'"

The others nodded, silently voicing words and looking surprised.

"Funny," Nat Grall said. "I guess I *have* been saying 'estabrish,' without noticing it."

"I say 'Engrish,'" Renee contributed. "I guess it should be— or used to be, 'English,' just the way it's spelled. Sounds rather awkward."

"In first school," Sugar said, "they told us it was 'the defective lateral.' Lots of kids noticed words like 'prane' and 'prease' weren't spelled the way they sounded. And there are others, too. Like 'knight,' and 'enough,' and 'phrase,' and 'island,' and 'could,' and 'lamb,' and 'through.'"

"Those are older," Jaxon said, "dating back to Old Historical times, when the scholars tried to 'reform' spelling to prove Latin or Greek derivation. They'd be pretty upset if they could hear 'prease,' and 'forrow,' and all the others. Still, some dialects continue to pronounce the K and the G in 'knight' centuries after it became unstylish. I suppose it's impossible to keep spelling and pronunciation in step. Spelling changes slowly. So we spell L and pronounce R—some of the time, at least."

"How long would it have taken, Captain," Sugar inquired, "for the amount of linguistic change we've observed here to have occurred?"

"Good point, Shyug," Tey said. "My guess would be a couple of hundred years anyway. At the minimum it's obvious that the *Omega* people survived their landing."

"And they're still alive and talking funny to prove it," Grall added. "Let's get this fellow in here and see what he's got to say for himself."

"Not inside the ship," Tey said. "We'll meet him on his own turf."

Accordingly Jaxon gave the stranger the pass wavelength, and the strange car resumed its approach. It was a one-man, Navy-issue two-wheeler contact-car of antique design, somewhat modified and poorly maintained, Tey saw at a glance on the direct-vision screen. "But," he commented, "it's a miracle it still functions at all at its age." Tey and Grall, bulky in suit-armor and wearing conspicuous side-arms, went out to make the contact.

The man who climbed awkwardly from the old-fashioned ground-only car was a wizened little fellow whose leather-brown face was so wrinkled it was impossible to discern his ethnic type. As the two men emerged from the great grey ship, he came scuttling forward, in a veritable cloud of unintelligible talk. Tey held up a hand, and the old fellow halted, still speaking volubly.

"We have a slight language problem," Tey cut into the tirade, his amplified voice drowning the other momentarily. As the echoes died, Tey noted with relief that the little man had fallen silent and appeared to be ready to listen. Tey repeated his statement.

Jittering and bobbing busily, the stranger responded, speaking more slowly now and with an apparent effort to enunciate clearly, first introducing himself as what Tey understood as Colonel-General von Shimo. The colonel-general went on to present verbal credentials as the accredited representative of the Council of One of New Ohio and all New Terra, restraining himself with visible effort from adding his full autobiography. Surprisingly, after a few minutes, his accent seemed hardly noticeable. Tey accepted the little man's speech gravely, then replied formally:

"I am Captain Tey, *Princeton,* five hundred thousand tons burden, on an extended survey run out of Terra. On behalf of my executive, I have the honor to convey greetings and await full briefing on the present status of New Terra."

After pointing out that he could of course offer no information of "miritary" value, von Shimo launched himself on a flood of detailed exposition regarding New Terra's economy, arts and sciences, benign intentions, and dislike of unwarranted intrusions. Tey quietly made accompanying commentary on his suitsteno, at the same time including those aboard ship in the briefing:

Light and heavy manufacturing to a value of a hundred thousand struggs per week (doubtful, considering his beat-up old car); agriculture: fully managed to limit surpluses to ten years' requirements (must be a better climate somewhere); birth rate: held stable at thirty-year replacement level; iron and coal resources: exceed estimated requirements for next century by tenfold; mineral resources: supply may be considered infinite, like that of timber, due to recovery/replacement programs far in excess of usage; nuclear fuel supplies: held at balanced level (if he's not lying, these folks have the technology they need back on Terra); and would the captain and his aide "kindry accept the invitation of the Councir to attend the annuar reception for Territoriar Councirors at Great Prime, even now in progress."

While expressing appreciation of the gracious invitation, before accepting, Tey explained, he had need to confer with Field Marshall, indicating Nat Grall.

"Some brag," Grall said, his voice ringing thin and tinny in Tey's ear-talker at such close range. "If half of that's true, this New Terra could wag old Terra like a tail."

"If we accept the invitation and go to this shindig," Tey pointed out, "we can probably find out."

"On the other hand, Jaxon and the girls can't con that tub out of here alone, if we wind up in an iron pot."

"With respect, Captain," Nat said, "this would be a good time for us to do something smart."

"Or at least not unnecessarily dumb," Tey agreed. "We have to make a move sometime: we've got to commit ourselves. What better time than now, while we have an opportunity so to do?"

" 'So to do,' " Nat mused aloud. "How can one dispute such elegance?"

"Nat, you're a frustrated pedant," Tey countered.

After a moment's discussion and a terse notification to Renee, who was manning the talker aboard ship, that they were about to accompany the spider deeper into his web, and with a final admonition to open to no one without a close inspection by direct vision at high mag, the two men turned to von Shimo, who had stood by jittering silently during the conversations.

"Prease, gentermen," he exclaimed, "we go now, at once, if you wirr?" The vehicle hatch stood invitingly open.

"Shall we, Captain?" Nat inquired as if in doubt.

"We have our side-arms," Tey said. "Let's go."

They climbed into the old car, and the voluble chauffeur set off at once, heading inland, toward the diffuse glow of the late sun.

SIX

Grand Tour

The ride in the elderly ground-car was astonishingly bumpy; at each dip the Terrans experienced disproportionate inertial pressure as the customary lift-and-glide of a modern stabilized vehicle failed to occur and the heavy machine clung doggedly to the surface.

"It's a genuine old-style ground-contact car," Grall commented. "No low-pressure air-cushion, even. It'd be worth plenty to the Smithsonian."

"And it's no new-manufacture replica," Tey said. "It's the real thing. They really built to last in those days."

"Over three hundred years old and still operating," Grall mused. "But where's all that light and heavy manufacturing the general was talking about?"

"Maybe he was lying a little," Tey suggested.

"By the way, Cap'n," Grall said, "thanks for promoting me to field marshall so I rank him. Might come in handy."

"Precisely," Tey said. "It's a legitimate rank, too. You're chief of our armed forces. Maybe you'd better ritz him a little, just to remind him to stay on your left and slightly to the rear."

Grall grinned. "It might help at that, if he has any unfriendly friends."

Soon they were into less level terrain of low, rolling hills. An hour's run out, Tey caught a glimpse of a long, sod-covered

160 –

mound, barely visible off to the right in the dying sunlight, but reflecting the side-glare from the brilliant headlight, oddly at variance with the monotony of the landscape. At that moment von Shimo casually angled left, giving the mound a wide berth, while busying himself with the terrain-display screen, muttering to himself. Then they were past the singularity and trending upward on a slight slope.

"Oh, drat, I nearly forgot," von Shimo exclaimed, giving the wheel a wrench to the right. "Up here fierd-office. Duty requires I check in. Take onry a moment." Then he became elaborately engrossed in steering.

The big, blurry yellow sun was on the horizon behind them when von Shimo took the car up a narrow, crooked trail to the top of a small, moss-green outcropping of what appeared to be granite. The tiny plateau at the summit was marred by a decrepit shack rudely built of corrugated synthetic panels such as were ordinarily used for temporary partitioning in large buildings. Dim, yellowish light, barely visible in the dusk, shone out through the many open cracks in the flimsy walls. The general turned, showed his passengers three gleaming gold teeth set in a row of blackened stumps, and rattled off something unintelligible.

"Roll that past again, if you will, General," Tey said. "I missed the last nineteen syllables."

"He spoke only twenty," Grall pointed out.

"I got 'prease,'" Tey said. "But he starts *every* sentence with 'prease,' so that doesn't tell us much."

"Funny," Grall said. "'Tell' sounds just right. I wouldn't try to say 'terr.'"

"That's why the word has resisted change," Tey said. "It's hard to say, just as your name would be, with the 'defective lateral,' 'Grawr': no, it's not the real you, Nat."

"Gentermen," von Shimo said, "this humber structure is my temporary fierd-office. I suggest you would be more comfortaber to remain here in the car, whirst I just attend to a few administrative detairs." Without awaiting a reply, the general scuttled across to a warped door which hung precariously by a single hinge; he made elaborate business of unlocking it with an old-fashioned electrokey, and went in. The lights brightened inside.

· 2 ·

Tey seized the opportunity to raise Oliver on his command talker, gave him an intensive briefing on the situation, concluding: "We'll stick with him until we've learned something of value. No point in turning back before then." Jaxon agreed, and they signed off with mutual exhortations to stay alert and take no unnecessary chances.

"What do you suppose that was, back there, that the general was so careful not to let us see?" Tey asked Nat.

"I guess the excitement of finding the field-office is supposed to keep our imaginations occupied, so we don't start imagining mysterious burial mounds," Grall said. "Let's take a sneaky look, Cap'n."

"That proposal, Field Marshall," Tey said solemnly, "does you no credit. First we'll check the hut. I'll take this side; you check out the others."

· 3 ·

In the still deepening twilight, Tey made his way silently to the door, which stood ajar. Inside, in the sickly glow of a single curled glare-strip, he saw boxes stacked on a rudely leveled dirt floor. Against one wall, apparently supporting it, was a large, old-fashioned and much-battered electronic chassis, of the type one associates with flake transistors. The bundle of conduits emerging from its side was less than a meter in length, ending in a ragged shear. Von Shimo perched on a three-legged stool of blackish wood, deftly manipulating a museum-piece keyboard. As Tey watched, the little man jumped up and accorded a piercing glance to a wall chronometer with an outsized face.

The clock, Tey saw, was stopped at 19:25. He wondered what year.

Now General von Shimo was at a desklike arrangement of boxes, pawing through heaped papers. At length he pounced on one, held it close to his face, angling it to catch the light. Then, apparently disappointed, he repeated the procedure; at last he chose one and settled down on a box serving as a chair to study his choice with an expression of satisfaction. As von Shimo stared at the small, pink document which he had so carefully selected, Tey moved around to the adjacent window, nearer the desk, from which point of vantage he could clearly see the pink paper. Under the printed heading, 'REQUEST FOR WORK ORDER,' it was blank. At last, von Shimo glanced at the large watch (or small clock) strapped to his skinny forearm. He then, in an elaborately casual way, opened a narrow metal wall-locker, lifted the lid of the wooden create therein, glanced quickly inside as if hoping not to notice himself sneaking a look. Then in a stealthy manner, he transferred to his pockets a regulation-issue emergency food packet, hesitated, then added two more, plus a flat flask marked 'MEDICINAL SPIRITS.' The last, he uncapped, sniffed at, and, after a momentary pause, recapped and tucked away.

Encountering Nat at the far end of the shack, Tey said, "Cover for me, Nat. Ten minutes." Then he set off at a jog downslope into the now-full darkness, steering by the last of the sun's glow. He sensed, rather than saw the mound, went to it, and followed its periphery, pausing only to place a glare-chip among the stiff grass blades. The length of the mound was just over two hundred paces; the width, only twenty. The sod made a smooth transition from the curve of the mound to the level terrain on which it had been erected. Tey realized he was assuming that it was not a natural formation. No irregularity broke the smooth curve as high as Tey could reach. He saw his glare-chip ahead, pocketed it, and returned to the dim glow of the shack, where Nat met him with an 'all clear.'

"Couldn't tell much about it in the dark," Tey said. "But why did the old devil try to keep it a secret?"

Feeling the cutting wind in spite of his heavy-weather suit, Tey motioned Nat to follow, and returned to the car.

·4·

As Tey closed the hatch, the hut door opened wide, and von Shimo came through it at a trot. After taking his seat and strapping in, the general turned to his passengers.

"Headquarters insist it is necessary now you give me more particulars of your esteemed persons," he said casually.

"What were you doing in there?" Tey asked as if in reply.

"Tiresome administrative routine, nothing more," von Shimo responded. "But now, prease, we proceed to your account of you." He switched on the interior lights, revealing the power gun he was holding aimed at Grall, resting it on the seat-back for steadiness.

"You prease to prace ceremoniar side-arms on carpet between feet," the general said casually. "Must to inspect, prease, formarity onry."

"What do you want to know?" Tey asked, ignoring the order, as did Grall. Von Shimo stared steadily at them.

"From where you come, prease?" he inquired mildly. "No vessel of *Conqueror* crass is known to be in this sector, so question is: from where you come?"

Tey hesitated, aware of the drama of the moment.*

"Direct from Terra," he said solemnly. Von Shimo's expression stiffened slightly, but otherwise he showed no reaction.

"What is it you seek here on Parasite, prease?"

"Parasite?" Tey repeated in interrogation.

Von Shimo looked confused, mouthing the word silently. "Excuse error, prease," he muttered. "Paratise. Very foorish of me to confuse name, but onry because not often have occasion to

---

*In this portion of the reconstructed narrative, it has been necessary extensively to edit the overabundance of inconsequential detail supplied by the transcription newly released from Terran archives. Only actual conversations are quoted in full, with notes added by Captain Tey at his subsequent review when preparing his famous *Journals* for publication.

use." He rearranged his wrinkles in a grin.

"Actually," Tey said, "we were seeking you—or anyone who could guide us to the settlement."

"Not to tell me more damned ries, prease, mister," the old fellow said abruptly, in a voice quite different from the crochety whine he had been affecting. He turned the gun to peer down the barrel, looked up with his usual bland expression.

"Where you come from, prease?" he said in his former whine.

"A place called Terra," Tey said. "As I have already told you."

"Prease do not experience the impatience with humber kern-er-genaru," von Shimo said tonelessly. "Inasmuch as that prace, Terra, is not known to me, kindry choose another."

Even as Tey was about to speak, von Shimo abruptly started up and gunned back to his usual 40 mph speed. The shack was at once lost to view in the gathering dusk. "Monotonous view, eh, gentermen? Same awr time," von Shimo commented airily. "Nothing much 'round here to see, onry frat rand, and, of course, humber fierd-office." Half an hour later the little man proposed a rest-stop, at once braked to a halt, and immediately demanded, "Now you terr me whence you come."

"Look, Grandpa," Grall said wearily, "it's not a matter of choice, like naming a baby. We come from one prace, and that's Terra."

"It's odd," Nat went on, speaking now to Tey, "since we've been with the general here, I've become more conscious of how often I used the defective L. I would have said I never did, before today."

"That's right," Tey said. "I've caught myself consciously not using it, when my speech mechanism was about to do so. But it's one of man's basic instincts, to mimic, so naturally, talking with von Shimo influences us."

"I wondered if we have any other little dialectical oddities we've never noticed because we've been using them all our lives?"

"It depends on what we use as a base-line," Tey commented. "Consider the Old Eng—Engr—English verb-ending, '-en', as in Chaucer: 'summer is acumen in,' etc. During the Danish occupation of Anglo-Saxon England, the Scandinavian '-ing' became familiar, and later the scholars decided the good old English 'walkin' and 'goin' and 'comin' or 'cumen,' was really 'walking,' etc., mispronounced. So we've been spelling it 'coming,' and pronouncing it 'cumen' ever since. The scholars put an L in cud, to match 'should' and 'would,' and for awhile, some people even tried to pronounce it, but now nobody complains when we say 'cud,' just as we always did." Tey paused, and added, "But perhaps a discussion of elementary linguistic oddities isn't precisely the primary order of business at the moment?"

Ignoring his passenger's conversation, von Shimo gunned the car back to its cruising speed and pressed on into the darkness, the course now corrected another seven degrees to starboard, Tey noticed. At last full darkness closed in. Few stars were visible in the overcast sky, and the moon remained below the horizon. Abruptly, von Shimo braked to a halt.

"Prease, we rest here some hours," he said in the bored tone of a tour-guide.

Five minutes later, having dined on von Shimo's aged but well-preserved G.I. rations and settled into heated sleep-pods under a low-pressure air-tent erected in the lee of the car, all three men slept immediately.

· 5 ·

They awoke in the murky dawn-light, and within three minutes were back aboard. At irregular intervals, von Shimo subtly altered course, always to starboard. With the automatic ease of the experienced navigator, Tey maintained a continuous awareness of their dead-reckoned position.

"How far are we going with this nut, Cap?" Nat inquired on his ear-talker toward evening. "From all the variety in the landscape, we could be sitting still."

"We might as well stay for the course," Tey replied, then leaned forward to address their chauffeur: "How much longer before we reach this big territorial shindig?" he asked.

Von Shimo gave him a look of patience overtaxed. "Just untir we come to Great Prime," he explained as one stating the obvious.

"Do I understand correctly that this is a meeting of representatives from all over New Terra?" Tey persisted.

"With regret," von Shimo came back, "humber kerner-genaru again points out, this prace cawr Parasite, or maybe Paratise—don't care which. I have no information of this Newt Era you persist so strangery in speaking of." With that he returned his attention to the monotonous view ahead.

"Why, do you suppose, is he pretending now he never heard of Terra?" Nat asked of Tey over his ear-talker. "His idea of being foxy?"

· 6 ·

It was late on the third day when the little old man next braked the car to a stop. Nothing was visible in the field of the single, center-mounted headlight but more of the same dry tundra. Von Shimo switched off the light and turned to eye his passengers coldly.

"You rike to get out here—or say what prace you come from?" he inquired coolly.

Nat shifted his weight as if to leave the car, then reached across the seat-back and came up with the weapon von Shimo had placed on the seat beside him.

"Very quick, so big a man serdom move so fast," the general commented calmly. "You pran shoot me now, prease?"

"We wouldn't find it convenient to get out here," Tey said.

"Kindry understand position of humber kerner-genaru," von Shimo said in a reasonable tone. "If I bring you—totar stranger —into top security instarration, awr wier set upon me, tear me rim from rim. Not a preasant business," he added. "Bit of a sticky wicket, prease, gentermen." He gazed solemnly at Grall, then at Tey, then out at the sub-Arctic night. "Kirr you, too," he added as an afterthought.

After brief discussion von Shimo set the car in motion and they drove on into the seemingly endless tundra. Day came at last, bringing no change in the monotonous view. From time to time Tey raised Oliver on the command talker woven into the rank-braid on his collar, and told him they were going on. ". . . until we get *some*where," he concluded. "Just keep tracking us, and keep those defense circuits hot."

· 7 ·

Then, late in the afternoon of day four, a streak of vivid green in the gray of the terrain ahead became apparent. As von Shimo altered course as if to avoid the novelty, Tey gently suggested he continue dead ahead.

"Taller vegetation," Nat said. "Maybe a crop." He passed the glass to Tey, who took a long look and commented, "Maize, I think. Ripe, too. And maize can't reseed itself; it has to be planted." He addressed von Shimo: "Who planted it, General?"

"Enemies!" the little man replied, predictably. "Not nice to poke about too crose. Better shear off now, prease, Captain."

Tey directed him to circle the tilled field at what he considered a safe distance. Grall snickered into his ear-talker. "Intrepid trio savaged by corn-on-the-hoof," he improvised solemnly; then to von Shimo: "Do you expect it to bite, or what?"

"Green prants do nothing, of course; onry good sometimes stear few ears. But enemies prant this, and those ferroes watch prenty crose. Better move on, now." As he finished his appeal, an astonishingly loud *sprong!* broke the somnolence, causing all three men to jump.

"A hardshot off the canopy," Tey said. "A primitive weapon against a Navy-issue war-car, even this plushed-up antique, but plenty effective against suit-armor."

"You see?" von Shimo yelped in truimph, hauling the car around in a tight one-eighty. "To get kirred now would be retting the side down, eh, gentermen?"

"All right, General," Tey said, "you're right. We have to be a bit more cagey, it seems."

A second round kicked up a puff of dust inches to the left of the left front wheel.

"That was just to encourage us—" Nat broke off abruptly, turning to look off to the right across the field. A plume of smoke was rising from the far side of the field, growing quickly until shredded by the ever-present wind.

"Somebody just set that, Cap'n," he said. "It wasn't there a few seconds ago."

"Let's take a swing around there and see what's going on, General," Tey suggested. "It's not whoever fired at us, that's clear."

Von Shimo accelerated without comment, swung a wide arc at the corner, racing toward the point from which orange flames now whipped upward. They saw a small group of men upwind of the blaze, which the steady breeze was pushing deeper into the ripe crop.

"Burns well," Nat commented.

One of the men at the site of the fire came running back along the edge of the field with a blazing torch, leaving a trail of new flames as he went. He was first to notice the oncoming car, and turned back abruptly to join his fellows.

"Anything we can do, Cap'n?" Nat inquired.

"Onry thing," von Shimo replied over his shoulder, "keep nose crean, stay out of whole sirry business. Damfoors poke naser organ in where should poke *out*."

· 8 ·

At a hundred yards from the fire, Tey told von Shimo to stop the car. The three men climbed out, von Shimo complaining bitterly the while. The arsonists stood their ground, six men of medium physique, with well-tanned faces, wearing loose whitish garments. The biggest of the group pushed one of his fellows aside, spoke curtly to the rest, and swaggered forward. Nat and Tey, their hands conspicuously empty, went to meet him. Von Shimo followed, well to the rear. Meanwhile, the fire swept deeper into the cornfield, leaving bare, blackened stalks behind it.

"We saw the fire and thought maybe we could help," Tey said by way of greeting.

"Don't need no hep," the stranger replied. "We can burn out these Little Diggers with no hep from Wheelers." He was a stocky, well-muscled man of middle years, with the bland, round face of an ancient stone Buddha. He advanced directly toward Nat Grall, and at a distance of three feet suddenly bounded astonishingly high, his left foot lashing out in a vicious kick at Nat's head. Grall leaned aside, caught the leg with both hands and slammed the astonished aggressor to the sod with a *thump!* Tey fancied he could feel through his boots. Still holding the leg by the ankle as its owner threshed in vain, Nat inquired of Tey: "Shall I tear it off, Cap'n, or just bend it into an interesting shape?"

"You better ret me up fast, Wheeler," the felled man snarled in as menacing a tone as he could manage while flat on his back with a sprained knee. "Ain't you got no respect for Champion of One Hundred?"

"One hundred what?" Nat inquired in a tone of deep interest. "Bunny rabbits?" He gave the leg a casual half-turn, and the man yelled in pain.

"What's the idea burning up the crop?" Nat demanded. "I'll bet my second-best diamond-studded spittoon you didn't prant it."

"You insurt me yet again, Wheeler! Of course a decent Walker would never deign to dig in dirt!"

"Deign," Nat repeated. "That's a fancy word for a poor sucker with only one leg."

The five other men, all vigorous-looking fellows with unfriendly expressions, came up and stood about, watching the proceedings indifferently.

"Better kirr him, Wheeler," one said carelessly. "If he lives he'll hunt you down."

"Why?" Nat demanded. "So I can bend his other leg to match?"

Tey stepped forward. "Why are you burning the corn?" he asked. Five vacant expressions were his only reply. "I like to get answered when I ask a civil question," he said gently, directly addressing the nearest man. "You. Why are you setting fire to somebody's crop?"

As no response was forthcoming, Nat said, "This one's going

to speak up like a litter genterman, aren't you, Bub?" He twisted the leg as he spoke, eliciting a mournful cry. Von Shimo crept closer and muttered, "Enemies."

After half an hour of active interrogation, Nat had elicited the information that decent Walkers always burnt the crops of Little Diggers, who were in any case subhuman. As to whence they themselves came, six arms waved vaguely toward the East. They had called Nat a Wheeler, they explained, for the obvious reason that he had arrived in a wheeled vehicle. None of the men had any idea who fired at the car. At last Nat shoved them away in disgust.

"Bub here can still walk pretty well," he stated as he put the man on his feet and pushed him forward. "And if he can't, his friends will be glad to carry him." Bub hobbled off, pausing at a safe distance to look back and shake his fist.

"Enemies," von Shimo commented in a satisfied tone. "Just rike I tore you."

"Maybe the old coot is right, after all," Nat said to Tey over his ear-talker. "Now let's find out who shot at us."

"What about the fire?" Tey countered. "Perhaps we could drive back and forth downwind and make a firebreak."

"We ought to try," Grall agreed.

· 9 ·

Over von Shimo's even-more-excited-than-usual expostulations, Grall took the wheel and made a hard left to drive directly into the massed corn-stalks at a point a few yards downwind of the raging conflagration. Vegetable juices splattered the transparent canopy, forming a pale-green film that ran down and out across the smooth flanks of the car. After some minutes of the battering progress through the heavy stalks, the car burst through onto the unploughed tundra. Nat executed a sharp U-turn and started a second pass, overlapping the first, the sheet of wind-whipped flame now licking out to within inches of the juice- and soot-covered canopy, blackening the translucent fluid into a tarry, black coating.

"What do you think, Cap'n?" Nat asked, as a gust drove red

flame, soot-edged, across his diminished field of vision. "Are we wasting our time?"

Tey, who had been studying the flattened stalks of their first transit, shook his head. "It might work," he said. "The high wind makes it chancey, but we'll at least slow it down."

After four passes Nat pulled the car well clear of the field, and stopped. Inside the nearly totally opaqued canopy, darkness was almost complete. Von Shimo, who had not stopped protesting except to draw breath, burst out: "You ferrpows have taken reave of your senses!" he screeched. "Rook at my car. Ruined. One cannot drive a car from which one cannot see out! Foorishness! Who knows what enemies rie in wait?"

"Maybe we'd better get out and take a look," Nat said as he released the blackened canopy, which sprang up to afford a view of wind-blown smoke and a delicious aroma of pop-corn. "Visitors," he said over his shoulder, as he stepped down.

· 10 ·

Tey followed, saw two men standing uncertainly a few yards distant. As Tey overtook Nat, who, after chipping a flake of tarry substance from the black-coated vehicle, had started toward the strangers, they advanced boldly to meet him. The two, like the group of arsonists at the far side of the field, were vaguely Polynesian in appearance and, like them, dressed in unwashed white pajamas of coarse cloth, and were bare of foot.

"More of Bub's boys, you think, Cap'n?" Nat asked quietly.

"I doubt it," Tey said. "From the looks of them, they've been fighting the fire."

At ten feet, the locals halted. "Why you rousy Walkers try to destroy the crop?" one demanded hotly.

"We're no Walkers," Nat replied. "We're honest—some of us —Wheelers! You can see that for yourselves." He motioned toward the blackened car. "And we weren't destroying your crop; we were helping you."

"Not content you burn up cornacob, you try fratten it out, too," the second man put in.

"Wrong, Junior," Nat cut him off. "Did you ever hear of a firebreak?" He looked past the men at the leaping flames now at the edge of the flattened area and fluttering as if confused. The fire ate into the fallen and compacted stalks, but only slowly, while behind, the last of the tall flames flickered on the blackened stalks.

"You've got a chance, now," Nat said quickly. "Throw dirt on the beaten strip, and you'll stop it. It didn't jump across."

The two turned, studied the situation for a moment, then spun and dashed into the still standing corn, calling out as they went. Other men appeared from among the burned corn, some carrying flat baskets, others shovels. They looked about, then converged on Tey and Grall, those with shovels foremost. The two intruders stood their ground. Tey drew his pistol and fired a burst into the turf at the feet of the foremost, who halted and downed his shovel.

"Are you boys by any chance Little Diggers?" Nat inquired in a casual tone.

"Damn right Little Diggers—but not boys. Grown men!" the nearest replied promptly.

"No offense intended," Nat reassured him. "There's a bunch calling themselves Walkers—over on the far side—that's starting fires," he added. "By the way, which one of you farmers shot at us?" No one answered.

Behind Nat, von Shimo, who had been creeping nearer, spoke up. "Enemies," he said contentedly.

"Hey, Ed," one of the shovel-bearers called over his shoulder, "it's that rousy rittu poacher, just like we thought—only, this time he's got a cupper of hired guns with him."

"You got that wrong, Junior," Nat said grimly. "And if you birds would get busy, you could still put that fire out."

"Already tore you—men, not birds," Junior came back hotly. But he went to the nearest patch of flame in the flattened strip and beat it out with his shovel. The others followed suit, a few digging up clods of damp soil to dump on the dwindling fire. They ignored the three outsiders as they went back to the blackened car. Meanwhile Tey used his beamer on its lowest setting to burn away the coating from the lower part of the canopy, while Nat cleared the headlight and von Shimo scuttled about, chattering of enemies.

· 11 ·

"Oh-oh," Nat said when he'd stood to admire his work. His eyes were focused on the far corner of the field, well beyond the burned area. "Looks like Bub and his pals want to play some more."

The group who had called themselves Walkers came into view, paused, then advanced with a look of determination; Bub, limping theatrically, was in the lead. Noticing them, the Little Diggers began to chatter excitedly, converging on the car. Nat watched them as they clustered in its lee, uttering ferocious threats. Meanwhile, Bub's group had spread out and entered the shelter of the cornfield.

"They're the firebugs I told you about," Nat said to Junior. "What are you going to do about it?"

Tey joined Nat, their backs to the car, as the agriculturalists, ignoring Bub and his Walkers, converged on them threateningly. As they closed in, their shovels at the ready, von Shimo ducked aside and disappeared from view. When the nearest man was close enough, Grall, with a quick grab, snatched the shovel from his grasp, casually broke the stout wooden handle in two, and handed half to Tey.

The Little Diggers paused, retreated out of reach, and Junior said loudly: "Your plan didn't work."

"Gosh," Nat said in mock chagrin. "Outwitted by a halfwit." He glanced back through the canopy behind him, clear now except for a slight haziness and a few flakes of dry tar still peeling away. Flames were rising from a half-dozen points near where Bub's group had been. Nat turned and caught Junior's bloodshot eye.

"There are your fire-bugs at work, Junior," he said. "What do you plan to do about it? I'd hate to see the crop burn after all my hard work."

Junior turned away with a sneer; he jumped as a gunshot

shattered the stillness. The slug struck the car and whined off.

"A hardshot," Tey said beside Grall. "Now we know who fired at us, or at least who didn't." The farmers had gone to earth, flat against the turf, all except Junior, who stood in the lee of the car staring from Nat to Tey with a hostile expression.

"It seems he never heard the saying about 'the enemy of my enemy,'" Grall said. "We might as well leave this bunch to themselves. They deserve each other."

"Where's von Shimo?" Tey asked. "I haven't seen him for some minutes."

"Maybe he dug a hole and got in it," Nat suggested offhandedly.

· 12 ·

Back in the car, Tey now in the driver's seat, the two men scanned the horizon. Their erstwhile guide was nowhere to be seen. Bub and his troops had formed up a ragged column and were headed southward. Von Shimo was not among them.

"I didn't look under the car," Nat said. "Or maybe he hid in the corn."

"If so, he'll be coming out soon," Tey said, as the renewed flames swept across the firebreak. "And Junior's boys, too."

The tall corn stalks burned splendidly until only two small patches at the downwind corners remained unburned. Still no one emerged from shelter.

"Something's fishy," Nat grumbled. "Or I'm dreaming. Tell me, Cap'n did I see eight Little Diggers take to the corn when Bub showed up, or was I seeing things?"

"They went in there, all right, Nat," Tey replied seriously. "Let's drive over there."

Nat pulled the car around in a curve and drove up beside the nearest patch of flame, dying now as its fuel was exhausted. Minutes later the corner was indistinguishable from the rest of the blackened area. One last bit of fire still flourished at the far corner. Nat drove over to it in time to watch at close range as it too died. No one had appeared.

"They went in, but they didn't come out," Grall stated the situation plainly, as if to examine it for flaws in his reasoning. "And there are no burned corpses lying around. And they didn't take off and fly—so that leaves one direction; they must have gone down." He popped the canopy, now clear as the last black flakes fell away. Tey followed.

· 13 ·

The two men walked across the spongy turf, which seemed to be fire-resistant, to the still-smoking triangle that had been the corner of the field. Without conversation both men began carefully to examine the charred ground. After quartering the small patch and finding nothing unusual, they turned by common assent to look across the rest of the quarter-acre of blackness.

"It won't have a sign on it that says 'lift here,'" Grall mused aloud, "but it has to be here somewhere. So we have the whole lousy field to check."

"Maybe footprints will help," Tey said, pointing to a faint one. "These hard clods don't leave much of a trail, but what we can find will give us a clue."

"Anyway it has to be below the firebreak," Nat pointed out. "That helps some."

· 14 ·

After nearly an hour of criss-crossing the devasted soil, Nat halted and called to Tey, pointing out to him a faint discontinuity in the otherwise homogenous surface: a roughly rectangular patch some two feet on a side, which appeared to be depressed a fraction of an inch below the general level.

After a few minutes of experimental probing, Nat uncovered a heavy latch mechanism of the nearly imperishable, synthetic trade-named Eternon, which Tey identified as a standard Navy-issue hatch dog.

"These folks have some cache of Terran manufactures to draw on. it seems," he commented. "Which doesn't say much for all that light and heavy industry von Shimo was talking about."

"Don't be shocked, Cap'n," Grall said in his best tongue-in-cheek manner, "but the thought occurs to me that the general is not above stretching the truth from time to time. Damnedest compulsive liar I ever met," he added.

"Gracious," Tey responded in kind. "Pray excuse the strong language, but one hesitates so to stigmatize even a lousy little sneak like von Shimo. I wonder what he's up to?"

Nat had cleared the rectangular outline of the hatch of its six-inch soil layer. He tried the latch, found it locked.

"Twice to the right, then hard left," Tey advised. "Some early models had somebody's idea of a tricky security gadget, but the Navy lost some good men before they realized that a man with a broken arm and flames licking at his aft end might have a little problem in remembering even a simple combination like that."

With the hatch open, they looked down a vertical shaft, metal-lined, with a wet floor at the bottom.

"Must be an opening down there, Nat," Tey said. "Shall we check it out?"

"What for, Cap'n?" Nat asked. "So these clowns can give us another hard time?"

"I suppose you're right," Tey conceded reluctantly. "But eventually we've got to find a native who'll stand still long enough to tell us a few things."

"Meanwhile," Nat said, "let's get the troops in out of the hot sun." He climbed back into the car and resumed the driver's seat, Tey beside him.

"Time to report in," Tey said and triggered the command talker. There was no response. After ten tries had failed to raise even a carrier hum, he said to Nat: "Looks like trouble. We'd better head back in a hurry."

"Must be awful sudden trouble, Cap'n," Nat countered. "They were OK half an hour ago."

"I've never known trouble to send engraved invitations," Tey said grimly.

"Could be we're out of range, Cap'n," Nat said. "That trick collar of yours is a handy item, but it's got its limitations. Still, I could keep my mouth shut for a long time before I start telling you about Navy-issue com gear."

"We're less than ninety miles from *Princeton*," Tey said. "Shimmy took us in a wide swing to the north, damn near full circle. We can be there in a few hours."

SEVEN

A Dead City

"**W**hat are we waiting for?" Nat said. "There must be some good reason for Ollie to forget to monitor communications."

"Were we waiting?" Tey asked in reply as he gunned away across the blackened clods. In minutes the former corn field was out of sight behind them. Abruptly Tey slowed up. "Look over there, Nat" he said, pointing. "If that's not some kind of structure, I've been out here too long."

"Right on both counts, Cap'n," Grall agreed. "I take it we'll give it a quick look before we head back."

"After five days another half-hour won't change anything," Tey agreed. "Let's go, and if anybody accuses us of stealing a car, we'll plead 'not guilty, by reason of insanity.' "

As they approached, the irregularity visible on the horizon, due north, resolved itself into the ragged silhouette of low buildings outlined against the pale sky.

In a fair imitation of von Shimo's reedy voice, Nat said, "Prease, gentermen, forgot about prace where enemies rurk in hiding and jump out to kirr me. Enemies."

Tey steered straight for the town. To Nat, he commented, "This was his destination all along. He steered dead for it. That was some fancy navigating, considering we've covered over eight hundred miles—but we're less than a hundred miles from *Princeton.*"

"Me, too," Nat agreed.

"I wonder why he didn't take the direct route?" Tey pulled the car up in the lee of a crumbling wall which seemed to be of concrete, with rusted iron rods visible where a corner was chipped away. Beyond, the skeletal roof structures of burned-out buildings were starkly silhouetted.

Alert for signs of life, the men descended from the car, keeping in the lee of the vehicle, black except for the canopy.

"Dead," Nat said briskly. "Enemies kirr other enemies. Good system we have here on Parasite," he added. "Awr enemies wirr die at rast."

"That's not *entirely* nonsense," Tey commented. "The place is fortified, but not well enough." He pointed out what was clearly a watch tower, complete with a smashed infinite-repeater barrel canted toward the low, gray sky. "Mark IX," he said. "Used in dismounted battery service. At least a hundred and fifty years since it was replaced by the X. Looks as if it blew up. They'd do that if a green gunner got eager and set the feed rate up too high. That's one reason they were finally condemned, in spite of having won the Jersey-Philly war for Banshire Nine."

They found an unbarricaded sally-port and entered, climbing over rubble to emerge at the end of a street of packed clay, pitted by the three-foot craters of antipersonnel mortar fire and littered with debris from the gutted buildings lining it on both sides.

"Shimmy said his immediate destination was the Imperial Summer Palace," Tey commented.

"So who lives *here?*" Grall demanded.

"The Emperor of all Paradise, of course, prease," Tey said as one humoring a fool.

"You have a monarchial form of government, then," Nat said, playing along with Tey.

"The present form of our government is compretery democratic in nature," Tey said solemnly. "All actions require one hundred percent accord of the erectorate—an arrangement not equar in recorded history."

"In that case, what does the emporor do?" Grall wanted to know.

"Like all others, he does as he pleases."

180 –

"This is getting us nowhere," Grall said to Tey.

Tey nodded absently, sniffing the air. "This place has been saturation-bombed with Verbot Nine," he told Nat. "Recently."

· 2 ·

Having surmounted a rubble-heap, Tey pointed to a cavelike opening in a heap of fallen concrete slabs halfway up the street. "A gunner's nest," he said. As if in reply, a single shot rang, echoing, and rock-dust spurted behind him.

Tey and Grall, without hesitation, split, one taking each side of the street for a house-to-house search. There were no more shots. Half an hour later they met at a larger-than-ordinary building with a quasi-classical portico littered with concrete chips. There was a faint sound near at hand as von Shimo emerged, dusty and gasping, from the heap of fallen slabs beside the dusty steps.

"Great big tunner down there," he said, dusting his knees. "Neary got rost—bit of a sticky wicket, that."

"General," Nat addressed the little man severely, "it wasn't by any chance you who took a shot at the Cap'n just now, I suppose?"

"Not me, Fierd Marshawr. Prenty sturdy rogues hide here in Parace grounds."

"Thanks for running out on us," Nat said without emphasis. "Good job you didn't get your feathers singed. By the way, how well do you know your way around this dump?"

"Know pretty werr, but awrways find new tunners; garbage mice awr time break new, sneaky ways."

"Fine. Let's take a look," Nat suggested.

· 3 ·

The three men spent the next hour silently prowling the formerly elegant corridors of the ruin.

"What happened to Junior and his boys?" Nat asked.

"Go every which way: tunners are awr over prace," von

Shimo explained in a tone suggesting the humble hero.

There had been no more gunfire, nor any other indication of life, with the exception of an almost invisible trickle of smoke from a small heap of embers on the carpet of a once-splendid room with rotted blue-wood paneling.

"Warm," Nat Grall said after he had touched the heap of gray ash.

"Fine," Tey replied calmly. "This proves we didn't imagine somebody shot at us—or at something."

"I tore you, enemies awr round!" von Shimo responded hotly. "Enemies!"

"Then, how come didn't we see 'em?" Nat needled the small man.

"Because this prace has prenty secret passages, hidey-holes, tunners, and these bad hats know the rot!"

All three men froze at a faint sound from a closed door across the big room, a heavy and ornately carved panel somewhat spoiled by scars where large chips had been violently removed, the exit holes of solid slugs, it appeared. The door opened, uttering a faint squeal of unoiled hinges.

The woman who appeared at the opening was tall, lean to the point of emaciation, yet with an appearance of haggard beauty, not quite obscured. She was dressed in a complicated and voluminous garment, faded to an uneven gray, which hung in folds about her. Her gray hair was arranged in a disordered attempt at an elaborate coiffure. She looked steadily at the handguns each man had aimed at her, then spoke, in a somewhat rusty contralto:

"Pray excuse me, gentlemen. I'd no idea—" she broke off and turned as if to withdraw the way she had come.

"Please don't go, ma'am," Tey said quietly. The woman gave him a level look.

"Not bloody likely, Captain," she said, closing the door firmly.

"Not 'captain,' " Tey said. "Not any longer. Ex-captain would be more appropriate."

The woman nodded, almost as if impatient. "Certainly; it figures, doesn't it? But as between us, I prefer 'captain'—if you've no objection."

"As you wish, ma'am," Tey murmured. "And now, if I may present his Excellency the Terran Ambassador, Nat Grall."

"Screw diplomats," she said casually. "And I see you have this wretched Jerry von Shimo in tow," she continued. "Doubtless he's filled you fur of ries about me."

"Well, at least she doesn't seem to be surprised at the mention of Terra," Grall commented sotto voce.

"Actually, ma'am," Tey demurred, "he's told us nothing at all. But he claims to be surrounded by enemies. Still, he brought us here."

"Umm. I'll keep that in mind at the court-martial. Now send the little bugger packing; we have matters of importance to discuss."

Without further urging von Shimo sidled to the open door by which the three men had entered and slid through and out of sight.

"You can wait at the car, General," Grall said after him.

The woman was looking with disapproval at the heap of embers which occupied a ring of char in the deep green carpet.

"Unfortunately, Captain, Mr. Ambassador," the woman said, "the council is in plenary session at the moment. Awkward, but perhaps you'd like a bit of refreshment while we wait."

"Make mine Scotch," Nat said. "Not too much ice." The woman merely nodded, and yanked at a braided cord hanging beside a rotted tapestry on the warped bluish wood paneling.

"Oh, boy," Nat said to Tey, "do you suppose she's really got some?"

"I prefer a good German beer," Tey said. "It seems a long time since the last one I had aboard *Princeton.*" With a subvocalized code-word he activated his command talker.

"We're intact, Ollie," he transmitted quietly. "Checking out a deserted-looking but inhabited town. Arano."

"Still no response, Nat," he advised. "But maybe I've just been catching the monitor circuit at switchover."

"Sure," Nat replied. "You can't expect even a sophisticated circuit to stay keen for a week without getting bored."

There had been no response to the woman's imperious tug at her signal cord.

"It figures," Nat said. His eyes ran up the heavy, braided velvet. At the top, it was tied in a bulky knot to a corroded metal bracket. The woman had followed his glance.

"I have many times reported the deficiency to the chief of maintenance," she said harshly. "It is clearly time for sterner measures."

"No doubt, ma'am," Grall replied gravely. "By the way, who are you, if I may inquire?"

The woman's expression hardened. "Really, Mr. Ambassador, one would expect that your Excellency would have presented his credentials before now." She looked defiantly from Grall to Tey and back.

"Sure," Nat said. "My boner. Must have left 'em in my other pants."

Tey stepped forward to intercept her reply. Inclining his head courteously, he repeated Grall's request that she identify herself. "We've been away for a long time, you understand, ma'am," he concluded.

"I'm Cleo Dulane, chatelaine of the demesne of Far Chicago," she stated proudly. "Now, you really must excuse me. I gotta go to the can." She swept from the room imperiously, the tattered hem of her draperies stirring up a small cloud of dust.

· 4 ·

Grall looked at Tey. "Another nut," he commented.

"Still," Tey pointed out, "she seems to be in charge of whatever the hell she's in charge of here." He went to the door through which the chatelaine had departed and found himself looking into a room as dusty and musty as the first, but distinguished by an elaborately decorative cornice of pierced fretwork. Cleo stood at the far end of a long rubbish-littered table to which were drawn up elaborately carved chairs, six to a side. On the seat of each rested a human skull. On the table, at each place, lay a powergun.

"Seems like the boys are having a hard time getting together," the woman said in a matter-of-fact tone. "So maybe we better go ahead and get down to business."

Tey nodded. "By the way, Madam Chatelaine," he said carefully, "by what title should I address you?"

" 'Hey, lady,' is traditional," she replied. "But let us dispense with formalities. You may employ the semiformal 'OK, sister.'"

"OK, sister," Grall said at Tey's shoulder. "Now let's get down to business."

Cleo turned an icy look on the big man. "Must I remind you, pal, that you still have not presented credentials to my Chief of Protocol?"

"Gosh," Nat said in a humble tone. "I must've forgot again. I knew there was something . . ."

"No matter," Cleo dismissed the matter with an airy wave of a clawlike hand laden with heavy rings with bright-cut stones of strange hues. "I presume you're from that nasty little swine Edgar—"

"Now, look here, lady," Nat protested. "That's no way to talk about good old Eddie."

"It's like the little skunk to try a sneak around left end, even as my glorious armies are confronting his cowardly hired guns. I'll not treat with you—it's far too late for that. Only unconditional surrender, now." Cleo's haughty gaze held on Nat's face. He allowed a grim smile to modify his look of resentment.

"Let's cut the comedy, sister," he suggested quietly. He jerked a chair back from the table, causing the skull on the seat to roll off and shatter. "Funny," he said, "just as much dust where Mr. Bones was. Looks like he just sneaked in." Nat raised his eyes to meet Cleo's. "Are you nuts, ma'am, or do you think we are?"

"It is the custom," she replied. "Our noble Council remains perpetually in session here in the museum, in commemoration of the fact that they were here, working desperately and in good faith to meet Thinker demands when the obscene Thinker air force struck, killing all at their posts of duty. They were alerted well in advance of danger approaching, but refused to flee."

- 185

"Look at this, Mr. Ambassador," Tey said quietly from the far corner of the long room.

Grall went across to Tey, and took a position beside him, flat against the wall.

"That's the idea," Tey said. "Unless I missed one."

"You think they're ready to sacrifice her?" Grall queried.

"Why not? She's said her piece. But I disapprove." He raised his voice slightly. "Hit the floor, Sister. Under the table. Fast!"

She turned a strained expression to Tey, but her voice was steady. "I prefer to stand," she said. "This is my post of duty." Her toe stirred the broken cranium at her feet. "Councilor Wellmax was my ancestor. Can I do less than he?"

"A lot less," Tey snapped. "Belay that nonsense. Being dead is a drag. Now move!"

With no further objection Cleo, with surprising agility, dived under the table, just as gunfire racketed from inconspicuous apertures in the decorative cornice high on each wall of the room, slugs smacking solidly into wood and plaster, raising an instant cloud of smoke and dust, filled with flying chips and criss-crossed with the streaks of tracers. The pattern spread from an initial oval which had at once reduced the carpeting to tatters, searching close to the corner where Tey and Grall had taken refuge, but unable, quite, to reach them.

· 5 ·

"Nice figuring, Captain," Nat said as the shocking thunder died as abruptly as it had begun.

"Noticing fields of fire is part of a naval officer's education," Tey replied. "It becomes automatic."

"I spent ten sweaty minutes doping it out," Nat said. "Why the lacuna here? Not accidental, I guess."

"It's usual—a safety device in case one of your own is caught out. At the first round, he knows where to go."

"But Cleo let *us* take it, with no kick. Quite a gal. I wonder how she made out." Grall ducked to look searchingly at the rubble heap under what was left of the table. As he did, Cleo's bracelet-hung arm appeared, groping out through the wood and plaster fragments. Grall went across to her, extricated her, and helped her to her feet. Her face was chalky with plaster dust, and a shallow cut on her cheek was vivid against it. Nat glanced down at the shredded veils of her voluminous garment, the last of which fell away, revealing a slim, lithe female figure clad in a close-fitting one-piece garment of a frosty-green color.

"Not bad, Cleo," Nat commented. "Why cover it up with grandma's old parlor curtains?"

Her reply was to turn away coldly, before she spoke: "We've been running Program Three on you fellows," she said wearily. "But to hell with that. If you're not from His Imperial Supremacy, just who the devil are you?"

"I'll say it again, slowly," Nat replied. "We're new arrivals here; just in from Terra on a load of hay, so to speak. We had in mind we might find a going colony here, calling itself New Terra, maybe, founded three hundred Terran-years ago. But all we've turned up is one old lunatic in an antique Navy-issue car, plus this setup, whatever it is."

Cleo was nodding calmly, as at a familiar tale. "Right," she said, "and you've got the true revelation—you and you alone, just like us." She turned to look defiantly at Grall, then at Tey.

Both men answered: "I'm afraid not, ma'am, I mean Sister," Nat said, as Tey spoke: "We haven't any revelations, true or otherwise."

"I've got one of my own," Cleo put in. "Unless we get out of here fast, we'll be joining old great grandpa Wellmax."

"Who fired at us?" Tey demanded. "And why?"

"The State Lifeguards man the gallery," Cleo replied. "At least that's what that bunch of bums call themselves—just Squatters who like to shoot at live targets."

Tey took her arm and half-led, half-dragged her to the nearest door and out into the corridor.

"You don't need to carry me," the chatelaine said in a tired voice. "I'm coming."

"You're a good-looking gal, Cleo," Nat commented. "Why the get-up?"

"Tradition." Cleo spat plaster-dust. "Screw tradition!" she

added. "They grabbed me years ago, when I came here, foraging. I fast-talked my way out of a rape-and-necktie party. They installed me as a kind of high priestess until they could figure things out. I had my hands full staying alive—no chance for me to do anything but play along. I wanted to warn you fellows, back there in the council room, but when I saw the captain, here, studying the loopholes I knew it would be OK." Cleo looked around uneasily, beckoned Nat closer. "This place is watched," she said quietly. "Galleries and peepholes cover every foot of it."

Nat nodded. "I wondered how you managed to be on hand to greet us as soon as we walked in."

"Now level with me, Nat," she said in a tone of warm fellowship. "Who *are* you boys and where are you from?"

"Have you heard of a place called Terra?" Nat inquired.

Cleo nodded. "Of course—but this is no time for fairy-tales. Guns are trained on you—on all of us—right now."

"Why?" Tey persisted.

"All right, I'll explain," Cleo said exasperatedly. "Here these Squatters were, settled down all cosy in the ruins, and one day —*blop!* They hit the place with all they had—the Thinkers, I mean. The few Squatters that lived through it got a little paranoid after that."

"Sure," Nat said. "But how long ago did all this happen?"

"I don't know exactly," Cleo said. "Several weeks, I imagine."

Nat looked at her. "You know, you go along sounding as plausible as a travel agent and then suddenly, you spin out. OK, I'll leave it at that."

Cleo caught his arm. "Please, Nat," she said earnestly, "just keep talking nonsense. If we can stall them until we reach the next intersection, we're home free—for the moment."

"Sure, honey," Nat said. "Here's the pitch: we stole a battleship back on Terra and came out here looking for a long-lost colony we happened to have found out about. We made it in four years, and got the old tub down ship-shape and stepped out to greet the welcoming committee—but they fooled us. There wasn't any welcoming committee—only poor old Shimmy, zeroing in on us like a bee to an outhouse. We're still trying to find somebody to complain to."

Cleo nodded brightly. "Of course, Nat, dear . . . Now—left!" As she spoke, her weight went against him—and rebounded. "You're as unyielding as a concrete abutment," she cried, and caught his eye. "Do go quickly in, dear Nat," she urged, and slipped past him and Tey into the narrow passageway. The two men followed, and at the same moment, a familiar voice rang out from somewhere above: "Stop where you are!"

"Forget it, Junior!" Tey's voice interrupted. "You forgot to cover your flank. You'd better find some other profession. Trying to be a big-shot heavy is beyond you."

Nat turned to see the hapless Junior, still a trifle sooty from his incendiary chores, drop a big old-model handgun, whirl, and run. Tey watched him go; then, at Cleo's urging, joined the others in the side-passage. Cleo explained breathlessly that there was a long-unused hatch leading into an emergency complex.

Inside the cramped and musty passage they encountered von Shimo, who greeted Cleo casually and at once began to harangue Grall.

"Madame Creo is a fine rady," he assured him, "but, aras, not to be trusted. Forrow me; I sharr take you direct to our car."

"How about it, Cap'n?" Nat said.

"So far," Tey said matter-of-factly, "the general seems to have played it square enough with us, except for a few harmless lies, and pointing one little old handgun just that one time. I think we should play along."

· 6 ·

The passage through cramped and littered ways was surprisingly short, though devious; and in less than half an hour daylight gleamed through chinks ahead and they emerged outside the town wall, a few feet from the blackened car.

Cleo expressed astonishment at sight of the vehicle, but seemed quickly to grasp Nat's explanation of its function. He assisted her to the seat beside the driver's position; the others followed. Von Shimo fussed a bit when Tey took the wheel, but subsided, grinning widely and chattering of enemies.

"Awr unfriendly, every way one goes," he stated.

"Why are they unfriendly?" Nat pressed the point.

"Prease, it is the nature of enemies to be unfriendly," von Shimo stated firmly.

"I'll put it another way," Nat persisted. "Why are they enemies? Or what makes you think— That is, how you know they're enemies? What do they do that's hostile?"

"Oh, prease, they rive as wild beasts, defy the emperor's raws, bring no taxes, some time shoot at me."

"Did you shoot back?"

"Oh, my, yes," von Shimo said, and flipped a small handgun from his sleeve into his palm. He fired—a vivid burst of pink light into the shadows, and tucked the weapon away again. "Prease," he said, "enemies."

"I'll steer 348," Tey said. "That's the direct route." He set off at the car's best speed, swinging in a wide curve to take up the course for *Princeton*.

"We've wasted a lot of time, Cap'n," Nat said. "I hope we get there in time to do some good."

"About two hours," Tey said. "Probably everything's OK. Just some problem with the equipment." He tried again to raise the ship. Nothing. They drove on through deep twilight in silence, except for a quiet conversation between Tey and Cleo, while in the back seat Nat relentlessly quizzed von Shimo.

·7·

Suddenly, von Shimo spoke up. "Prease to hart now. The parace of His Imperior Majesty ries near at hand."

"We're in a hurry right now, General," Tey said. "We can catch His Majesty next trip."

"Best you take this opportunity to request audience straight away," von Shimo protested. "Pray hart now whirst I check with the major domo. Besides, I wish to take a reak. Urgentry."

"Well, that's an appeal one can hardly refuse," Tey conceded, and slowed to a halt and opened the hatch. The night was still and cold. All around lay an expanse of tundra not apparently different from the rest.

"Where is this palace?" Nat asked. As if in reply, von Shimo hopped nimbly down and darted away to be lost at once in the darkness.

"Maybe he'll just keep going," Nat said, in a tone which was more hopeful than apprehensive.

"Doubtless," Cleo said coolly. "The little wretch has some devious scheme in mind. Don't be fooled by him and this imaginary emperor of his. This territory lies under the rule of Edgar, in any case."

"All we want to do is get out of it," Tey commented. "I trust he won't object to that."

"If not, he'll find something else to which to object," Cleo said glumly. Abruptly von Shimo reappeared at a lope.

"Prease, gentermen, and rady," he began in his reedy voice, "His Imperior Majesty command you may now come arong. I wirr read you to a most preasing rounging area, there to await His Majesty's preasure."

"We don't feel like it just now," the big man said, easing casually into the little man's path, which caused the latter to ricochet off Nat's hip to dodder a few steps and halt. He turned, his expression unreadable, but before he could speak, Tey said, "His Majesty's jurisdiction doesn't extend to the Terran fleet. Let's go talk to somebody a bit more accessible."

Von Shimo shook his head sadly. "No one erse," he said. "Onry enemies."

"Where do these enemies stay?" Tey persisted.

"All 'round," von Shimo said, with a sweeping gesture. "Onry fear of His Imperior Majesty keep them at a distance."

"Are they human?"

"Oh, no. Onry beasts. But cunning, you understand." With a surprising swift motion, the old man whipped the small, but deadly-looking powergun from the folds of his capelike garment, and held it steadily aimed between Tey and Grall. The latter half-turned away, then lunged past von Shimo, causing the old fellow to pivot to follow him, thus placing his back to Tey, who quite casually reached over the general's shoulder to pluck the weapon from his hand—all this in a fraction of a second. As he stepped back, von Shimo uttered a squawk and leapt sideways, only to encounter Grall's massive arm, which gathered him in and held him immobile by the neck.

"Shall we throw him away, or keep him around for possible future use?" Grall asked, as if pondering the point.

"Enemies," von Shimo said, "Awr 'round—enemies." He made jerky motions, as if miming an effort to escape the iron grip on his nape.

"No, no, General," Tey said, "we're not enemies. We just arrived, remember?"

"Arrive? From where you arrived?" the general sputtered. "Rong time, many years nothing there on Boondock. Then—poof! One day I see you there!"

"As I mentioned the last time we discussed this point, General, we came from Terra."

"Rousy joke," von Shimo replied sharply. "Terra onry prace we hear about in fairy-tares."

"The general field marschall and I are living proof to the contrary," Tey said. "Now, let's move on to your own people. Just where are they? They don't all live underground, I assume?"

"Rissen," von Shimo said. "My people are underground, most. But don't rive underground. Dead, buried. Awr but a few. Rast three, four—I was too sick—had to ret them rie. Very sad time for me. Had woman, one of rast to desert me. Awr arone, many year now. Arone, I, trying my best, but too many enemies."

"These enemies, where do they come from?" Tey persisted.

"Come from no prace. Rive here. Awr around, on Parasite. Try to kirr me many times, but I was a young chap then, fastest gun in east-southeast."

"What is it they want?" Grall asked.

"They never say, onry come, make war, kirr many, not ret me sreep rong time. Enemies!"

"Do you know how mankind came to be here on Paradise?" Tey asked the old man, who stopped his listless jerking to give Tey an indignant look.

"You perhaps take me for a foor, prease? Mankind originated here, of course."

"You don't remember the Omega colony?" Tey pressed the

point. For a moment von Shimo was silent; then he said, in an entirely different tone:

"Aha, the Mysteries! I was never a communicant of the Cult. practicar sort of chap, I am. If others choose to bereave, ret them."

"Three hundred Earth-years ago," Tey said, "a colonization venture was dispatched from Terra, a very distant world where fossil evidence of the origin of man is found. Any human being on this planet, including yourself, is a descendent of those original colonists. With the exception of ourselves, of course; we are new arrivals."

"To be sure," von Shimo said coolly, as one brushing aside a trivial point. "A pity none of this is susceptiber of objective investigation."

"On the contrary," Tey said. "I can prove every word I've said."

"Prove to you, maybe. Not to me, prease, as I know Mysteries are awr nonsense."

"This is no mystery. But to Hell with it. Let's go, General. I want to see these enemies of yours."

· 8 ·

Repeatedly Tey attempted to elicit a response from the ship; once, he caught a faint, crackling carrier hum, instantly cut off.

"Cap'n," Nat said hesitantly, "are you dead sure about this heading? We can't afford to miss it." He went on at once: "Don't count that one, Cap'n; I just seem to have to say something stupid every so often. That takes care of this month, I hope."

"It's a natural enough question, Nat," Tey replied mildly. "Actually I wasn't consciously aware of monitoring our course —I do it automatically. That's one trick the Academy drilled in to stay. By the way, we've drifted half a degree to port, but it won't matter. We'll have her in sight any minute now." He took up the small multiplier-glass and scanned the empty horizon, then lowered the glass slowly.

"No joy, Nat," he reported. "She's gone—sure, I know it's

impossible—but from here she'd be clearly in view." Ten minutes later, there was still no welcome glimpse of the needle-shape.*

Tey halted the car. "If it were where we left it, Nat, we'd be within fifty feet of it," he said. "I recognize the track I made on my recon." He indicated a faintly differentiated strip against the dull gray-green of the tundra turf.

"Sure," Nat said. "I can see the scar where she sat. So—what do we do for an encore?"

"Nat," Cleo almost wailed. "Why did you— And, do you know, I *believed* in you. I thought somehow you were different." She sniffled.

Grall patted her hand awkwardly. "Now don't go getting all upset, Cleo," he urged. "We'll—Cap'n and I—get it straightened out somehow. Just take it easy."

"Now what?" von Shimo crowed. "Your bruff has fropped—as awr such ries must do at rast. You're foorish ferroes so to make yourserves rook a pair of proper Charlies! You come here to torment me in a big vesser from fabered Terra indeed. Perhaps now you wirr ret good sense prevair."

"What do you think, Cap'n?" Nat inquired of Tey.

As Tey hesitated, von Shimo resumed brightly: "Kindry reave matters to me, gentermen, and Madame Creo," he suggested. "Onry ret me take over the driving chair, and matters will be crarified straight away."

"We might as well," Nat conceded. "I'm fresh out of good ideas—or even bad ones." Tey exchanged seats with the little man.

"We go!" von Shimo stated. He started up the car and with no hesitation dug off in a sweeping curve to head out across the total blackness ahead.

---

*It must be remembered that primitive war vessels were deeply influenced in design by traditional concepts of the correct "streamlined" look of a water- or air-vessel, since these first large ships were intended more to impress a neighboring warlord than actually to engage in space combat.

Far ahead a faint point of light glowed, flickering. At first Tey was unsure whether he actually saw light or if it was an aberration of eyes straining for vision in utter blackness.

Then Grall commented: "He's steering straight toward it." Then to von Shimo: "What is it up ahead, General?"

At this, the little man started, causing the car to veer sharply.

"Excuse prease," he said glibly. "I had quite forgot I am not arone as usuar."

"Sure, but what is it?"

"Ah, you refer to faint grow in distance, no doubt." He looked over his shoulder with one of his wrinkled expressions. "Enemies," he stated calmly. "Awr around, every way, awrways enemies."

"Then, why steer straight at them? Why not go around?"

"Not to go around, prenty more enemies, any way I steer. Better to face them at once. Besides, I never ret pass an opportunity to wipe their eye. Oh, my, no." The car rolled smoothly on, the glow very slowly becoming more distinct.

"It's a fire," Nat said. Tey agreed. The flicker of leaping flames was distinct now.

"My enemies never rest from attack, you see," von Shimo commented calmly. "Now they try to ignite the drybog, in hope to cause me a spot of bother."

"Cap'n," Nat said quietly, "do you think this vegetation would burn?"

"Not without a lot of encouragement," Tey replied. "It's packed pretty hard; no air circulation. Like trying to light off a coal-field. It will burn, but it'll take plenty of heat to get it started."

"They think to burn me out of my stronghold, expose me naked to attack," von Shimo explained in a matter-of-fact way.

"Is it just you they're after?" Grall asked the old man, "or the Emperor and his suite as well?"

"Want to destroy awr. Envy greatness, you see. Bit of a sticky wicket." Von Shimo reached casually for a switch, and the searchlight mounted atop the car stabbed out; the blue-white beam illuminated what appeared to be an encampment of small, ragged tents.

Men, women, and children, caught in the sudden glare, stood frozen for an instant before bursting into feverish activity, running in all directions like ants in a broken hill.

"They're human!" Nat exclaimed. He reached across the seatback to grip the old man's upper arm. "Why did you lie to us? You said they weren't human."

"Oh, perhaps a matter of definition onry," von Shimo replied as one brushing aside details. "Prease to ret go my arm, sir. Need have free hand to direct gunfire."

As Nat released him, his hand jumped at once to a well-worn lever below the instrument panel. A deafening bellow of sound burst out, the car bucking under recoil at the roar of a heavy needler at full bore. Tracers were flat streaks ripping into tents, a low shed; sweeping the area around the now-abandoned fire; sending gouts of soil, splinters of wood, and rags flying, to be torn and shredded by the continuing fire. All this in the instant before Grall slapped von Shimo's hand from the firing lever.

A single burst of white light exploded near the fire, the car rocked sharply, and the beam of the searchlight died. Now again, only the campfire was visible in a night that seemed even wider and blacker than before the brief, incredible outburst.

· 10 ·

"Where did they go?" Grall queried. "One second there were people running in every direction, and the next, those needles were sweeping bare ground."

"Enemies," von Shimo said as if supplying an obvious answer.

"Slit-trenches," Tey observed. "Apparently they were prepared for attack; everyone had his assigned hole to roll into. Very smartly executed, too."

"Incruding attack on me—on us. I should say, as you gentermen—rady, too—equarry dead if they had scored a vitar area hit. Rucky bad shots. Onry destroy right."

STAR COLONY

"Academic," Tey said. "They aimed for the light. Damned good marksmanship."

"You see, enemies—as I said. Prease, never to accuse me of rying again."

"Anyone who shoots back at you is an enemy—is that the way you work it?" Grall asked the old man, who seemed quite calm and content, as if he had demonstrated his thesis beyond doubt.

"Enemies," von Shimo murmured. "Awr around, enemies."

"You said all these enemies of yours were dead," Tey reminded the old man.

"Onry a manner speaking, sir. You see, anyone who oppose the emperor is—good as dead."

"Let's go, General," Tey said. "Some of those people must be wounded. Let's go take a look."

Von Shimo objected strenuously, but Tey boosted him out of the car, suggesting to Nat that he stay behind with Cleo to man the guns, in case of difficulty. The big man consented reluctantly, conceding that it would be unwise for both Tey and himself to place themselves in the hands of the "enemies", and simultaneously under von Shimo's guns.

EIGHT

Jonesu-san

The fire, still blazing in a low metal firebox, undiminished by the hail of needles which had swept it, was some hundred yards distant. As Tey, with von Shimo reluctantly preceding him, approached, people appeared, one by one, from their shallow hiding places, mere folds in the nearly flat ground. They stood uncertainly, it seemed to Tey, peering into what for them was utter darkness from which the two were gradually emerging into the fire's faint ruddy light. When only a few feet from the metal firebox, von Shimo, who had forged ahead, halted suddenly and began to harangue the people upon whom he had fired so savagely a few minutes before:

"Rucky peoper, you," he yelled in his cracked voice. "You cross treaty rine awr the time, to try to kirr me. But you find out I'm not so easy to kirr. You fire on imperior war-car, break my big right, but I got a spare firament, fix it soon. Right now awr you peoper rine up, and me and my correagues rook you over."

"Never mind all that," Tey cut in on the old man's speech. "Is anyone hurt?" he called across the fire. Now at close range he saw that they appeared to be Hawaiians, male and female, of all ages, from a toddler holding his mother's finger and sucking his own to a gnarled ancient nearly as wrinkled as von Shimo. None had any visible wound. No one replied to Tey's question.

"I tore you, rine up," von Shimo repeated irritably, but Tey silenced him again with a curt gesture.

After a momentary pause a man with close-cropped gray hair and a larger-than-average physique stepped forward, his eyes on Tey. He nodded in von Shimo's direction and introduced himself to Tey as Jonesu-san.

"This poor orde maniac we know very wear," he said in a medium baritone voice. "But you, sir, are a stranger to us. May I ask how it is you traver in the company of the Mad One?"

"You may," Tey conceded. "It happened he was the first person I met after my arrival here."

The spokesman's bland expression reflected momentary puzzlement. "I fear I don't understand, sir. You appear to have arrived together, in yon devil-cart. It was myself and my famery you met here, and greeted with the noisegun."

"No, no, I mean my arrival on Parasite, or Paradise, or whatever you call this world. You see, we saw no signs of human habitation, until this man—Colonel-General von Shimo—appeared. He led us here. He fired before we were able to interfere."

"We call the world New Terra—" the gray-haired man said, "or, alternatively, Omega."

· 2 ·

"I don't get it," Nat Grall said, when Tey—after a brief talk with the nomads' spokesman—had prodded von Shimo back into the car and had given Nat and Cleo the astonishing news. "If the original Omega people actually survived—or at least the tradition—why don't we see signs of civilization? They've had plenty of time to build roads, plant crops, open up mines, and everything else you'd expect. Instead, we find one old dement and a crowd of primitives traveling on foot. I suppose we may as well give up any grandiose ideas—if we ever had one—of a hero's welcome and a triumphal parade into the capital."

"Nat, Captain," Cleo said urgently, "do be careful. These are no doubt a band of outcasts from some nearby Squattery, liars and murderers—worse even than Squatters. Better to wipe them out at once, while you've got the drop on them."

Tey thanked her solemnly for the advice, but declined to follow it.

"I'm not sure, from what Jonesu-san said," Tey commented, "but I think they still maintain a tradition that someday a marvelous ship is going to come to Omega and solve all their problems. When Jonesu-san started in on the Mysteries, he lost me. I asked him to hold while I came back for you, and he liked that all right, but I think we'd better tell our story in small doses, so as not to exceed the credibility quotient."

· 3 ·

While all around the members of Clan Jonesu deftly and efficiently struck tents and rolled packs, their leader sat with his three guests, as he insisted on regarding them, quietly discussing their incredible meeting, while von Shimo hovered nervously in the background. The main camp area, unseen in the darkness a hundred yards from the bonfire, had received minimal damage from a few ricochets, and Jonesu-san had quickly produced a flask of a powerful and evil-tasting home brew in honor of the occasion.

"Very fine, very old stuff, you know, gentlemen," said Johnny, as Grall had nicknamed him. "My word, it *is* quite something, you know, being first, or almost first (with a nod in von Shimo's direction), to greet you here. I think we have much to discuss, and many prans to make."

"Your people seem surprisingly incurious," Tey commented. "Not one has come up to ask questions—or even to stare at us. Strange."

"Not really," Johnny said calmly. "They know quite wear that any man, woman, or child who should defy my instructions to stay, I can shoot on the spot."

"It's curious," Tey said, concealing his revulsion at his host's remark, "that with an entire planet to choose from, we parked right in front of the general here—and only a few day's march from your group."

"I dislike to dispute the point, Captain," Jonesu-san said, just as von Shimo darted in to comment:

"I, of course, hurried to extend His Majesty's greetings." He glared at Jonesu-san. "And I don't mind terring you, it was a trifer hectic reaching you before anyone else so as to ensure a correct contact."

"You mean, so as to have an opportunity to prejudice our honored guests before we of Primary presented ourselves," Johnny corrected.

"You see, Captain, all is not well here with the Omega colony," Johnny added.

"How did you know we were here?" Nat inquired bluntly. "You people look as if you've been on the trail for some time. How far are we from this Primary you mentioned?"

"Not so very far," Jonesu-san replied blandly.

"By the way," Tey put in, "you folks didn't by any chance attack our ship any time in the last few days, did you?"

Jonesu-san gave Tey a troubled look. "Certainly no one representing Primary has committed any hostile act," he said. "As for Squatters, Big and Little Diggers—all that rot—who can say? . . . though one doubts they would have the intestinal fortitude to attack anything more formidable than von Shimo here, say."

"But it was this Primary of yours that saw us first," Nat pointed out. "How did you find us so quick?"

"We maintain the traditional surveillance net, Herr General Feld Marschall," Jonesu-san said. "We are reduced now to a single, automated, off-planet picket vesser, but it detected your approach some forty days since, though I realized only at the last day that you had chosen the Deadrand on which to alight. Very puzzling, Captain. May I know why?"

"It all looks the same from a few hundred miles up," Tey replied. "Why do you call this area the Deadland?"

"Because we found no life here, Captain, in old days. Now Squatters and Big and Little Diggers, even Walkers, roam here. But it happened I was the one, of the hundred and nine technicians studying your path, first to deduce your precise point of landing; thus I was given the honor of coming to make the first contact. Pity von Shimo managed to stear mamarch and reach you first. I *do* hope his erratic behavior hasn't unduly prejudiced you."

"What is all this conflict between you and von Shimo?" Tey asked bluntly. " 'Enemies,' he calls you."

Johnny made a gesture of dismissal. "He fires on us without warning, and if we repry in kind, we're crassed as enemies," he said wearily. "Who can exprain the actions of a madman?"

"Enemies," von Shimo said firmly. "Not half crafty, this rat."

Tey eyed the bland, regular features of Jonesu-san. "If one of your group—a child, perhaps—happened to wander over this way, would you really shoot him?"

Jonesu-san smiled in a contented way. "Would the captain rike me to demonstrate?" he asked genially.

Even as Tey shook his head, the leader caught the eye of the plumpish, middle-aged woman who happened to be closest at the moment, though well outside the hundred-meter line; she dropped the pack she was adjusting and came hurrying toward them.

Jonesu-san, with a flick of the wrist, produced from his bulky sleeve a small handgun. As he aimed and steadied it, Nat Grall's hand, striking with shocking speed, knocked the weapon flying. Jonesu-san scrambled to his feet to find himself facing the big man, who had risen even as he struck.

"Captain," Nat said, "I really think this son of a bitch would have fired." He fixed his eyes on those of the native. "Starting now, no more killing, understand, you blood-thirsty skunk?" He stood facing Jonesu-san now, his back to the embers of the fire.

"My word," Jonesu-san said stiffly, "you go too far when you ray hands on my person."

"I'll disassemble your damned person," Nat said.

Ten feet behind him, the woman whose life he had saved brought out a long, slim poniard from a sheath on her arm and advanced at a clumsy trot. Tey moved quickly to intercept her. She shied at his approach—

Tey staggered, but kept his feet, half-dazed by the kick the woman had delivered to his head. Now she moved in, board-hard hands ready; shifting her weight as Tey feinted right, she took his left 'sword-hand' square in the ribs of her thick weath-er-suit. The padding absorbed most of the deadly thrust; she gasped, but resumed breathing strongly after a moment. Tey followed with overhand chops at the base of her neck, which halted her in her tracks, her motherly face contorted in pain or rage. She still held the knife. Tey ordered her to drop it. As she did so, she lunged, meeting Tey's knee with the top of her head. She fell on her face and lay unmoving, the knife under her.

· 4 ·

"Take care, Captain," Jonesu-san called, as Tey bent over her solicitously. That's a tricky one; don't let her—" He broke off as the inert woman moved feebly, then lunged upward at Tey, swinging the knife in a vicious arc, missing him by a fraction of an inch as he jumped back. A sharp report sounded from behind Tey, and the woman went inert, lying twisted, half on her face.

Tey looked around to see von Shimo calmly tucking away a gun in one of the many folds of his garment.

Jonesu-san spoke up apologetically. "You see, Captain, per-haps there is good reason for my precautions."

Grall replied first. "Pray accept my aparogies, Jonesu-san. I was wrong."

Tey was watching von Shimo, who met his eyes boldly while tucking away his gun.

"You could have taken over any time you wanted to," Tey said, "or tried to. But you went along. Why?"

"Rife is far too comprex, Captain," von Shimo replied, "for any person to imagine he understands it. My poricy is rate and see what deverops."

"Congratulations, Captain," Johnny was saying as he came forward. "You came crose to defeating a Champion of One Thousand." He nudged the corpse with his foot. "But it is as well the Mad One shot her down. Had you turned your back—as I suspect you would have, thinking her unconscious—she'd have had you." The body had flopped on its back at the chief's prod, revealing that the right hand still held the slim knife, gripping it even in death.

·5·

The people of the clan had not failed to observe the incident and had gathered in a loose circle just outside the limit imposed by their chief. They gazed back impassively as Tey scanned their faces for some indication of their reaction to the brief episode of violence.

Jonesu-san waved his hands in a shooing motion. "Now we march," he called. "Up packs and form coromn of march." His people instantly set about obeying the command, the picture of docility.

"Every one of us, Captain," Jonesu-san said quietly, "is armed and dangerous. Prease, I suggest you do not turn your back on any one. The temptation might be too great. Some have never killed; they rong to achieve status."

"Tough people," Nat said to Tey. "But I guess they have to be, to survive on this tundra." He turned to the leader. "Johnny, where are you headed?"

"*We*, not second person," Jonesu-san corrected. "It is best you accompany us, as I think you yourself weir concede."

"We'd like to see your hometown, Johnny," Tey said. "But maybe we ought to ride in our car. We can follow you."

"Or better yet," Nat Grall put in, "we can scout ahead on the flanks. Why don't you ride with us, Johnny?"

Jonesu-san inclined his head in a stiff, formal bow. "Prease, I will accompany you—on foot, so as to keep an eye on these people." He gazed distastefully at his obedient clan.

"You do all your traveling on foot?" Nat asked. "Why not use powered vehicles?"

"You suggest that I should profane the Mysteries?" Jonesu-san inquired coolly.

"It might not be a bad idea," Nat said, "if the Mysteries have you folks walking all over the landscape when you could be doing it faster and better on wheels."

"It is not for us to question the Mysteries," Jonesu-san intoned stagily. "But frankry," he added in a hushed tone, as if to avoid overhearing himself, "it *is* a kind of pain in the sitz-fleisch to see the Guardians touring arong in ruxury, wire the rest of us do it the hard way."

"Tell me, Jonesu-san," Tey put in, "does the name 'Greylorn' mean anything to you?"

The native chief turned sharply to meet Tey's eyes. "I am not a Schismatic, Captain, I assure you." His expression changed. "Prease to tear me the truth now: from where do you come? Who sent you here to spy on us?"

Tey shook his head. "Try to get that idea out of your mind, Jonesu-san," he said patiently. "I'll repeat: we came here to this planet of which we knew nothing but the location on the Galactic grid, from Terra, the prace from which your own ancestors came. We came looking for the descendents of the people who came here three hundred Terran-years ago, on a vessel named *Omega,* the same name you have told me you sometimes apply to your planet. That seems to confirm that we've found what we were looking for."

"Nonsense, old boy," Jonesu-san replied briskly. "I've heard oar that rubbish before. But as I said, I'm not a true devotee of the Mysteries. One has one's reservations, you know—though I am no iconoclast. I recognize the societar value of the Faith. So just be a good chap and tear me why you're here. Perhaps I can even help you to make your task easy. I have nothing to hide."

"That's your line and you're stuck with it, it seems," Tey said less patiently. "We had hoped to find a thriving colony, based on the report of Commander Greylorn, who made contact last century—with your picket boat, it now appears. He was led to believe that Omega colony had thriven exceedingly, and had even established outposts on the nearby planets of the system. I begin to suspect that he was misled."

"Oh, yes, the mysterious 'contact,' which, I can tear you, neary caused the corrapse of the Temper of the Mysteries.

Paradox, perhaps, that after ages of preaching the Return, when an outside source—the Picket Service is notably free of Mysteries sentiment—seems to confirm their predictions—chaos. To preach the mystic 'return' of godlike creatures who came here from outer space is all very well, but to be abruptly confronted with the reality of imminent invasion by these same super-beings—that, I can assure you, my dear chap, is another outcropping of zeldstone altogether."

"We're not in any way super-beings," Tey said. "In fact, we're in some distress and hoped to find help here for Terra's most pressing probrem: overpopuration. We planned to begin shipping our excess people as soon as proper arrangements could be made. Surely this world is underpopulated. In only three centuries you can hardly have increased to more than a few hundred thousand individuals—which, I think, explains the undeveloped appearance of the land."

"You may as well drop it, Captain," Cleo put in. "You'll never change this ferrow's mind."

"What you propose is unthinkaber," the chief replied, less casual now in his manner. "We have prans for the systematic deveropment of every acre of our world, except, of course for Deadrand. We have no prace for outsiders!"

"But—" Tey protested, "you're in desperate need of population, in order to develop the planet. You'd be getting experts in minerals, agriculture, transportation, power sources—everything you need!"

"If aur these peoper came here and do awr these things, they make a fine world, it is true—for themselves. We would be shunted aside, shut out. Better by far to do awr things ourselves, though it take ronger. But when awr is finished, it berong to us arone!"

"You can't deverop a world with a handfur of people with no modern equipment and technology," Tey pointed out, determinedly.

"By Jove," Jonesu-san countered. "But you've no knowledge of our technorogicar resources, prease."

"If the equipment you're using is any examper—" Tey started.

"It isn't," the chief cut him off. "For excerent reasons. We traver right, don't you know, old boy? But soon you see Cache One. Very fine prace, prenty erectronic, you bet." He strolled away.

Tey turned to Nat. "Let's try one more time to raise Ollie. The car-talker has a lot more punch than my command unit. Maybe he's held a two-way on us, and he may be getting nervous."

"Ollie, nervous?" Nat laughed. "He gets nervous rike a five-ton hellbore."

· 6 ·

No one interfered as they went to the car, beside which von Shimo sat dejectedly, guarded by two powerful-looking native men holding scatterguns with the apparent negligence of the expert. As Nat engaged the old fellow in bantering conversation, Tey slipped inside the car, and tuned for the tell-tale carrier hum of a two-way beam. To his astonishment, he found it almost at once. Jaxon's voice came through, faint with distance, excitedly:

". . . been sweating hard-slugs, Captain. Wait—"

"Ollie," Tey said as calmly as possible, "I'm reading you about Nine. What happened?"

"I'm not sure," Jaxon replied. "The perimeter alert went off a couple of times, but I couldn't pick up anything on the scanner."

"Ollie," Tey persisted, "how did you move the ship? And where are you now? Nat and I have been growing white whiskers since you disappeared."

There was a momentary pause before Jaxon replied. ". . . as if you said you'd been back here and couldn't find the ship. But that's nonsense of course. No fear, Captain, I couldn't move this vessel if I wanted to—and I don't want to. We're sitting tight—and now that you've called in at last, we can relax. Renee is beside me, crying and laughing. Some relief, to hear from you. I'll hold this beam on you, now that I have a hard fix."

"Stay buttoned up," Tey advised. "We've contacted, among other things, a group of fifty-one—correction: fifty—people, the first half-way sane folks we found, present company excepted. No signs of a high technology, but the boss-man, Jonesu-san, claims they've got plenty of stuff back at home base. They're doing a simple primitive number for ritualistic reasons as far as I can interpret Johnny's rather cryptic remarks. He doesn't give direct answers, just rambles on, covering the same ground. He's heard of Omega, brought up the word himself—but rejects the idea of our off-world origin. 'It's a big pranet,' he says. 'No tering what some misguided Guardian may be cooking up on the other side of it.' He's heard of Greylorn, but considers the story a myth. He ties everything I ask him into something called the Mysteries, apparently some sort of religion.

"We're about to set out—on foot—with his bunch, to see their hometown, which he calls Primary—probably the same prace von Shimo mentioned. We're not exactly prisoners, but nobody's yet offered to scratch wrists and do a blood-brotherhood number. But as long as you're all right, there's no point in our hurrying back without making the contact with this Prime or Primary."

"What sort of fork are they?" Jaxon wanted to know, his voice faint, as with distance. "Do they seem to be Omega descendents?"

"Hard to say," Tey replied. "You know how it is when you breed the old strains back together—everybody looks like the preprimary split type. They'd look right at home in the Bronze Age."

"It figures," Jaxon commented. "Any clues as to the size of the native population?"

"Not yet; but it's only a few days' hike to the big town, the boss says. He calls this one 'Cache One.' I'm not doing any heavy prying until we get there and I can see for myself. We'll be moving out any minute now; the gang is formed up in a column of ducks. Try to hold that beam on us. My best to Renee and Sugar—"

"Be careful, Cap'n," Renee's cool voice came back. "Tell Nat he's going to have to give Sugar a full, personal account. I think he has a real fan back here worrying about him."

"Not worrying," Sugar's youthful voice came in. "Just very eager to know all about it. Good luck, Captain."

· 7 ·

Cleo, standing by, had listened with interest to the exchange. "I've heard of such talkers, Captain," she said coolly, "but I always thought it but part of the so-called Mysteries, the silly superstition all them ignorant savages make so much of, with their Grand Gatherings, and imaginary Picket Service and so on. Who were the women?" she concluded abruptly.

"Our fellow crew members," Tey said. "Renee is a mature woman, but Sugar is only a child."

"One sometimes longs for the company of a cultivated fellow-woman," Cleo commented without conviction.

Tey rejoined Nat and von Shimo. One of the guards spoke up. "If you gents would like to take over responsibility for him, we'll check out."

"Of course," Tey said, and the two casually strolled away.

"Strange sort of discipline old Johnny keeps here," Nat said, watching the self-relieved guards fall in at the tail of the double column waiting patiently in ranks awaiting the order to march. "But it seems to work."

"It works," Tey said, with a glance at the unburied body of the woman. "It works just fine."

NINE

Banshire's Man

Glancing back from a hundred feet at the deserted campground, Tey saw nothing to indicate that fifty people had camped there for some hours, but the glow of the fire-pit, from which the cold fire-box had been removed and disassembled for packing. Barely visible in the faint glow, the corpse lay where it had fallen. Von Shimo was mumbling to himself.

Jonesu-san, walking beside Tey and Grall at the tail of the column, noticed Tey's glance, and himself looked somewhat disapprovingly at the dead woman. "I suppose I reary should have buried—or posserbry cremated her," he said as if thinking aloud. "She was me mum, you know," he added without emphasis.

Von Shimo's muttering focused into audible speech. "We must go at once, ere we drown with this rabber—"

Tey stopped in his tracks, causing von Shimo to collide with him. The little man backed away, uttering apologies mingled with curses, then turned and darted away. Grall took a step after him, but Tey caught the big man's arm.

"Did you hear what this cold-blooded little devil said?" Grall demanded, eyeing Jonesu-san coldly.

"Let him go, Nat," Tey said. "I have a feeling Johnny can find him if we need him."

"Damn right. Damned good show the bounder left," the

chief said. "Saves one the trouber of dearing with him."

"He'll take the car," Nat protested to Tey. "Cleo's back there —alone."

"She can take care of herself, Nat. And we don't need the car. We can run him down and settle with him later. The first item of business is to reach Prime and find out what's going on."

At that moment, the running lights of the ground-car winked on; its spinners whined up to speed.

"Get ready to hit the dirt," Tey said, "if old Shimmy has an impulce to play with his needer pump again." But the car merely executed a sharp turn and sped away across the flat tundra.

Nat Grall stared for a moment after the vehicle, then at the dead woman. "Is that really your mother?" he inquired of Jonesu-san.

"Aras, the rady is dead," the latter replied. "Nothing wier be changed by ramenting the fact. In any case, she deserved it. And we awr have to die at rast." After a pause, he intoned:

'The sun is born and dies and comes again;
The moon is born and dies and comes again;
Man is born and dies and comes not again.'

"Jonesu-san," Tey addressed the chief, "since you and your people originated here on Omega, how is it that we speak the same ranguage?"

"What else? Onry one possiber ranguage can exist. It is inherent in man to speak."

"Au contraire," Tey said. *"Det finns många språk i världen."*

Johnny stared at him in astonishment. "You made a sound rike speech," he said. "But it was not speech. How very strange."

"That little verse you recited," Tey said, "it's an old saying from Africa, back on Old Terra."

"One need not suscribe furry to the Mysteries in order to appreciate the beauty of some of the Sayings," the chief stated as if expecting contradiction.

"Someday," Nat said, "I want to get a furr briefing on these Mysteries of yours."

"Not mine," Johnny said sharply. "Fear not, General Feld Marshall, when we arrive at Prime, you share rearn perhaps more than you rike from the Guardians."

"Gosh," Nat said in mock alarm, "how long will that be?"

"Onry one more march, perhaps," Jonesu-san replied. "Maybe two, depending on, uh, circumstances."

"It's my observation," Nat said, "that around here, the circumstances never change."

· 2 ·

They marched on through the long night, and dawn, pale yellow-green in the East, came at last. Still, Jonesu-san signaled no rest-stop, and his people seemed as fresh as ever, plodding doggedly on, skirting occasional puddles.

"Nat," Tey said, "have you noticed that the ground seems to be getting just a little softer?"

Nat paused to dig a heel into the turf.

"Maybe," he said. "A little spongy, maybe."

"Exactly," Tey said, moving a little aside from Jonesu-san. "Nat, we're on what is known as muskeg. It's like peat that hasn't consolidated yet. We've talked about how the wind doesn't seem quite as cold as it did at first—and it's *not* our imagination, or getting acclimatized. It's almost Summer. The picture is this:

"In the dead of winter, this kind of soil, with its high albedo, gets a hard chill. Permafrost forms, perhaps to fifteen or twenty feet down. At that point, all incident precipitation is blocked from penetration: an instant water-table. So the soil above becomes saturated. At its worst, it becomes a sort of jelly, a true quicksand. After that, the permafrost thaws, and the surface water sinks in. The surface then becomes compacted and dry —hard as concrete. Then the cycle begins again."

"And at what point in the cycle are we now?" Nat asked.

"A week ago, the ground was hard," Tey said. "Now it's softening. Next comes the jelly phase." He turned to scan the broad expanse of monotony. "See if you can spot any reflections from puddles or surface water," he suggested. "I think that should give us at least a warning."

Nat scanned his side of the horizon. "You know, Cap'n, it's a funny thing," he said calmly. "Since we started talking about the 'defective lateral,' I've been noticing it more and more, both in your speech and mine. I guess I've been doing it awr—all my r—life, but I never really paid any attention to it. I remember as a kid wondering why words weren't sperred—spelled the way they pronounced, but I soon forgot that."

"No doubt being in the company of von, Shimo and Jonesu-san, we're unconsciously conforming to their dialect," Tey commented. "I just noticed I didn't say 'diarect.' So we'd probably sound a bit odd to Renee and Ollie and Sugar now."

"What's wrong with L?" Nat asked. "Why avoid it? It's not hard to say."

"Why do we say 'tea' instead rather than 'tay,' as it was originary?" Tey asked rhetorically. "Or 'Performance,' instead of 'perfur*n*ance'? Or 'join' instead of 'jine'? Languages change, and this is just one of the changes. I suppose we'd never have noticed it, if we hadn't been thrust into the company of someone who carried the change even farther than we do, another familiar phenomenon. There are millions of people on Terra today, who say 'moight' and 'oirland,' by analogy with 'join.'"

Nat caught at Tey's arm. "Oh-oh, look there, Cap'n!" He pointed. Far across the monochrome tundra, watery sunlight glinted from a string of bright patches.

"I hope this Prime base of Johnny's is either very close, or built on a rocky outcropping," Nat said. "Neither of which appears likely."

Tey and Nat had closed up the space between themselves and Jonesu-san, who marched along at the heels of the rear rank of the tribe, plodding silently and stolidly ahead, either not noticing, or not concerned by the evidences of imminent dissolution of the ground underfoot.

"Jonesu-san," Tey addressed his host, "I assume you realize we're soon going to be swimming in a thick soup."

"Captain," Nat cut in abruptly, his voice tight, "what about the ship? That's the same kind of ground, isn't it?" he paused, then added: "I have to assume we were hallucinating, and she's still parked where we left her, since Ollie reports so."

"Maybe he or the gals will figure it out and move in time," Tey said stiffly. "But we can't count on it. All we can do for now is try to reach this Primary as soon as we can."

"A curious observation, Captain Tey," Jonesu-san belatedly replied to Tey's query. " 'A thick soup,' you say. Among us, soup is to be eaten. Since you imagine the ground is about to turn to food beneath your feet, I infer you are hungry. That being the case, I suppose I'd best order a dinner-hart."

"Never mind the heavy sarcasm, Johnny," Nat put in. "How far is it to solid ground—the shortest way?"

Jonesu-san halted abruptly and mimed testing the turf underfoot.

"Cap'n," Nat said, "is it possiber this clown doesn't know what he's standing on?"

"I doubt it," Tey replied. "He's just reluctant to admit to himself that *we* know."

Jonesu-san was gazing from Nat to Tey and back again with an expression of honest puzzlement on his handsome features. Tey caught his eye with difficulty.

"We've got perhaps a few hours, perhaps onry minutes," Tey said sternly, "it's time to cut out the drama and do something smart. What wier it be?"

Jonesu-san muttered, half-turned, and motioned to the man who had been acting as trail-boss to the marching tribe; he at once barked a curt order, and the two files diverged, curving outward to come around in a wide arc and rejoin, in the form of an only slightly lopsided circle. They downed packs, and busily began laying out their contents.

"Look, Johnny," Nat addressed the chieftain earnestly, "this is no time to settle down for the afternoon—"

"Wait," Tey interrupted Grall's protest. "Maybe he knows what he's doing."

·3·

The clan, rather than pitching tents, were unrolling large groundcloths, crowded so close together as to overlap, and then began busily to lace the edges of the heavy tarps together, while others distributed the other items in what was quite apparently a planned arrangement, on the tarps, leaving aisles at close intervals.

"Will it work?" Nat inquired of Tey rhetorically.

Tey glanced at Jonesu-san, who was blandly watching this curious activity. "It's probably a well-tested technique," he said.

Jonesu-san turned to Tey, now wearing an expression of well-bred curiosity.

"Tear me, prease, Captain," he said in the tone of one being consciously reasonable, "how did you know that the Great Dragon was about to awaken?"

"I know nothing at all about any dragon, great or smawr," Tey said. "But anyone can rook out there—" he waved a hand toward the flat expanse around them, "and see the puddles forming. As soon as all the ice crystars that are mixed up with the sand thaw, we'll be walking on slurry."

"Not so simple to dismiss Mysteries in this fashion," the native countered. "My word, one hardly knows what to make of you, Captain. Who are you? What do you expect of me?"

"I'm what one of Lord Banshire's best boys called 'a misbegotten dog of a broken officer' of the Terran Navy," Tey answered. "With the herp of others, I stole a deep-space vessel and followed some hundred-year-old information that we happened to intercept—and came here. We have records of a coronization attempt here, three centuries ago. It was given the name *Omega*, because the rast retter of the ancient Greek alphabet seemed appropriate for a desperate rast attempt. We were red to berieve we'd find a thriving corony here, with a high rever of technorogy. Only the facts that you and your people are obviously human, speak archaic Standard, and sometimes call your world Omega, tend to confirm that we did, indeed, find whatever it is that old coronial venture has evolved into in three hundred years."

"Except for the fact that the human race originated here on Parasite, that of course we speak as we do because there can be no other manner of speaking, and that awr you've said is the most utter rubbish I've ever heard," the leader said. "Your manner is most convincing, but reary, Captain—" Jonesu-san broke off with a shrug. "You reave me no option but to assume you are in the hire of the Guardians."

"Let *me* try," Nat said. "Rook here, Johnny, we never heard of these Guardians of yours. We've crossed over fifteen lights of space to reestablish contact with a long-lost corony. You ought to be a rittu preased and excited about meeting people from back home!"

"Never mind, Nat," Tey said. "You can't reary blame him; it's a rather mind-browing concept to come upon suddenry."

· 4 ·

"How far is it to solid ground?" Nat demanded of the leader. "That canvas raft of yours might give you a few more minutes before the goo croses over your heads, but it won't save you."

"There's only one alternative," Tey said. "How about it?" His gaze slipped past Grall, out across the featureless expanse they had crossed, now thickly spotted with light-reflecting puddles. "Hey," he said softly, "wait a minute . . ."

Tey put a hand on the big man's shoulder. "We'll have to try for a hard spot," he said, loudly enough for Johnny to hear, "so to speak," he went on, feeling his boots sinking into the rapidly softening surface. Grall followed closely, and had taken two steps when Jonesu-san spoke behind him:

"Stop there!" the usually mild voice cracked. Neither Grall nor Tey paused. There was a sharp detonation; mud gouted, inches from Tey's advancing foot. He went on. Grall turned in a lazy way. "What—" he started, and was on the leader before he had time to so much as shift the aim of the old hard-shooter he held, pointed slightly offside. It fired, the round

216 -

going wild. Nat plucked the gun from the leader and tossed it aside; Jonesu-san lunged after it, and Nat released his grip while hooking the other's ankle with his toe. The leader fell face-down with a squashy splash. Nat put a foot on his back.

"Yes, Johnny? You wanted me to stop, isn't that right? What for? So we could go down with the ship, or the canvas bag, or whatever that arrangement might be called?"

Now Tey was at his side. "You saw it, Nat, didn't you? What do you think?"

Nat, still holding Jonesu-san helplessly pinned to the ground, turned his head to look toward the east.

"A car," he said. "No doubt of it. A ground-effect car coming more or less this way. Von Shimo's wheels wouldn't get ten feet in this." He turned to meet Tey's eye. "That means Ollie," he said. "He wouldn't have let Renee come alone."

"Or Sugar," Tey said with an indulgent grin. "She'd do as she pleased." Tey glanced down at the prostrate man, whose half-hearted struggles had intensified.

"Let him up, Nat. Breathing muddy water doesn't seem to agree with him."

Nat removed his foot and caught Jonesu-san by the neck, brought him to his hands and knees, and then to his feet so he could look him in the face.

"You were saying?" Grall prompted. The leader's mouth was open, mud running from both corners. Glancing past him, Nat saw that the clan members were proceeding calmly with their work—all but the trail boss, who was looking worriedly toward his leader and the two outsiders.

"I'm going to remove my thumb from your windpipe," Nat said quietly to his captive, "to allow you to tell your wrangler to get busy."

As the pressure on his throat relaxed, Jonesu-san sucked in air convulsively and went into a coughing fit. Nat slammed a hand against his back, which elicited a violent explosion of air and water from his mouth. Nat lowered him until his feet found purchase and took his weight. Still coughing, Johnny looked at

Grall with red-rimmed, bloodshot eyes. "Ret go, Grall-san," he said in a choked voice, between coughs, "and I shair do as you say."

Nat released his grip. Jonesu-san staggered, but retained his feet, eyeing Grall reproachfully.

"Sorry to have given you discomfort, Johnny," Nat said, "but when you pulled that gun and splashed mud on my britches, it made me angry. It's not considered porite this season." As Jonesu-san's eyes went to the gun, barely visible in the mud, Nat stepped on it.

"You won't be needing it," he said. "Now, do you have any more good ideas?"

"I have shown you nothing but kindness," Jonesu-san said rather shrilly. "Now you attack my person unexpectedry. This is outrageous! My word!"

"It won't happen again, Johnny," Nat said patiently, "at least not unexpectedly, because from now on anytime you fire a weapon in our general direction, you can expect a return." He turned away from the man and went to Tey, who had moved a few feet on to watch the approaching vehicle.

"A great victory for our side, General Feld Marshall," Tey said. "We can consider this moment the true beginning of diplomatic relations with Omega, since no one was killed."

"In that case, Cap'n, you'd better change my title to Ambassador Extraordinary and Minister Plenipotentiary."

"At least," Tey agreed. He glanced toward Jonesu-san, who had now apparently noticed the approaching vehicle and was watching its progress with a stiff expression.

"It seems he's not expecting anyone," Tey commented.

· 5 ·

Now at a quarter of a mile, the car was close enough to be identified as the fast-scout vehicle from the ship, or its twin. Behind the grayed-out windshield, the driver was not visible. It was still approaching at unabated speed, following approximately the track taken by von Shimo on his departure, though no trail was apparent across the sodden turf.

"Gentermen," Jonesu-san called after them, "I suggest with some urgency that you return to safety and rie prone, as my peoper and I are about to do."

When Tey looked back, not a man, woman, or child was visible on the rumpled canvas surface.

The car had made no change of course, but came on as if to rush blindly across the makeshift mat; nor did it appear to react to the phenomenon of Nat and Tey standing apart therefrom. Then, at a hundred yards, it slowed, and curved in toward the two waiting men, splattering a fine mist of mud as its steering jets cut into jellylike soil. Whipping the surface into froth, it slowed sharply, glided past Tey and Grall, and came to rest almost overriding the edge of the mat, its rotors whining down to a faint growl.

The two men waited. The emplacement above the hatch, Tey noted, was closed and locked; the gun muzzles depressed. Then the hatch opened, and a man dressed in what appeared to be a patchwork quilt stepped down and looked at them keenly. Tey's scattergun was in his hand. He held it as if negligently, aimed at the newcomer's chest. The man was a total stranger.

· 6 ·

"Cutting it a trifle close, are you not, gentlemen?" he inquired in a voice deeper than those of von Shimo or Jonesu-san. His features appeared to be those of a Mediterranean type, Tey thought. He carried no visible weapon.

"So it seems," Tey replied to the rhetorical question. "Our genial host, Jonesu-san, claims to be leading us to a prace named Prime Base, but it appears his timing is off."

The stranger glanced at Tey's pistol, then across the quarteracre of canvas; if he saw anyone, he showed no reaction.

"Jonesu-san, eh? Goofy name. Who is he? How does he fit the picture?"

"All we know of him is that we encountered him here and he

persuaded us to accompany him. We were, and still are, eager to make contact with the authorities."

As the muddy turf grew noticeably softer underfoot, the three men stepped, without comment, to the uncertain stability of the canvas and continued their casual conversation, ignoring the aimed pistol.

The newcomer told them that his name was Constable Billingsly and that they were in his area of jurisdiction. "So, it appears," he commented, "you've made the contact with authority, which you claim you desire."

"We were thinking of a somewhat higher level in the local hierarchy," Tey replied smoothly. "Perhaps," he glanced at the constable's vehicle, "you could conduct us to your headquarters."

Nat caught Tey's eye. "Wot the 'ell, Captain," he muttered in a meaningful tone. "Why muck abaht wif this bloke?"

Tey grinned. "Perhaps you're right," he said.

Billingsly's face had lost its relaxed, genial smile. His gaze was now openly fixed on Tey's weapon. "You'd best put that away, my dear fellow," he said sternly. "No reason for it in any case, you know. And of course, insofar as gunplay is concerned, my car is fully equipped with automatic defenses."

"I don't think your discriminatory circuitry is sufficiently sophisticated to know whom not to gun down," Tey replied coolly. "The pistol is just to make it clear where the advantage lies."

"Get at least half-smart, Tey," the stranger said in a crisp tone. "Did you really imagine Lord Banshire would let you steal his best battlewagon?"

"Get this, Billingsly, or whatever your name is," Tey replied tautly, readjusting his point of aim to the center of the man's chest, "at your first wrong move, you'll collect seventy-five new holes in your anatomy—*if* I can hold it to a short burst."

"This won't do you any good, Tey," Billingsly said in a tone of weariness. "One man—even two men—against the entire Space Arm won't have a chance." He put a hand against the side of the car and leaned on it casually.

"What is it you want?" Tey demanded, ignoring Grall's inobtrusive move beside him.

"You're under arrest, of course," Billingsly said. "Hand over that weapon, and I'll be able to write up a more favorable report than if I have to use force."

"Go ahead," Nat said. "Use force."

As Billingsly casually shifted the hand which he had placed against the side of the car, there was a sharp *click!* from within the car.

"Naughty," Tey said, and smiled sadly at Billingsly. "You stand right there, Bill; His Excellency and I have something to talk over." As he turned away, Billingsly took a convulsive step to one side, as if preparing to duck around the car. Nat knocked him down without looking at him.

Tey held the gun aimed steadily at the man's head and backed up a few steps, Grall beside him. Then he put the weapon away and turned. "You can get up now, mister," he said over his shoulder.

Billingsly got up, looking resentful, and slapped at the mud on his much-patched shipsuit.

"You might even be lucky enough to cancel that antipersonnel blast before it goes off," Nat added. But even as he spoke, the charge of light buckshot *whoof*ed from the aperture in the rocker panel, riddling Billingsly's legs; he fell with a curse and lay with his face in the mud. A few spent pellets rattled against the boots of Tey and Grall.

"Now, there, Mr. Ambassador," Tey said disapprovingly, "is an example of what happens when one ignores basic safety precautions as prescribed in Fleet regulations."

"He was a pretty careless fellow," Nat agreed. "Still, I would've enjoyed asking him a few questions before he outsmarted himself."

"Never mind, Nat," Tey said, "we'll backtrack him and get into just as much trouble as if he'd told us where to look for it."

· 7 ·

Jonesu-san, who had been hovering in the shelter of the car, came around holding his hand over his mouth. "Who was this —" he managed to stifle a snicker, "Constable Birringsry? When you reft him standing there right in the rine of fire, he rooked a proper Charlie. My word, yes." He went to the man and rolled him over with his foot. "Bit of a rum go," the leader said. "He's dead, from a charge of buckshot in the shins. Spot of bother, that. Can't tell where he came from, with his shiny, new cushion car."

"That vehicle is of the type carried by class-A units of the Navy," Tey said. "There'll be a cargo flat where that came from. With a bit of ingenuity, we could use it to get your people out. It's the only chance I see."

"Not to worry, Captain," Jonesu-san replied smoothly. "I assure you, we shall be quite awr right. As for finding a cargo flat, our Constaber Birringsry is hardry in a position to betray the rocation of his vesser."

"No need," Tey said. He waved a hand toward the clearly discernible trail of froth left by the air cushion across the muddy tundra. Jonesu-san glanced from Tey to Grall and ducked his head in a rudimentary bow. "Good ruck, gentermen," he said.

"We'll be back as soon as possible—or before," Tey said.

With no further formalities, he and Grall stepped into the car, started the engine, and swung away in a wide curve paralleling Billingsly's foam trail, then gunned across the black plain.

TEN

Old Grove

For half an hour they hummed along in silence; the air car's trail, though faint, was clear enough, stretching on and on ahead. Nat was first to break the silence:

"And we were wondering about how to let them know we'd found Omega," he said contemptuously.

"He came straight to us," Tey said. "His course doesn't waver worth a damn."

Nat nodded. "What do you think, Cap'n? A newly arrived vessel, or what?"

"He was no local, of course—and hadn't met enough locals to fake the dialect—as you so subtly pointed out."

"Consider all the obvious queries asked," Nat said genially.

"We'll know some answers soon," Tey replied. A moment later the local-communication radio uttered a harsh noise and spoke:

"All right, Stutz, the admiral would be real appreciative if you'd let him in on a few things—like what you found over there, and why you're hot-footing it back to base instead of finishing the sweep as ordered. Owanoh."

Tey flipped switches with practiced ease. "Roger. Tell the admiral to keep his britches on," he said lazily. "I found what I was looking for; why waste fuel?"

"You just told him yourself, Stutz; he's standing right beside me—with smoke coming out of his ears.

"And by the way, he'd prefer full radio discipline. G, over and out."

"Look, G," Tey said tiredly, "I've been around long enough you don't need to try that old gag on me. You hurt my feelings. The admiral is standing beside you like I got Miss Universe sitting on my lap. Stutz, over and out."

"Aw right, that's enough comedy, Stutz. You sound tired. But I've got news for you. You're to divert right now on a heading of three-six-oh, and approach with caution fix thirteen point one, by twenty-eight point oh, arbitrary. The admiral *does* hope you attended the briefing."

"I'm reading you, G," Tey said. "Now go ahead and fill me in on the rest of it."

"Thirteen twenty-eight is listed number two on your A list. You know, Stutzie—either a major construction or a class-A bogie, grounded—or maybe Analysis is seeing things. Go see, huh? And be nice about it, just in case."

"Sure, sure," Tey replied, "what about that small, fast-nearing fix? Everything jake with that? Or do we just chalk it up to a local breed of horse that holds a steady twenty-five knots?"

"That's somebody else's problem, right, Stutz? And what's the matter with your voice? You sound like you tried to swallow some issue stew without blowing it first—" the voice broke off abruptly.

"It must've dawned on him he wasn't talking to Stutzie," Tey said. "But we got a little."

"You did very well, Captain," Nat said with mock formality. "Practically pumped him dry. So—do we divert, or bore in on G?"

After a brief discussion they agreed to investigate fix thirteen twenty-eight.

"It might be *Princeton,*" Nat voiced the thought.

"They'll be all right," Tey hoped aloud. "Probably this admiral just posted a guard on her while he went looking for the nearest big city."

"Sure," Nat agreed readily. "But how did they manage to follow us out without our spotting them on our tail?"

"I don't remember looking behind very much," Tey said. "We were otherwise occupied. And of course, Ollie's out of range—if he really has moved the ship, and we weren't hallucinating."

"It's just as well," Nat commented. "We *did* get to meet good old Stutzie." He glanced back at the encamped clan, now barely visible behind them. "Cap'n, they're just sitting there, doing nothing. I've got a hunch Johnny's expecting . . . something."

·2·

As they sped along due north, conversing idly, the character of the countryside changed subtly.

"It seems we've passed out of the muskeg area," Bat pointed out. "No more puddles."

Tey's eyes were fixed on a slight irregularity on the far horizon. As they approached, the outline became more distinct. "Trees," Tey said.

Nat agreed. "You said it, Cap'n; I didn't. I thought I was making them up."

"We've been climbing a few inches per hour," Tey pointed out. "With all the pollen around, there had to be some ground somewhere high and dry enough for major vegetation."

"Only another mile or two to go," Nat commented. "Should we buzz right in, or hang back and do a recce first?"

"The trees seem to match our target area," Tey said. "I feel like barging right into the middle of Sunday dinner and to hell with it."

Nat glanced at him, smiling. "You've got that fine, careless feeling, eh, Cap'n? Don't care whether school keeps or not."

"If all the admiral's intelligence section spotted was our little group, and missed *Princeton*, we've got an ace in the hole—and two more in the cuff, Nat. I'm ready for something to happen. They aren't likely to blast good old Stutzie without at least chewing him out first, even if they've noticed he's us."

The trees were immense, gray-needled conifers, which rose without branches for the first hundred feet. Above that, spreading boughs formed a roof which left the flat ground below in deep shadow. In the gloom, points of light glinted here and there, and one blue-white arc made a brilliant disc which reflected from the underside of the foliage overhead. Men moved about, casting long shadows.

"I guess the big shot with the fancy porch light will swallow his toothpick when I put this go-cart right in the middle of his show, " Nat said.

People looked up with startled expressions and made fast decisions to withdraw as Nat bored in among them, slowing barely in time to come to a dusty halt under the big arc-light.

"It's no time to act cautious," Tey said, and opened the clamshell hatch on a chilly rush of dusty glare. Half blinded, the two men stepped down and stood fast, listening to confused yells and snappy commands over the dying whine of the rotors. An overweight man in a rumpled set of Fleet-issue fatigues came groping in through the thinning dust with an expression on his meaty features which indicated that he was prepared to be masterful. His mouth opened and quickly closed as he recoiled at sight of Nat Grall's boulderlike presence.

"Stutzie couldn't make it, chum," Nat said. "He sends his best."

"Look here," the plump man said harshly, "I don't suppose I need to tell you two fellows—"

"Gentlemen," Nat corrected. "Now you may go."

"We'll be ready to see your flag officer in a few minutes," Tey added. "Meanwhile, you may take the car to the motor pool for routine maintenance; otherwise, nobody is to touch it."

Two harder-looking men in stained workalls came up beside the fat man. The dust was settling rapidly; through the remaining veil, a ring of men was visible, all staring toward the car that had so suddenly arrived among them.

· 3 ·

As the three men stood before Grall, uncertain, he reached for the two newcomers, dragged them closer, cracked their heads together, and pitched them away. Then he turned to the plump man, who moved away a step, then turned and was quickly swallowed in the crowd.

"Well," Tey said, "now that we've stealthily insinuated ourselves into the group, do you have any other ideas?"

Before Nat could answer, two men in faded Deck Police uniforms closed in. One held an unholstered cratergun at his side; the other offered a piece of paper.

"Looks like that's it, gents," he said glibly. "Major Teech got the idea somebody was bending, or maybe even breaking, two or three—or possibly a hundred and nine and half—Fleet regs, not to mention a dozen or two Station Rules and maybe the Articles of War; so if you don't mind—"

Nat took a careful grip on the fellow's neck with one hand, while plucking the cratergun from the other's slack grip. He tossed the weapon carelessly aside and lifted the cop to eye level.

"You boys seem like you're a little mixed up," he commented mildly. "Now, as I remember it, I drove in here under my own power; you didn't put the arm on us and drag us out of our hideout in the mountains after a game resistance in which losses on both sides were heavy. OK?" He dropped the man and turned away. Both cops withdrew without further encouragement.

"Hey!" Nat called after them. "We dropped in to see the admiral, remember? You may escort us to his headquarters."

The two men paused, turned back reluctantly, and stood waiting, eyes downcast.

"That's how you teach a cop a little common courtesy," Nat commented to Tey. "They'll be nice boys now, eh, fellows?" He addressed the last words to the two discomfited officials.

"This here way, gentlemen," the one with the papers said diffidently; he moved back a step, turned and set off, the audience opening a path for him.

"Ready, sir?" Nat inquired gravely of Tey, who nodded briskly.

"Any time, Mr. Ambassador," he said.

The remaining cop stepped back and Grall and Tey went past him, following the other man, who had paused and was looking back. They threaded a devious path through the thinning crowd—all, Tey noticed, dressed in shabby Fleet-issue garments—then among trees and brush and at last to an issue fieldhut, where two armed men stood sentry duty by the sprung door.

As the guide turned to speak, Nat brushed past him and kicked the door open.

· 4 ·

Inside, barely visible in darkness relieved only by a greasy-smelling candle, a man sat behind a desk improvised of crates. He was a heavy-shouldered, thick-necked man with gray-flecked hair and hard features into which a cigar fitted as if it had been hammered in between the clenched jaws. He wore the filthiest set of whites Tey had ever seen, with polished gold buttons and the shoulder boards of a vice admiral. He held an issue side arm, its butt on the desk and the muzzle trained squarely on Tey's chest.

"Nagle," the admiral said past the new arrivals, "Williams . . . report to the detention officer on the double. Oh, as you were—just take it easy, but be there in sixty seconds, and report yourselves on ten days basic. Do it!" He shifted his eyes to meet Tey's.

"Not smart, boys," he said in a slightly lower tone. "Not even practical. You're Tey, ex-officer." He glanced at Grall. "Who's this fellow? I didn't have anything on . . ." he hesitated, "a second man," he finished lamely. Tey nodded, as if the man had said something profound.

"Better hide the Mark IV," Tey said. "You don't want to shoot anybody, not even Williams and Nagle." Tey glanced toward the open door, where the two guards stood peering in uncertainly, ignoring the admiral's orders to report themselves under arrest.

"Sure," the admiral said, "discipline is falling apart—but you can hardly blame 'em; this cruise has been bad news all the way."

"Still," Tey said, "you got here. Now what?"

"Getting here was the easy part," the admiral grunted. "We

did a full-coverage on the damn planet, and the only sign of life we saw was the jungle over on what we called Big Continent. Rather a letdown, you know."

"What does that have to do with us?" Tey demanded.

"Damn if I know. I'm Carstairs." His tone changed: "Vice Admiral Thomas Y. Carstairs, FSA."

"You're a damn liar," Tey said casually. "Not that we can't get along anyway," he added smoothly. He watched Carstairs deciding whether to take offense or not.

·5·

"You know," Tey said casually at the correct moment, "we haven't a whole lot of time to spend horsing around. I presume your geology boys have informed you of the tectonic situation . . ."

"Earthquakes?" Carstairs said, jerking at his soiled collar. "Or omegaquakes, or whatever—that would just about cut it."

"Precisely," Tey said comfortably. "That's why we're here in the Deadlands, of course. Quietest area on the planet. There. Did you feel that?" He looked inquiringly at Carstairs, then glanced at Grall, who nodded. "About force seven this time, I'd estimate," he commented in a matter-of-fact way.

Carstairs came to his feet, knocking over the crate on which he had been sitting. He removed the cigar stub from his face, glared at it, jammed it back in place. "How long do you think I have, to lift the boat before . . ." He looked at Tey with an expression that mingled hope with intimidation.

"Perhaps one hour," Tey said carelessly. "The cliff is an old fault line, so . . ." He let the sentence trail off, as though the rest were obvious. "We're on an island, you understand," he added. "Rather interesting, actually. It appears that when East Continent and Big Continent corrided, some hundred and eighty million years ago Standard, thrusting up the Barrier Range—you can barely make out the peaks from here on a fine day—" Tey waved a hand in the general direction of his arbitrarily designated north, "the mountain-building incident caused East Continent to rotate fifteen degrees clockwise, and so opened up a V-shaped gap south of the foothills, where the plate edges diverged.

"Much later, say fifty million years ago, a wedge of oceanic plate which had existed as an offshore minicontinent for over a hundred million years, rode into the gap and was wedged in with such force that the entire two-hundred-mile-wide slab was bowed upward, raising a big expanse of old sea-bottom above sea level. Treacherous stuff: turns to jelly at odd intervals, as you've no doubt observed."

Carstairs glared from Tey to Grall. "And you'd have me believe that the Omega people picked *this* region to plant their colony?"

"I didn't say that," Tey replied. "The facts speak for themselves."

"Then the facts are damned liars," Carstairs said. "Which brings me back to why you have the audacity to sit there and call *me* a liar. Damn outrage. No way to address a Fleet flag officer." He turned his back.

Grall leaned close to Tey to whisper: "Where did you get all that geological stuff?"

"Jonesu-san told me part of it," Tey said. "I made up the rest, but who knows, it might even be true."

"You know," Grall said soberly, "I *did* feel a tremor a few minutes ago."

Carstairs whirled to face Tey, his expression grim. "I don't know why I haven't already brigged you two damned mutineers," he snarled.

"That's an easy one, chum," Nat said. "You're a pretty stupid fellow, but you're not *that* stupid. A: you can't; B: you're a damned mutineer yourself; and C: you need us."

Carstairs recoiled. "Eh? How do *I* need you, mister?"

"Think about it," Nat suggested genially. "Here you are, stranded at the back end of nowhere, with a crew of incompetent eightballs. You don't know where you are, and you don't know how to get back, and if you went back you'd be shot before you told the first lie."

"You're insane," Carstairs commented, as if casually. "What makes you think I'm lost? That's foolish."

"Maybe the tank aboard your vessel knows where it is, but—" Nat made a careless gesture. "What good does that do you when the poor old tub is lying in thirty feet of water with her hull broached in three places?"

In the distance someone was shouting.

Carstairs ground his teeth audibly. His heavy features were dark with space-tan and fury.

"That takes care of point A," Nat said. "Shall I go on? Or shall we quit wasting time and make a deal?"

· 6 ·

Before Carstairs could respond, the scene was thrown into confusion by the arrival of two men who entered the hut at a full run, collided, ricocheted, and began shouting simultaneously:

"My gawd, Admiral, a big rock slide!"

"Caught Hymie and Spud, too—right where she went over!"

"I seen it from right yonder!" The smaller of the messengers turned to point wildly.

The other knocked his arm aside. "Don't nobody give a damn where you seen it from, Archer!"

Archer replied with a swing that went wide as his target ducked and hit him solidly in the abdomen.

Carstairs was shouting.

Tey and Grall stood aside and waited until the noise ceased, except for Archer's wheezing. Then they quietly left the hut. No one interfered as they started across toward the cliff-edge visible through the trees, and marked by a clump of great trunks leaning outward at a perilous angle. The camp's inhabitants were streaming past them—all, it seemed, shouting. The two intruders moved aside into the lee of a small, dense thicket which parted the crowd. In the distance, apparently from below the cliff-edge, a dull explosion sounded. Bits of debris rose into view beyond the fallen trees and fell back. The crowd noise changed tone.

"Corky!" a young woman shouted, near at hand. "Corky's down there!" She ran on.

"Time for a council of war, Cap'n?" Nat proposed. Tey nodded.

"Apparently we *were* followed," Tey said. "This Carstairs was probably a staff officer. The men got unhappy with the long cruise—just as Commander Greylorn's did, a hundred years ago —and instead of backing his captain, this Carstairs joined up with the mutineers. He saved his neck for the time being, but look at this crew of his: slack, dirty, insubordinate, and they can't go home again. So Carstairs has been sitting on a powder keg.

"No doubt the mother ship is still in orbit. Carstairs probably brought this party down in one of his dispatch boats, because he had no one he could trust to do it for him. He had to leave the ship in the hands of one of his boys he thought would be safe. Technically it takes a full crew to operate a capital ship, but it takes guts to navigate across fifteen light-years of space—and all that would be waiting would be a court-martial and a death penalty." Tey paused thoughtfully.

Nat nodded. "It figures, Cap'n—only, let's not get carried away. Let's see: he parked the lander in the lee of the cliff for security reasons—harder to see, and he's covered on one side. Only, he didn't know about the tectonic activity. So scratch one sideboat."

"Probably," Tey said.

At that moment Carstairs burst from the brush beside them. "All right, I heard most of that," he said, scowling around his cigar. "Stutz had to spill his guts, I suppose?"

"All Stutzie said was 'Good morning,' before he killed himself," Nat replied.

"Killed hisself?" Carstairs yelled. "I got a good mind—"

"No, you haven't," Nat cut him off. "*We* still have long-range space capability, remember? You want to make friends."

"Well, uh," Carstairs muttered, and sidled past Nat. "You two wait right here," he said. "I got to see to my command." He hurried away.

·7·

The dispatch vessel, a slim hundred-yard long modified high-speed craft designed for atmospheric work as well as deep-space navigation, lay on its side in the surf, among jagged rocks and newly fallen boulders. The buckled hullplates amidships revealed that its spine was broken. Men worked in the surf and on the heaped gravel of the rock slide, manning cables they had managed to secure to the ship's hull.

As Tey and Grall watched, a man started out in a rescue sling, crossed halfway, was briefly submerged by a giant comber, and signaled to be hauled back, as the stricken vessel's captain yelled orders and gestured wildly, ignored by the salvage crew.

"They're not accomplishing anything, in spite of Carstairs's help," Tey commented. "It wouldn't matter much if they did get inside. She's not going anywhere without three months in a class-one maintenance depot—and maybe not then."

"Too bad," Nat said. "It appears we'll have to share the planet with this mob of lightweights." He sighed. "Of course we've already got von Shimo and Cleo's crowd, plus Johnny and his gang—already it's looking like a small planet."

Yells sounded as more rubble from the crumbling cliff-face rained down onto the wreck. People near the cliff-edge withdrew hurriedly.

"What's your theory, Cap'n?" Nat asked. "What happened here—back at the beginning, when the Omega people made planetfall three hundred years ago?"

"It's pretty clear, Nat," Tey said, "there was some sort of disaster—maybe a crash landing. At best, putting a vessel the size of the colony ship down on a planetary surface is a tricky business—and when you consider they didn't have the experience or the refinements in equipment we have today, it would be close to impossible. So picture a ship made of eggshells, steered by explosions of TNT, guided by periscopes—and run by a crew more inept than the freshman class at the Academy today.

"It's amazing anyone survived. But we have von Shimo and Jonesu-san and company as clear proof they did. But there was a disagreement, right at the beginning: maybe some wanted to stay with the ship and try to repair it, while others said they had to leave it and learn to make a living off the countryside. So they split into at least two factions. Probably fell out over who would get control of all the supplies and equipment aboard. From that point on—who knows? At any rate they didn't start in building roads and towns."

"Still," Nat said thoughtfully, "they had enough space capability left to set up their picket line off-planet. I wouldn't put much trust in what von Shimo said—but Greylorn's story confirms it. So what did they do?"

"They acted human," Tey said. "They started fighting. As a result, three centuries later, we have bands of nomads like Jonesu-san's bunch wandering around the countryside, plus whatever sort of opposition group von Shimo represents. He claims he's the last survivor of his crowd—and he doesn't consider the nomads human."

"Too bad we let old Shimmy drive off into the sunset in that antique car of his," Nat said. "There are a lot of highly pregnant questions I would've liked to ask him—now that it's too late."

"We'll see to him later," Tey said.

"And I'll bet the story we squeeze out of him will make the rest of this madhouse look routine."

"Where we can have no preconceptions," Tey said, "nothing should surprise us."

· 8 ·

As the two men talked, the crowd had gradually quieted, many of those on the outer fringes wandering off to resume their regular duties. Tey noticed activity around the car in which he and Grall had arrived. It had been moved to the edge of the flood-lit area, where a long, low shed had been improvised from tree branches and canvas. They started toward it. Behind them, Carstairs's voice was still audible, though flagging somewhat, as he harangued his crew.

A stocky man in a stained, but neatly pressed coverall came forward to meet them. His attitude was diffident as he approached. He cleared his throat, half-saluted, then turned the gesture into a careless wave of greeting.

"Yessir, fellows," he said. "Maintenance never sleeps. SCPO Mullen reporting. Have her ready for you in five minutes, topped-off and signed-off, ready for action wherever duty calls. Uh, will you be taking her out right away, sir?" He eyed Tey mournfully, as if expecting the worst.

"That's right, Chief," Tey said. "I'll see that you're mentioned in dispatches."

The mechanic fell in beside Tey. "If you don't mind, sir," he began, "I'd like to ask a like favor. Me and the boys, well, we're kind of wondering what's going on. Ever since the admiral passed away—the real admiral, I mean: Hayle. Not to say Captain Carstairs isn't the finest skipper a man could ask for, but it seems like things have been deteriorating. Chow is bad; supply takes a week to deliver, no maintenance, except of course, us fellas in the motor pool. Some pool: one recon car, and that hadn't been in for PM one time until you turned her in, sir. Good job you did—main fans both cracked, bad bearings on the converter, all that. And now *this* foul-up." The man glanced back toward the scene of activity above the fallen vessel. "Me and Black both put in a protest, under Article Nine, sir, strictly IAR—but poor Jim got two weeks on standby, and I got called things guys get killed for calling people." He paused, deep in thought. "One lousy scooter and six guys—and back at Luna, I had four hundred men in my section, and we were prime for wagons." Mullen spat. "Never thought I'd want to get back there," he added.

"You say the admiral passed away," Tey stated. "Suddenly? Or was he a sick man?"

"Fine on Monday, sick on Tuesday, dead on Wednesday, out the hatch on Thursday. He used to come around the sections, you know; boosting the old morale and all. He was a fine old man. Course it figures he had to get sick sometime, him being eighty years old, or something. Anyway, he made us *want* to soldier right. Now this Carstairs—oops! I mean Cap'n Carstairs or I guess 'Admiral' he calls hisself now—he was the Exec. Then one watch he made a announcement about the admiral, 'line of duty' and all. And had us observe sixty seconds of silence. I tell you, I seen guys crying that was as hard as a hullplate. But since we've had Cap'n Carstairs, nobody seems to care much about anything anymore—and he's a funny kind of brass. You get the feeling he's scared of *you*—" Mullen glanced at Tey as if to see if he had said too much.

"What's the favor you mentioned?" Tey asked.

"Well, you know, sir, 'keep the troops in the dark, they ain't paid to think,' and all that. But we all wanna know where we're at. What *is* this place?" Mullen looked at Tey desperately.

"Weren't you given any orientation before you signed on for the cruise?" Tey inquired.

"They told us it was a regular colony—we were going to meet people out here that built cities and roads and all—and what do we find?" Mullen waved his hand wildly. "Nothing but a big mud flat and one patch of jungle. Some colony!"

"The planet *was* the target of a colonization effort three hundred years ago," Tey explained. "For good reasons the top authorities back home got the impression the colony had been a big success. But—let's face it: it wasn't. There are still some surviving descendents, but they're at war with each other, so nothing's been done to develop the planet. I suppose Captain Carstairs is as confused as are you all, Chief. He doesn't know what to do—especially now, since he's lost his boat. And with the kind of discipline I've seen here—yourself excepted, Mullen —it appears that nothing much will be done about it."

Mullen looked grim. "You're sure right about the discipline, sir. And this was a good bunch—as long as Admiral was in charge. You know, sir, a gang of crew on a long cruise is kinda like a bunch of kids; you know, they get bored and they want something to happen, even if it's bad. They start testing the rules to see how far they can go—what they can get away with.

They *want* to be slapped down, so they know where the boundaries are. Makes 'em feel more secure and all that, you know?" He eyed Tey, who nodded.

"But this Carstairs," Mullen went on. "He yells a lot, but then he don't back it up. If he court-martialed half the guys he said he was gonna, there wouldn't be nobody left to guard the jail. So you can see, sir, why things are bad. We'd been here about a week—and I don't mind telling you we were plenty glad— when we heard Com Section had picked up an R trail; rumors was rife, like they say. We'd've even been glad if it was the inspectors right on our tail, but the com chief said we was out here to track down some damn fool stolen ship of the line—all that jazz. But anyway, Stutz won the toss and plotted an intercept. He was back in two local days—long mothers." Mullen paused.

"Said the bogie was a museum-piece model-C scooter—the kind that was Fleet issue for admirals a few hundred years ago. Guy in it was some kind of Chinaman—talked crazy—but he told Stutz the people he was looking for had thrown in with the 'enemy.' He kept talking about the enemy, you'd've thought you was in the middle of a battlefield, Stutz said. Anyway, he come back in and reported—I got to hear the debriefing tape —and Cap'n looked like he wasn't gonna make a move, so us fellas talked it over and we decided Stutzie better follow up on what this old guy told him.

"So—next thing we know, he comes back—it was his car all right—but you two gents was in it. So we don't hardly know whether to spit or go blind." Mullen spat. "By the way, how *did* you two get ahold of Stutzie's car? Well, not—it ain't Stutzie's, but he was signed out fer it."

"He gave it to us," Nat said. "In his will," he added.

Mullen swiveled to face Grall; as he looked at the big man, he visibly changed his mind about what he was going to say. "Not meaning to stick my nose in," he commented mildly, "but the odo's got more'n twelve hundred miles on 'er, and 'er fuel cell's flat. You timed it close, gents. She's got another five miles on that cell. I'll check over what I got in the back and see if I got a live one. I reckon I do."

"That's excellent news, Mr. Mullen—the last part, I mean," Tey said. "As for our possession of the car, Spaceman Stutz quite accidentally activated the antipersonnel equipment and neglected to station himself in the safe zone."

"That ain't like Stutz," Mullen said. "He was a skunk, but he was a spaceman."

"A local chief was present," Tey added. "He doubtless accorded the remains the same respect and ceremony he would his own mother."

"It ain't Stutzie's remains I'm worried about, sir," Mullen stated. "You know," he added, "we're getting low on chow, Messarnt says, and his *bad* news is always on the square. We have to find a local source, or we'll be down to long pig and water." He looked with disapproval at the surrounding foliage, backed by great gray-leaved trees. "Says ain't nothing grows here we can eat, neither." He paused.

"Hey, look yonder," he said, pointing.

A small animal had emerged from the deep shade of the 'jungle,' and paused in a patch of sunlight. As it stretched its limbs, one at a time, six small duplicates of itself came tumbling into view and arranged themselves in a row beside the larger creature, which flopped on its side to permit its young to lunch.

"Looks kind of like a beaver," Mullen said. "How come they got beavers way out here on this God-forsaken mud-ball? I reckon a feller could eat beaver," he added.

"Hold everything, Chief," Tey said. "It must be descended from whatever kind of animals the *Omega* people brought along. They probably had the seed stock for all the useful farm animals."

"Yessir," Mullen said. "And I never seen a vessel over fifty ton yet didn't have rats aboard."

"Some rat," Grall said. "The babies are bigger than the full-grown *Rattus rattus* I saw at the zoo once."

"And *they've* apparently found something to eat," Tey commented.

"Funny I never seen one before," Mullen mused. "Been here a Standard week or more, and seen no signs of 'em." He stopped, came up with a fist-sized stone. "A fella can't eat rats," he said. Tey restrained him from pegging the stone at the animal.

"What are the chances of salvaging the boat?" Tey inquired of the maintenance chief.

"Not good with the manpower on hand, sir," Mullen replied. "I don't reckon she's hurt too bad—spite of the buckling." His voice grew enthusiastic: "If I had the equipment . . ." He let it trail off. "Might as well say, 'If it wouldn't of fell over in the first place.'"

"Still, I suppose you'll have to try," Tey said.

"Not me, sir!" Mullen responded at once. "Not with Carstairs jumping up and down on me, and no tools and no help." He glanced at Tey to judge his reaction to the insubordinate remark.

Tey nodded. "I understand how you feel," he said. "But with your ship waiting in orbit, the boat's your only way home."

Mullen looked dejected. "Reckon I got to do some thinking," he said. "Main item's a hoist, of course. And that water in her antiac box ain't gonna help."

"Don't you have land-based communications?" Tey asked.

"Must have," Mullen replied, more brightly. "Carstairs would have a setup in his hut yonder."

· 9 ·

They had arrived at the improvised maintenance shed, where, beside the car, three grimy men eyed them, tools down, as they came up.

"All right, Jackson, report!" Mullen barked. One of the three came forward; Mullen went to meet him, and the two engaged in a low-voiced exchange. Mullen turned back, looking cheerful.

"Got a new cell in her, gents," he stated. "Jack says she's in good shape: I'll inspect her now and see for myself." He got into the car and started up.

Tey caught Nat's eye and they moved off into the deep shade of a giant tree and sat on a plank set up there for the purpose.

"We'd better decide on a course of action," Tey said. "So far, we've been drifting with the tide."

"Say, Captain," Grall replied, "somebody's been working hard to lead us astray. Look at this." He showed Tey a small, greenish nodule, looking very insignificant lying alone in his callused palm.

"It's an acorn," Tey said. "Strange. There was no oak pollen in that soil test we ran."

"One test isn't much," Nat commented.

"No doubt," Tey said, "the *Omega* expedition brought along seeds of many kinds, probably including a few by accident—like the rats. Eventually they'd have a need for timber, and by then it would be available." He took the acorn from Grall's hand and examined it closely.

"Let's plant it," he suggested. "We'll call it the Decision Oak, because right now we've got to make some very important decisions."

A few feet away the car started up with a howl, and a blast of air and dead leaves.

"At this point," Tey said seriously, "we can throw in with Carstairs and count on finding an opportunity to take over his vessel, with or even without the use of force."

"Or we can go on blundering around the landscape," Nat commented, "running into one set of nuts after another, until we hit pay dirt."

"Exactly," Tey said. "I vote to keep on as we have, maybe getting a little better at it as we go along. Somewhere on this benighted dirt-ball, there *has* to be somebody who can give us a few sensible answers. Maybe at this Prime we heard about."

"Suits me," Nat said. "Somehow, I don't think Carstairs and I would ever become real pals." Nat looked out across the featureless tundra. "Someday," he said, "all this will be developed into farms and cities and golf courses and roads; and some forlorn little band of nature nuts will be staging a campaign to get the government to buy up a few square miles of the original, unspoiled tundra so they can fence it in and let the tourists come to look at it at so much a head."

"We may be standing on the future Manhattan of New

Terra," Tey suggested. "They'll be saying, 'If I'd just had the foresight to buy a few lots off Seventh Avenue here, back before they paved it, I'd be a billionaire now!' Picture it, Nat: crowding, smog, noise, uncollected garbage, bad smells, people jostling each other—all the benefits of civilization."

Nat looked glumly at the patch of woods, into which the small animals had disappeared.

"Don't kid me, Captain," he said in a level tone. "You're no 'aren't-we-humans-terrible' cynic. In fact you're the only really starry-eyed romantic I ever met. Naturally civilization's not all tulip gardens and little girls in party dresses—but it's not all Recpark and treachery, either. How about, say, a farm about ten miles square, with a big white farmhouse full of healthy people who love to farm, and a big red barn full of hay for happy cows, and a big, shady woodlot, and a forty foot well with a crank and a bucket, and lots of pretty white fences . . ."

"So that's your dream," Tey commented gently. "Here on Omega, you might even have it one day."

"Let's call that a Decision, Cap'n," Nat replied. "I don't know where I got that farm from; all the farm I ever saw was a clay pot with one red geranium in it." His eyes were still on the bleak landscape. "It's going to take some work, Cap'n," he pointed out.

"It's strange how in our culture 'work' has become equated with 'bad,'" Tey put in. "I suppose the biblical remark about 'eat(ing) thy bread in the sweat of thy face' has something to do with it. Physical exertion feels good to anyone in good health, and after our work-haters have gotten themselves a spot where they can sit all day, they go out and spend their time off walking all over a golf course, or cranking in swordfish, or even hiking up mountainsides. But that's not 'work,' so it's OK."

"A few hundred years ago," Nat said, "every small town—and they *were* small—had a tailor and a shoemaker and a black-smith, and all of 'em were craftsmen who could take pride in their work—and don't tell me they didn't get a lot of satisfaction out of what they did. Then somebody thought up factories and mass production and cheap materials, and pretty soon only the big shots could have tailormade suits and hand-lasted shoes, and the factory workers got the worst shafting of all—they lost the satisfaction of doing a job they could be proud of."

"You had me fooled, Nat," Tey replied. "I had no idea you were a lay sociologist."

"I don't know about that," Nat said, "but we had an old family heirloom when I was a kid: a big wrought-iron door latch and lock that was hammered out of a bar of raw iron by my umpteen-greats grandpa. It was pretty crude compared with a modern cyberkey, but you could see the skill and the pride the old man had put into it. It was kept because it was his masterpiece —the item he made to prove to the guild that he should be promoted to the rank of master blacksmith. Funny . . . we use 'masterpiece' as if it meant the crowning achievement of a master, when it's really student work. Anyway, I used to rook at that thing—I took it apart once, and looked at the works— and wondered how he could do it, with no plans and no patterns —just him and his hammer and anvil and a piece of iron. Maybe here on Omega we'll have the chance to try it all again—and get it right this time."

Now it was Tey who studied the vast sweep of monotonous gray-green before them.

"A whole planet," he mused. "It's so damn big, and we're so small. It doesn't seem we could ever see all of it, much less cover it with concrete."

"And palace gardens and swimming pools and parks," Nat amended. "But whatever we do, we have to start somewhere, and sometime."

The two men turned their attention back to the group of mechanics standing by the car.

ELEVEN

Decision and Disaster

SCPO Mullen seems like a good fellow," Grall said. "I suggest we tell him the situation before we run off in his only vehicle." He spat out a fragment of leaf, squinting through the settling dust cloud.

Tey nodded. "By all means," he said.

The two men rose and went over to the car, which was now idling, bobbing slightly on its air cushion a few inches above the bare humus exposed by the air blast. Mullen grinned at them, gave the ancient A-OK sign with thumb and forefinger. He climbed out, looking pleased and glum simultaneously, an expression too complex for his broad, simple features to cope with.

"Dammit, gents," he said, "she's lined up to a RCH, but she's still got that wobble on idle. But I'd be willing to sign her off serviceable." He patted the sleek gray flank of the car. "Uh," he began, "you gents *did* say you were taking her out right away, din't you?"

"Mr. Mullen," Nat said genially, placing a large hand on the mechanic's shoulder to draw him aside, "permit me to introduce myself. I'm Nat Grall, and my friend is Captain Taliaferro Tey. He looks like an easy-going sort of chap, but don't ever try to con him. Just a friendly tip, you understand."

"Tey . . ." Mullen repeated dully. "Ex-captain Tey, that's the maniac they said run off with Lord Banshire's showpiece new cruiser." Mullen eyed Tey surreptitiously. *"He doesn't look crazy,"* he told himself reassuringly.

"Mr. Mullen," Nat said soberly, "Captain Tey is the least crazy man you'll ever meet. I don't know, naturally, what story you were given about the crazy man who stole a battleship, but the facts are, he didn't come directly to Omega by chance. Actually, a human colony has existed here for three hundred years. That fact has been known to the authorities for over a century. Yet the overcrowding of Terra has continued unabated, because a few selfish men feared an emigration program might upset their power base."

"Gosh," Mullen said.

"Captain Tey learned of this situation, which is the real reason he was publicly discredited and cashiered. He then took matters into his own hands, the only way to pinpoint Omega."

"And you helped him," Mullen added.

"I certainly did, to the fullest extent of my ability," Grall said. "The question at this point is: are you with us?"

Mullen turned his head to gaze in the general direction of Carstairs's headquarters tent.

"Between you fellas and *him*," he said, "that's easy."

"Don't make a snap decision, Mr. Mullen," Grall cautioned. "You'll be bucking the Navy, Lord Banshire, and common sense. Captain Tey and I are going to get the news back to the Terran public, somehow. Lord Banshire won't like that. You'd be putting your life on the line."

"I'm with you," Mullen said steadily. "Let's get started."

· 2 ·

Tey used the car's radio to call *Princeton* on the agreed emergency band. There was no reply. He set the transmitter on automatic, to repeat call and reply codes.

"Something's seriously wrong," Nat said to Tey. "Otherwise they'd be monitoring that band on automatic, at least."

"Let's find out," Tey said. Mullen was at the wheel. Tey gave him a heading, having, by long habit, at all times maintained by dead reckoning a precise knowledge of his position relative to that of his ship. They hummed along, skimming the surface of the bog at cruise, which the car could maintain indefinitely on its fully charged power core. As they sped south, the unbroken shallow-water surface gradually yielding to occasional dry ridges, all lying at right angles to their course. The ridges grew more distinct and at last merged, as the soil level eventually rose above sea level, an expanse of shiny black muck, densely matted with short vegetation, now sodden and limp. Ahead, there were only interconnected ponds now, and beyond, a broad sweep of undrowned tundra.

"How many of Jonesu-san's folks could we load onto the crawler?" Nat asked Tey.

"Under ideal conditions and using emergency evacuation procedures, with a cargo flat in tow, we can haul three hundred and nine, according to FSAM 119-6B," Tey replied.

Mullen, who had been squinting against the glare of reflected sky on the wet ground while scanning the horizon for the first glimpse of the ship, spoke up:

"Cap'n, with respect and all, what's the use of doing the rescue number on this Johnny-Sue bird? From what you told me, sounds like they could be awfully hard to handle if they decided to get rough."

"Simple humanitarianism, Mr. Mullen," Grall said in mock rhetorical style. "Beside that, we need help to get that side-boat of yours in shape."

"Well, yessir," Mullen said. "But . . . I guess it ain't up to me to be second-guessing you fellows, but this amounts to siding this Johnny against whoever it is he's scared of."

"Scared of?" Nat echoed. "I don't recall our saying he was scared."

"Sounds like a scared man to me," Mullen persisted. "He's running from somebody. I'll bet you my next three promotions against a Y-ration steak."

"I tend to agree with you, Chief," Tey said. "And it's not Colonel General von Shimo he's worried about. We've been postulating two factions, represented by Johnny and von Shimo —but on consideration, while they evinced a sort of routine of mutual hostility, they didn't strike me as taking it very seriously."

"What about these Guardians you say both of them mentioned?" Nat suggested.

"We don't know enough to make any intelligent plans," Tey said. "All the more reason for getting to Johnny for a heart-to-heart talk and some plain answers."

"Uh, Captain," Mullen said, "how far away did you say this ship is?"

There was a moment of silence as all three men looked out at the featureless wetlands that stretched into hazy distance on all sides.

"She's gone, all right," Tey said. "We're within a mile of where we left her, and she'd not only be visible, but conspicuous, at three times that distance. So she's really gone," he repeated, "from any angle. Mr. Mullen, do you see a ship of the line anywhere around here?"

"Not me, Cap'n sir."

"Strange," Grall said. "Ollie wouldn't have lifted her short-handed and said he didn't, without a very good reason—and I can't think of one."

·3·

Slowly the car approached the patch of disturbed ground, a roughly circular depression now filled with brown water, where the great vessel had been.

"If it's here, gentlemen, it's very cleverly disguised," Mullen said in mock solemnity.

"Time to break out Plan B," Tey said. "But unfortunately we don't even have a Plan A."

"No use getting back to Johnny and his band of slowly sinking citizens," Nat said. "All we could do would be stand by and watch."

"We've got to find von Shimo. He might have resources."

"Where do we look?" Grall eyed Mullen. "Your man Stutz who saw him didn't get a line on him, did he?" The driver shook his head. "If it was the same dude," he commented. "Didn't get his name."

"Let's try to raise *Catrice* on the car com here," Nat suggested, and turned to the Standard Fleet band. There was a little star static, but nothing more.

Mullen supplied his mother ship's emergency code, called it a dozen times with no response, then a flat voice came in:

"—here, about time. Identify."

"SCPO Mullen here," he replied. "We got plenty problems down here, Tubby. We need help in the worst way."

"And that's the way you'll get it, if I know Light Commander Gross. What's eating you?"

"It's what we *ain't* eating, Tubman," Mullen came back. Then, aside to Nat, he explained, "Tubman's Com Section NCOIC. A pretty good man; buddy of mine."

Ignoring the idle chatter, Tey prepared to debark. Warmish air struck his face as he opened the hatch.

"I'm going to look over the ground," he told Nat.

"Careful, sir," Mullen advised. "We don't know how solid that ground is." He peered out at it, looking doubtful. Tey stepped down, felt firm soil under a half-inch squashy layer.

"You gents were plenty lucky to pick a hard spot," Mullen said. "Or maybe it wasn't luck."

"The albedo analysis said vegetation," Grall responded. "We imagined something like Nebraska. But it was frozen solid when we put down."

"Funny country," Mullen commented. "We looked all over, hunting for that patch of woods. Seems like the high ground is all around the edge of the island. There's more trees spotted along the shore farther east, above the cliffs."

"Apparently the island plate is overriding the continent," Nat commented. "We're high and relatively dry here because the island has a slightly domed configuration. Subject to earthquakes, or omegaquakes."

"Yessir, we felt a couple tremors just before the big one flipped the boat," Mullen replied. His expression reflected disapproval. "Don't see how anybody picked this lousy place for a colony," he added. Then, into the microphone, he said, "I'll get back to you, Tubby," and switched off.

"From near-space it looks good," Grall pointed out. "Surface gravity, solar intensity, atmospheric composition—even that deceptive albedo."

"Sure," Mullen conceded. "But the whole place can't be like this island with its bag of tricks. How come they didn't settle in over on the mainland? On a clear day a fella can see the trees over there."

"That's the old element of luck, I suppose," Grall said. "Or maybe they *are* established elsewhere."

· 4 ·

While Grall and Mullen were speculating, Captain Tey had been reconnoitering the area around the ship's former parking space. He paused to study a series of small water pockets of declining size which extended in a curve away from the central puddle. Abruptly he returned to the car.

"Somebody with a very fine hand jet-walked her away from here," he told the others. "About a hundred yards out there's some chewed-up soil that could mean anything from a normal liftoff to a necktie party." He climbed in and took the driver's seat which Mullen had vacated. "Let's go," he said. "Take your last looks, men."

"What at, sir?" Mullen inquired.

"Where to?" Grall inquired. "You sound as if you have a destination in mind, my captain."

"The mainland," Tey said. "Where else is there?"

"What about the cliff, sir?" Mullen asked. "A cushion car can handle water with no sweat, but how do we get down that fifty-foot drop?"

"I think we'll find that the cliff doesn't stay strictly with the shoreline," Tey replied. "I explored to the west from here and came to what must surely be the same fault line well up on the slope. The island is dome-shaped, you know; only a few feet of difference in elevation, but it's enough to give us this relatively high and dry ground near the center; and the cliff is a fault relieving the stress of the island plate compressing between East Continent and North Continent."

"Oh," Mullen said. "I guess all that high-level geology stuff is over my head, Cap'n," Mullen said. "The whole place is screwy to me."

"To me, too, Mr. Mullen," Nat said. "Nonetheless, I'm content to accept the assurances of Captain Tey that we can probably find a way down—or more accurately, a level beach."

"Sure," Mullen agreed. "I didn't mean— Oh, hell, I don't know what I mean."

"Chief," Tey addressed the puzzled mechanic in a change-of-subject tone, "this car being assigned as the admiral's gig, I assume it has class-four capability."

"You mean the transmitting graphic materials and all?" Mullen inquired rhetorically. "Sure, sir. First-class outfit." He looked inquiringly at Tey.

"Get back in touch with Tubman, please," Tey directed the SCPO. "Tell him to transmit a high-resolution vertical centered on our fix, corrected orthographically, of course. Any convenient scale."

Max nodded and flipped switches. "Listen, Tubman," he said without preamble, "I got a hot-G item. Shoot me a stretched straight-down, with all garbage filtered through three. Got that? Do it. Out."

·5·

Less than a Standard minute later the class-four unit hummed briefly, and the required document dropped into the hopper below the instrument panel, smelling of volatiles, but clearly delineated in finely detailed black-line. It showed the northern half of the island, including the areas of contact with North and East Continents. The three men studied it in silence for a moment before Tey spoke:

"The plate is oceanic no doubt, so it's thin, which is why it's bowed up under the pressure. The bowing means the uppermost rocks are in tension, and the basement is in compression. The small quakes are undoubtedly due to the slipping proceeding along the M-discontinuity interface. As for the tension, there'll be thinning and eventually a major rupture." He ran his finger along a band of faintly lighter color which ran from near the apex of the island down across what would necessarily be the crust of the shallow dome.

"We're close to the maximum stress zone," Tey said. After a moment's consideration he addressed a question to Mullen:

"What's the periodicity of the quakes, Max? According to Stelzl's hypothesis, there's a direct ratio of adjustment frequency to the time of failure in tension."

"Irregular, Captain," Mullen said. "I timed the first few close: twenty-six hours three minutes plus, peak-to-peak for the first three; then we skipped one and got the biggy that started the slide that dumped the gig at fifty-three hours."

"If I'm recalling Stelzl's equations correctly, and I am," Tey said, "and assuming we get the next shock back on your twenty-six hour schedule, which I expect, she's due to crack wide open within two hundred and fifty Standard hours. We should make it a point to be a long way from here by then."

· 6 ·

With that, Nat took the driver's position and gunned the car forward in a cloud of fine mist thrown up by the small high-speed starting rotors.

Tey broke the glum silence of the last few minutes by addressing Mullen. "Chief, do you suppose your mate Tubby would break one more reg for us?"

"Sure, Cap'n," Mullen replied confidently. "Long's he don't have to get off his butt to do it."

"How about asking him to use his long-range IFF gear to see if he can raise *Princeton*?"

"Just gimme the numbers, sir," Mullen said. "Old Tubby thinks he's a hot shot when it comes to bottle-feeding a signal that almost ain't there."

A moment later Tubman breezily confirmed: "I'll put her right in your lap, gents—if she's inside a .00019SU volume centered on this here planet."

After long minutes of white noise, Tey thought he heard Jaxon's distinctive voice. ". . . what to do. Try . . . soon as possible. . . ."

"Or did I imagine it?" he asked Grall, who confirmed that there had indeed been a snatch of speech mingled with the static.

Abruptly, the voice came in loud and clear; "—our screens have all gone dead. I sure wish you were here, Captain. It's beyond me—and Renee and Sugar, too, for that matter. Instrument readings are crazy, and the lock is jammed. This is something the manual doesn't cover, Captain!"

"Stand fast, Ollie," Tey replied. "We'll get to the bottom of it. Don't try to open the hatch. Just sit tight. Ohano."

"—hear your voice. Faint, but read you about sixteen. Arano," Jaxon came back, then added: "Thank God you're all right. You *are* all right, aren't you?"

Tubman's voice cut in. "My arandee says three and a half hey you, on a line with Altair 2. Who do you know way out there, Mull?"

Nat shook his head, not in negation, but in puzzlement. "Got any ideas, Cap'n?" he grunted. Tey addressed Mullen: "Perhaps there's some mistake," he said almost hopefully.

"Tubby could be wrong about a lot of things, sir," the NCO stated firmly. "But com gear—no sir, Captain, sir. If he says three and a half Sols, three and a half Sols is where it's at."

"Cap'n," Nat said grimly, "they're in trouble. Big trouble."

"Talking about it won't help them," Tey said. "Let's go find this Prime and get a few answers."

"Cap'n," Nat said, "we don't know the questions."

"All right, Nat," Tey said. "We'll start with those." He was still studying the photo map. "Look here, Nat," he said, pointing to the delineation. "We'd better stop." Grall complied. As the wiper-field dispelled the last of the mist that had collected on the canopy, Tey adjusted the map so as to smooth the upper right portion, and switched on an interior light. "Right here," he indicated an almost featureless area. "Am I seeing things, or is there a configuration of very fine lines converging here? We're near the edge of it."

"It's there, Cap'n," Grall replied thoughtfully. "Or maybe radiating from the blurry spot there. But what do you suppose it means?"

"Trails," Tey said without hesitation. "For comparison, look over here: you can barely make our own backtrack across the bog area. Those lines look about the same. And you can see the big loop Jonesu-san was making. Looks like he was trying to avoid the spider's web, maybe."

"This must be Shimmy's line in to us," Nat commented, pointing. "If it is, he gave that patch a wide berth, too."

"It looks like that must be question number one," Tey commented. "Or maybe one through four hundred and sixteen."

"I'll bet you made that up, Cap'n," Nat said. "The four hundred and sixteen, I mean. Anyway, I quit when I got to three hundred and twelve, because I was getting duplication."

"I'll split it with you, Nat," Tey said, and swinging the car in a wide circle, he set off across the empty landscape.

·7·

It was half an hour before Nat, who had been studying the terrain closely, said:

"Not bad, Cap'n; about two degrees port to line up with this track here."

"I'm making a beeline, Nat," Tey replied. "I noticed on our map that the trails diverge around an outcropping of some sort, a few miles ahead."

"Pardon me," Nat said. "Someday I'm likely to learn that when it comes to navigation, you're pretty near as good as Tubby is at tracking down ghosts." He frowned. "What in the nine hells do you suppose they're doing way out there?"

"On second thought," Tey said, "I think maybe we ought to check out this outcropping. It ought to be visible any time now." Even as he spoke, a vague bulk, tiny with distance, became apparent on the otherwise featureless horizon, slightly to the left of dead ahead.

"More ruins?" Nat murmured. He took the small binocular from the car's equipment rack. "Looks like somebody started to build a garbage scow and quit in the middle," he commented, passing the glass to Tey, who examined the structure.

"A curious way to go about assembling a pressure hull," he

said. "As if they'd begun with a quadrant of the main frame and finished it up, from life-support volume interior deco right out to ablative, like a long wedge of melon."

· 8 ·

As the distance closed with surprising quickness, it became apparent that the structure was indeed a sector seemingly cleanly sliced from a deep-space hull of antique design. Nat halted the air-cushion car ten feet from the object.

"Even has space burn on the exposed hull metal," Tey commented as they climbed out. "And what look like rock burns, as if she'd put down on a planetary surface—which is highly impractical, as well as a violation of Space Arm regulations. Some sort of parade float, maybe, made of papier-mâché."

The turf close to the up-looming curve of the realistically scarred pseudohull was marked by the wheels of contact vehicles as well as footprints, the latter marked lightly against the previously well-flattened tundra growth. Tey was examining the curved surface which ended so abruptly above.

"How far up is that edge?" Nat inquired.

"Fourteen feet, three and a half inches," Tey responded promptly. He turned to the mechanic. "Mr. Mullen, do you think you could stand on my shoulders?" he asked and turned to face the hull. Mullen looked puzzled but said, "Sure," and stepped closer. Nat lifted him overhead at an arm's length, and after a moment of uncertainty, the SCPO put a foot on Tey's shoulder and, steadying himself with both hands against the out-curved metal wall, brought up the other. He groped higher on the wall. "Too high," he reported. "We need another three feet."

"Climb down, Mr. Mullen," Nat said. Then he made a stirrup with both hands, Tey stepped in, and seconds later he and Mullen were standing on Grall's shoulders. Mullen grabbed the metal edge, pulled his weight off the human ladder, and Tey jumped down. Above, Mullen leaned out over the edge.

"It's the same on the inside," he called down. "All here, right down to the I-burns around station ninety-seven—" He broke off abruptly, uttering a choked cry.

Tey and Grall exchanged glances; then Tey, two yards from the hull, dropped to one knee and put the other knee and both fists on the damp sod, bracing himself. Nat turned and walked away a few paces, then turned again, crouched briefly, and dug off like a sprinter leaving the blocks. Two astonishingly quick bounds, and the third off the platform of Tey's back, then high against the hull, the thick fingers of one reaching hand grabbing for purchase on the edge, and he was up and over. Sounds of violence followed at once. As Tey stepped back and looked up, a man came over the top, silhouetted for an instant against the verdigris sky in the spread-eagle pose of a leaping frog. A strangled yell accompanied his flight, cut off abruptly as he slammed into the turf with a squashy *thud!* and lay face down.

Tey went to him and saw at once that he was breathing strongly. One leg was in a curious doubled-under position not attained by intact bones. The man, clothed in worn garments of anonymous cut, was small, with a scrawny neck and tangled black hair, hacked short. He opened his eyes, blinked, and attempted to rise, then emitted a screech and subsided, sobbing.

"Never even seen them other six fellers," he complained.

"Never mind that," Tey said without sympathy. "You broke a leg when you jumped. Just sit still, and we'll get it set."

· 9 ·

Mullen's face appeared above the gunwale, looking shocked. A trickle of bright red emerged from his hairline to trace a brilliant, crooked line across his dusty cheek.

"Came at me like a wildcat," he commented. "Clobbered me with a number five grab-wrench." He reached up to touch the top of his head tenderly. "Time I threw the sucker up against the wall, saw one more, and he was just leaving. Old Nat—uh, Mr. Grall—hardly got himself warmed up."

Nat's face appeared beside Mullen's. "Scared up some garbage mice, looks like, Cap'n," he said mildly. "Looks like they been camping here for a long time. Wish you'd come up and take a look, Cap'n;" he concluded, and leaned far out to extend a hand. Tey took two quick steps toward the hull, jumped, and his hand slapped Nat's and was at once enclosed in a grip which easily lifted him over the side.

"What about that sucker, gents?" Mullen asked, nodding toward the man below who was busily inching his way toward the ground-car. Mullen went over the side. Tey glanced at the scene and said, loudly enough to include the injured man, "If he touches it, Mr. Mullen, jump on him. Break the other leg and a couple of arms. Save the neck for later, so he can tell us a few things." The scrawny man at once became still, playing possum with one eye half-open. Mullen stood over him. The injured man twisted his head to look up at the husky SCPO. "I'm—" he grunted, "tellin' you nothin'."

"You're gonna be prenty sorry you crossed the rine," he added in a hoarse voice.

"That was the Third Army, Buster," Mullen corrected. "What's Hitler's War got to do with it?"

The man, as if emboldened by Mullen's jocular response, raised himself on one elbow, wincing as he did. Mullen put a foot on the back of the fellow's neck and pressed him back, comparatively gently. "Just stay put, Buster," he admonished mildly.

"Name's not Buster, Pokker," the prone man objected, his speech blurred by a mouth full of wet turf.

"You may address me as 'sir'—" Mullen informed him, "when I give you permission to speak, that is," he added.

"You'll find out prenty quick we don't mess around with any suckers tryin' to pass over the Don't Rine."

"I've heard of the Dew Line," Mullen said in a relaxed way, at the same time pressing the fellow's face firmly into the sod.

"In case I didn't make it clear, Buster, keep your yap shut until I tell you to speak."

Buster made muffled sounds, and Mullen relaxed the pressure of his foot slightly.

"OK, shoot, Buster," he said in a tone of command. "But keep it short—and porite."

"We'll show you 'porite,'" Buster snarled. "Take maybe two, three minutes, then rook out!"

"Aboard the hull-slice," Mullen called.

Tey's head and shoulders came into view at once.

"Seems like Buster here is expecting reinforcements, sir," Mullen reported. "He says about two minutes."

"Talkative fellow," Tey commented.

"A real blabbermouth," Mullen agreed, "but not very porite."

"See if he won't suppry a few detairs," Tey suggested. "Watching all sides at once is a nuisance."

"Sir," Mullen said, "I predict he's going to suppry prenty of detairs. In fact, he's eager to." He glanced down at the gaunt face glaring up at him. "Right, Blabby?"

"Tell you nothing, Pokker," Blabby snarled.

Mullen shook his head. "I don't know who Pokker is, Blab," he said, "but I'm not him. You may call me 'sir.'"

Blabby made no reply, except to comment: "Better get busy watching all sides, rike your boss said."

"Oh, Cap'n," Mullen called to him. "Blabby says they're going to hit you from behind."

"From inside this stage set, I assume you mean," Tey replied. "Anything more? Where are they hiding?"

"Hidin' no prace," Blabby rebutted at once. "Rive there, pretty big tunners—come up everyprace."

"OK, Blabby, that's all I need from you," Mullen said briskly, and pressed the man's face down firmly into the soft, moist sod.

"Now don't move, or I'll break whatever I see that's not still," Mullen cautioned. Blabby's reply was a bubbly grunt.

· 10 ·

Mullen returned to the hull, and Tey hoisted him over the side.

"Seems we're sitting on top of an outret to a tunner system," he reported. "Must be a hatch here somewhere.... Sure! Should be an access to the backup auxiliary emergency bypass circuitry for number five close-support battery. Got to be right over here beyond bulkhead Forty-one." He moved toward the archlike structured number.

"Don't be too confident, Mr. Mullen," Tey suggested. "This is just a dummy, remember."

"Sure, Captain," Mullen replied. "But here it is. Shall I open it up, sir? Looks like it's been used right recently," he added. "No dust on the hinges and all."

"Right, Mr. Mullen," Grall put in. "I was sure there was more than one of those boys. That's their bolt hole."

"Look here," Mullen said excitedly. "Where this here bulkhead ends: conduits, tubing, wires, V-guides—everything's here, all cut off clean at the same level. She's built to Navy specs, right down to the supply code on the insulation."

"But one thing is very clear," Tey commented. "Whatever this thing is, it certainly wasn't built by a human being."

TWELVE

In the Vaults

Faint sounds from below indicated the imminent counterattack. All three men moved back flat against the hull.

"What'll it be, Cap'n?" Nat inquired. "Hit the first sucker through, or let 'em think they're pulling a fast one, and then clobber 'em?"

"The latter," Tey said shortly. "We don't want to give any tail-end Charlies a chance to go back home to think it over."

At that moment, with a dry rasp, the hatch flew open and a face much like Blabby's emerged, glanced about in a cursory way, failing to see the three men to his left rear, ducked back, and yelled shrilly. An instant later he came through with a bound and encountered Nat's hand, which clamped over the lower half of his thin face at the same moment that he was lifted and pitched over the side. The second man got so far as to have one knee on the deck; Tey lifted him and boosted him over the side so quickly that the two men's yells blended. Mullen took the third, paused to administer a sharp rap to the jaw as the astonished newcomer kicked frantically at the knees of the burly NCO. Mullen lifted him over the side, glanced below, and dropped him atop his two predecessors, who were just rising uncertainly, knocking them flat again. They responded with yells and blows.

Beyond, Blabby lay as instructed, his eyes rolled toward the heap of his comrades. Mullen caught his eye, and made a cutting motion across his throat, even as another man joined the melee. As Mullen turned to resume work, he was, for an instant, face-to-face with Tey. "Looks like the boys are having a little misunderstanding, Cap'n," he reported briskly.

"Fine," Tey replied; he offered his powergun. "If any one of them touches the car, wing him."

The violence, though intense, was brief. When the eighth and last man had been put over the side, the three defenders at once went through the still-open hatch, ignoring the yells of the evicted men and the shower of damp clods lobbed over the side at them. The passage, at first a metal-lined tube, soon debouched into a cold, damp, moldy-odored chamber with smooth stone walls. From it a low tunnel led away into total blackness.

"Looks like a natural cave system," Tey commented. At the captain's request Mullen lit the red disaster lamp which was a part of every noncom's standard suit issue. Without further delay or discussion, they set off, crouched awkwardly, Tey in the lead. It was clear that they were in a natural water-cut cavern. It twisted gently, but continued on a basically eastward course.

·2·

"It trends downward at a ratio of about 1:100," Tey commented. "We're not far from the coast. Presumably we'll emerge at the cliff-face."

There was no evidence to suggest that nine men had come this way a few minutes before. The air was fresh, with a slight flow uphill. After half an hour Tey called a halt, and the men gratefully stretched their limbs. Lying on the smooth floor, they could see a hint of cold light gleaming far ahead. Another five minutes' clumsy progress brought them into a rough-hewn chamber, where with great relief they were able to stand at last. It was clearly a storeroom, its walls banked with shelving of unplaned grayish-green planks, heaped with what at a glance appeared to be pipe fittings, electrical connectors, switchgear, and the like. By the inadequate illumination from a light-well aided by Mullen's lamp, Tey examined a few of the unpackaged articles, noting that each bore a stock number.

"Looks like we've stumbled onto somebody's supply depot," he commented. "Maybe a government installation: all this stuff is obsolete Navy issue. But it's no official depot—not with everything dumped at random. No bin numbers, even. So it's *not* an official installation—more likely a thieves' cache."

"Look here," Mullen blurted, holding out a nine-ounce power-pistol for the others' examination. "Whole box of 'em," he added, "still in neolene."

Tey took the weapon and looked it over carefully. Mark X Browning patent," he commented, "replaced by the Colt 8.5 in '38. Precisely the same weapon Shimmy was carrying, and also the one Johnny had, before you mashed it into the mud, Nat."

"Whoever's manufacturing handguns, even out-of-date ones," Nat commented, "is somebody we want to meet."

· 3 ·

Tey nodded and they resumed their progress, encountering, in this next short stretch of tunnel, a few bits of litter, suggesting that this part of the cavern received more usage, and less inspection, than the outer leg to the surface. The light grew stronger, and at last they climbed a flight of rough-hewn steps to emerge in a wood-paneled chamber that clearly was in current use as a packing-and-shipping department, with larger bins, heaps of empty crates, and coils of baling wire. A skylight of irregular shape shed light on the scene.

"Can't be far now," Mullen said, edging toward the exit passage. He paused at a bin half full of what appeared to be second-hand clothing.

". . . Westrat issues better stuff than this to DU's,*" he commented, holding up a worn duty jacket.

---

*'Designated Undesirables' was the term applied by the then-regime at Granyauk to political agitators whom, for policy reasons, it chose not to kill outright (Captain Taliaferro Tey being an example).

"Hold it," Tey said in a tone that was low, but clearly of command. Mullen nodded and in a stage whisper said: "Coming. More'n one. Close."

At Tey's terse "Take cover" each of the three men quickly selected a narrow space between bins and wedged himself in. Footfalls sounded loudly near at hand, and a heavyset man in a bleached and much-patched issue coverall entered the room and went briskly to the clothing bin. He picked through the garments, some scarcely less worn than his own shabby costume, muttering as he held up one after another and tossed it scornfully aside.

Mullen had selected a hiding place close to a roughly cut archway opening on a second chamber. The heavyset man went past him, less than a foot away, dragging a dirty rag that had once been a shipsuit. He seemed to pause momentarily, then went on into the other room. By this time another man, taller and thinner, and similarly garbed, had arrived and passed through the storeroom without pausing, to continue along the downstream passage. A moment later the profound silence was broken by a hoarse yell.

· 4 ·

"Hank! Where'n herr ya got to? Rooky here, Hank! Pokkers been in here: shooter rayin' here, here amongst the warrs and awr!"

"Shut yer head, Splinter," Hank's deeper tones came back. He reemerged from the side-room and went down the steps to join the tall man. A low-muttered conversation followed.

Tey emerged silently from his cranny and stationed himself beside the passage to overhear what he could.

". . . no Pokkers here. Ya know Harney and them went out to check up—"

"And ain't come back yet," Splinter retorted. "See here, Hank! Shooter was took off the shelf yonder and put in here, where it don't belong. Wasn't there a hour ago, or Porky'd had somebody's guts for garters. You know that."

"Porky prolly stuck it in there himself. Maybe just to check on how sharp we are. Well, we're sharp!"

"Ain't sayin' we ain't sharp," Splinter conceded. "But I say let's purge the system."

"Cain't do that without no orders—ya know that, Splint."

"This here's a emergency, Hank. Go ahead and mask up. I'll seal off and let her rip."

Tey risked a look along the passage, saw the tall figure of Splinter opening a gray-painted wall panel which he recognized as a standard Navy-style valve closet. Hank was starting back along the passage. He halted abruptly, at the foot of the stair, backed two steps, looked over his shoulder at his partner, and called, "Hold it, Splint, it's another damn test!"

· 5 ·

Tey emerged casually into as full a view as the dark tunnel afforded. Hank was facing him now, peering uncertainly into the gloom.

"What about Harney and his squad?" Tey demanded harshly. "Porky wouldn't like it if you kirred them without orders."

In reply Hank went quickly to the tall man and thrust him roughly away from the panel, which he slammed shut.

"I ain't ret him do no harm, did I?" he demanded defensively, glancing into the dark passage whence the strange voice had issued. "Anyways, who are ya?" he growled. "Ya better show yourself."

"That's 'show yourself, prease, sir,'" Tey corrected him sharply. "Now you and Splint better douber time back to your duty station."

Hank stood uncertainly at the foot of the steps, looking up into darkness. "Who are ya, anyways?" he demanded, but with diminished authority. "Don't know yer voice, mister. Hey, Splint," he called over his shoulder.

The tall man came over, glanced up, said, "Ret's go, Hank," and started up, but Tey placed a boot in his face and thrust him back; he fell against the stocky man, cursing.

". . . no damn Guardian due here this lesslight," Hank protested. Then, getting to his feet, he came to a rough approximation of the position of a soldier, and said, "We're coming up, whoever ya are, and both of us got our tapers in active mode, so we can prove ya never answered our challenge. Now, one more time: Who's there? Name, rank, and serial number—"

"Very well," Tey replied coolly. "Taliaferro Tey, ex-Captain, F037537978."

"What's that 'ex-Captain' 'pose to mean?" Hank put in from behind Splinter.

"Tell me about 'purging the system,' " Tey ordered the man.

Splinter made an "aw, shucks" gesture with his shoulders. "Nothin' to it," he said. "Close off the watergates both sides, and pump in the pink stuff."

"You, too?" Tey inquired. "Kamikaze number?"

"Naw, we safe-up right here. Anyways, it's only Verbot Five; makes ya pretty sick, but less'n one percent fatal."

"You did good to change your mind," Tey said briskly.

Hank, who had come up behind Splinter, spoke up abruptly:

"OK, Splint, that's enough." He pushed the taller but lighter man aside and assumed a *do-ari-imo* stance, ready for either attack or active defense.

"Better get that left foot back another one and three eighth inches," Tey suggested mildly. "Otherwise you'll be flat on your back as soon as I pump a couple of fast snap-kicks into your solar plexus."

Hank muttered and relaxed. "Splint thinks you're a Guardian; maybe you are; but until I see some proof, I'm still a duly constituted sentry on active duty. Come down nice and slow."

"Let's have a little talk," Tey proposed easily. "You two clowns may sit on the bottom step. Snap to it!"

Muttering, the two men squatted in the designated position, still staring up into what was to them total darkness.

· 6 ·

"Why were Harney and his squad sent out to attack harmless strangers without warning?" Tey inquired. "And who sent them?"

"Whoever ya are," Hank snarled, "yer no Guardian."

"I haven't claimed to be," Tey pointed out. "Nevertheless, you're going to answer me. Fast."

Behind him, Tey heard Nat Grall and Mullen emerge from their crannies and converse in whispers:

"What's happening, Nat?"

"Cap'n asking questions. We'll stand fast and listen to the answers."

Tey heard them move to positions flanking the stairhead. Below him, the burly Hank shifted his position slightly, then lunged for Tey's lower legs, yelling, "Let's take him, Splint!" His yell was cut off sharply as Tey's boot crashed against his face. Splint, coming in over him, met a large fist where no fist should have been, and fell back across his partner.

"Sorry about that, Cap'n," Nat said softly. "I just got a little eager, I suppose. No offense intended."

"None taken," Tey reassured him. "Let's bring 'em up where we can see better." He went down, stepping carefully across the two groaning and feebly moving men. Nat followed, less carefully; he bent and lifted Splint, stepped back over Hank, and tossed the man up as lightly as if he were pitching hay. "Here's one for you to sit on, Chief," he called to Mullen. "Don't squeeze him too hard, unless you want to."

"Yessir," Mullen's reply came promptly, followed by soft sounds of a brief scuffle terminating with a sharp impact.

"Hey, Nat, Captain," Mullen called excitedly. "I seen this sucker before. Coming out of headquarters, same day we clobbered in."

"We'll be right up," Nat replied. "As soon as old Hank here is ready. You ready now, Hank?" he inquired in solicitous tones as he lifted the man by his bushy black hair. Hank got his feet under him and tried a kick to the knee, but intercepted the hard edge of Nat's boot across his shin instead.

"Naughty," Nat commented in the tone of mild reproof of a teacher whose pupil has muffed an easy one. He went up the steps, Hank's knees bouncing on each step as he was dragged limply. Tey came behind.

Mullen had hauled Splint to his feet and thrust him back against the overcurving wall, causing the tall man to crook his neck awkwardly.

"How does it figure, Cap'n?" Mullen asked as Tey came up.

"It seems we've been taking too many things for granted," Tey replied. "Such as that *Princeton* arrived here ahead of Banshire's boys. How about it, Mr. Splint?" he inquired casually. "What's the connection between you and whoever runs this place?"

"That's 'Mr. Patucci,' if you wanna get formal," Splint muttered. "I tell you nothin', Mr. Terrible Tey." He spat, missing Mullen's shoe, and received a short, stiff punch to the ribs from the latter.

While Splint worked on his breathing, Tey said, "It seems we'll have to do it the hard way." He grabbed Splint by the collar and slammed his head against the stone.

"Better get started, Mr. Patucci," he growled, "while what you use for a brain is still behind that homely face of yours— instead of all over it."

"You spill your guts, and I'll see you down the spill-hole myself," Hank yelled at Splint to no avail.

Splint had already begun speaking.

·7·

". . . told us was we had this like Prime Depot to draw on, and we could help out with some specialist manpower, so Hank and me come on over. Damn funny kinda place. You seen that slice of a *Viking* class laying out on the moor. Hank and me ran a couple tests: it's one hundred percent organic matter, and it's exactly thirty-one Standard days old."

Splint paused and Tey commented, "That's surprising news, considering the well-established pattern of trails that are oriented on the spot."

"Used to be some kindofa—like a shrine ya might say, on that spot. Then, couple months back, *that* thing. You birds couldn't a never punched this outa me, but no Hank Burko's gonna get the idea he can top-dog *me* and tell me what an' what not to do."

Mullen spoke from behind Tey: "Motor pool over here in the next cave, Captain. Request permission to investigate, sir."

"Permission granted," Tey called over his shoulder. "Provided Messrs. Burko and Patucci have no objection."

"We ain't no messers," Burko growled, and broke off as Nat prodded him.

"Now, ya don't wanna get to pokin' around too much," Splint said, almost briskly, starting forward as if to intercept the NCO. He subsided when Tey intercepted him and slung his head back against the curving stone wall.

"No objections, hey, Hank?" Splint blurted. "Already got a sore place last time you done that," he went on, eyeing Tey aggrievedly, fingering his skull.

"Tell me more," Tey urged gently. "What is this place? Who is it that's squirreling away all this obsolete Navy property? And why did they send a squad out to attack us? What are they afraid of?"

"Scareda nothin'," Splint blurted. "Standin' orders: soon as Porky seen the way you was headed, he posted a crew, rike he 'pose to. Routine. This here is Prime Depot, is what it is. Anybody knows *that* much. Folks here are Custodians, what they are. They stay here. Born and raised right here, don't like no Crawlers comin' around. Rike you." Splint decided against spitting on the floor and swallowed hard instead. He looked at Tey solemnly.

"Go ahead, Patucci," Hank called. "Might's well. Time I'm done with ya—" Nat's hand in his angry face stilled the stocky man's threat.

Splint gulped again and resumed: "Old Carstairs said it was Banshire One hisself made the deal—here a hunert years back or something; but these here Crawlers, like you guys, all the time takin' stuff. Got to put a end to that, Carstairs said. Reason old Porky's so jumpy and all. Nothin' to it." Splint fell silent, rubbing his head and eyeing Tey resentfully. "Rike you," he resumed abruptly. "Rook at that new all yer wearing. Took it right outa three, didn't you? Him, too, and the other one," he added, glancing at Nat Grall, who had placed Hank face down on the floor and was holding him there with one booted foot on the back of the neck.

"Anything you'd care to add to that, Mr. Burko?" Grall inquired solicitously, looking down at the struggling man beneath his foot.

"Breathing all right now?" he asked gently. "If you want any air, just let me know. Seems like your associate, Mr. Patucci, has run out of information for the moment. This is your chance to make a good impression—or should I just squash your scrawny neck flat?"

Hank flopped his arms and uttered gargling sounds. "Might —" Nat eased off the pressure slightly, "—as well, now that Patooch already blew his gaff. So what the hell!"

· 8 ·

"Where does this tunnel lead?" Nat inquired curtly.

"Comes out, oh, right at Plenum, like all these damn caves. Go ahead, barge in, you'll find plenny folks to talk to."

"Who are these Custodians your pal was gossiping about?" Nat glanced up and met Tey's eyes as the latter stood over Splint, now collapsed on the floor. "Plenum. That's a funny name, eh, Captain?" Grall commented. "Remarkably intact after a few hundred years of oral transmission."

"Custodians?" Hank repeated. "Guess you're havin' your rittu joke. Custodians are the ones got awr the stuff; you know, rike suppries on hand. Got to keep a sharp eye out fer these Crawrers. Ya try'na rob stuff awr a-time. Makes it tough for the Custodians, and them try'na do a job."

"Sad," Nat agreed. "And just what job is it these Custodians of yours are doing?"

"Ain't *mine*," Burko objected. "Been ona job since before— anyways old Banshire One—I mean his Rordship, a-course— made a deal; they been sticking to their end good. Rotsa compraints this trip, though; seems rike guys over on North—Big Diggers, mostly—havin' trouble with Jumpers and Walkers and Maxies and Gosh knows what all."

"I don't think I ever heard of those Maxies before," Nat said easily. "What's their number?"

"Oh, Maxies? Heck, everybody knows they're the nuts say the

Exarted is a fake—get that; a fake! The Exarted hisserf! Crazy, huh?"

"Slow down, Hank," Nat cautioned. "You're shedding more heat than light. What is this exarted? I've heard of it before, but never did quite pin down what it meant."

"You try'na joke me, Big Boy?" Hank replied with a sneer. "OK, I'm going arong, ain't I?" he added defensively. "Awright, the Exarted is the source of all. The Exarted made Parasite here, and the sky, and the tunnels and all the stuff in 'em. That's right. Guys rike you breathe air and never wonder where it comes from, and you wear your clothes—sure, some of 'em's a rittu wore out—and some days it's cold and wet, and ya ride in a car and ya never stop to give praise to the Exarted, which He's the one made it!"

"Seems to me you've got this Exarted of yours mixed up with General Motors," Tey commented.

"Sir," Mullen said calmly, sounding strange after the excited voices of the two men under interrogation. "Really wish you'd take a rook here, Cap'n, sir. Something mighty funny." As Mullen emerged from the side-chamber he had been investigating, both Burko and Patucci spoke up:

"—bad news pokin' around there. That's Place, you damn fools!"

"—nobody viorates the Sanctum. Musta went off your track. Old Porky—and even the Sayer, and maybe the Exarted hisserf —" Splint gobbled.

· 9 ·

Ignoring the clamor of protest, Tey and Nat converged on the arched entrance, which appeared to differ in no way from the others they had passed. Beyond, in the deep gloom relieved only by the white glare of a light-well, could be seen row on row of brand-new recon cars of the same obsolete design as the one which von Shimo had appeared in, how many days since, Nat was unsure.

"Just like old Shimmy's," he commented. "How long we been on this rousy pranet, Cap'n?"

"Thirteen days, four hours, twelve minutes, and a bit, approximately," Tey replied. "Why?"

"I lost track," Nat said. "One of those nuts who fix up old junk cars would give birth to a litter of pre-Bang Volkswagens if he could see *this* stash. Shall we take a look?"

Mullen went ahead, passed along the line, and paused by a gleaming prow at the end of the line.

"Back here, Cap'n," he said, and moved to the rear of the vehicle. Tey followed and at once observed the anomaly: the car *ended* abruptly just aft of the air dam.

"Just like that fake *Viking* class," Mullen said. "Ends in a straight line like it was cut with a knife."

"Not cut, Chief," Tey demurred. "Just not finished; like a C-ray tube display when the power cuts."

"Nobody manufactures things that way, Cap'n," Mullen protested.

"Not 'somebody,' " Tey said. "Some *thing.* " He glanced back at Hank and Splint, standing in the entry, still protesting. "They don't much like our being in here. Maybe that means there's something we ought to see here."

"Want me to go back and keep an eye on them suckers, Cap'n?" Mullen offered. Tey's glance lingered on the two chastened men.

"They'll be all right," Nat reassured him. "I explained the facts of rife to them."

"I'm not so sure, Nat," Tey demurred. "It looks to me as if they've got their heads together. Their morale is a rittu too good to suit me." He went across to the two men, who looked a trifle haggard but unmarked by their interrogation. They addressed Tey simultaneously:

". . . tell ya we gotta—"

". . . don't want ta brame *us,* fer crapsake . . ."

As Tey eyed them coldly, they broke off and addressed each other accusingly:

". . . was I s'pose to know—"

- 269

". . . gave you the high sign!"

"Never mind, men," Tey said calmly. "It doesn't matter; it didn't work." He glanced back into the room behind him, and called quietly to Nat, who came to his side at once, a frown on his blunt features.

"Cap'n," he started, eyeing Burko dubiously, "I've got a kind of feeling—"

"Me, too," Tey cut in gently. "It seems we've been had—or almost."

Nat nodded, then suddenly grabbed Splint and Burko by the hair, left and right. He wacked their heads together and gave them a shove. The two staggered off a few steps, uttering dismal sounds.

"What have they cooked up, Cap'n?" Nat inquired expectantly.

Tey shook his head. "No details, Nat, but they've held us here very effectively, for two hours and forty-one minutes, Standard."

Nat nodded briskly, as at good news confirmed. He looked around the water-worn chamber, with its various outlets. "We ought to start waiting as fast as we can," he suggested. At that moment there were faint sounds from an unexplored archway. Burko and Patucci fell silent at once, and the stealthy rustlings and faint metallic clickings became more audible.

"Must be up to no good," Nat said pontifically. "The way they're sneaking up silently, I mean."

"Good thinking, Tey commended dryly. "Shall we run or hide?"

"No," Nat answered. "I want to see the fun when Porky finds Hank and Splint, here, drunk on the job."

"Not drunk," Burko spoke up defiantly. "Ain't seen so much's a empty gin bottle in better'n—worser'n a year. Where'd I get any drunk stuff?"

"Out of Stores, of course," Nat replied blandly. "Got a rittu of everything aboard ship, stashed someplace."

Hank and Splint exchanged glances, then collided as they crowded out together through one of the many openings. A moment later Splint reeled back into view, in time nearly to collide with a short, red-faced man in a fantastic headdress who had abruptly emerged from the adjacent aperture followed by three men.

· 10 ·

"Drunk on duty," the short man accused.

"Me, too, Pork," Splint replied, regaining his balance with a wild lurch. Porky snarled and waved him away as Burko came up.

"Me and Mr. Patucci—" he began.

"You and Mr. Polluted Patucci are under arrest," the short man yelped. He turned toward Tey, the feathery adornments on his hat swaying. "Now, just how did you get in here, you—whatever you are?" he demanded. "No excuses, mind, just the facts: I've got over four hundred sentries posted, and you appear to have waltzed right through them without even setting off a screamer. That's interesting. I want to know how it was done!"

Tey turned slowly to give the fellow a close scrutiny, head to toes and back. "It strikes me, my man," he said coldly, "that you don't know whom you're addressing."

"Yeah, well, sir, you see," Porky started, then changed his mind. "I stand on my rights," he declared decisively. "I'm Looker Two this here turn, and I got a right—"

"Wrong," Tey cut him off. "You're relieved. Permanently. Now see to these two before you report to the Sayer." He turned away.

"Hey!" Porky exclaimed, a stricken look on his fat features. "How come—the Sayer! Cripes, I ain't— Rook, ret's just settle for a nice rittu company punishment, hey? I don't want to have to go see the Sayer!"

Tey halted and looked at the man over his shoulder. "Prefer to take the matter direct to the Exarted, eh? Perhaps you're right: two designated Lookers, drunk on duty right in midturn."

"Say, I didn't mean—" Porky fell silent, nibbling his lower lip.

"That's enough nonsense for now, Porky," Tey said almost

genially. "I'm not interested in seeing you busted back to Looker One, just because you're a rittu stupid."

Porky bridled, took a deep breath, and changed his mind. "You there—" He pointed with his thumb at a lanky fellow nearby. "Put clamps on all of 'em. All four of 'em," he emphasized. He glanced at Tey, and Nat, who had come up beside him. "I've got men posted in every tunner outa here. Armed and ordered to fire at will. So be nice, and ret's get this straightened out peacaber."

Tey turned casually to Nat. "Will your Excerrency honor me with an opinion?" he inquired mildly. "What shall we do with this funny little man?"

· 11 ·

Everyone stood fast for a minute, then Porky's squad began moving about busily, arranging themselves around the periphery of the chamber. One, beside the entry to the garage, leaned to thrust his ear into the dark archway.

"Wise up, Herky," Mullen's voice hissed. "Admiral Carstairs wouldn't like it if you clowns insulted his new diplomatic mission the first day out."

"I heard that!" Porky bawled, and whirled to peer into the adjacent room. "Come outa there and let's have a look at you!" He was holding his powergun now. Mullen emerged, blinking, into the brighter though still dim light.

"You're the chief grease monkey," Porky accused, putting his weapon away. "I seen you three! You're a funny kind of ambassador."

"I'm Their Profundities' driver," Mullen explained diffidently.

" 'Their Profundities'?" Porky echoed in dismay. "These two fellas are Chief Guardians?"

"You heard me, Herky," Mullen replied positively. "Hercules Adams, fresh out of Old Terra with Lord Banshire's greetings. You can hear they still got a Terry accent."

"Wise up, Porky," Patucci put in contemptuously. "You don't

think we'd open up the Prace to just any two stumblebums happened arong, did ya?"

"You shun't oughta call me 'Porky,' " Herky complained, "me being Looker Two and all, and you only a Looker One."

"Report, Looker," Tey snapped. "Make it fast and make it complete."

Herky/Porky looked sorrowfully at Tey. "Well, Yer Profundity," he started, "course we've been on blue alert here at Prime ever since we got that Code Able One from His Excellency the Admiral, here a week ago. Awr about some crazy man tryna mess things up, tamperin' with the Rubes and awr. . . ."

"What Rubes?" Tey demanded.

"*All* the Rubes, Profundity—"

"You needn't keep calling me 'Profundity,' Looker. First encounter of the day is what protocol requires; after that, 'sir' is correct."

"Yessir. Anyway, bein' on arert an awr, Speaker says double the watch. So then Rack One pipes Warkers snooping around Site Beta, and next thing you know, I get a Shout One from Patucci here—good man, Pattuch, when he ain't drunk onna job, I mean, an—"

"Wait," Tey said, "go back. As Mr. Mullen mentioned, we're just out from Terra, and our briefing didn't cover Prime or Site Beta, and most of the other things we've encountered here."

Porky looked mournfully at Mullen. "If I wouldn't of saw you myserf right outside the admirar's tent, I'd say there was something here I oughta take to Speaker."

"Never mind that, Looker," Tey chided gently. "We're going to have a nice talk, that's all. No need to stir up any grave consequences, such as personnel disposal actions, for example."

"PDA's?" Porky echoes in a tone of outrage. "Me, PDA'd? Well, even Speaker wouldn't—or maybe he would, the skunk. All right, a little talk can't hurt none."

For some hours Tey, Grall, and occasionally Mullen, questioned the bewildered noncom. At last Tey told the chunky fellow to rejoin his squad, who were waiting restlessly in a side-passage. Gratefully the exhausted fellow did so, quieting a greeting chorus of demanding voices with a curt "Shaddup!"

Tey looked at Grall questioningly.

"The picture I get," Nat said, "is that *Omega* made it intact. But discipline must've been lost, because they broke up into factions, and then the factions broke into factions—all bitter enemies. Dunno why."

"Something to do with the ship itself," Tey suggested. "It seems each bunch is accusing the others of stealing it, silly as that sounds. Then there's apparently an indigenous life form— or an artifact left behind by a life form—that helped out in some way. Apparently they managed to get some sort of factory going and started manufacturing, but only at the level of the then state-of-the-art technology. No progress."

"Then why haven't we seen any of these helpful natives?" Nat wondered aloud. "And no signs of industry: no mines or smokestacks—no roads, even—and only a few remains of towns . . ."

Further questions elicited the statement that "all them guys —Big Diggers* and all—are over on North Continent. Got their Source of All over there, and won't share with these here Easters."

Tey asked about von Shimo and was assured by Porky that he knew no one of that name.

"What about this big powwow supposed to be going on here at Prime about now?" Nat Grall put in. " 'The Reception for Territorial Counselors at Great Prime.' "

Porky/Herky snickered. " 'Great Prime,' " he echoed. "That's what these Easters call some clearing they grubbed into the woods. They pretend it's the real Prime. But this here is Prime Depot, only real Prime there is. Reception is right," he

*A reference to miners, as distinct from Little Diggers, or farmers.

added. "Them suckers is going to get *some* reception, all right. Got a crawler—great big mother—with a pair of repeaters on her. Gonna clear up these Easters once and for all." Porky broke off abruptly, as if suddenly aware that he was speaking too freely.

Nat urged him on: "Don't stop now, Porky, just when it's getting interesting. Lord Banshire will want to know all about it."

"Well, yeah," Porky conceded. "No harm in reporting to you fellas—yer Profundities, I mean. After all, it's His Lordship's orders and all, ain't it?"

"You mean it's Lord Banshire's orders for you boys here at Prime Depot to keep things stirred up, don't let the Easters and Northers get together," Nat clarified by inference.

"Sure, and the same with the locals," Porky amplified. "No telling what these bums might manage to do if they'd once get together. Maybe try to jump Prime here and clean out Stores —Exarted wouldn't like that." Porky fell silent for a moment, looking as thoughtful as his porcine features would permit, then resumed. . . .

Editors' Note: The board, after careful consideration of Hercules Adams's lengthy discussion with Captain Tey and Nat Grall, transcribed from newly released tapes,* believes that the literate public has no need to hear again in detail the familiar account of the state of affairs obtaining on Colmar under Terran control, long known from other sources, though denied by Terran officials.

*The originals are of course available to scholars by written request one year in advance. This passage is included in RRm31-(reel 14):.28.2, now stored at Archive One at New Conference, North Continent.

THIRTEEN

Genocide at Prime

"**I**t's no wonder all these Walkers and Goers and Stayers and What-have-yous are at each other's throats," Nat commented when Rooker Herky had at last exhausted his store of confidences and fallen silent.

"Not with this crowd making sneaky forays in their fleet of museum-piece ground-cars, hit-and-run, and leaving plenty of clues to somebody else," Nat agreed.

"Not harf crafty," Mullen commented.

"It sounds as if the population of North Continent has done somewhat better," Tey put in. "Apparently they've got their own industry, and don't take much stock in the Exarted."

"This big 'Territorial Conference,'" Nat went on, "sounds like a fine spot for a massacre; all the rocal yokels in one prace, all mutually hostile, and with Porky—and a rot more rike him —adding the necessary incidents to get the riot going."

Tey looked at Porky. "After they've wiped each other out, I presume you boys and your Exarted will take on North Continent next, so as to put in loyal Banshire men all around, and own the whole planet."

"Sure, yer Profundity. Me, I'm loyal, you bet!"

"What's your share going to be?" Tey asked.

"Every man gets a hundred thousand acres of prime farmrand, or the mineral tract of his choice—and the slaves to work it. And this here soil is good, sir—oughta see the crops some of these Rittu Diggers are raising—and *we* harvest."

276 –

"Sir," Mullen spoke up, "'cording to my calcs, the big ruckus is scheduled in just a couple days, so—"

"Nineteen hours and a bit," Tey agreed. "We just about have time to make the scene before things hot up."

"Now, uh, yer Profundities, sir," Porky started, "better not. Even if you *are* Chief Guardians, Speaker ain't gonna be preased to hear somebody's mixing in his show, after he spent the rast year and more working out the timing and awl."

"That will do, Rooker," Tey said sternly. "You may go now and make your report. Be sure to clear the passages within five minutes, because I'm going to purge the system then—"

"Hey, how'd you know about the purge setup? That's classified so hot I don't hardly even know about it myserf—but I guess you Chief Guardians get all the inside dope . . ."

"Oh, we have the rittu picture," Nat supplied. "It's just the big picture that's a trifle obscure."

Porky nodded. "His Rordship ain't no dummy," he said contentedly. "Don't ret nobody but hisserf have the *whole* picture, eh, sir?"

Tey turned to Nat and said, "We'll go out the same way we came in, Nat—that is, if you gentlemen don't mind another few hours walking in a crouch."

"Best way," Nat agreed, while Mullen nodded and Porky began a protest, cut off as Nat eyed him meaningfully. "Let's go," he said.

The area of the car was deserted when they reached it at last. "Just as well," Tey commented.

"Which way, Cap'n?" Nat inquired as he took the driver's seat.

"Off the map, to the west, as well as I can guess from what the boys said," Tey replied. "That and Jonesu-san's route." He put aside the aerial photo. "No help here; if the clans are gathering, they're blazing their own trails. No pattern."

"I'll backtrack our trail for awhile," Nat said, and set off.

Within minutes they spied a forlorn-appearing foot caravan at extreme range to the south, on a convergent course. Half an hour later another straggling group was in sight dead ahead. Nat steered wide of them.

"They remind me of poor old Johnny," Nat commented. "Do

you suppose Speaker will really do anything about them, or was that just more hot air?"

"We'll check as we pass the area," Tey said. As they neared the area where *Princeton* had last been seen, Tey swung to the east.

· 2 ·

Following approximately the route of their initial reconnaissance, the trail of which was faintly visible in the dryer stretches, in three hours Nat had brought the car to the low cliff Tey had discovered on the first day. He maneuvered down the rock slide to the lower level. Here the ground was only slightly softer than above. Nat noted and commented on the faintly visible two-trail, which extended due east from the slide until it faded in the misty distance. Otherwise the plain was as featureless as was the higher level.

Another hour's high-speed run roughly paralleling the visible trail brought them to a pebbled beach, where the transition from flat wetland to flat sea was marked mainly by banks and clots of dry foam. Without hesitation they crossed the pebbled strip, cutting a wide swath through the spume, and slid out on the air cushion upon the barely riffled surface of the slack sea.

Now the far shore was visible as an irregular, dusty blue-gray mass stretching along the horizon. The car's proximeter indicated a distance of eight miles. Through a small binocular carried as standard equipment in Fleet VIP cars, Tey could distinguish gray-greenish foliage. He passed the glasses to Nat and Mullen, who declared unequivocally that they, too, could distinguish trees.

The crossing required less than half an hour and brought them to a wide, flat beach of pale yellow sand, where half a dozen, grayish metal rowboats lay, as if abandoned, among strands of dry seaweed, sun-bleached shells, and bits of driftwood.

"Well, Cap'n," Nat commented as Tey steered the car carefully among these artifacts, which appeared identical, except for some of the more recent-looking dents. Tey climbed down and examined the nearest boat, then quickly glanced at the transom of the next. "Duplicates of a Navy-issue survival-kit item," he announced. "They even have the same serial number."

"Footprints," Mullen pointed out. "Above the tideline. Looks like these boats haven't been here too long."

"It seems the party hasn't started yet," Tey commented. "Assuming we're right about this being Prime."

"Hasta be, sir," Mullen said firmly. "Only place in sight with boats."

"It could be a decoy," Tey pointed out. "If so, we're buying it anyway."

· 3 ·

Above the high-tide line, beyond the trampled strip, vegetation began with sparse grasses, backed up by a belt of dense shrubs, over which towered the odd, barkless trees with their shiny trunks of indigo and tangerine and vermilion. Rough-barked Terran species spread their green canopies, vivid against the dull verdigris of the native foliage. Bright green or purple blossoms lent a touch of holiday decoration to the grim, dull-foliaged mass of indigenous growth. Tey pulled the car up onto the grass and shut down. The eyes of all three men were on a rough-hacked tunnel cut through bush and saplings, leading into the interior of the forest.

"Might be booby-trapped," Mullen commented.

"We'll have to find out," Tey replied. "It's wide enough for the car—maybe."

"Let me check it out first, Cap'n," Nat suggested. "I'll be *very* careful, you may be sure."

"Better you than me," Mullen observed contentedly. Tey nodded, wasting no time and breath on ritual objections. Nat Grall knew what he was doing.

Grall went to the opening, paused at its mouth, then stepped inside, and was at once lost to view in the darkness there. Large butterflies of a polished metallic yellow fluttered their gold wings or floated lightly around the car. One perched on the cowl, precisely before Mullen's face.

"That's a Terry bug, Captain," he stated firmly. "Look at them six legs and them big compound eyes and them feelers and all. And that segmented abdomen. Got to be reg'lar Earth-style butterflies."

"So it appears, Max," Tey agreed. "Later we can perform a dissection and determine whether it has a ventral, ladder-type nervous system."

"Damn right," Mullen confirmed. "Got a reg'lar chitinous exoskeleton, anybody can see that, eh, Captain?"

Before Tey could reply, Nat Grall burst from the tunnel, holding clamped under his arm a much smaller man who was threshing desperately. Nat's expression was calm as he came to the car and dumped his prisoner on the ground, casually pressing him back to a prone position with one foot as the man attempted to rise. Tey opened the hatch, receiving a gush of warm air and a torrent of shrill vocalization, which Grall stemmed with a light kick.

· 4 ·

"Look what I found," Nat said calmly, and Tey studied the excited captive. He was small in stature, skeletally thin, wrinkled of face, and dressed in now mud-stained white pajamas.

"Our old associate, the colonel-general," Nat said genially as he removed his foot from the old fellow's back.

At once von Shimo scrambled to his feet, but before he could resume his ululation, Tey took the initiative:

"Where's Cleo? Where's the car?"

"Crazy femare wreck car," von Shimo mourned. "Could have kirr me!"

"Where is she now?" Nat insisted.

"Crazy woman drive off, reave me stranded *here!*" Von Shimo looked about him as if incredulous of his surroundings.

"Tricky riar, too," he added hotly. "Said she never rode in a car before! Then drives rike mad sonabitch!"

"Which way did she go?" Nat pressed. Von Shimo pointed vaguely along the beach, then stared up at Nat.

"This prace is Prime, where big meeting scheduled to pran war," he stated impressively.

"Sure. That's why we came," Nat said.

"You ferrows are making a serious error," von Shimo yelled. "I tried to warn this—" he gestured his frustration at Nat, "—this unkind chap," he finished lamely. "Here you must not come bursting in unescorted. Forbidden territory, for awr except the erect, incruding myself."

"Who erected you?" Tey asked.

Von Shimo's reply was to jump up and down and redouble his screeching. Abruptly he fell silent for a moment, then spoke in a reasonable tone:

"See here, gentermen, you are making a dreadful error. You wirr rook a pair of proper Charlies when you rearize you have savaged your one true friend, who has tried from the beginning to herp you. Was it not I—"

"Who turned us over to the most blood-thirsty pack of liars and killers you knew of," Grall finished the little man's sentence for him. After at first nodding agreement, von Shimo, belatedly grasping the import of Grall's words, broke in with excited protestation:

"—who came to give you warning, spirited you swiftly away, and placed you in the protection of known enemies of all Walkers?" von Shimo furnished his version of the conclusion of his interrupted sentence. For a moment he appeared to be considering renewing his tantrum routine, but as Nat Grall glanced at him and said quietly, "I wouldn't," he changed his mind.

"The time has come, Colonel-General," Tey stated, "to tell us more about these mysterious Guardians to whom you refer so obliquely from time to time."

Von Shimo stared at Tey as if dumfounded. "Obriquely?" He exhaled in tones of astonishment, then stepped closer to Tey and lowered his voice. "You are very foorish ferrow indeed," he stated, sounding nervous now, "to come *here*, to bait the Guardians. This is an intrusion they cannot overrook!" von Shimo concluded.

"Oh, did I forget to tell you?" Nat asked casually. *"We're* doing the overrooking from now on—and damn little of it."

"Skip all the double-tark, and get right down to essentiars," Tey commanded the colonel-general. "Just spit it out: who are these Guardians?"

Von Shimo looked shocked and lowered his voice to a hiss. "Not so roud!" He looked around as if checking for eavesdroppers. "It is not good to disturb the Exarted One."

Grall, standing behind von Shimo, unhurriedly gathered a wad of the coarse cloth of the little man's garment in his fist and lifted him until his toes cleared the ground by six inches, at which von Shimo emitted a shrill yelp, trying in vain to turn his head far enough to get a glimpse of the cause of his sudden levitation.

"Tell it," Nat said. "If you get tired trying to breathe past that pressure on your windpipe, just spill it to the captain, and you'll get to take a deep breath. No real hurry, you understand. Any time within the next microsecond will do; then I take another turn." So saying, Grall slowly rotated his fist a quarter-turn, eliciting a squeak from von Shimo.

"I terr awr," he blurted. "But you crazy man to come here to bait the Faithful One." Another few degrees of rotation brought about an abrupt change of tone.

·5·

"We poor ones are bressed to enjoy guidance and support of the Guardians. It is they who guard our rives, give us of their bounty—awr out of sheer benignance." He rattled the words off as if reciting a litany.

"Where are they?" Tey demanded. "Where do they stay? I want to meet these wonderful fellows."

Von Shimo hissed. "One does not *meet* the Guardians. . . . One is privereged to enter into their Presence—perhaps, if . . ." the little man trailed off doubtfully.

Nat Grall leaned over his shoulder. "Time for another lesson?" he inquired genially, gathering in another wad of dirty cloth just under von Shimo's left ear.

The little man yelped and looked around hastily. "Rerease me," he demanded. "Am I not terring you everything?"

Nat carried the little man into the tunnel from which he had emerged a few moments before, set him on his feet at the spot where the wire noose had barely missed him. Van Shimo looked around innocently, then registered surprised pleasure at the sight of a cluster of small, pale green blossoms, which he plucked and sniffed at contentedly.

"You didn't know who was coming, or you'd have set it lower," Grail said. "You have a great deal of hostility in you, General. Who is it really aimed at? Cleo?"

"Ret us go quietry, Fierd Marshar," von Shimo cautioned, pretending not to have heard Grall's question.

· 6 ·

They had now reached the spot where Grall had plucked the little man from his perch on the rude platform of a low bough screened in by gray foliage. Beyond, sunlight gleamed in a clearing in the forest. This was no mere fringe of trees like the jungle across the water where the *Catrice* party was encamped, Nat saw. He sensed that he was at the edge of a vast, primeval forest which stretched on and on across an unknown continent.

A few steps ahead, something lay on the trampled sod of the trail—a scrap of some synthetic, he guessed, half an inch thick, dense in texture, iodine-colored, polished on the smooth, outer curve, dull along the shattered edges and the pebbly underside. A fragment of a manufactured object, it appeared obvious. He picked it up, found it to be as hard and stiff as one of the metal-polymer alloys. The scrap offered no hint as to the size and shape of the destroyed object of which it was a small part. He glanced around for more pieces, proceeding slowly forward into the clearing which, though shallow, stretched away to the left and right in the dazzle of sunlight for a considerable distance, hemmed in on all sides by flat barriers of undisturbed forest. The ground here was like a once-smooth lawn now in need of mowing.

Tey came up beside Grall, while von Shimo hovered, jittering and emitting a steady stream of mumbled protest: ". . . genter-men, one *must* observe the niceties. I have to insist, it is for your own good. . . ."

Nat handed the shard to Tey. "What do you think, Cap'n?" he said. "Man-made, eh?"

By no means, someone said. *Go away.*

Tey was rubbing his thumb thoughtfully on the smooth sur-face of the object. "Don't rush me," Tey said absently as he examined the fragment. "It's not, I think, any material listed in *Naval Resources.*" He tried to bend the scrap, scratched at it with a fingernail, then with the blade of a small folding knife, all without effect. He handed it back to Grall, who turned to the nearest tree, wedged the fragment into a narrow cleft between thick boughs, set himself, and applied pressure with the heel of his big hard hand. The sound of splitting wood was quite audi-ble. He retrieved the object from among splinters.

"Somewhere on the tough side of stellon," he commented, then paused to peer into the underbrush beyond the tree. He ripped aside a leafy branch to expose a neat stack of small cylinders piled against the tree, apparently of the same material as the fragment. Von Shimo dithered, darted forward, ineffec-tually thrust the broken foilage back in place, and turned his back on it, rejecting its exposure.

You must not intrude here! the same soft voice said.

"Nat!" Tey spoke quietly but with a note of stress that caused the big man to whirl—and freeze. Across the smooth lawn, something moved, a gelatinous, opalescent bulge which thrust out from behind the screening leaves, a quivering hulk which seemed more to grow than to change position.

"Captain Tey," Grall said quietly. "Sir, I submit that the time has come for us to take our departure, just as you said." As he spoke, he reached out to grab von Shimo, who had begun to edge away, his eyes fixed on the grayish-pink bulge among the gray leaves.

Tey looked thoughtful, not quite smiling.

Get out now! The voice was sharper.

"A proposal, Mr. Ambassador, which I myself was about to

make," Tey said. "Shall we?" He started back along the green-gray tunnel through which they had entered. Grall followed, dragging von Shimo, who found his feet and matched pace, leaning awkwardly to accommodate Grall's grip on his collar.

"I tried to warn you ferrows," he shrilled. "It is not a prace for one to come poking about uninvited. . . ." He trailed off when Nat lifted him, held him at arm's length, and shook him gently. Giving Grall a cold look, von Shimo stated with dignity: "You prace me in an impossibur position."

"I sincerely hope so," Grall said, as if acknowledging a lavish compliment. "Maybe after a while you'll get it through that pointed head of yours that we're not only bigger than you are, we're also smarter. Then perhaps you'll abandon the idea that you're going to do us in."

"I perform my bounden duty, nothing more," von Shimo said dully. "In the end it is you ferrows who wirr find you cannot defy the raw of the Exarted."

· 7 ·

None must violate the place of Beginnings . . . the voice warned, and then from a near distance a yell sounded and was quickly cut off.

"What was that about 'beginnings'?" Tey asked.

"I thought *you* said that," Grall said. He dropped von Shimo, who scuttled back toward the clearing.

Ahead, clear of the thicket, Tey halted. "I see you threw him away," he commented. "And I think we're going in the wrong direction, after all. Listen."

Grall nodded. "People," he said. "Excited people, at that." He stood, his head tilted, concentrating his attention on the muffled shouts and yells now emanating from the tunnel-mouth behind him.

"Sounds like they're coming into the clearing," Tey suggested. "They don't seem to like what's going on any better than we do—so presumably, they're not responsible for it."

At that moment a man dressed like von Shimo—in dirty-white pajamas—emerged from the tunnel at a dead run. Noticing Tey and Grall, he skidded to a stop, paused, and, ignoring von Shimo, ran back into the tunnel. Moments later he—or another man of the same size and shape and pajamas—appeared, this time advancing cautiously toward Nat Grall, who took a few steps to meet him.

· 8 ·

"Good morning, Johnny," Grall said easily. "I'm glad to see you didn't sink all the way in." '

"Smawr thanks to you, Mr. Ambassador," Jonesu-san replied sharply.

"Looks like the big conference is beginning to shape up," Grall commented. " 'And thick and fast they came at last, and more and more and more.' Why did you hide when you saw us coming?" He frowned thoughtfully. "By the way, what's going on back there?" He nodded toward the tunnel, from which more men had emerged amid the yells and threshing sounds from the clearing. "Sounds like it's hotting up," he added.

"You pretend you do not know, whereas in fact you know very well," Jonesu-san said coldly and turned his back.

Three of the men who had fled the clearing had gravitated toward Jonesu-san. Abruptly they closed in on him, one tackling him with an arm around his throat, one seizing his arms, the third having knocked his legs from under him and clamped them hard, though not before taking a solid kick to the jaw. Awkwardly they hauled the struggling man to his feet. Ignoring Grall, they started to haul Jonesu-san away.

"I'm not quite finished with him," Grall spoke up at last. "We were just beginning what promised to be a most interesting discussion."

One of the men looked back at Grall. "The swine decoyed us into ambush," he growled. "That gives *us* priority."

"Think again, prease," Grall replied. Then he stepped forward and brushed the three men away like flies as he grabbed Jonesu-san. "Now, tell me, Johnny, how did you get out of the muck?" he demanded of him.

"Our friends arrived and withdrew us to safety," he muttered, then gave Grall a hot look. "Would you have me revear *awr* in the presence of *these?*" He gave the three attentive bystanders a haughty look.

"Sure. Go right ahead and revear awr," Nat echoed his words. "Don't worry about these ferrows, Johnny—they're going to be nice." He released Jonesu-san, who at once bolted for cover.

"Rook here, I don't know if—" one man blurted.

"I say, we can't have—" another contributed.

"This is quite outrageous," the third commented and took a step toward Grall.

"Clear out," Nat said. "Scat! Be missing. Get hence. Dangle. Begone!"

"Sir," the least excited-looking of the trio began, "doubtless unknowing, you intrude in a matter of the greatest importance to all Omega."

"Swell," Nat said in a contented tone. "You've made a nice start: Now, go ahead; tell me all about it."

There was a stir at the far side of the clearing as a familiar voice called: "Hey, Captain, you want this sucker?"

Tey looked up to see Jonesu-san struggling in the easy grip of Cleo, slim and graceful in her fitted suit, emerging from the underbrush. Tey greeted her, while Grall went forward to embrace her briefly and take delivery of her captive.

"Now how about it, Johnny?" he said, laughing lightly. "Ready to tell all?"

· 9 ·

One of Jonesu-san's attackers had been staring up at Grall, the Hawaiian features of his face set in a look of indignation. "You intrude here!" he said, then added, "Who *are* you?" in an intent tone, looking Nat over as one inspecting a curious specimen.

"I'm still Nat Grall," the big man said. "Who're you?"

The smaller man fluttered his hands as if brushing away Nat's words. "Names are of no importance," he sputtered. "*What* are you?"

"Back to that?" Nat commented. "Just as I said, I'm a new

arrival, fresh from Terra. Some people call me Profundity," he added genially. "But I guess you wouldn't care about that. In any case I'm getting very tired of interrogating nuts and trying to find out where the head man is around here."

"If by 'head man,' sir, you mean to refer to our Special, Mr. Ohara, I can tell you that doubtless he remains, as is correct, at his post of duty."

"And where would that be?" Nat asked. "It seems right here is where the action is."

To Nat's astonishment, the man suddenly uttered an inarticulate yell and launched himself at him, like a furious Pekinese attacking a bull.

Three other pajama-clad men dashed from the tunnellike path and raced to join the assault. Grall gently fended off the first aggressor, who was vigorously applying judo techniques to the big man's oaklike arm, to no effect. As the reinforcements arrived, Nat picked up his original assailant and rolled him, log-wise, across their paths. All three went down and instantly became entangled in a screeching, furiously hacking melee, which subsided almost at once.

· 10 ·

Mullen had strolled over to the edge of the woods and was absorbed in examining various of the many kinds of saplings sprouting there. Using his suit-knife, he busied himself cutting lengths of representative specimens, which he took back to the car.

Grall was deep in conversation with Cleo as Tey strolled to Nat's side, and, over the background screeching, quoted: " 'Some guys has got wrong ideas about when to get tough.' "

Nat smiled. "Right, Cap'n. And maybe my style is a trifle too abrasive for these boys. Would the captain care to have a go?"

Tey nodded and addressed one of the men whom Nat had been questioning: "We're both quite reasonable men, I hope," he said in a pointedly reasonable tone. "No doubt we are both laboring under certain misapprehensions. So in order to clarify matters, I suggest we exchange facts. Are you agreeable to that?"

"Of course," the man replied evenly, making his display of reasonableness in turn. "First," he began, "from where do you come?"

"We came here from Terra, your own ancestral home. We had only a few rumors—no more than legends, actually—as to the location of the old colony, but we were fortunate. We found you."

The man was shaking his head. "We Siblings do not subscribe to the superstitions of the Croom men," he said with a hint of severity. "We are reasonable men, after all, and recognize the fact that we all—even Croom men—sprang from the Great Mother. That was at the dawn of time, several centuries agone."

"Three, to be exact," Tey said. "But the 'Great Mother' you all sprang from was the planet Terra, or Earth as it was called in the prespace era."

"Prease, spare me these ritual formulations, ah, Cappin, I believe your colleague addressed you." He ducked his head in a literal nod to formality. "You may address me as Fox-san."

"Very well, Fox-san," Tey replied. "But we're not going to get very far if you challenge every statement I make. Consider: what advantage could I even theoretically gain by lying to you?"

Fox-san looked vaguely troubled. "Prease, no riddles," he muttered. "How can an honest Sibring divine the motives of those who are sraves of the Erect?"

"Try to grasp this," Tey said patiently. "I have never heard of either the Siblings or the Elect."

"You speak of strange things," Fox-san commented indifferently.

"I am a strange man," Tey replied. Then: "What is the battle about?" He added the question as the shouts from the clearing redoubled.

Fox-san's bland face registered a number of emotions, as if he had only now become aware of the din. "Crever," he muttered;

then raising his voice, he said, "You think to distract me from my duties, but your pran fairs. I shall confute your insidious prans!"

Behind Fox-san, Nat commented, "You'll eliminate, too, if you eat reg'lar."

"Never mind, Nat," Tey interceded mildly, taking the excited Fox-san's arm gently. "Fox-san and I are about to have a most enrightening talk." He steered the small man away as Nat caught the other two by their collars.

"Let's you and me have an enrighting rittle tark of our own," he suggested, his big hard face six inches from one of his captives. "OK, pal?" He shook the fellow gently, as if to jar loose a reply, which he received in the form of vigorous nodding of the head.

"Ret me roose, you great ugry creature," the man's high-pitched voice squeaked, then paused for breath.

"Gosh," Nat said, assuming a stricken expression. "And me a three-time winner at Atlantic City." The man dangling from his other fist attempted to kick Grall in the groin, a maneuver which netted him a shift of Nat's grip from collar to neck, plus a painful rap on the shin.

"Naughty," Nat commented mildly. "I think you've got the odds figured wrong, my man. Be nice and we can get along. Right?"

Another vigorous nod. "Ret go of my neck, and we'll more rikely resolve interpersonal frictions," Nat's captive proposed.

Editors' Note: The journals of Hon. Founders Captain Tey and Freddy Shi-matsu show that full mutual understanding was reached only after some three days of acrimony, during which Captain Tey was instrumental in arranging an armistice to the ceremonial, yet literal, war between the Siblings and the faction known as the Backers, with all comers cordially invited to join the fray. The situation into which Tey and his companions had blundered, so to speak, can be summarized as follows in the light of present knowledge:

After making a safe planetfall, the crew and passengers of

Omega had fallen out and formed two basic factions: the crew, led by Hon. Founder Captain Brill; and the colonists, under Hon. Founder Jake Colmar. The legend holds that the great vessel—the nature of which is only vaguely understood by the bards—on which all had depended for life support had then mysteriously disappeared, each faction accusing the other of treachery. At this point a superhuman Presence, it was generally believed, had revealed itself to the colonists on East and had miraculously assisted them through their first winter—though not without loss of life—and had thereafter supplied all needed artifacts on request, a practice which gave rise to the Easters general taboo on manufacture of any sort. Life was not easy for those on barren East, but with the devoted help of the Exalted One, the colony survived.

On North, where the presence of the Exalted was not felt, the colonists were soon driven to experiment with local materials to supply their needs. They, too, lost many to cold, starvation (until the farms began to produce), and internal strife.

In spite of this initial difficulty, the two parties had succeeded in surviving the early years, planting crops, including a few trees, and had established herds of beef and sheep. Seeds escaping into the wild had soon established Terran flora over a large portion of East Continent, with a scattered representation on North, to which a party called Backers had, quite early, succeeded in crossing (the soil of Island proved too alkaline for Terran species to thrive there), and had there established an independent culture, uninfluenced by the Exalted.

At the point during these early years when contact had first been made (by Easters only) with the alien intellect known as the Mancji, referred to also as the Exalted One(s), the colonists had, according to legend, been on the point of abandoning their efforts to survive in the then alien milieu of early Colmar, and had organized a mass prayer-and-suicide meeting, to which, it seemed to them, the Exalted had responded, urging them to carry on and providing assistance.

After this first contact It held Itself aloof, reappearing from time to time, always in moments of crisis: during the Great Forest Fire, the earthquaking, and the 2500-year-Period

Glaciation. This interference, benign though it clearly was in intent, had the effect of conditioning the colonists on East Continent to rely on anything other than their own efforts, even to the extent that the manufacture of any artifact, or any form of construction, came to be regarded as heretical; whereas on North, the local raw materials were freely exploited in primitive fashion, high technology being soon forgotten. The need for slaves at last brought the two populations into contact again, most raids being from the North on the East, until East in some fashion acquired sufficient boats to attempt the twenty-mile crossing.

Shortly after groundfall, the colony vessel's fast courier boat had been ordered into distant surveillance orbit by Captain Brill, either to warn of the approach of searchers or to bring glad tidings thereof, the attitude of the colonists being ambiguous.

Self-reliance had by then become an article of dogma, at least to an inner circle of extremists calling themselves the Blowers. This fanatical faction elevated the legends of Earth origin to the status of a religion, commonly called the Mysteries, and only vaguely understood by the rank and file. For a century there was no contact between East and North.

Further factionalization of the divided Easters was inevitable, each new splinter group following the example of the older established doctrines in considering itself a closed group and alone in holding true to the Directive, an apparently imaginary document specifying policy for the colony. Each group continued to believe (or pretended to believe) that one or more of the other (by now multitudinous) factions was responsible for the theft of *Omega,* each sect reconciling, in its own way, the existence of an original colonizing vessel with the paradoxical doctrine of man's origin on Omega, as the planet was then called on East, while North preferred Colmar, which, of course, eventually prevailed—although "Omega" continues to linger on among rural populations to this day.

Exchange of personnel between factions by defection or capture in war occurred at a very slow rate, which resulted largely in refinement of differences of doctrine rather than any resolution thereof.

Quite naturally, the mutually hostile groups often met and clashed in the great empty spaces of the undeveloped planet. Since few effective weapons had been salvaged from the colony ship before its disappearance—presumably for hunting or protection against possible hostile indigenous life—combat was soon limited by custom to hand-to-hand encounters, a few wooden weapons and effective shields gradually coming into use. Casualties were few, but captives for conversion (and slavery) were eagerly sought.

In time these battles became ritualized and were purposefully arranged in accordance with a complex schedule worked out by the Croom group, all such events taking place at the site of the original campground, a curiously regular but natural clearing in the then-lone patch of thick native woods, a spot traditionally known as Prime and believed by many to be the spot where Man came spontaneously into existence, but which was later discovered to be the traditional hatching ground of the Mancji.*

It was during this period of ritualization—approximately (the precise date of *Omega*'s landfall being unknown) eighty-four years after Discovery—that an exploratory vessel from Terra, dispatched by His Lordship Enguerrand Banshire III as a part of a general sweep of the Solar neighborhood, secretly landed on East Continent near the site of present-day Old Grove on the north coast of Province, East Continent, and cautiously established liaison with the first Colmarites encountered (who happened to be a small party of Blowers) and through them vigorously spread among the scattered Omegans (some of whom, prior to the tabu on construction, had by then reached the cultural stage of small, permanent towns and tilled fields) the doctrine of the New Mysteries, the primary element of which was the Commandment of Mutual Hostility, in accordance with which the previously mild and sporadic skirmishes were soon elevated to the state of full scale Declared War. Contacts—and thus conflicts—were now being eagerly sought, rather than casually avoided, by all sects seeking Elevation thereby, with the inevitable result that intersect rivalry soon devolved into a

---

*This is, of course, the popular recreation-park now known as Playground One.

contest for supremacy among the half-dozen or so most advanced towns—and into their subsequent mutual destruction as well.

This policy of constant agitation by Terran agents calling themselves New Guardians* was designed by Lord Banshire, it now appears clear, to prevent the possibility of development of a planetary power base which could come to rival his own grip on Old Terra. Since at the Beginning his agents had access, by chance, only to East Continent, the spread of the Mysteries was confined there, while development on North Continent proceeded with little interference, the continent itself assuming the aura of East's taboo among its simple tribesmen, nomads, and ruin-dwellers. Still the Northers had little need for—or interest in—the savage wilderness across the water, other than the previously cited slave raids, which gradually became less frequent as the developing North technology reduced the need therefor.

At the moment of arrival aboard *Princeton*† of Hon. Founders Captain Tey and Nat Grall, the sects calling themselves the Siblings and the Backers were engaged in their decennial ceremony, which was being prosecuted with unusual vigor because the Backers had denied primacy to Prime, insisting that another less-regular clearing a few leagues distant was the true Prime and that the Siblings' Prime was actually Secondary.

It was remarkable that no weapons were in use; yet with fists, feet, knees, and elbows, and hard skulls alone, while seldom killing or permanently disabling a man, the combatants had soon expended their initial fervor and it was difficult to determine which mob of panting, bruised, and exhausted warriors could be considered the winner of the affray.

At that point Hon. F. Captain Tey and Hon. F. Nat Grall, two against two hundred, stepped in—both rhetorically and physi-

---

*This designation is not to be confused with that of His Profundity the Guardian, High Pontiff of the Church of the Mysteries Revealed.

†The *Princeton* is now in permanent orbit and open for viewing at all times, free shuttle service being provided by the Recpark administration. It is estimated that over 35,000 tourists per annum visit this fascinating relic still officially in commission by the Navy of Colmar as a number one ship of war.

cally—to impose an armistice. The Pacification was accomplished in stages over a period of one month, during which the two doughty peacemakers, by one-by-one singling-out of the most persistently aggressive individuals for intense interrogation and education, at last forced the leaders of the dominant sects to face the fact that they were mauling each other uselessly, over academic questions which would be better settled by archaeological methods.

It was then, in circumstances of relative quiet, that Captain Tey and his companion were at last able to elicit information regarding the piratical (to the Easters) Northers, equipped with terrifying magical devices and bent on slave-gathering.

Forced grudgingly to tolerate each other's presence, the newly reconciled Siblings and Backers immediately hatched a scheme to use their newly acquired strength by entering into an alliance directed against the Croom men, the next sect scheduled to arrive at Prime to face the colonists. Hon. Founder Captain Tey scotched this plan by the simple expedient of binding the limbs of the two sect leaders and hoisting them into adjacent trees, where they dangled, face-to-face, for five hours until both swore eternal pacifism and mutual regard.

When the first Croom scouts arrived, Hon. Founder Grall captured them and brought them to the clearing, their cursing and vows of reprisal falling silent only when they were presented with the astounding spectacle of heretic sects quite apparently associating on a nonlethal basis. They were then released to report this ominous development to their First Officer, who at once deployed his forces to ambush the approaching colonists, in stark defiance of tradition. Hon. Founder Tey, together with Hon. Founder Mullen, used the car to intercept the Croom leader, much to the astonishment of the latter, who, of course had never seen an advanced air-cushion vehicle.

[Summary ends.]

"I suggest, Mr. Brill-Smythe," Tey proposed to the first

officer, "that you examine your motives. What benefit will accrue to your mission from attacking these people? Omega needs every man if she is to establish a viable local economy."

"My interest, my dear fellow," Captain Brill replied coolly, "is not in what you said—but rather in harvesting scum to serve the New Mysteries."

As he spoke a massive wheeled box of gray-wood planks heaved into view, crashing through the jungle foliage, propelled by a perspiring but disciplined team of men, straining at heavy pegs protruding from the sides of the vehicle. At Captain Brill's gesture it halted.

"Captain, sir," Mullen put in to Tey quietly, eyeing the ordered ranks at the heels of the first officer, "I got an idea. Our boys can't handle trained troops like these fellas, not barehanded. They need an edge—and I think we can give 'em one."

Encouraged by Tey's nod, Mullen went on. "What we can do, sir—well, I been checking over some of the local woods, and I'm pretty sure the ones they call wishitwood and trapweed will do it. Archery, I mean. You know, archery's on the Navy's training list as a standard option for PE. Not many fellas pick it, but I did —regular orange-wood bows we had, just the simple kind without pulley wheels, and regular bason arrers."

"'Errors,' Mr. Mullen?" Tey responded. "I don't believe I understand."

"Not mistakes, sir, arrers—air-rows—you know, like on traffic signs and all."

"Ah, yes," Tey said at last. "Red Indians and all that, eh?"

"Just the bows and ar-rows, Cap'n, sir," Mullen persisted. "And it wasn't just them Injuns. All the primitive folks used 'em, seems like. And I got pretty good at it. I been working up a bow, sir, whilst you and Mr. Grall were busy."

"I noticed you scratching away at a stave of wood," Tey said, "and assumed it was simply a nervous habit."

"Let me show it to you, sir," Mullen proposed. "Bowstring was a problem for awhile, but like I said, the trapweed works OK."

Tey gestured to Mullen to wait for him and then turned his attention back to Captain Brill, who had now been overtaken by Burko and Patucci who were now hovering near him.

Seeing that Tey was about to speak once again to the Croom leader, Burko stepped forward determinedly and spoke up first:

"Mr. Speaker, sir—" he addressed his chief. "Uh, me and Patooch here, sir—What we had, sir, about these here gents is —They's Chief Guardians, sir. Thought you might like to know —"

Captain Brill whirled to face Burko. "Why do you make that astounding statement, my man?" he demanded. Then over his shoulder, attempting an awkward head-bob: ". . . overlook it, Profundities, if I missed any fine points of protocol. Nobody informed me! Outrageous!"

"No harm done, Mr. Speaker," Tey soothed the man. "And now you know."

"Still," Captain Brill temporized, "one has one's orders." He waved a hand, and the wheeled box rolled into the clearing with a groan and squeal of wooden axles. The men at once formed up into a ragged column of fours behind it. Both Patucci and Burko, after yelling drill-sergeant orders, took places flanking the head of the column.

"Really, Profundities," the Speaker said, "I must get on with my attack—coordinated with air cover, you understand. With your permission," he ducked his head and went to take up his place at the head of the column.

"I suppose we'd better get back and make what preparation we can for the assault," Tey said. "The boys aren't going to like that war wagon, but at least if they know what's coming they may not run at first sight of it."

"Captain," Mullen inquired, "do you suppose these Croom boys are ready to violate the taboo and use those handguns we saw back at the depot?"

"We'll have to wait and see. In the meantime maybe we've got a secret weapon of our own." He went into conference with Mullen, walking beside him.

FOURTEEN

Slave Raiders

At the car, again parked at the water's edge out of harm's way, Nat Grall listened with interest to the report of the coming attack by war car. He pressed Mullen for the details of his homemade weapon, and the SCPO extracted the bow from its stowage place beneath the car's front seats. It was of straight-grained, pinkish wood, nearly six feet in length, two inches thick at the center, tapering both ways to notched tips. Tey and Grall watched with interest as Mullen bent the springy stave and fitted the looped ends of the trapweed vine into the notches.

The taut string hummed when Tey plucked it. "What about arrows?" he asked, and Mullen reached again, and brought forth a quiver improvised from the rags of a pseudoleather garment of the kind stocked at Prime Depot. It was packed half-full with straight, two-foot-long shafts, tipped with odd bits of glass, metal, or mollusk shell, and at the notched end, bearing three small vanes clearly snipped from a Navy-issue stiff-plastic placard. Tey and Grall handled the objects carefully.

"I saw one in the museum at the Academy," Tey said thoughtfully. "I recall that at the time it seemed pretty complicated for something made by pretechnological man, but at the same time pitifully feeble for facing big cats and dire-wolves, and stone axes as well. A miniature spear-thrower is all it is—but now suddenly it seems to have an air of potency about it."

"It's all relative, sir," Mullen put in eagerly. "Up against even stone-tipped spears, it's better than nothing."

"Let's see a demonstration, Mr. Mullen," Tey suggested. Back on the ground, Mullen indicated a foot-wide Leave-Me-Alone Tree,* with a patch of black, terrestrial fungus at head height. Smoothly he plucked an arrow from the quiver now slung behind his left shoulder, fitted it, drew it back until its hammered sheetmetal tip barely cleared the bow, and let fly. At the *twang!* of the released string, the missile leaped up and out with an audible hiss, flashed across the fifty-yard range, dropping just enough to impact on the fungus-patch with a businesslike *smack!,* and fell away.

Grall gave Mullen a hearty clap on the back which almost felled the archer. "These comedians aren't as tough as wood, Chief," he reassured him. "But maybe you need to bend it a little farther." He took the bow, which Mullen had unstrung, restrung it with a single deft motion, casually bent it into a deep arc, and flexed it a few times.

"Nice springy wood," he acknowledged. "But you'd need longer arrows, eh?"

"Right, sir," Mullen agreed. "But most of these fellows couldn't bend it as it is. I'll make theirs smaller."

At that moment a ragged yell went up from the listless combatants, only a few of whom were still doggedly tugging at each other, too tired to complete a throw. As they turned to stare, the man-propelled tank crashed through a final screen of shrubbery and nosed into the clearing.

The surprised Easters gave ground, except for a bold Walker "armed" with a swagger-stick, one Shigemura Schmidt, who, it was later determined, advanced direct   of the monster and idly poked his stick into th   in the box, a foot-wide, two-inch-high

*The popular name of this familiar species was, c
when its intractable working qualities became

300 —

front plank. The tank at once halted. As Schmidt turned his back to it, grinning, the inimitable rasp of a powergun on tight aperture sounded and Schmidt fell face-down, revealing the great charred wound in his back. A yell went up and the Easters crowded into the surrounding brush, leaving the clearing vacant but for the corpse, and, on the opposite edge of the open area, the three Terrans.

Mullen glanced at Tey with the raised eyebrows of the interrogative and received a brief nod. He plucked an arrow from its quiver, nocked it, drew, squinting along the shaft, then elevated it and let fly. The slim arrow shot out and up, too high it seemed, then dropped, still horizontal, with astonishing swiftness, and passed through the observer's slit to half its length, where it paused, and was then drawn quickly in, even as a thin yelp came from the mysterious box.

A few Easters emerged from the brush, yelling and shaking their fists. At first few spared a glance for the Terrans, whom they apparently did not connect with the tiny spear that had elicited the cry of pain from the monster—but now, made bold by this evidence of its mortality, they crowded around the intruder, shouting threats and shaking fists. As if cut by a knife, the mob-roar ceased as the rasp of the powergun sounded again. The man directly before the open slit, from which the arrow had been drawn in, fell, his face bloodied, and the others took to their heels.

"Hold your fire, Mullen," Tey ordered, and a long, silent moment passed. Then a hatch lifted atop the box and a man's head and shoulders appeared. There was a bloody wound in his neck.

· 2 ·

"I could nail that sucker," Mullen said quietly, bow in hand and arrow nocked.

"No. I want to talk to him," Tey said. He took a step forward icked his collar communicator to PA mode, at which the swiveled toward him, bringing up his gun.

"Better drop that," Tey called, his voice booming. "The next one won't be in your shoulder. It'll be right through your neck." As the man hesitated, Tey turned to Mullen and mouthed silently: "Give him a close one and reload."

The arrow whined past the Croom man's ear. He started convulsively and dropped the gun—and at once ducked back inside the wooden car.

"You said you wanted to talk to that sucker, Cap'n?" Nat Grall inquired rhetorically, and walked across the clearing toward the menacing plank-sided tank. The draft-crew had faded away into the underbrush. There was no response as Grall inserted his hand into the observation slit, and, with a mighty heave, ripped the two-inch-thick board from its place and tossed it aside. Within the dark compartment revealed, two men in dirty whites crouched. At Grall's command they crept forth, dropped down to the trampled sward, and hurried across to where Tey waited beside Mullen with his bow drawn.

". . . what King Edgar will say when he sees his magical war car," one was babbling as he halted before Tey. "His revenge will be terrible."

"You may speak when spoken to," Tey told him curtly. "You're finished threatening people and shooting unarmed men from inside a box."

Nat, who had scooped up the pistol before following the two tankers, arrived then and showed Tey the gun. "Same old reliable Mark X," he commented. "That colony ship must've carried arsenal enough to supply a division of infantry."

"A couple of corps," Tey corrected. "Only the noncoms carried a handgun then. But I think there's more to it than that. They must be manufacturing them locally somehow."

"It seems that way, Cap'n, but these clowns won't even pick up a stone to pound with; that's their number one taboo—"

"I know, Nat, and that's going to be our problem—getting them to adopt the bow and arrows to counterbalance North's tanks and Mark X's. Still, the guns are here—and a lot of other little trifles—and they're coming from somewhere."

Both men fell silent, listening.

A distant hum had become audible, a distinct beat developing as it steadily grew louder. Mullen came over.

"What is it, Cap'n?" he asked anxiously. "I thought old Smitty was bluffing. If these Croom boys have really got air cover, we're in trouble."

The Croom captives spoke up simultaneously:

"—not ours. —kill us too. Must all run away now, before—"

"Cowardly Northers, and their familiar demons—"

Tey gave them a thoughtful look.

"The Northers have aircraft, eh?" he prodded. "Tell me more."

"It is the Guardians, come from the Grove," one said sullenly.

"They bring many New Things," the other added. "Things not of the Mysteries—" he touched his forehead in the now-familiar antidemon gesture. "Yet like the Mysteries for strangeness. This is a most terrible Thing—a being which comes now, beating great vanes, riding the very air." The Croom man shuddered.

The *whop-whop!* of the approaching craft now dominated conversation, drowning the clearing in menacing sound. The former combatants had fled again into the brush, all but the two who lay dead on the smooth-trampled grass. A fantastic thing swung into view, making a low pass above the clearing. It was like an immense dragonfly, with frantically beating wings. It dropped below treetop level at the far end of the long clearing, hesitated in midair, hanging there impossibly, a whirlwind spinning a dust cloud beneath it. Then it came on.

"It's an H-1001," Tey commented mildly. "Only a few decades off the active equipment list. It has to be a new import."

"I've seen that sucker before," Mullen said, as the copter pilot's face became clearly visible, now only fifty yards distant. "Never knew his name. One of Carstairs's broom-and-pan men."

Tey turned to the more talkative of the two captives.

"I'm going to take that thing in one piece," he told the terrified man. "Do you think you and your friend here could cooperate with these Easters long enough to save your necks?"

". . . to take it—" the man gulped. "I don't understand what you mean, sir. No man can 'take' such a thing—or even approach it. To attempt it is to die. *It* takes men, carries them off—to devour them in its lair—none is ever seen again."

"Still, we're going to take it. Mr. Mullen—" Tey turned to the SCPO, standing by with an arrow nocked, "Can you skewer his arm, without really damaging him?"

"Sure thing, Captain—if I can get a clear shot at him."

"I'll tease him out into the open," Tey said, and set off to intercept the craft, now barely moving as it hovered a foot above the sward. He heard the rotors change pitch, and the machine drifted to a stop, still hovering.

Tey gestured with his open hand extended, palm down—a sharp downward motion. He was looking directly into the face of the pilot, who frowned and then, as if by reflex, responded to the standard hand-and-arm signal. As the dusty wheels touched, Tey made a sharp slashing motion across his throat with his forefinger. The engine died with a clatter, and the long rotors became visible, slowing to a halt. Through the dusty canopy, the pilot frowned quizzically at Tey, who motioned him out and waited with folded arms.

The canopy opened, and the pilot stepped out onto a narrow footplate and raised a pistol. Tey heard the twang of the bow and a finned shaft stood in the man's right shoulder. The pistol fell with a clatter off the plate and dropped into the grass. Tey had continued his slow advance and now quickened his pace. He reached the man as he collapsed, caught him, and eased him to the ground. The wounded man was staring incredulously at the arrow buried in his body.

"It is a New Thing," he gasped. "Yet an officer of His Majesty is ready to face even such strangeness."

"You've already faced it, sir," Tey said comfortingly. "It's painful, but it's not fatal. We'll get it out as soon as you and I have our little talk."

"Pain is nothing," the young pilot stated, then fainted.

Two days later a second copter appeared, coming in low over the clearing. It hastily aborted, trailing smoke, when Mullen sent an arrow through the aluminum wall of the engine compartment at a precise point indicated by Hon. Founder Captain Tey, who immediately called a council of war, attended by, in addition to Grall and Mullen, the Sibling and Backer leaders Fox-san and Pugliese, the Croom Speaker, Captain Brill-Smythe, other lesser tribal leaders, including Jonesu-san, and the captive Norther pilot, Racy Muldoon, whose mood had brightened considerably after his wound had been tended and he found himself, to his surprise, alive and intact.

"We all need information," Tey said by way of opening the conference. "Each of you has his own distorted concept of the true situation here on Omega."

"Colmar," Brill-Smythe interrupted. "Only the savages subscribe to the superstitious designation 'Omega.'"

"Very well," Tey responded. "But at this time questions of nomenclature are secondary to our substantive problems, as I'm sure you'll agree."

"I agree to nothing," the Croom man said haughtily. Tey curtly told him to remain silent until called upon to speak, and then to speak fully. Brill-Smythe subsided.

"You have been victimized," Tey went on. "And the exploitation continues, as Mr. Muldoon's activities attest. By his own boast he is a slave raider—and personally responsible for the delivery of over one hundred captives to the gang of pirates you all refer to devoutly as the Guardians. These Guardians of yours are nothing but hoodlums sent out here and supplied from Terra by a big shot who calls himself Lord Banshire. Their job, it seems clear, is to keep you people stirred up, constantly at war, bickering over the details of your so-called Mysteries. Most of you don't have any idea what you're fighting about—it's just a habit you don't know how to break. As for you Croom men, you seem to have lucked into a supply of Navy-issue items somehow, and you use them to maintain your supremacy over the rest of your fellow Omegans—or Colmarites, as Mr. Brill-Smythe prefers."

At this mention Captain Brill pushed forward importantly and addressed Tey:

"It is not a matter of personal preference, mine or another's," the little man said with dignity. "Our Guardians"—here he sketched a ragged B in the air with his left hand—"have revealed to us the proper name for our world."

Tey designated two of the more quarrelsome aides of Fox-san to escort the Speaker to a nearby tree, bind him to it, and to prevent him from making any further vocal disturbance. The short, plump Croom leader went silently, eyeing his guards and traditional enemies nervously. No one made any move to interfere.

·5·

After half an hour of calm and reasoned address to the unresponsive faces around him, Tey summed up:

"An original colonial vessel named *Omega* arrived here some three centuries ago. There was dissension over the disposition of the vessel, probably an argument as to whether to cannibalize her for her materials or to maintain her intact as a line of retreat. Presumably the former view prevailed, since we now see evidence of some of her supplies still in existence among you, as well as the curious legend that some among you stole her —a highly impractical theft, considering her bulk.

"Thereafter further schisms occurred and reoccurred until the first-generation descendents of the pioneer group were hopelessly divided and barely holding on at subsistence level, although sufficient Terran flora and fauna had been established at the beginning to make possible a hunting-and-gathering subsistence.

"At that point, it seems, a second Terran vessel arrived here, evidently a party of Greenbacks dispatched by 'Lord' Banshire I, a find the exploitation of which enabled him to establish himself as supreme among the robber barons of the day. Banshire's policy has been one of divisionism, encouraging and deepening the hostility he found already existing among the several various factions you had already established among yourselves. This of course greatly simplified the task of enlisting slave labor from among you 'native' Omegans, labor which was needed to develop the rich mineral and other natural resources found especially on North Continent, and perhaps other continents unknown to us.

"East Continent, meanwhile, continued as a totally undeveloped wilderness, while Island, due no doubt to the treacherous nature of its unstable surface, became a taboo area, self-forbidden to Omegans, a taboo respected out of fear by nearly all.

"The time has now come to put an end to this dismal situation. And that task . . . can be done *only* by you, yourselves."

· 6 ·

"But—" It was, surprisingly, the lanky Patucci who rose to protest: "—what about the Exarted? Do you not know that the Exarted controls all affairs on Omega? His will be done."

"I have deliberately ignored the Mysteries," Tey replied, unruffled. "It is clear that the original Terran technology has assumed the status of a religion among you. Calling it 'the Mysteries' excuses you from any impulse to investigate that technology rationally and to establish sciences of your own. But in order to throw off the yoke of these 'Guardians' of yours, it will be necessary for you to face the fact that nothing will be done unless you do it for yourselves."

Jonesu-san rose and seemed about to speak, but subsided silently. However, Grall, at Tey's side, muttered the question: "How *did* Johnny and his bunch get out of the soup?"

"I suspect," Tey replied, "that when we have the answer to that, we'll know more about the whereabouts of *Princeton,* including Oliver, Renee, and Sugar."

"Funny thing," Mullen put in. "These here natives got a legend about a full-size space vessel disappearing, and now we got the same problem."

Emboldened by Jonesu-san's unrebuked interruption, others rose with a variety of rebuttals of Tey's interpretation of events, mostly petty points of doctrine.

"What it boils down to," Grall said, cutting across the chatter, "is that you people need to start doing something for yourselves —and the first thing is self-defense. The old slave-raider tactics can't do much against archery—not without killing off the slaves. Right, Mr. Muldoon?"

The copter pilot looked baffled, but replied, "I don't know what that word is," he commented, "but nobody can fly with a sharp stick in his arm—or shoot, or anything else."

"Thus," Nat said gravely, "we demonstrate the chink in the armor of technology. In other words, let's get started."

Von Shimo, until then silent, rose to say: "Chink in armor, incorrect. No Chink here; mostly honorober Yapanee ancestry."

Tey called upon the leaders present to arrange their people in groups of ten, while Mullen went to the undergrowth at hand and busied himself cutting a four-inch-thick sapling. Tey and Grall, working opposite sides of the assembled clumps of restive Omegans, directed their pupils' attention to Mullen's technique of girdling the tough young tree to a depth of half an inch, using his Navy-issue belt knife, a type known to the locals. As he broke off, trimmed, and split the two-yard length of wood, then resplit the halves into four long narrow staves, the audience began to mutter and draw back:

". . . it is a new thing."

". . . magical miracle more fitting to the Exarted."

". . . see, he makes more miracles."

·7·

All watched nervously as Mullen shaved the first of the rough lengths, tapering it both ways from the center. Soon he had roughed out a crude but serviceable bow stave. The crowd observed carefully as he notched the ends, then laid it aside to begin pulling long, ragged lengths of trapweed.

". . . not only a new thing," Burko's voice rose above the

chatter to intone solemnly, "but a New Thing. Such cannot be!" Others took up the protest as Mullen worked quietly on, stripping leaves and suckers from the tough strands. With a deft motion, he strung the bow, then looked up to see the menacing locals closing in on him, hesitant, frightened, but determined, the Croom men in the van. He nocked an arrow from the quiver still slung across his shoulder, drew casually, and fired an arrow into the trampled turf precisely between the feet of Burko, who leapt back protesting.

"—coulda went right through a feller's gentrails," he yelled. "Magic! Blasphemy! Don't you see, you idiots? It is a new Thing! Destroy it and the fiend who made it!" As he whirled to face Mullen, the crowd surging forward with him, Mullen let fly a second shaft, which struck Burko's wrist, penetrated it, and pinned his arm to his hip. The excited mob recoiled as the Croom agitator stared down in horror at the stick protruding from his body, tugged tentatively to free his arm, screamed, and fell, out cold.

"Any more objections, boys?" Mullen asked, his next arrow ready.

Editors' Note: At this point the journal of Captain Tey loses continuity, as only scattered lengths, much damaged by weather, have been recovered of this, the fourth and final reel of his field notes. On the basis of early oral history recordings, sparse official records, and personal reminiscences of Mrs. Nathan Jaxon-Tey, the following has been reconstructed:

After minor scuffling and another arrow, this one through both thighs of a Croom straw boss as he attempted to slip away unnoticed into the forest, order was restored. Working briskly the three Terrans, aided now by Jonesu-san and one other local, reshaped the churning mob into groups of ten, irrespective of tribal affinity, and assigned a small class of five to Mullen for intensive training as instructors in bow-making. Hesitantly at first, then with grinning enthusiasm, the hand-picked cadremen—who had been selected on the basis of what the Terrans had observed of their behavior, assisted by the advice of the former tribal bosses—took wood and knife in hand and watched, astonished, as, following Mullen's tutoring, their hands shaped the new material. Cries of "it is a New Thing!" were frequent and increasingly sounded with a note of pride rather than fear.

Soon all five were excitedly flexing their bows and looking longingly at Mullen's quiver. He allowed each one to fire one bolt into the underbrush, and at each wobbly and uncertain shot, a shout went up, not from the trainees alone. Others were gathered close, watching hungrily, their hands unconsciously mimicking the action of drawing and firing.

At last Mullen called together his graduating class, told each one to teach two others, and retired. Less than a day later, with every adult and half-grown child in possession of his own self-provided bow, Tey authorized Mullen to demonstrate the manufacture of arrows.

Once armed, it soon occurred to one of the former tribal chieftains, one Sven Mbuto, a swarthy Downer, to organize an attack on the now-dissolved tribe's former archenemies, the even blacker-skinned Uppers, a move which the Terrans had anticipated and immediately stifled by confronting the outraged Mbuto with a solid wall of tribally mixed Easters, bows drawn, arrows aimed. Sven Mbuto subsided, muttering about "tribal purity," and "congenital inferiors." In this minor altercation Brill-Smythe, surprisingly, lent his still not-inconsiderable authority to the pacification.

"You suckers—and even we Croom men, too, I admit it—have been on the losing end long enough," he bawled. "I don't know where these Great Guardians—" he inclined his head toward the Terrans, "—came from or why. But I know a good New Thing when I see it, and we're through fighting each other. We'll fight the Northers—and even the Guardians, if that's what it takes!"

Even as Tey and his illustrious colleague, Mullen conferred with the Croom leader, an alarm was given as an abrupt shadow fell precisely over the clearing. A few yards beyond, the pale sun continued to gleam on grayish foliage. The so recently pacified bowmen gathered in restive clumps, casting apprehensive glances alternately upward and toward the two Terrans conferring with Brill-Smythe. The latter, noting that he was haplessly included in the focus of the suspicion and hostility so rapidly growing among the frightened men, stepped back a pace, disassociating himself from the strangers. The shadow grew denser, accompanied by a faint whirring sound and a sense of doom impending.

"O zarm!" Brill-Smythe shouted. "O zarm!" Having thus invoked certain primitive idols, he briskly set about disposing the men around the periphery of the frightening shadow, bows at the ready. Brill-Smythe rounded on Tey.

"I hold you fully accountable, Captain, for the safety of my men!" he yelled. "You will find you can't so easily trick us into your traps."

"What traps?" Tey returned sharply.

"This—this unnatural darkness in full day," the little man yelled.

"Whatever it is," Tey commented, turning away, "it appears that Mr. Mullen and I are equally affected—though I have never known shadows to be dangerous."

At a curt gesture from the former Croom Speaker, the ragged ring of bowmen closed in, arrows nocked and ready, aimed directly now at Tey and Mullen, who stood fast as the shade grew denser.

"What do you figure, Captain?" Mullen muttered the question.

"No idea, Chief," Tey replied. "I suppose we'll find out soon."

"It appears, Cappin," Brill-Smythe said lazily, "that your tenure as usurper and dictator has come to an end." He paused to pull at his lower lip and eye Tey distastefully. "As well make an end altogether," he added, and moved off through his circle of ready executioners to take up a position well out of range. "You, my dear Cappin, are, it seems, hoist by your own petard, as the saying has it. Having provided me both incentive and means to dispose of your interference, I should be a bit of an ass should I fail to take advantage thereof."

"Appearances can be so deceiving at times," a bass voice rumbled behind the Croom Speaker.

As Brill-Smythe jumped in startlement and reached to his quiver for an arrow, the large, scarry-knuckled hand of Nat Grall closed over the slender shaft. While Brill-Smythe stared in indignation, Nat snapped the arrow between his fingers and dropped it to the brambly ground. Then he plucked the bow from the hands of its owner.

"Primitive weapons can be effective against sophisticated ones," Grall stated. "But of course, every weapon has its weakness. In this case the bow is useless for close-in work." He used both hands to bend Brill-Smythe's bow almost double before it snapped with a sharp *crack!*, at which the short Croom man uttered a yell and launched himself at Grall like a terrier attacking a Bolo Mark IV.

"You were naughty," Nat said, taking his favorite grip on the excited man's thinning waffle-cut, lifting him so that his feet threshed frantically six inches above contact. After a few seconds of this fruitless exercise, Brill-Smythe fell silent and hung, breathing hard, eyeing Grall with a venomous expression on his round face.

"Now what?" he cried at last. "At my command my loyal troops will execute your friends—then you, you great ruffian!"

Grall bounced him, almost gently, up and down, the tension on the Croom man's scalp pulling his features into a distorted grimace, and eliciting a shriek at each upward jerk.

"I was telling you," Grall continued as if there had been no interruption, "that the penalty for misuse of bows is the loss thereof." He threw the broken weapon aside, and dropped its owner, who snatched up the pieces and gazed mournfully at them.

During this distraction, Tey, with Mullen at his side, had

brushed casually through the encircling bowmen, most of whom had already unstrung their bows. Brill-Smythe confronted Tey, backing to maintain his position facing the bigger man as Tey advanced steadily.

"Now I want to know, Cappin," the game little man yapped, with a glance upward into darkness, and just as quickly returning his gaze to Tey's face, "I want to know just what effect you imagine you will achieve by this charade?"

At last Tey, now beside Grall, spoke: "The present effect is sufficient, I imagine."

· 9 ·

Men with restrung bows were now crowding close again. Nat Grall reached casually and plucked the weapons from the hands of the two nearest, in the process snapping off the arrow shafts just below their heads. He broke both bows and tossed the fragments into the faces of their bereaved makers.

"Slow learners," Nat scolded them. "I've already explained that you're not allowed to misuse these new weapons we've given you. Anybody else?"

The men shrank back, those nearest unstringing bows, returning arrows to quivers, and assuming "who, me?" expressions.

"Nice work, Nat," Tey commented. "But after awhile it will occur to them to get out of range of those dainty hands of yours and fire a volley."

A yell went up. Tey and Grall looked upward.

A curious phenomenon was now visible through a fine mist at the center of the hovering darkness, descending silently amid shadow from above: an immense bulk in the form of a blunt cylinder—clearly a material object of gigantic mass, yet it was alighting as lightly as a feather.

As the blunt end of the huge thing pressed down relentlessly through the treetops, Brill-Smythe jabbed a finger upward. "That *Thing*," he stated, "is impossible. Impossible things do, by definition, not occur. Ergo, there is nothing there. 'Tis but an illusion induced by your demonic arts! I shall ignore it, as shall my troops. You there—" he broke off to yell at the nearest of the bowmen, now standing about, fingering the bows. "You there, O'Toole, Shaw, Burko, Banniver, Joule: O zarm!"

Abruptly breaking off his incantations, Brill-Smythe, who had worked his way back to Tey's side, inquired in a conversational tone: "Just what in the devil *is* that damned thing, Cap'n?"

Tey replied quietly that he was as surprised as anyone at the spectacle, though, he conceded, he *did* recognize the object. It was a deep-space vessel of the Terran Navy, his own late command, *Princeton*, in fact.

"Sure, it's *here*, all right, Cap'n," Mullen commented. "But why the silent approach? And how? A sharp copter pilot might be able to con her in that slow on full emergency blast, but not like a falling leaf."

"Clearly," Tey said, "she's not operating on her own power. Let's wait and see." By common consent, all present had backed away, leaving the center of the glade clear.

· 10 ·

Have no fear, Tey Mullen, someone said clearly, over the whistling of wind and the crunch of collapsing foliage, as the immense bulk of the vessel descended irresistibly until its great grasshopper landing jacks contacted and pierced the humus layer of the forest floor, shifting nervously for a few moments until satisfied that equilibrium had been achieved. It took seconds before the fact that movement had ceased penetrated the consciousness of the watchers.

"She's down!" a man yelled, and started forward, to be curbed by a barked order from Brill-Smythe, who took up a prominent position on a fallen tree and addressed all present.

"By some miracur, peeper, we see before us the great ship of veneraber regend. We of awr men are priviliged to witness this historic moment." He turned to Tey and Grall. "Doubtless, the coming of you gentermen is no mere happenstance, but is direckry associated with this great event. Gentermen, what are your instructions?"

Neither Tey nor Mullen hurried forward to correct the first officer's impression.

"As it happens," Tey said quietly, "we have reason to berieve the vesser to be under the contror of friends." He turned to Mullen. "Did you hear it, too—or was I harrusinating?"

"He called us by name, sort of," Mullen replied. "I thought I'd burned my linings: Said 'Have no fear,' but I'll be candid, Cap'n—I had some fear anyway."

"Me, too," Tey confided.

It is not to worry, the same bland voice spoke again. *All is well with your Sugar-Renee-Jaxon unit.*

"What's that mean?" Mullen inquired of Tey.

"My friends aboard ship," Tey explained. "I was just getting ready to try pounding on the hull in Morse to try to make contact."

"Dames, sounds like," Mullen commented in an awe-struck tone. "You know, Cap'n, aboard *Catrice* we had two female crew: one ninety years old, the other a three-hundred pounder. What's this Sugar and Renee look like?"

"Sugar is a mere child," Tey said. "Renee is a thoroughly married lady."

The Croom men fell silent as a sound from above signaled the opening of the rear, emergency personnel hatch. A moment later Jaxon's head and shoulders appeared.

· 11 ·

"Which way to the Emerald City?" he called genially. "If you see a shoe with a foot in it sticking out from under my basement, pay no attention: it's just the Wicked Witch of the West—or is it East?" Then, directing his gaze at Brill-Smythe, who was still holding his ground atop the fallen log,* Jaxon said sharply—

---

*A reconstruction of this historic scene, cast in durlon, can be seen today at the Regional Museum.

quite apparently not yet noticing the three Terrans standing inobtrusively aside—"You seem to be the big shot among our welcoming committee, sir. Will you be so kind as to indicate the direction of the nearest town?"

"We should have known Ollie wouldn't let the side down," Nat Grall commented. "From Tey to Grall to Jaxon—the classic triple play."

Brill-Smythe responded to Jaxon's request by inhaling deeply, in spite of the still-settling dust, and uttering in a shrill yell: "What the meaning of this outrage might be, I don't know—"

"Too right, Jack," Jaxon cut him off. "That's just the top of a long list of what you don't know. Don't you recognize gods making a miraculous descent when you see them?" With that, Jaxon withdrew.

Renee's pert face appeared. She saw Tey at once and smiled. "Thank God," she said. "I don't understand it, but I accept it. Do board ship at once, Captain," she added coolly. She withdrew, and Jaxon reappeared in the opening.

"Right, Cap'n," he called cheerfully. "I'm right 'round the bend, you know. Renee's not much better. Shuggie's been holding things together."

"Wow, some dame," Mullen said reverently. "Is that the old lady, or what?"

"Neither," Tey said shortly. "Apparently they've been through some harrowing experiences. But I'll wager they'll be able to give us a reasonable explanation. Let's get aboard her."

While the responses of your Oliver-Renee-Sugar unit seems more incomprehensible than ever, be not alarmed. All is well.

Tey and Mullen exchanged inquiring glances.

"I guess if we both hear it, we're not really winging it, eh, Captain?" Mullen remarked, and turned at once to the business of scaling the rungs on the heat-tarnished, atmospheric guidance vane near at hand.

Brill-Smythe ordered men forward to help him, and a moment later, Mullen caught Jaxon's outstretched hand and was drawn inside. Tey followed. One of the Croom men attempted to follow, but Jaxon gently advised him to wait.

Tey was unprepared for the impact of the face-to-face confrontation with the ravishing youth, beauty, and above all, femininity of Renee, who in turn seemed almost drab in contrast with the full-blooming radiance of the prime young beauty beside her, whom Tey barely recognized as Sugar. *If she's like this at almost sixteen,* his dazed mind wondered, *what can the future hold?*

The development of your Sugar unit is proceeding perfectly normally, Tey. Be not dismayed.

" 'Dismayed' is not the word for it," Tey muttered.

"Say, Captain," Mullen spoke up, "now which one is the kid and which one is the old lady?"

Both women laughed. Tey made introductions. Mullen managed to gulp and utter apologies for the gaucherie of his question. Sugar smiled at him, and the rugged veteran, as he later stated, almost fainted.

"I'll try to bring you up to date, Captain," Jaxon spoke up. "First, after the first few days after you dropped off the screens, I thought I'd better try to follow you in the utility car. The girls talked me out of it." He glanced at the pretty pair. "Then," he went on, "I went bananas. Started hearing voices. Even answering them. Had some fine conversations, too. All about somebody named Mank-chee and his mother. Weird stuff. Otherwise I seem to check out 'still functional.' "

Renee spoke up: "If Ollie is unbalanced, so are Sugar and I." She put a sisterly arm about the girl, who was still artlessly studying Mullen, the first male human stranger she had any memory of seeing at conversational range. Mullen, in turn, was quite unable to get his eyes off the heavenly young beauty who had appeared so unexpectedly in his life.

". . . and I don't for one minute believe any of us is insane. There *is* a voice," Sugar stated firmly.

"Certainly there is," Tey confirmed. "If we all hear it, we must accept it as objective fact."

*We've been all over that, long ago, very long ago. Surely it's
not necessary to begin again.*

"Just how long ago?" Tey murmured aloud.

"You *did* hear it," Renee exclaimed. "I wondered too."

*In terms of planetary revolutions, two hundred ninety-seven
and one half. Your Brill-Max unit was a most stimulating one.
Indeed, it stimulated a revolutionary change in Mancji life.**

"Then after I blew my main panel," Jaxon continued, "I imagined I was conning the ship by mind control. We had a fine,
silent, vibration-free tour of the countryside. Pretty poor visibility, but I even imagined I photographed some roads and villages
and tilled fields and whatnot over on North. I'll show them to
you later. Anyway, it seems we picked the most deserted part
of the damned planet to touch down on. The colony made it!
I was looking for you—or for that museum piece you drove off
in—and finally Sugar spotted movement near here. So I decided to move in to fifty miles and take a good look. I saw what
looked like a trail party, so I put her down—and here you are.
That's all lies, of course. Actually I'm strapped to a frame in sick
bay, being fed intravenously."

*This last, it appears, is an example of the curious, nonlinear
phenomenon you call "humor." It defies analysis by my (our)
logic segment.*

"Of course," Jaxon went on, "logically I realize it's just my
subconscious trying to find a way out of a situation which I'm
impotent to change."

"Still," Tey commented, "if everybody else hears the same
things—"

"I've got a very resourceful subconscious, Captain," Jaxon
pointed out. "I can imagine everybody hearing voices just as
easily as I imagine *I* hear them."

"Yet," Tey persisted, "the ship *is* here."

"Very well. Suppose that for the moment we accept that as
objective fact. It simply means that somehow I've tapped a

---

*This statement, as repeated by Captain Tey for the log, represents the earliest
occurrence on record of the myth of Mancji planetary origin.

psychokinetic ability I didn't know I had. It does nothing to convince me that everything is proceeding normally in my head." Jaxon put his hands to the sides of his head, elbows high, like a man lifting off a helmet. "Still screwed on tight," he commented, as if matter-of-factly.

"Please, Oliver," Renee said in a stricken tone, "do abandon this silly idea that you've gone mad. It's very distressing."

"Renee is quite right," Tey said crisply. "You've indulged these fancies long enough. Now, snap out of it, Ollie, and give some consideration to the strain you've been putting on Renee and Sugar."

Beside Tey, Sugar took a step toward Jaxon. "You can knock off that charade right now, mister!" she said in an uncompromising tone. "You *know* you're not crazy!"

"You mean," Jaxon replied uncertainly, "all of you can really hear that damned Mank-chee—or whatever he calls himself?"

Mancji. As for the maneuvering of your immense carapace, I did lend assistance. Nonetheless, I found you to have a fantastic aptitude—well up into the third stratum of organization— and you, a mere lone life unit! Quite astounding!

"Telekinesis!" Jaxon and Sugar said together. "Then it really does work." Jaxon went on: "With this, there's no limit to what we can accomplish."

"And the first item," Tey put in, "is to stop this insane internecine warfare." Briefly he told Jaxon and the two women of the curious custom of mutual hostility that had, for three centuries, prevented the descendents of the Omega colonists from progressing beyond subsistence level.

Editors' Note: In the above reconstructed segment of Hon. Founder, Captain Tey's journal, all quotations of actual speech are attested to in at least two independent citations in other authenticated journals, diaries, and log entries. [Reconstruction ends.]

· 13 ·

Tey and Mullen, with Sugar, all armed, descended to find the Croom troops patiently waiting. Tey quietly gave the first officer a no-nonsense ultimatum to cease all hostilities immediately—and permanently. Presented with the awesome threat of the great warship looming over them—plus an occasional silent suggestion from Mancji, as Tey and the other Terrans now called the voice—Brill-Smythe addressed It as the Exarted One —and, at Its specific order, agreed to give up his plans for independent command. It was for this peace-making achievement, which of course formed the basis for the Concord on which our present government is based, that Hon. Founder Captain Tey, and others, was awarded the nonhereditary rank of Prince of Omega, and the great estates which remain as showplaces of what can be accomplished in landscape architecture by blending Terran and Omegan plant forms.

FIFTEEN

The Ship Is Found

"We've made a beginning," Tey continued his briefing. "This crowd—the main spark plugs of Mutual Hostility, it seems—are pretty well covered, I think. Brill-Smythe has some influence among the tribal chiefs—and Oliver has put the fear of the Exarted into him, with the help of my conscience, or some other still, small voice."

"Conscience"—with-knowledge; a fascinating concept, suggesting as it does that you possess multiple minds, which do not always agree, and yes, fantastic though it is, you do, indeed—please, my good fellow, no need to shout. Heavens, let's just let that fellow remain comatose. As to your primary mind—the one you think of as Conscious—it's time now to accept my existence as a normal—though unprecedented in your experience—phenomenon. As for the Brill-Smythe unit, it (he) will henceforth lend all his (its) considerable talents to the support of the Tey complex.

"Lord Banshire had been even sneakier than we suspected," Tey continued. "Somewhere along the line, about eighty years back—that would be Banshire Five—they did what Greylorn thought *he* was doing—traveled out and found the planet they then called Omega, after the original colony ship. Instead of using the discovery to relieve the pressure back on Terra, Banshire kept it secret and used it to consolidate his power. Now he had a source of raw materials and local labor to draw on, virtually free of charge, and as long as no one on Omega could talk to anyone else, he had nothing to worry about.

"Eventually of course, someone was bound to get a toe in the door. Some months before my court-martial, I noticed some curious discrepancies in what should have been routine operational reports, and started a little snooping. I of course was swatted in a hurry—which was a mistake—Banshire's first major one—because it only made me snoop a little more, and after a bit of cops-and-robbers, we came poking in here; then of course Carstairs, out here on a regular run, got the word to slap us down. Unfortunately for Enguerrand Nine, Carstairs is an incompetent. So now we know where Banshire's local command post is, and it's next on our schedule, as I see it. Anybody disagree?"

"What about North, Cap'n?" Grall asked casually. "That's where the slavers operate from."

"Still," Tey replied, "they're 'native' Colmarites. We need to get them on our side. How about it, Mr. Muldoon? Is there anyone over there in a position to call off the slave raids and cooperate with East to throw Banshire out?"

The captured copter pilot nodded glumly. "For years there's been an underground movement afoot, preaching just that. They've been getting stronger. A fellow named Thorvald-Kyoso is the head honcho. I could get to him, and with what I can tell him, I think he could stage a general strike and from there go on to take over North. Most people'd go along. None of us really like mining and purifying minerals—including some remarkable gem-stone deposits and plenty of metals—to load aboard foreign cargo hulls that take off and come back empty, hungry for more. I never volunteered for anything, but I know how to follow orders, Captain."

"So ordered," Tey said. "You still have plenty of range left on your copter, I assume?"

"These new power cells are something—I'll give the Terries (no offense to present company) that. They came up with some great technology."

Editors' Note: Since numerous accounts exist of the subsequent events leading swiftly up to Unification, available to all at any data station, it would be inappropriate here to do more than outline the sequence of major events at that pivotal time.

Major General (then Lieutenant) Muldoon was entirely successful in his mission, and within a period of less than one month, Hon. Founder Kyoso sent emissaries to look into the matter of these surprising Easters, who had caused two North copters to fail to return. This temporary alliance was of course the beginning of the fruitful association which soon overran the Terran encampment at Old Grove, on the north coast of East Continent in the area now known as the Province, and continued thereafter to eventually form the basis for Unification.

· 2 ·

There was for a time the question of the religious issues involved in the new Omegan autonomy. As Brill-Smythe put it in a well-known statement:

"We have not been keeping the faith for the last two centuries just to abandon the Quest now. What is going to be done to force the miscreants to disclose the location of the ship?"

Tey reassured him that he too was just as determined to get to the bottom of the old mystery.

Unsatisfied, Brill-Smythe appealed to the other former tribal leaders, reminding them that it was the nominal purpose of existence of every one of the multitudinous sects to find the ancient ship and to uncover the identity of the thieves, those actually responsible for the theft, rather than the possible mythical Thieves, whom all had sought in vain for so many years.

"And when you find *Omega,* what then?" Tey asked mildly. "Surely you don't entertain any idea of finding anything much aboard that will be of use to you."

"We are not looters," the first officer replied heatedly. "It is a holy mission. The Mysteries demand we find it."

At once acrimonious voices were raised. Each sectarian, though formally in agreement with the policy of cooperation and the burying of differences, when abruptly presented with the prospect of the climax of the Quest by another than himself, reflexively fell back on his own accustomed dogma:

". . . sacred mission!" blurted a Stayer.

". . . known to us alone!" a Loner yelled.

". . . our destiny!" contributed a Talker.

"Silence," Tey ordered quietly. Beside him Nat Grall reached out and seized the nearest loudmouth, lifting the angry little man by the hair. The latter's screeching at once modified to a lower level.

"The captain said 'silence,' Buster," Nat told the fellow, who winced and fell silent. "Don't forget, Junior," Nat said and dropped him. He dealt with two more noisy ones, and an island of silence grew around the group.

"We," Tey said, addressing the now only muttering crowd, "are newcomers to Omega. We have no partisan position regarding the Mysteries. Accordingly no one need feel disloyal to his mythos if we strangers show all of you at once the location of the vessel."

"Cap'n," Nat said diffidently, "I guess I'd sound pretty silly reminding you not to bite off more'n you can chew."

"Don't worry, Nat," Tey replied. "I'm on firm ground—I think. . . ."

"You can show these fanatics where their Holy Grail is?" Nat queried incredulously.

"I can give you a definite 'maybe' on that," Tey replied coolly. "Meanwhile, do you have any better ideas?"

"I don't even have a worse one, Cap'n. These babies want trouble—they think those bows are atom bombs—and there's just too damned many of 'em."

· 3 ·

After conferring at length with Ollie and the women, Tey again called together the former sect leaders, including the North Ambassadors, making it clear that he did so solely to ensure that all shades of opinion were represented, and that it would be the last time any recognition would be given to the former existence of the now illegal sects. Some forty bruised, tattered, and exhausted men and a few sturdy, and equally battered, women grouped before him.

"I am now going to the location of starship *Omega,*" he told them without preliminaries. "Those of you who wish to accompany me on foot are free to do so." He nodded to Nat.

"Let's go. It will be better if Ollie, and the girls stay with *Princeton.*" Mullen elected to stay. Without ceremony the two men set off to the north, followed by some forty-four former sectarians in ragged line astern, von Shimo among them.

At the shore, they looked over the battered boats drawn up on the pebbles, selected one with no obvious holes and with two sets of oars, and pushed off at once. Behind them their retinue, after considerably agitated talk and arm waving, took to the boats in twos and threes and, rowing with more energy than coordination, followed in a confused flock which formed very slowly into two more or less orderly lines, with much splashing and shrill chatter. One boat, bearing von Shimo and two women turned back, almost swamping in the process, and returned to shore. After von Shimo had alighted, talking vociferously the while, the other two pushed off and rejoined at the tail of the squadron, while von Shimo gesticulated from shore.

· 4 ·

It was a tedious two-hour crossing. Tey and Grall spoke very little. As they grounded on the island's gravel shore, Nat said, "I guess you know what you're doing, Captain, bringing this bunch into taboo territory."

"And so do you, Nat," Tey replied curtly. "Let's not make something mystical of it." By the time the two had reached the vegetation line and started upslope, the other boats were discharging their passengers in the shallows to wade ashore both eagerly and uncertainly.

"Here's our old trail, Cap'n," Nat said, after moving off a few feet to scan the grass. Tey nodded and joined him. Behind them on Shimo, by sculling frantically, had passed the main body, nded, and was now hurrying along in their wake.

"You're a navigating machine, aren't you, Captain?" Grall inquired rhetorically. "How do you do it? I've been looking for a landmark, but the whole damn thing looks the same to me."

"I don't know how I do it," Tey said. "I don't even know I'm doing it. But somehow I never get lost."

"Like a pigeon," Grall said. "They're tuned in to the G-field, I read someplace." Tey nodded.

"Maybe that's it. We want to go *that* way." He pivoted slightly to the right and pointed.

The walk across the spongy turf was easy, almost pleasant, in spite of the dull gray sky and the too-cool breeze and the pressure—implacable pressure from the no longer noisy crowd behind, and a more immediate sense of pressure within. *If he were wrong*— Tey cut off that line of thought. He could only go ahead now as if he knew rather than guessed.

Grall was silent, his big blunt features unaccustomedly grim.

"I've been guessing same as you, Captain," he said at last. "What makes you so sure? But I guess that's a dumb question. You're not sure—you've just got plenty of guts."

"Prenty big foor!" von Shimo's screech cut in. Breathing hard, the colonel-general trailed them closely, far in advance of the rest.

·5·

They hiked on in silence across an unchanging landscape. The faint trail they had followed out had almost disappeared with the thawing of the soil, but Tey needed no trail. He *knew*. The network of reflecting puddles was gone now, only a glint here and there remaining as reminders of the treacherous nature of the terrain. As they hiked, the sun set. Darkness fell quickly.

Arriving at the slope of fallen scree by which, outbound, they had descended from the higher level above the fault line, they scaled it easily.

"Captain," Grall said at the top, "that's not a natural formation; slump angle's wrong. That cliff was blasted. I spent a few years in heavy construction, back before the Grab. Somebody blew that. I wonder what's under it." He kicked at loose gravel.

"Maybe someday we'll excavate it," Tey said.

· 6 ·

Another hour brought them in sight of a low mound far ahead, outlined against the sky's last glow.

"That's the underground palace old Shimmy showed us, I bet," Nat said.

"You win, Nat," Tey said. "Another half hour and we'll get to meet the emperor." He motioned von Shimo forward.

The ragged group behind Tey and Grall had fallen silent as they came up to the low, turf-covered mound, long and narrow. Tey went to the point at which he once had seen von Shimo enter the subterranean structure, and at his gesture the former guide came forward reluctantly. After a moment's groping, von Shimo found an invisible handle, which he grasped and turned. There was a faint rasping sound, and at a tug a round plug of sod, backed by a panel, swung open, hatchlike. By the pale light that sprang up, Tey saw metal treads that led down. Von Shimo scurried down and after a moment, Tey followed into darkness and musty air. He paused to cough explosively. Behind him Grall said, "We need breathers, Cap'n."

"It doesn't matter," Tey replied. "We've come far enough." He shone a tiny clip-light on the gray vinyl-clad metal wall beside him, searched across it until he found a small embossed metal plate riveted to the bulkhead.

NOTICE: THIS EJECT PORT FOR DISCHARGE OF CLASS-ONE WASTE ONLY. SAR MAN 128-D-913, A AND B. MANUAL OPERATION BY WRITTEN COMMAND ONLY.

"Ye gods," Nat said reverently, after he and Tey had returned aboveground, where the huddled Easters waited in silence. "It figured, but actually to know . . ."

Then von Shimo was back, popping out like a small animal guarding the entrance to its burrow.

"The hour is rate," he announced. "Not surprisingly, His Imperior Majesty decrines to grant an audience tonight. In the morning—only a short wait, prease, perhaps."

"Swell," Grall said. "What do we do? Stand here for the next fifteen hours?"

"Prease, no necessity to stand when not in actuar enthroned presence."

"Gee, that's liberal of His Majesty," Nat muttered with mock humility.

"No, prease, onry practicar way," von Shimo said seriously.

"Tell us about His Nibs," Grall proposed. "Why does he stay out here in the boondocks?"

"Enemies," the general replied, crisply. "Enemies of the state. Criminar types who roam the frats rike wired beasts."

"Strange, we didn't see any today," Nat commented.

"Today," von Shimo said, "we passed through prenty enemies, conceared. They are expert at hiding, prease. Not ordinary enemies, rike these trash—" he indicated the waiting group. "*Rear* enemies, well-armed chaps, with modern equipment. Sent by Guardians, no doubt. Best we prepare for batter. They are sure to attack."

The locals, led by Brill-Smythe, who had continued to hang well back from the mysterious opening, surged forward as Tey, close behind Grall, closed the door, plunging all into total blackness.

"Your Mystery is solved," Tey said steadily. "This is the colonial vessel *Omega*. It was moved here somehow during cold season. When the thaw came, it sank below grade. In time the turf reformed over it, and then it was upthrust, probably by hydraulic pressure from the high water table, and stabilized at its present position."

Suddenly the silent voice of Mancji was speaking:

I (we) made a serious error. We (I) misunderstood the nature of your ship, having had no experience of artifacts. It was not unlike a Mancji brood mother—and we (I) presumed that was what it was. Accordingly since you folk had preempted the brooding-ground, we (I) moved her here—to safety and comfort as I (we) thought. You understand that it was—and is—nearly impossible for me (us) to conceive of discord among larvae-individuals, that is to say—or of lack of communication. Thus we (I) only now grasp the nature and magnitude of the disservice I (we) have done you. I (we) hope for your pardon.

"No pardon is needed, Mancji," Tey replied. "It was one of those unavoidable misunderstandings—"

You mean—such errors have happened before?

Tey sensed the shock felt by the compound mind of the alien(s).

"Human history is made up of such mistakes," Tey said sadly. Your intentions were good—but your information was inadequate."

Brill/Max should have informed me.

"They didn't know what you were contemplating," Tey guessed aloud.

Correct. I reviewed my memory gestalt just now, and I find that, curiously, I did not inform Max/Brill of my (our) benign intentions.

The small crowd of Croom combatants had received Tey's solemn announcement in silence. Then their voices broke out:

". . . all this time, just about a dumb misunderstanding—" growled a Talker.

". . . matter, anyway? We've got all we need, really—" a Keeper protested.

". . . get word back to Prime!" cried a Croom man.

". . . better look inside," a Norther declared importantly. "How do we know—"

Tey and Grall moved to block the entrance.

"It will be better," Tey said over the rising clamor, "to leave everything *in situ*, for careful study by qualified specialists."*

---

*When the ancient vessel was explored, some weeks after its discovery, by an official party led by Hon. Founder Captain Taliaferro Tey, all was found to be in precisely the condition that would be expected after a hasty evacuation—

One man headed determinedly for the now closed hatch, attempting to dodge behind Nat Grall, who picked him up and threw him at another enterprising fellow. The crowd closed in about them, then fell silent and edged away.

"Fellow colonists," Tey called loudly enough to be heard by all, "the unfortunate early history of Omega has now ended. A future devoted to constructive effort lies before us. Let's get started."

Editors' Note: This passage is the latest that can be reliably reconstructed in detail. However, at this point, happily the Standard histories pick up with adequate accuracy the account of the great spurt of development, including most importantly, the establishment of the land-section system, still in use today, and the intensive improvement of Area One, formerly referred to as Prime.

Within a year of the de facto unification of the people of Colmar, an assembly had been called, delegates elected, and policy established regarding basic matters such as relations with far distant Terra; future colonization; Terraforming versus conservation of native species, which tended to quickly fail in competition with imported forms; the status of the Mysteries; relations with Mancji; and so on.† North Continent was selected to be first for intensive development, since a start had already

with the exception of certain traces of more recent occupation by some foraging individual, such as the remains of a wood fire built in a radar oven, traces of food scraps, including bones of the mutated Terran species *Rattus giganticus*. A mummy was found aboard, on the bridge, still clad in the deteriorated remnants of an issue decksuit, lying before the main com screen, which the man had apparently been attempting to operate at the time of death. The ID tags identified the body as that of Lieutenant Ohara, a crew member. It is postulated that he was aboard on a retrieval mission (a container of small hand tools and the like was beside him) when the vessel was teleported by the well-intentioned Mancji and that thereafter, rather than deserting the vessel, Ohara remained at his post in the ancient Terran naval tradition. His remains were interred, with the posthumous rank of Fleet Admiral, at the Grand Plaza at Colmar City, in OY 283.

†See *A New Standard History of Colmar,* Authorized Edition, Colmar City, 2581T.

been made there. The problem of manpower arose as soon as large-scale engineering projects were scheduled, and only after long and acrimonious debate was the decision taken to open the planet to colonists from Terra. Since the Terran vessel *Catrice*, fully manned and in spaceworthy condition, was still in orbit at that time (OY 12), it was at the direction of the chief assembly-man, Hon. Founder Tey, ordered its then-commander, one Lieutenant Commander Gross, to make planetfall. Those of its landing party, who had for eleven local-years been stranded on the surface of the undeveloped planet, were enthusiastic about an opportunity to return to their native world, with the exception of HF Brevet Colonel Mullen, newly wed under a curious singular contract to Blessed Mother Sugar.* A number of native-born Colmarites also volunteered for the opportunity to see the world of their ancestors.

Resolution of the ancient mystery of the ship served to consolidate the temporary alliance. After appropriate deliberation, contact with Terran authorities was made and, with the assistance of Mancji, a treaty concluded, setting up moderate quotas with highly selective criteria for annual acceptance of Terran colonists—transport to be provided by Terra; and adequate reception facilities, by Colmar.

This arrangement functioned satisfactorily for some forty Terran-years before falling into desuetude, due to administrative atrophy at both ends. During this period, just over one hundred thousand selected immigrants arrived on Colmar with minimal fatalities—except for the incident that befell the early immigrant carrier designated as Special Auxiliary Hull 731, one of the last of the Initial Phase transports.†

Of the many surviving accounts of the origins of First Families, perhaps the most representative (with the exception of loss

---

*In a double ceremony, HF Assemblyman Grall at the same time took as his bride the Lady Seneschal Cleo, founding the illustrious clan Grall, still a leading force in Colmarian affairs today (see Appendix II).
†The remains of the vessel, which was irreparably damaged upon landing, are believed to lie within the mound known popularly as Tell Meemore, near the present-day limits of Terry City on North Continent.

of life due to meteorite impact in transit, which at the same time lends drama to an otherwise routine narrative) is that of Colonist Augustus Addison I, reproduced in its entirety (see Appendix I) in the colonist's own language, from his diaries, which have been carefully preserved by the family over the years and only recently—upon the death of Augustus Addison IV—presented to the Museum of the Council. It has been the decision of the editors to include the passage in this form in order to communicate the sense of urgency with which the early immigrant program was conducted.

APPENDIX I

Extract from the Journals of Augustus Addison I

The girl said, "No." She shook her head and turned her ice-chip blue eyes back to the programming console that almost filled her work cubicle. "Have some sense, Gus."

"We could live with my family for awhile—"

"You're already one over legal. And if you think I'd crowd in with that whole bunch—"

"Only until I get my next step-increase!"

Her fingers were already flickering over the keys. "See my side, Gus. Mel Fundy's offered me a five-year contract—with option."

"Contract."

"It's better than no marriage at all!"

"Marriage! That's a lousy business proposition!"

"Not so lousy. I'm accepting. It'll mean a class-B flat for just the two of us—and class-B rations."

"You and that dried-up—" Gus pictured her with Fundy's crab claws touching her.

"Better get back to your slot, Gus," she dismissed him. "You've still got a job to hold down."

He turned away.

A small, balding man with a large face and a curved back was coming along the two-foot aisle, darting sharp looks into the cubicles. His eyes turned hot when he saw Gus.

"You're docked half a unit, Addison! If I find you out of your position again, there'll be charges!"

"It won't happen again," Gus muttered. "Ever."

The shift-end buzzer went off at 8 AM. Gus pushed along the exit lane into car 98, stood packed in with the other workers while it rocketed along the horizontal track, halting every twelve seconds to discharge passengers, then shot upward three-quarters of a mile to his flat level. In the two-foot wide corridor, a banner poster showed a Colonization Service Officer looking stern, and the slogan: FILL YOUR BLOCK QUOTA! Gus keyed the door and stepped into the familiar odor of home: a heavy, dirt-sweet smell of human sweat and excrement and sex that seemed to settle over him like an oily patina.

"Augustus." From the food-prep ledge at the far end of the living aisle his mother's collapsed, sagging face caressed him like a damp hand. "I have a surprise for you! Mock giblets and a custard!"

"Evening, son." His father's jowly head poked from the study cubicle. "If you don't especially care for your custard, mind if I have it? Stomach's been a little feisty lately." As if to prove it, he belched, then grimaced.

Three feet from Gus's face, the curtains of the dress-in alcove twitched. Through a gap, a pale, oversized buttock showed. It moved sensuously, and Gus saw the curve of a full breast, the soft, pink nipple peering like a blind eye past the edge of the curtain. Libido washed up through him like sewage in a plugged manhole. He turned his eyes and saw a narrow, rabbity face glaring at him in feeble ferocity from the washing nook.

"What are you staring at, you young—"

"Tell her to keep the curtains shut, Uncle Fred," Gus grated.

"You young degenerate! Your own aunt."

"Gus didn't do anything," an uncertain voice said behind him. "She's done the same thing to me."

Gus turned to his brother, a spindle-armed, ribby-chested lad with a bad complexion. "Thanks, Len. But they can think what they like. I'm leaving. I just came to say goodbye."

Lenny's mouth opened. "You're . . . going?"

Gus didn't look at Lenny's face. He knew the expression he

would see there: admiration, love, dismay. And there was nothing he could give in return.

The silence was broken by a squeak from Mother. "Augustus—" She spoke quickly, in a false-bright voice, as though nothing had been said. "I've been thinking, this evening you and your father might go to see Mr. Geyer about that recommendation for class-C testing—"

Father cleared his throat. "Now, Ada, you know we've been all over that—"

"There may have been a change—"

"There's never a change," Gus cut her off harshly. "I'll never get a better job, never get a flat of my own, never get married. There just isn't *room*."

Father frowned, the corners of his mouth drawing down in an unwittingly comic expression. "Now, see here, son," he started.

"Never mind," Gus said. "I'll be out of here in a minute, and leave the whole thing to you—custard and all."

"Oh, my God!" the woman wailed.

Gus saw his mother's face crumple into a red-blotched mask of grief, a repellent expression of weak, smothering, useless mother love.

"Say something to him, George," she whimpered. "He's going—out *there!*"

"You mean . . ." Father elaborated a frown. "You mean the colonies?"

"Sure that's what he means," Lenny burst out. "Gus, you're going to Omega!"

"Catch *me* volunteering for anything," Uncle Fred shook his head. "Stories I've heard . . ."

"Augustus, I've been thinking," Mother began babbling. "We'll leave the whole flat to you, this lovely apartment, and we'll go into Barracks, just visit you here on Sundays, just come and bring you a nice casserole or soup. You know how fond you are of my lichen soup, and—"

"I've got to go." Gus backed a step.

"After all we've done for you!" Mother keened suddenly. "All the years we've scraped and saved, so we could give you the best of everything . . ."

"Now, son, better think this over," Father mumbled. "You'll never see your home again—or your mother . . ." His voice trailed off. Even to his ears the prospect sounded attractive.

"Good luck, Gus," Lenny caught his hand. "I'll . . . see you."

"Sure, Lenny."

"He's going!" Mother wailed. "Stop him, George!"

Gus looked back at the faces staring at him and tried but failed to summon a twinge of regret at leaving them.

"It isn't fair," Mother moaned.

Gus pressed the button and the door slid back.

"Say, if that custard isn't cold . . ." Father was saying as the panel closed behind Gus.

·2·

Recruitment Center Number Sixty-One was a white-lit acre of noise and animal warmth and tension and people packed elbow to elbow under the low ceiling with its signs reading CLASS ONE—SPECIAL and TEST UNITS D-G and PREPROCESSING (DEFERRED STATUS) and its glowing arrows cryptic in red and green and black. After an hour's waiting Gus's head was ringing dizzily.

His turn came. A woman in a tan uniform thrust a plastic tag at him, looking past his left ear.

"Station twenty-five on your left," she intoned. "Move along . . ."

"I'd like to ask some questions," Gus started.

The woman flicked her eyes at him; her voice was drowned in the chopping of other voices as the press from behind thrust Gus forward. A thick-shouldered man with reddish hair put his face near Gus's.

"Some mob," he shouted. "Geeze, it's a regular evacuation, like."

"Yeah," Gus said. "I've heard Omega was next best to hell, but it seems to be popular."

"Hah!" The redhead leaned closer. "You know the world population as of Sunday night stat cutoff? Twenty-nine billion plus—and the repro factor says she'll double in twelve hundred and four days. And you know why?" He warmed to his subject. "No politician's going to vote to cut down the vote supply—"

"You— Over here." A hand grabbed Gus and thrust him toward a table behind which sat a pale man with thin, wispy hair. He pushed two small cards across.

"Sign these."

"First I'd like to ask a few questions," Gus started.

"Sign or get out. Snap it up, Mac."

"I want to know what I'm getting into. What's it like out on this Omega? What kind of contract do I—"

A hand closed on Gus's arm. A man in Ground Corps uniform loomed beside him.

"Trouble, fella?"

"I walked in here voluntarily." Gus threw the hand off. "All I want—"

"We process twenty thousand a day through here, fella. You can see we got no time for special attention. You've seen the broadcasts; you know about New Earth—"

"What assurance have I got—"

"No assurance at all, fella. None at all. Take it or leave it."

"You're holding up the line," the thin-haired man barked. "You want to sign, or you want to go back home . . ."

Gus picked up the stylus and signed.

· 3 ·

An hour later, aboard a converted cargo carrier, Gus sat cold and airsick on a canvas-strip seat between the redheaded man whose name he had learned was Hogan, and a fattish fellow who complained continuously in a tremulous tone:

". . . give a man time to think. Big step, going out to the colonies at my time of life. Leaving a good job . . ."

"They washed a lot of 'em out on the physical," Hogan said. "Figures. Tough out on Omega. Why haul freight that can't make it, eh? Costs plenty to lift a man four light-years."

"I thought they took anybody," Gus said. "I never heard of anyone who volunteered coming back home."

"I heard they send 'em to labor camps." Hogan spoke confidentially from the corner of his mouth. "Can't afford to send malcontents back to the hive."

"Maybe," Gus said. "All I know is, I passed and I'm going—and I don't want to come back, ever."

"Yeah," Hogan nodded. "We made it. To hell with them other guys."

". . . no time to think it over, consider the matter in depth," the fat man was saying. "It's not what I'd call fair, not fair at all . . ."

· 4 ·

They debarked on a flat, dusty-tan plain that stretched away to a distant rampart of smoke-blue mountains. Gus resisted an impulse to clutch the railing as he descended the ramp—the open sky made him dizzy. The air was thin, after the pressurized city and the transport's canned air. Gus felt lightheaded. He hadn't eaten all day. He looked at his watch and was astonished to see that it had been less than five hours since he had left the flat.

Uniformed cadremen called orders up and down the line; the irregular ranks of recruits started off on foot, following a dun-colored car. After half an hour Gus's legs ached from the unaccustomed exercise. His breath was like fire in his throat. The car moved steadily ahead, laying a trail of dust across the empty desert.

"Where the hell we going?" Hogan's voice wheezed beside him. "There's nothing here but this damned desert."

"Must be Mojave Spaceport."

"They're trying to kill us," the plump man complained. "What do you say we fall out, catch some rest?"

Gus thought about dropping back, throwing himself down, resting . . . but he pictured a cadreman coming over, ordering him back.

Back home.

He kept going.

They marched on through the afternoon, with one brief break during which paper trays of gray mush were handed out. Marching, they watched the sun go down like a pour of molten metal. Under the stars they marched. It was after midnight when a string of lights appeared in the distance. Gus slogged on, no longer conscious of the pain in his feet and legs. When the halt was called on a broad sweep of flood-lit blacktop, he was herded along with the others into barracks that smelled of new plastic and disinfectants. He fell on the narrow bunk pointed out to him and sank down into a deeper sleep than he had ever known—

—and awoke in the predawn chill to the shouts of the noncoms. After a breakfast of brown mush the recruits were lined up before the barracks and a cadre officer mounted a low platform to address them.

"You men have a lot of questions to ask," he said. His amplified voice echoed across the pavement. "You want to know what you're getting into, what kind of handouts—jobs, farmland, or gold mines—you'll get on New Earth." He waited ten seconds while a murmur built up.

"I'll tell you," he said. The murmur stilled.

"You'll get just one thing on Omega: an even chance." The officer stepped down and walked away.

The murmur rose to angry mutter. A noncom took the platform and barked, "That's enough, you covvs! When the major said an even chance, that meant nobody gets special privileges! Nobody! Maybe some of you were big shots once; forget all that. From now on it's what you can *do* that counts. Only half of you are going to Omega. We'll find out which half today. Now—" He dictated orders.

Gus found himself in a group of twenty men tramping out across the pavement toward a tall, open-work structure. A lean, black-haired man marched beside him.

"These boys don't give away much," he said. "A man'd think they had something to hide."

"No talking in ranks!" a wide-faced cadreman with gaps between his teeth barked. "You'll find out all you need to know soon enough, and you won't like it." He leered and moved on. There was no more talking.

· 6 ·

At the tower the men were herded into a large open-sided lift that lurched as it rumbled upward. Gus watched the desert floor sink away, spreading out below like a dirty blanket. He shied as the gate whooshed open beside him at the top.

"Out, you covvs!" the burly noncom shouted. Nobody moved.

"You," the cadreman's eyes fixed on Gus. "Let's go. You look like a big, tough boy. All it takes is a little guts."

Gus looked out at the railless paltform, the four-foot wide catwalk extending across to a wider platform twenty feet distant. He felt his feet freeze to the car floor.

The noncom shook his head, brushed past Gus, walked halfway across the catwalk, turned and folded his arms.

"Omega's that way," he jerked his head to indicate the far end of the walk, then went on across.

Gus took a breath and walked quickly across. Others followed. Three stayed behind, refusing the walk. The noncom gestured.

"Take 'em back!" The car door closed on them. The cadreman faced his charges.

"This scares you," he said. "Sure it's something new, but out on Omega everything'll be new. You covvs'll have to adapt or die."

"What if somebody fell?" the black-haired man asked.

"He'd be dead," the noncom said flatly. "That's real rock down there. If you're going to die, it's better to do it here than after His Lordship's wasted the cost of shipping you four lights into space."

· 7 ·

Next there was a climb up a tortuous construction of bars and angles, a maze on edges that led to dead ends and impasses that forced the climber to descend, find a new route, while his hands ached and his legs trembled with fatigue.

Then there was a water hazard: locked in a large cage suspended over a muddy pond, Gus listened to instructions, held his breath as the cage submerged, rose, dripping, submerged again . . . and again. When the torture ended, he was half drowned. Two men were carried away unconscious.

An obstacle course confronted them now, with warning signs posted. Several men ignored the signs—or forgot—or lost their balance. They were carried away. Gus stared at one blood-spattered face, unbelieving.

"They can't go this!" Hogan said. "By God, these birds have gone out of their minds! They . . ." He fell silent as the gap-toothed noncom strolled past.

There was a half-hour break while the candidate colonists ate another mush ration; then the day went on. There was a run across rock-strewn ground where a misstep meant a broken ankle, or worse; a passage through a twisted, eighteen-inch duct where panic could mean entrapment, upside down; a ride in a centrifuge which left Gus dizzy, shaking, soggy with cold sweat. None of the trials was particularly strenuous—or even dangerous, if the subject kept his head and followed instructions. But steadily the roster of men dwindled. By nightfall only Gus and eight others were left of the twenty who had started together. Hogan and the black-haired man—Franz—were among them.

· 8 ·

"Haven't you caught on to what's going on here yet?" Hogan whispered hoarsely to Gus as the survivors tramped back toward the barracks area. "I heard about this kind of place. They brought us out here to do away with us. The whole deal—free trip to a new planet, the whole colonization program—it's a phony, a coverup for killing off everybody who's not satisfied with things."

"You're nuts," Franz said.

"Yeah? You've heard the talk about euthanasia . . ."

"A little gas in the hive would be easier," Gus said.

"That pond! If I wouldn't of seen it," Hogan said, "I'd of called the man a liar told me about it!"

"Sure, it's a screwy setup," Franz conceded. "But this is a crash program. They had to improvise . . ."

A murmuring sound had grown unnoticed in the distance. Now, as it swelled, Gus thought of distant thunder, and his imagination pictured cool wind, a cloudburst after the misery of the day's heat.

"Look!" Men were pointing. A flickering white star at zenith grew visibly brighter, and the sound grew with it. The rumble rolled across the plain, and the light brightened into a glittering play of fire at the end of a trail of luminosity.

"Stand fast!" the noncoms shouted as the ranks broke. A jet plane thundered across from the east, shot upward and dwindled toward the descending ship, which grew, waxing like a moon, as a hot wind sprang up, blowing outward from the landing point ten miles distant. A glint of high sunlight showed on the flank of the great vessel. It sank gently on its pillar of fire, dropped again into darkness, a moving tower of lights, sliding down to settle in its bed of roiling, fiery cloud. Slowly the bellow of the titanic engines died, the glare faded. Echoes washed back and forth across the plain.

"Starship!" the words ran through the ranks. Gus felt his heart begin to thud in his chest. Starship!

· 9 ·

There was no sleep that night. "You'll get plenty from now on," the cadreman told the recruits as they formed up into double lines leading to a white-painted building that gleamed pale in the polyarcs.

It seemed to Gus that the plain was filled with men, shuffling toward the lighted doorways. Hours passed before he reached the building. He blinked in the greenish glare of the long, antiseptically bare room. Teams of surgically masked men and women worked over rows of tables.

"Strip and get on the board," a voice chanted. Technicians closed in around Gus. He backed, gripped by a sudden panic. "Wait—"

Hands caught him. He fought, but cursing men forced him back. Hyposprays jetted icy cold against his arms. Questions clamored in his brain, but before he could form them into words he felt himself sinking down into the fleecy softness of sleep . . . Too late now. . . .

· 10 ·

Someone was talking urgently. The voice had been going on for a long time, he knew, but now it began to penetrate:

". . . you understand? Come on, Covv, wake up!"

Gus tried to speak, said "Awwrrr . . ."

"Come on, on your feet!"

Gus forced his eyes open. It was a different face that bent over him, not one of the technicians. A half-familiar face, except for the half-inch beard and hollow cheeks.

"Sergeant . . . Berg . . ." Gus got out.

"That's right, Covv. Come on, let's move; there's work to be done. You ought to be feeling good: this is your fourth day of rehab."

"Wha' went wrong . . . ?"

"Hah? What didn't go wrong? Hull damage, mutiny—but that's not for you to worry about, Covv. We're ten hours out; you've had your sleep—"

"Ten hours . . . from Earth?"

"Hah? From Omega Prime, Covv! Eighteen hundred and fourteen days out of Terra."

Gus rocked as though he had been struck. Almost . . . five years.

"We're almost there," he said wonderingly. Berg was urging him to his feet.

"That's right. And you've been tapped for ship's complement —you and a few other Covvs—to help out during the approach. Coolie labor. Follow me."

Staggering a little, Gus trailed the noncom along a tight gray corridor, green-lit by a glare-strip running along the low ceiling. Passing an open door, he caught a glimpse of a wrecked wall, sheet-plastic partitioning bulging out of line, broken pipes and tangled wires, a scatter of debris.

"What happened?" he asked.

"Never mind," Berg growled. "You're just a dumb Covv. Stay that way."

· 11 ·

They rode a lift up, walked along another corridor, came into the Christmas tree brilliance of the bridge. Silent, harried-looking men in rumpled tan peered worriedly into screens and instrument faces. Officers muttered together; technicians chanted into vocoders. A young-looking officer with short blond hair gestured Berg over.

"This is the last of 'em, sir," the noncom reported.

"I'll use him as a messenger. No communications with sections aft of Station Twenty-eight now. The tub's coming apart."

"Stand by here," Berg told Gus, and went away.

"Lieutenant, take over on six," a gutteral voice called. The blond lieutenant moved to a gimbaled seat before a screen that showed a vivid crescent against velvet black. A moon was visible at the edge of the screen; a tiny blob of greenish white. No stars showed; the sensitivity of the screen had dimmed in response to the blaze of the nearby sun.

Gus moved back against the wall. For the next hour he stood there, forgotten, watching the image of the gray-green planet grow on the screens as the weary officers worked over the maze of controls that swept in a twenty-foot horseshoe around the compartment.

". . . we're not going to try it—not while I'm on the bridge."
The words caught Gus's attention. A lean, hawk-faced officer
tossed papers onto the floor. "We'll have to divert! She'll break
up if I try any category-two course corrections now!"

"You're refusing to carry out my instructions?" The squat,
white-haired man who Gus knew was the captain raised his
voice. "You press me too far, Leone—"

"I'll put her down for you on East Continent," the first officer
shouted him down. "That's the best I can do!"

The captain cursed the tall man. Other voices joined in the
dispute. In the end the captain bellowed his capitulation:

"East Continent, then, Leone! And there'll be charges filed,
I guarantee you that!"

"File and be damned!" The argument went on.

· 12 ·

Pressed back against the wall, Gus watched as the crescent
swelled, grew to fill the screen, became a curve of dusty-lighted
horizon, then a hazy plain dotted with the tiny white flecks of
clouds. Faint, eerie whistlings started up, climbed the scale;
buffeting started. The men on the bridge had forgotten their
differences now. Crisp commands and curt acknowledgments
were the only words spoken.

Under Gus the deck bucked and hammered. He went down,
held on to a stanchion as the shaking grew; the scream of air
became a frantic tornado—

Then quite suddenly the motion smoothed out as a new thunder vibrated through the deck: the roar of the engines waking
to life.

Minutes crawled past while the Niagara rumble went on and
on, then seemed to fade. A shock slammed the deck and sent
Gus sprawling. Half-dazed he got to his feet and saw the officers
swinging from their places, whooping, slapping each other's
backs. The captain bustled past, leaving the bridge. The big
general display screen showed a stretch of dull, gray-green hills
under a watery sky.

"What in the devil are you doing here?" a voice cracked at Gus like a whip. It was First Officer Leone. "Get off the bridge, you bloody Covv!"

"Sir," Sergeant Berg said, coming up. "Captain's orders—"

"Damn the captain! Damn the lot of you." He waved an arm to include everyone on the bridge. "Reservists! The bunch of you wouldn't make a wart on a regular officer's rump!"

· 13 ·

Gus made his way alone back down to the level where he had been brought out of coldsleep. A cadreman greeted him with a curse.

"Where the hell have you been, Covv? You're on the defrost detail. Get aft and report to Hensley in the meat room—and don't get lost!"

"I wasn't lost," Gus said, returning the noncom's glare. "But I think a fellow named Leone was."

The noncom gave him terse directions; he followed them, and emerged in a narrow, high-aisled chamber, bright-lit, frosty. A bowlegged NCO waddled up to him, pointed to a rack of heavy parkas, assigned him to a crew. Gus watched as they undogged a thick, foot-and-a-half square door and drew out a slab on which the frost covered body of a man lay under a thin plastic membrane.

"Automatics are out," the foreman explained. "We got to unload these Covvs by hand—what's left of 'em."

"What do you mean?"

"We took a four-ton rock through the hull, about fifty hours ago. Lost a bunch of officers and some crew—and before Leone got around to checking, we lost a lot of Covvs. Splinter right through the master panel." The man lifted the plastic, which peeled away from the waxy flesh with a crinkling sound. "Spoiled, you might say—like this one."

Gus looked at the drawn, hollow face, the glint of yellowish teeth behind the gray lips. The plastic dropped back and the crew moved on to the next door.

In the next five minutes Gus saw twenty-one more corpses. Three hundred and forty-one presumably intact colonists were rolled into the revival rooms. Gus caught glimpses of the gagging, shivering men as they responded to the efforts of the Med crews.

"Where are the women?" he asked.

"One deck up," the noncom replied, grinning. "I got duty there tomorrow."

"It ain't easy to die and come to life again," the bandy-legged corporal conceded, watching as a man retched and bucked against the hold-down straps.

The work went on. The horror had gone out of it now; it was simply monotonous, hard, bone-chilling work. He had learned to spot the symptoms of tragedy early: a bulge of frost around a door invariably meant a dead man inside. The trickle of life of a living coldsleep subject generated sufficient heat to prevent frosting inside the capsule.

There was a telltale trace on the next door; Gus approached. He opened it, tugging to break the ice seal, and slid the tray out. There was a heavy layer of ice over the plastic. Gus leaned close, his attention caught by something in the face under the ice. He stripped the sheet back from the body and felt an icy shock that locked his breath in his throat.

The face was that of his younger brother, Lenny.

· 14 ·

"Tough," the corporal said, flicking an eye curiously at Gus. "According to the tag, he was in the draft next to yours; musta come into Mojave the day after you. We was five weeks loading . . ."

Gus thought of the screening trials, the torture of the dunking cage, the walk across emptiness on the catwalk. And Lenny, trying to follow him, going through all of it, and dying like this.

"You said by the time Leone got around to checking, some of the colonists were dead," Gus said in a ragged tone. "What did you mean?"

"Forget it, Covv. Let's get back to work. We got the live ones to think about." The corporal put a hand on the small pistol strapped to his hip. "We're not out of the woods yet—any of us."

· 15 ·

The ship had been on the ground twenty-seven hours when Gus's turn came to walk down the landing ramp and out under the chill sky of a new world. A light, misty rain was falling. There was a sour smell of burned vegetation and over it a hint of green, growing things, alien but fresh, not unpleasant.

The charred ground was a churn of black mud trampled by the hundreds of men who had debarked ahead of him. They were lined up in irregular ranks, row after row, that stretched out of sight over a low rise of ground. Gus's group was formed up and marched off toward the far end of the bivouac area.

"This don't look like much to me," Hogan said. His red hair looked wilder than ever. Like the other colonists, he had acquired an inch of beard while in coldsleep.

"This isn't where we were supposed to land," Gus told him. "We're on the wrong continent."

"Hah? How do you know?"

Gus told him what he had heard during his stay on the bridge.

"Cripes!" Hogan waved a hand at the treeless, rolling tundra. "The wrong continent: might as well be the wrong planet! That means there ain't no colony here, no housing, no nothing!"

"As the man said," Franz put in, "we're on our own. We can carve our own town out of this—"

"Yeah? With no trees for lumber, no running water—"

"Sure there's running water. It's running down my neck right now."

"We been had!" Hogan burst out. "This ain't the deal I signed on for!"

"You signed like the rest of us, no questions asked."

"Yeah, but—"

"Don't say it," Franz said. "You'll break my heart."

16

"No shelter," Hogan said an hour later. "I always heard the best food all went to the colonists. Where is it?"

"Wait until the ship's unloaded," Franz said.

"Nothing's come off that tub yet but us covvs." Hogan rubbed his hands together for warmth, looking toward the grim tower of the ship. The damage done to the hull by the meteorite was clearly visible as a pockmark near the upper end.

"They're probably still busy doing emergency repairs," Franz said.

"Don't look like a little hole like that could of done all that damage," Hogan said.

"That ship's nearly as complicated as a human body," a man standing by said. "Poking a hole in it's like shooting a hole in you."

"Hey— Look there!" Hogan pointed. A new group of parka-clad colonists was filing over the brow of the hill.

"Women!" Franz whispered.

"Females, by God!" Hogan burst out.

"It figures," someone said. "You can't make a colony without women!"

"Boys, they kept that one up their sleeves!"

17

The men watched as squad after squad of female colonists toiled up the hill, forming up beyond the men. Then the men turned at the sound of car engines. A carryall towing a small trailer came along the line and stopped near Gus. A cadreman jumped down, pulled back the tarp covering the trailer, and hauled out a heavy bundle.

"All right, you Covvs," he shouted as the car pulled away. "You're going to dig in. File up here and draw shovels!"

"Shovels? Is he kidding?" Hogan looked around at the others.

"Dig for what?" someone called.

"Shelter," the corporal barked. "Unless you want to sleep out in the open."

"What about our prefabs?"

"Yeah—and our rations!"

"There's power equipment aboard the ship! If there's digging to be done, by God, let's use it!"

The corporal unlimbered his foot-long club. "I told you Covvs," he started, and his voice was drowned by the clamor as the men closed in on him:

"We want food!"

"To hell with digging!"

"When you going to hand out the women?"

"I . . . I'll go see." The noncom backed away, then turned and went off quickly downslope.

Voices were being raised all across the hill now. Gus saw other cadremen withdrawing, one with blood on his face and minus his cap. The uproar grew. A carryall raced up from the ship, took cadremen aboard. Clubs swung at colonists who gave chase.

"After 'em!" Hogan yelled.

Gus grabbed his arm. "Stop, you damned fool! This is a mistake!"

"It's time we started getting a fair deal around here! We're not convicts, by God!"

"The power's all theirs," Gus said. "This won't help us!"

"We outnumber them a hundred to one," Hogan crowed. "Look at 'em run! I guess the digging party's off!" He shook off Gus's grip, looked toward the women. "Boys, let's pay a call. Them little ladies look lonesome—"

Gus shoved the redhead back. "Start that, and we're done for! Can't you see the spot we're in?"

"What spot?" Hogan began to bluster. "We showed 'em they can't push us around!"

"They're loading up, going back aboard." Gus pointed. Heads turned to watch the last of the cars wheeling up the ramp.

"They're scared of us—" someone said.

"We jumped them, forced their hand—" another said.

"Yeah." Hogan frowned ferociously. "So they ran from us."

"You damned fool," Gus said wearily. "Suppose they don't come back?"

· 18 ·

"They can't do this to us," Hogan whined for the fortieth time. The sun had set hours before. The rain had turned to sleet that froze on the springy turf and on the men's clothing.

"It must be five below," Franz said. "You think they'll leave us out here to freeze, Gus?"

"I don't know."

"They're in there, eating our rations, sleeping in soft beds," Hogan growled. "The dirty bloodsuckers!"

"Can't much blame 'em," Franz said. "With boneheads like you roughing 'em up. You expect them to come out and let you finish the job?"

"They can't get away with it!"

"They can get away with anything they want to," Gus said. "Nobody back on Earth knows what's going on out here. It takes ten years to ask a question and get an answer. And in ten years the population will have tripled. They'll have other things to think about besides us. We're expendable."

A ripple of talk passed through the ranks of men squatting on the exposed hillside under the relentless sleet as darkness fell. Dimly seen figures were advancing from the direction of the women's area.

"It's the girls," Hogan said. "They want company."

"Leave them alone, Hogan," Gus said. "Let's just see what they want."

· 19 ·

The leader of the women's delegation was a strong-looking blonde in her late twenties, muffled in an oversized parka. She planted herself in front of the men. They closed in, gaping.

"Who's in charge over here?" she demanded.

"Nobody, baby," Hogan started. "It's every man for himself . . ." He reached out with a meaty paw, and the girl brushed it aside.

"Pass that for now, Porky," she said briskly. "We got important things to talk about, like not freezing to death. What are you fellows doing about it?"

"Not a damn thing, honey. What *can* we do?" Hogan jerked a thumb toward the lights of the ship. "Those lousy crots have cut us off—"

"I saw what happened—you damned fools started a riot. I don't blame them for pulling out. But what are you going to do about it *now?* Let your women freeze?"

"*Our* women?"

"Whose women you think we are, Porky? There's even one for you—if you can keep her alive."

"We've got a few shovels," Gus said. "We can dig in. This sod ought to be good enough to make huts of."

"Dig holes for over six hundred people, with a couple dozen shovels?" Hogan jeered. "Are you nuts—"

· 20 ·

A crackle like nearby lightning sounded. "Attention-un," a vast voice boomed across the bivouac. "This is Captain Harississ-iss . . ." Floodlights sprang into life at the base of the ship.

"You people are guilty of mutiny-any," the great voice rolled. "I'd be justified in whatever measures I choose to take at this point-oint. Including leaving you to suffer the consequences of your own actions-shuns." There was a pause to allow the thought to sink in.

"However, as it happens, I have repairs to undertake-ache. I'm shorthanded-dead. Time is important-ant-ant."

"Tough," Hogan growled.

"I want twenty volunteers to aid in the work of preparing my ship for space-ace. In return, I'll see to it that certain supplies are made available to you people-ull."

A mutter went up from the men. "The son of a bitch is

holding us up for our own rations!" Hogan yelled.

"At the first sign of disorder, I'll clear a one-mile radius around the ship," the captain's voice boomed out. "I'm offering you mutineers the one chance you'll get-et! I suggest you think it over carefully! I want you to select twenty strong workers and send them forward-herd!"

"Let's rush the crots when they open the ports," Hogan shouted over the surf-noise of the crowd. "We can take the ship and rip those crots limb from limb! There's enough supplies aboard to last us for years! We can live in the ship until a rescue ship gets here!"

Faces were turning toward Hogan. Greedy eyes glistened in half-frozen faces.

"Let's go get 'em!" Hogan yelled. "Let's—"

Gus stepped after him, caught him by the shoulder, spun him around, and hit him square in the mouth with all his strength. Hogan went back and down, and lay still.

"I'm volunteering for the work crew," Gus called, and started forward. A path opened to let him through.

Franz walked at Gus's side, leading the small troop of volunteers down the slope to the ship. The big floods bathed them in bluish light. Gus could feel the muscles of his stomach tighten, imagining guns aimed from the open ports. Or maybe it would be a touch of the main drive . . .

· 21 ·

No guns fired. No flame blossomed beyond the gigantic landing jacks rising from the mud. A squad of crewmen met them, searched them for weapons, detailed them off, and marched them away. Gus and the blond woman were escorted to the Power Section and handed over to a bald, grim-faced engineering officer.

"Only two? And one of them a woman? Damn the captain's arrogance! I told the—" He shut himself up, barked at a greasy-handed corporal who gave the newcomers a ration of mush and set them to work disassembling a fire-blackened mechanism.

"What's the rush?" the girl asked the NCO. "Why work all night? We're all tired—you, too. How long since you've slept?"

"Too bloody long. But it's captain's orders."

"What's he doing for the colonists? Has he sent out the food and shelter he promised?"

"How do I know?" the man muttered. "Just stick to the job and can the chatter."

Half an hour later, with the corporal and the engineer busy cursing over a frozen valve at the far end of the room, the girl whispered to Gus, "I think we're being double-crossed."

"Maybe."

"What'll we do?"

"Keep working."

Another hour passed. Abruptly the engineer threw down the calibrator with which he had been working, then stamped out through the outer door.

"Try keeping the corporal occupied for a few minutes," Gus hissed at the girl. She nodded, rose, and went over to the corporal.

"I feel a little dizzy, handsome," she said, and folded against him.

Gus went quickly to the door and out into the green-lit corridor.

· 22 ·

He emerged in the darkened anteroom outside the bridge.

". . . nine hours at the outside!" a harsh voice was saying. "We lift before then, or we don't lift!"

"I don't trust your calculations, Leone."

"I showed you the fatigue profiles; check them for yourself—but do it fast! The structure is deflecting at the rate of one inch per hour. We'll have major strains in three hours, and buckling in eight—"

"I'll need six hours, minimum, to unload cargo, after the priority-one work is out of the way—"

"Forget unloading, Captain. Your first job is to get your ship back, intact!"

"And you with it, eh, Leone?"

"The other officers feel as I do."

"After you've browbeaten them! What about the colonists? Their equipment, their rations—"

"We can't spare the food," Leone said crisply. "You know what the damage inventory showed. We'll be lucky if we make it ourselves. The covvs will manage—they'll have to. That's what they're here for, remember?"

"They were slated for an established colony on North—"

"They can survive on East. It's chilly, but no worse than plenty of areas of Terra."

"You're a cold-blooded devil, Leone."

"I do what I have to."

Gus stepped back and departed as silently as he had come.

· 23 ·

The engineer whirled with an oath as Gus appeared. Gus stepped directly to him and, without warning, hit him hard in the stomach, hit him again on the jaw as he doubled over. Behind him the corporal yelled and jumped, tugging at his gun. He went down hard as the girl threw herself at his legs. As he started up, Gus knocked him cold with a kick to the jaw.

"Let's get out of here!" Gus helped the girl up; her nose was bleeding. He led her into the corridor, and they headed back toward the loading deck. They had gone fifty yards when a crew of armed men burst from a crossway and cut them off. It took three of them to hold the girl. Gus saw a club swinging toward his head, then the world burst into a shower of fireworks.

·24·

Bright light glared in Gus's face. He was lying on his back on the floor, his hands locked behind him. Across the small room a tall man in a tan uniform sat at a desk. Gus sat up painfully; at the sound, the man turned. It was the first officer, Leone. He gave Gus a sardonic look. His eyes were red, his chin unshaven.

"I could've had you shot," he said. "But I wanted to learn a few things first. Speak freely and I may be able to do something for you. Now: who was in on the scheme with you? Are those —" he tilted his head to indicate the planet outside, "poor grubbers planning some sort of attack?"

"I'm on my own," Gus said.

"Come on, man, speak up! You're already in deep enough: striking an officer, desertion—"

"I'm not in your army," Gus cut him off. "I want to see the captain, if you haven't eaten him for breakfast."

Leone laughed. "To claim your rights, I suppose."

"Something like that."

"There are no rights," Leone said flatly. "Only necessities."

"Like food and shelter," Gus agreed. "Those people out there came here expecting a decent chance. You plan to abandon them here—with nothing."

"Ah, so that was what was behind your little dash for freedom." Leone nodded as if pleased. "You need to adjust your thinking, Covv—"

"My name's Addison. Calling us covvs won't take us off your conscience."

"Wrong on two counts. I have no conscience. As for names, they imply family ties, a place in a social structure. You have none—except what you might have made for yourself, out there." Leone shook his head. "No, 'covv' it is. It's the role you were born for—you and millions like you." He poured himself a drink from a bottle on the desk, tossed it back with a practiced flip of the wrist.

"There was a time when I wondered at the purpose of it all —man's slow climb up to the present mad carnival of spawning that's turned a planet into nothing more than a surface on which nameless, faceless nonentities breed endlessly, in a doomed effort to convert the entire mass of the world into human flesh. It seemed so pointless. But now I understand." Leone smiled crookedly. He was very drunk.

"Ah, you're wondering, but too proud to ask! Proud! Yes, every little unremembered mote of humanity has his share of that fatuous delusion of self-importance! Funny; very funny!" Leone leaned toward Gus, waving the glass in his hand. "Don't you know your function, Covv?" He grinned expectantly.

Gus looked at him silently.

"You're a statistic!" Leone poured again, raised the glass in a mock toast. "Nature brings forth millions, that one may survive. And you're one out of the millions."

"Now that you have it all figured out," Gus said, "what are you going to do about us? Those people will freeze out there."

"Perhaps," Leone said carelessly. "Perhaps not. The toughest will survive—if they can. Survive to breed. And in time, devour this world, and jump on to a new star. Meanwhile it hardly matters what happens to a statistic."

"They were promised an even chance."

"Promises, promises. Death in the end is the only promise, my boy. As for those ciphers out there in the cold—think of them as fish eggs, if that will help you. Spawned by the million so that one or two can live to spawn in turn. Life goes on—as long as you've got plenty of fish eggs."

"They're not fish eggs. They're men, and they deserve simple justice—"

"You call justice simple?" Leone leaned forward, almost rolled from his chair before he caught himself. "The most sophisticated concept with which the mind of man deludes itself —and that's the only place it exists: in men's minds. What does the universe know about justice, Covv? Suns burn, planets whirl, chemicals react. The fox devours the bunny rabbit with a clear conscience—just the way Omega Prime will devour those poor crots out there." He waved an arm. "And that's as it should be. Nature's way. Survive—or don't survive. It's natural—like an earthquake. It'll kill you without the least ill-will in the world."

"You're not an earthquake," Gus said. "It's you that's holding back the food those men need."

"Don't come whining to me for your lousy justice!" Leone shouted, swaying in his chair. "We were having a well-earned drink in the wardroom when the rock hit. Killed half the officers of this damned tub—killed my friend, my best friend, damn you! After five years, cruise almost over—and all for the sake of a load of caviar . . ."

Leone gulped the rest of his drink and threw the glass across the room. "Don't chatter to me about what's fair," he muttered. "It's what's real that counts." He put his head down on his arms and snored.

· 25 ·

It took Gus five minutes to reach the desk and grope in the drawers until he found the electrokey which unlocked the cuffs on his wrists. There was a crew-type coverall in the closet. Gus donned it and added a small handgun from a wall chest. In the passageway all was silent. Most of the crew were busy, Gus knew. He made his way down to the lower levels and finally encountered a familiar corridor leading to the Power Section. He passed two men on the way; they hardly glanced at him.

The red-painted inner door to the Power Control Room stood ajar. Gus slipped past it, closed it silently, and dogged it down. The engineering officer yelped when Gus poked the gun in his back.

"Quiet," Gus cautioned. He prodded the man along to a parts locker, then motioned him inside.

"What do you hope to gain by this, you madman?" The man's red face blazed almost purple. "You're asking to be shot down —"

"So are you. No noise."

Gus shut the door and locked it. He went on to the room that housed the control servos. Three technicians worked over a disassembled chassis. They whirled when Gus snapped an order at them. Their hands went up slowly. Gus herded two of them into a parts locker. The third backed away, trembling and sweating, as Gus pressed the gun to his chest.

"Show me how this setup works," Gus ordered.

The technician began a confused lecture on the theory of cyclic fusion-fission reactors.

"Skip all that," Gus told him. "Tell me about these controls."

The technician explained. Gus listened, asked questions. After fifteen minutes he indicated a red plastic panel cover.

"That's the damper control unit?"

"That's right."

"Open it up."

"Now just a minute, fellow," the man said quickly. "You don't know what you're getting into—"

"Do as I said."

"Tamper with that and you can throw the whole core out of balance!"

Gus rammed the gun hard into the man's chest.

"OK, OK." He set to work with fingers that shook.

Gus studied the maze of exposed circuitry. "What happens if you cut those conduits?" He pointed. The technician backed away, shaking his head. "Wait a minute—"

Gus cuffed the side of his head hard enough to send the man sprawling.

"The whole revert circuit will be thrown on the line! You'll get a feed into the interlock system, and—"

"Put it in Standard!"

"She'll climb past crit and blow! Believe me, she'll blow the side of the planet out!"

"What if you just cut that one?" Gus indicated another lead.

The technician shook his head. "Nearly as bad," his voice broke. "She'd run away and the core would begin to heat. She'd be running red in an hour—and slag down in three. The gamma count—"

"Any way to stop it, once it starts?"

"Not once you let her climb past critical! You redline her, and we're all finished!"

"Cut that lead," Gus commanded.

"You're out of your mind—" The man launched himself at Gus, who hit him with the gun and sent him reeling. There was a heavy pair of bolt-cutters on the nearby bench. Gus used them to snap through the pencil-thick lead. At once a bell sounded stridently. Gus tossed the cutters aside and dragged the groaning man to a tool locker; then he went to the wall phone, punched a code from the list beside it.

"Captain, this is one of the fish eggs," he said. "I think we'd better have a talk about a choice you're going to have to make."

· 26 ·

Gus stood with Captain Harris on a hillside a mile from the ship, watching with the others as the spot of dull red grew on the side of the gleaming tower that was the stricken starship. A sigh went up from the men as a long ripple appeared across the flawless curve of the great hull.

"Broke her back," the captain said tonelessly.

"She'll cool down enough by spring for us to go aboard and salvage whatever might be of use to the colony," Gus said. "Meanwhile, what we took off her before she got too hot ought to last us."

Harris gave Gus an ice-blue glare that reminded him of a girl left behind on faraway Terra. The memory seemed as remote as the planet.

"Yes—you should be able to survive until then—"

"*We* ought to survive," Gus corrected. "We're all in this together, now."

"When the story of your treachery gets out—"

"It's to your advantage not to let it," Gus interrupted the threat. "Better stick to the story we agreed on, about my lucky hunch and your heroic action, saving as much as you did."

"My officers would tear me apart if they knew I'd come to terms with a mutinous, sabotaging scoundrel!"

"The colonists would rip all of you apart if they knew you'd planned to maroon them."

"I'm still wondering if you'd have made good your threat to blow her apart."

"Either way, you'd have lost. This way, you have a certain

- 359

amount of good will going for you with the colonists. They think you chose to lose the ship rather than abandon them."

"If there'd been any other way . . ."

A tall figure staggered across toward the two men.

"Cap'n—" Leone blurted. "I tol' you . . . tol' you she'd buckle."

"Yes, you told me, Leone. Go sleep it off."

"Last cruise," Leone muttered, watching as the weakened structure yielded to the massive pressure of gravity. "My retirement, flat of my own, wife—all gone, now. Stuck here, on this . . . this cold desert!"

"We'll march south," Gus said. "Maybe we'll find better country."

"I'm not sure we should leave this area," Harris said. "If we're to have any chance of rescue—"

"We're pollen on the wind," Gus said. "Nobody will ever miss us. It's up to us now; what we do for ourselves. Nobody else cares."

"My authority—"

"Doesn't mean a thing," Gus cut him off. "We're all covvs together, swimming in the same waters."

"Shark-infested waters!"

Gus nodded. "We won't all make it, but some of us will."

Harris seemed to shudder. "How can you be sure?"

"We have a chance," Gus said. "That's all any man can ask for."

Editors' Note: While the experience of the passengers and crew of SH 731 was anomalous in its severity, nonetheless even the most fortunate of the early Selected Immigrants suffered—though usually in lesser degree—from virtually the same hardships on arrival, a circumstance which was of course, in the long run, most fortunate for the development on our planet of those qualities of toughness and ingenuity which form the basis of our present, thriving economy and robust culture. A journal from the Era of Development, while reflecting the unfortunate intercontinental hostility which existed for some decades before formal Unification, nonetheless communicates a sense of the vitality and personal involvement of even obscure individuals, a fact which is well known to have been indispensable to Omega's exemplary success.

APPENDIX II

Extract from the Journals of Andrew Grall

They were waiting for Andy Grall as he left the Weather Control Complex at the end of the dawn shift: Pinchot, sleek and dandified even in a survey coverall; young Colmar, big and soft, with a worried look on his too-small face; Hogan, lean as a ferret, bright-eyed, nervous; and Halland, silent as usual.

"You've heard?" Pinchot said. "They did it." Grall nodded.

"Some East politico who's never been within five rawks of North Continent decides we need to open another hundred miles of desert," Hogan said. "So five hundred of us are gonna be drafted and shipped out to the plateau to play hardy pioneers."

"We knew they were going ahead with it," Grall said. "Why act surprised?"

"There was always a chance they'd take our warning and back down," Hogan said. He had a thin, high voice, a mouth that seemed always to be grinning a secret grin.

"It couldn't have been more blatant if they were *trying* to goad us beyond endurance," Pinchot said. "It's as if they were thumbing their noses and daring us to do something."

"We told them," Colmar said, sounding frightened. He swallowed. "We held off until now to give them a chance to see reason. They didn't. Opening a new sector now is a smack in the teeth to every man on North Continent."

"It's not just a little kick in the mouth," Hogan said. "It's slavery for all of us who are tagged to go out on the advance team. And for what? To give the East-controlled Development Bureau a nice growth rate to brag about."

"To fill politicians' pockets back on East," Pinchot corrected. "We're supposed to give up our homes, families, friends, move out into the desert, live in lash-up hutments, eat issue rations, work like horses fourteen hours a day—"

"I'm not afraid of work," Grall said. "If it were on a voluntary basis, I might even sign on."

"But it's not voluntary, Andy. It's compulsory. *They* decide who goes—and for how long."

"Even here in town it's serfdom," Hogan said. "Look at you —with an advanced degree in administration—putting in your two years on a board at Weather like any clod. And Pinch, here, with a Master's in personnel dynamics—"

"What about the petition, Pinchot?" Grall cut off the complaint impatiently. "Didn't you get an answer?"

Pinchot took a paper from an inside pocket and handed it over. It was a letter on the stationery of the Development Administration, formally—and patronizingly, Grall thought— thanking the addressee for his interest in Administration policy.

"It was addressed to me by name," Pinchot said, "not to the Committee. Don't ask me how they knew. But it doesn't matter now." He tore the letter in two and tossed it aside. "So much for appeals to established authority. We tried the peaceful way. Now we're taking matters into our own hands. So, are you with us, Grall—or against us?"

"He doesn't have to be either," Halland spoke up. "He's got a right to be neutral."

Pinchot shook his head. "Not any more," he said. "The time's come to take sides."

"The Committee of Fifty," Grall said, "consisting of forty-one members by actual count, out of a population on North of a hundred and twenty-five thousand—"

"What percentage of French peasants staged the French Revolution?" Hogan demanded. "How many Americans actually fired on the Redcoats? How many Bolsheviks tossed out the czar?"

"We can do it," Pinchot said, his eyes narrow and intent. "We move in fast, take the port and the com center, the generator and pumping stations, the depot and warehouses, grab Admin House—and we're in charge."

"What about the Security Force?"

"We'll bottle them up in their barracks."

"Spacearm could blow us off the planet."

"But they won't. BuDev wants profits; that means operating mines and plants. We'll cooperate with them; they won't get rough. They'll accept the fait accompli."

All heads turned as the soft *whirr* of a turbodyne sounded. A police cart came into view; the men stood silent as it coasted to a stop beside them. A tall, loose-jointed man in Security uniform swung down and sauntered over. He was a stranger—too tall, too pale—over from East, not a Norther.

"Ret's see your IDs, ferrows," he said in a nasal East accent. His partner sat stolidly on the cart, watching. The men handed over their tags, which were scrutinized cursorily and handed back.

"What are you doing here?" the Security man asked in a lazy tone, as if he didn't much care but was asking anyway.

Grall felt his face tighten. He shook off Colmar's restraining hand. "Minding our own business," he said harshly. "Why?"

The Security man looked him over casually. "Come over to the frat," he said easily.

"What for?" Grall said.

"Move," the cop snapped and flipped a small rod from his belt.

Grall walked over to the cart.

"Turn around, get your hands up behind your head."

Grall followed orders. Careless hands slapped down his sides, then deftly turned his pockets inside out. The Security man grunted.

"That's all. Break it up now. I don't want to see you hanging around in the streets after five bells."

The cart rolled away. Pinchot came over, picked up the items the Security man had dropped on the pavement, and handed them to Grall.

"They're nice fellows," he said softly. "Just doing their jobs."

"When?" Grall asked tightly.

"Tonight. Be at the Oak at midnight, ready for action," Pinchot said.

"I'll be there," Grall said.

· 2 ·

Walking through the dark street, Grall thought about it. He remembered stirring stories he'd read in grade school of hardy pioneers of half a century earlier—his maternal grandparents among them—who had come out from Terra during the Population Riots to cast their lot for themselves and their families on the virgin world called Omega Prime.

It had been a terrifying crossing. Before coldsleep was developed, five thousand men and women were transported in the hold of a marginally spaceworthy freighter, packed like sardines with barely space to move, fed on minimal rations, three bodies alotted to each bunk, sharing community toilets, with no amusements, no privacy, no relief for the long months of the voyage.

And arriving at the end of it not on the soft green world of open spaces and fresh air they'd been led to expect, but on the harsh tundra of the New Province on North Continent. There'd been riots then, and killing. But in the end the survivors had voted to stay, to take their chances on the new world, to conquer or die.

Very melodramatic, Grall thought to himself. But what's it got to do with today? They worked out their lives to give us— their descendents—something better. But do we have it? We've seeded the oceans, stabilized the soil, planted crops. Today we can walk in the open air without respirators, eat our home-grown vegetables; we have a town with an auditorium, a sports arena, and a public library . . .

"But we're still slaves," he said aloud. "We've been used; we dance to East's tune. The best of our products go east in return for a bare subsistence level of imports. And the time has come for a change."

They were a vague crowd in the darkness. Grall pushed his way through, turning his face away from a beam of light from a pocket flash. Pinchot appeared, a white sweatband around his forehead. His face was taut; his tongue flicked restlessly at his lower lip. He handed Grall a small plastic-boxed talker.

"You're on Team One, hitting Admin House. You worked a summer there as a messenger, so you know the layout. Lie low until it's secured. If Hogan—I mean, when Hogan and his team secure Port, they'll call in. Same with Mullen, Pyle, Bergson—all the teams will report to you when they've pinned down their objectives. I'll coordinate with you—"

"Where am I supposed to hide while the rest of you are winning the war?" Grall asked, feeling surly.

"You take cover in the park while the rest of the team goes in. When you see their signal—you know we've got those survey flares—move in fast and take over the switchboard." Pinchot beckoned a tall, lean man. "Fry's your team leader. You stick close to him until they move in. Okay, get going."

Grall followed Fry and the other members of his team—two men and a girl named Teresa—as they threaded their way through the now-dispersing throng, turned east along the Outer Drive, heading for the park. The talker box muttered and crackled, monitoring terse conversations.

As they turned into Park Way, Grall caught Fry's arm. "That's a cop-flat parked up there." He pointed to a police cart under a pole-light a hundred yards distant.

"There's nobody near it," Fry said and shook off Grall's hand. "Come on. We've got three minutes to get in position."

The party went on, entered the park via a service gate, and crossed toward the line of trees behind which the lights of Admin House glowed peacefully. They halted beside a fountain which tossed sprays up into colored light.

"There's a gap in the hedge." Fry pointed. "As soon as you see my flares, come in at a run."

Grall nodded and took up his post behind a screen of shrubbery as the others slipped away silently. They reached the street, started across. A fine mist of spray from the fountain dampened Grall's face.

An accidentally imported, and highly mutated, but harmless Terran insect called a skiddoo alighted on his neck. He brushed it away.

The spotlights lanced out simultaneously from two points; one was aimed downward from the roof of Admin House, raking across the lawn, pinpointing the gate through which Fry and Teresa were just passing; the other, from the parked cop-flat, struck the group horizontally, and threw stark shadows against the hedges. The two conspirators caught outside the gate froze for a moment, then turned and ran, their feet noisy in the silent street. An amplified voice boomed out.

"Stop where you are! Davies, Henderson! We know you, you can't get away—" The voice broke off as light winked and a shot crashed from the gate. Fry was lying flat in the shadow of the ornamental gatepost. Grall saw another flash, but the second shot was drowned by the short, savage roar of a police bullet-pump. Fry's body was flung a foot into the air and hurled ten feet back like a bundle of rags. The two runners skidded to a halt and threw themselves face down in the street. Grall saw Teresa reach the front entrance of the government building; as she ran up the steps, the door burst open and two uniformed Security men gathered her in.

Men in battle armor, handguns ready, were swarming into the street, clustering at the gate and around the captives. Heavy footsteps sounded behind Grall. He hugged the ground and ducked as lights glared, playing across the shrubbery around him. A man went past less than six feet away.

At that moment Grall's talker box uttered a burst of static and a small clear voice said, "Power station secured. One man hurt and a couple of windows broken—otherwise no damage."

The Security man who had just passed halted; gravel crunched as he swiveled, playing his light about. Grall eased back. The light flicked closer. He reached a large tree and got to his feet. A twig crackled.

"Stop there," the Security man barked. Grall ran. A shot sang through foliage. He heard sounds ahead, veered right, and crashed through a head-high hedge into a bricked path. Two uniformed men standing fifty feet away turned toward him; he plunged around a bench, dove into massed foliage. It yielded and he was in the clear.

A tremendous blow on the calf of his right leg sent him tumbling. He rolled, tried to jump up, fell on his face. His leg was hot, numb, a dead weight. Scrabbling frantically with his hands, he dragged himself under a spread of juniper and felt the ground crumble beneath him. He rolled, then fetched up with a thump in drifted leaves at the bottom of a drainage ditch.

The voices and footsteps came closer, but they seemed remote and unimportant now. Grall's thoughts had leaped ahead, quite calmly, to the trial, the conviction, the prison sentence, the loss of his citizenship. . . .

· 4 ·

The dark was quiet now. Listening closely, Grall could hear distant voices over the rustle of foliage in the light breeze, but nothing stirred nearby. He moved his injured leg tentatively and discovered to his surprise that it responded, though painfully. He sat up, explored the wound. There was a neat hole in the mass of muscle below and behind the knee, a less neat hole to the left of the shin. A small-caliber solid shot had gone through without hitting bone. He rose to his feet. He could walk. He brushed leaves away, climbed out of the ditch, and was confronting the hedge that bordered Government Street. Through a gap he could see the lighted front of Admin House. Uniformed men were on the terrace, on the lawn. The front doors stood open, brilliantly lit. Floods illuminated the lawns. A dozen cop-flats were in sight parked along the street.

At first Grall didn't see it; then he did: sellout. Two-thirds of the Security Force was here, posted two deep around the front of the house; and he could see that the rear service entrance was equally guarded. But the small and inconspicuous entry at the side was shrouded in shadow. Insofar as Grall could see, no Security men were near it.

The talker crackled: the Power Complex was in rebel hands. Pyle, at the port, called in: all was secure. Bergson, sounding elated, reported the virtually unopposed seizure of the pumping station. The uprising had gone well—all but the most vital part. Administrator Brill and Major Jensen had concentrated all their forces here. They hadn't been fooled for a moment. They knew all about the Committee's plans and had been ready.

But there was that side door. Grall's mouth was dry; his heart pounded painfully. It could be a trap. There might be half a dozen Security men lying in wait for the mouse to take the cheese. But on the other hand, the door was little used, a delivery door; it was just possible that Jensen had overlooked it.

Grall could slip away now, return home, and be as surprised as everybody else when the news came out. Or he could put his neck solidly in the noose.

With a curse that was half prayer, he left his vantage point and, limping, slipped away along the hedge line.

·5·

From a clump of shadow between the library and the Agricultural Experimental Building, Grall studied the scene. He had a better view of the side door from here. Nothing stirred there. To anyone not intimately familiar with the building, there appeared to be an unbroken mass of shrubbery along the east wall. Grall took a deep breath and stepped out and crossed the street openly, two hundred yards from the lighted gate of Admin House. He went back past the west wing of the elementary school, crossed the playground, came up along a path to a point fifty feet from the rear corner of Admin House, paused for a moment, then ran across a strip of open ground to the door. There was no alarm. He tried the latch, then pushed with his shoulder. The panel yielded slightly. He stepped back and kicked straight out at the lock. Plastic and metal shattered, the door bounced in. Grall slid inside, shut the door, and stood in darkness, listening.

Voices sounded from the front of the house; somewhere a radio crackled and a toneless voice droned, too faint to make out the words. Feet clumped to and fro. There was a stair a few feet ahead. Grall felt his way in darkness, found the newel post, and started up. He saw dim light above. On the second floor he looked along a carpeted hall. At the far end a man in mufti with a paper in his hand emerged from a door, then hurried away. Grall went on up.

The third floor corridor was illuminated. A uniformed Security man stood twenty feet away, fiddling with the mechanism of his blastgun. The man holstered the weapon, walked to the far end of the hall, lifted a house phone from its hook, and began an inaudible conversation. He turned his back to Grall's position, still talking.

Grall slid out, then eased silently along the passage to the intersection with the wide corridor off which the administrative suite opened.

Four Security men were in sight—two posted beside the ivory-enameled double doors, the other two at the main staircase. One of the men guarding the stairs descended a few steps to carry on a conversation regarding the whereabouts of someone named Katz. His partner leaned over the rail, his back to Grall. The two men on the door had their heads turned, following the exchange. Grall stepped out and walked silently and swiftly toward the door adjacent to the guarded portal. He was six feet from it when one of the men glanced his way, gave a startled grunt and grabbed for his slung blastgun, then fumbled it.

"Here you, where you think you're going?" he blurted.

"Special messenger," Grall said crisply.

He reached the door for which he had been headed as the second guard swung his gun round. Grall tried the knob; it turned. He plunged through as two shots racketed in the hall, gouging molten plastic from the doorframe. He spun, slammed the door, tripped the security lock system, and heard armor sliding into place as a heavy body struck the panel from outside.

Men hammered and shouted as Grall ran across the room, then paused for an instant at the connecting door, picturing the slugs that would rip into his body if the administrator had posted guards inside his office as well as in the hall. Then he opened it and stepped through.

Administrator Brill was a plumpish man with graying hair; he sat behind his desk, his eyes on the hall door, an expression of surprise on his face. As Grall appeared he whirled and reached for a desk drawer. Grall dove, knocked the older man's hand aside, and scooped up the 2 mm needler and aimed it at Brill.

"What—what—" Brill said, then collected himself. He straightened his clothing, fixed a stern expression on his round face, and looked challengingly at Grall.

"Well? You've forced your way into my office for a good reason I suppose, Grall, since you'll most certainly be taken into custody before you leave here."

"Your Security men are overpaid," Grall said. "They're expert at harassing citizens but not so good when it comes to something complicated—like watching both sides of a house."

Brill's features flinched.

"I suggest you give yourself up at once, Andy," he said. "You've made your point. I'll personally look into the conduct of Security Affairs—"

"I'm not here to complain about inefficient police work," Grall said. "I'm here to take over the government."

· 6 ·

Brill stared across the desk at Grall, who pulled a chair around and sat down. The pounding at the door went on, while an intercom screen on the administrator's desk buzzed insistently until Grall reached across and switched it off.

"Andy," Brill said in a reasonable, kindly tone, "I've known your parents for thirty years. I remember the day you were born—"

"Make it 'Mr. Grall,' Micky."

Brill jerked as if he had been stung by a wasp. "I hardly think disrespect will advance your cause—whatever it is. Now, if you don't mind, tell me why you're here. I suggest you hurry, since my Security forces will be in here at any moment—"

"I doubt that. Your locks are pretty solid."

"You can't believe you can succeed in this abortive uprising!"

"We have the port, the power plant, and Com Center. The major seems to have overlooked a couple of bets while he concentrated on Admin House."

"See here, Andy—*Mr.* Grall. You were always a levelheaded lad, a good scholar, potentially a fine citizen, and a valuable colonist. You come from a distinguished family. What are you doing mixed up with these anarchists? People like Daniel Pinchot—known radicals, soreheads, agitators—"

"Dan is a Sector Scholar. He may be impatient with established order, but he's no fool, Mr. Administrator. I'm mixed up with him because it was that . . . or go on the way we've been going—and that wasn't good enough."

Brill's face shifted to a look of grim determination. "I hardly think it's the function of a handful of malcontents to determine unilaterally what is or is not good enough for the welfare of Omega Prime."

"And you are?"

"I was duly appointed by the Colonial Administration to carry out my function; I've been trained for this work; I have more years of experience in administration than you have of life."

"*I* didn't appoint you."

"You're intelligent enough to recognize the fact that specialists who've devoted their lives to the problems of government and administration are better qualified to run matters than a pack of—of amateurs who regard any restriction of what they consider their freedom and rights as intolerable burdens!"

"A pack of profit-minded bureaucrats and politicians who tell me I have to give up everything that makes life livable and devote years of hard labor to opening up new territories that we don't need or want."

"You're a fool, Grall. You don't know what you're talking about! The economy must expand or—"

"Or certain big corporations back on Terra won't make as

much as they'd like out of our blood, sweat, and tears."

"That's a childishly simplistic version of matters. Why—"

"You mean Parson's Bay and General Logistics and North American Materials won't show a profit from opening up the new sector?" Andy demanded.

"Well—of course they hope to! And why shouldn't they? They funded the great bulk of the developmental work, provided most of our specialized equipment, supplied technical experts —and still do."

"All at a nice return on their money. And we do the work. Especially the five hundred names that got pulled out of a hat to open Sector Twelve."

"So, like impatient kindergarten children, you're going to take over the nursery and make it all one long play-time, is that it, Andy . . . Mr. Grall?"

"The mines will continue to operate, Mr. Administrator. We'll still export—and don't tell me how good and kind Terra is to buy our products. I know how scarce nonorganically contaminated chemicals are today."

"Suppose a squadron of Peace Enforcers arrives to restore order—"

"That won't open any mines."

· 7 ·

Brill gazed at Grall. It was quiet in the corridor now. A call light blinked on the big desk, ignored.

"You want all the advantages of what other men have built," Brill said slowly, "but you want them without working for them, without effort, without commitment or obligation. Well, the Universe doesn't work that way, my young friend. Nothing is free. Society isn't withholding your birthright—not in the sense you're apparently demanding."

"I have the same birthright any animal in the wild has," Grall said. "To take what I can get and hold."

"So you'll seize the granary and eat until it's empty. But who'll refill it for you, eh? You'll grab the trideo set you've always wanted—but who'll repair it, who'll supply the power to run it, who'll do the programming and the performing, and who'll pay the bills?"

"We will. We're prepared to work as hard as required. But we intend to keep the rewards for ourselves, for Colmar—including for you, Mr. Administrator, if you decide to stay, instead of sending it off-world for the benefit of corporate executives we've never met, who've never seen Colmar and never will."

"It's the arrogance of it that astounds me," Brill said wonderingly. "We all have our obligations, Grall, whether it pleases us or not. The food you eat, the clothes you wear, the entertainments you enjoy, the education you were given didn't pop up out of the desert. Someone made them. They represent human ingenuity and effort—the struggles of our pioneers—and you've reaped the benefits."

"That's a debt that's passed along from generation to generation, Mr. Brill. A man owes nothing to the past. Life can't demand payment for itself."

"I've always thought you were a young man with a sense of decency, of justice, of regard for the rights of others. Tell me, Andy, if this . . . revolution of yours succeeds by some wild chance, what then? Will you rest easily with your loot? Can you justify theft on a grand scale and settle down to enjoy your stolen goodies until they run out?"

"You're taking the position," Grall said, "that because the government exists—"

"Legally," Brill put in.

"Because the government exists legally, that I'm therefore obligated to support it—or at least obey it. But I challenge that statement. Suppose the government were an outright tyranny —would I be obligated to connive at my own enslavement?"

"That's absurd—"

"No. A man has a natural right that supersedes legal obligations. Overthrowing a legally constituted government is treason—unless you win. Because if you win, you change the laws. Then anyone who supports the *old* government is the traitor."

"This is mere sophistry, Grall. You can't mean—"

"The right to revolt," Grall said slowly, as if thinking aloud, "is the most basic right a man has."

"Activist jargon," Brill snorted.

"Not if we win—and we *have* won, Mr. Administrator."

Brill's face flushed. "Nonsense. A pack of rabble-rousers couldn't possibly have—"

"Wrong. We're not rabble-rousers, we're the rabble itself, Mr. Administrator. Mr. *ex*-Administrator. Check for yourself."

Brill turned to his communicator panel and poked keys. His face tightened as no lights responded to his calls.

"You can still get through to Security barracks," Grall said. "Call Jensen and tell them to put down their guns."

· 8 ·

Brill punched out the code. The angry face of Major Jensen appeared on the desk screen.

"Mr. Administrator, thank God you're all right!"

"Never mind that," Brill said. "What's the situation?"

"These hoodlums have invaded a number of installations, Mr. Administrator, but I can clean them out. Just the same, I'd suggest you get through to CDT Sector and request a pair of PE's, triple GUTS priority."

"I'm afraid I'm not precisely at liberty to do that, Stig," Brill said. He angled the pickup to include Grall, gun in hand. Jensen's face jerked.

"What—"

"The, ah, Revolutionary Committee seems to have out-flanked us," Brill said.

"Stand fast, Mr. Administrator," Jensen said between clenched teeth. "My boys'll blast their way in there and—"

"Lay down your arms, Jensen," Grall cut in, leaning forward. "We hold every strong point on the continent—"

"I've got forty trained men on the grounds of Admin House," Jensen grated. "You'll never get out alive, you damned bandit!"

"Don't talk like an ass, Stig," Brill said calmly. "He's out-maneuvered you. It's checkmate." He looked at Grall. "What do you want from me, Andy?"

"Capitulate. Hand over control to the Committee and step down. I'll guarantee your safe conduct—and Jensen's too, unless he does something stupid, like firing on our men."

Brill stared levelly across at Grall. "Are you sure this is what you want, Andy? The responsibility—"

"Tell him," Grall said harshly.

Brill turned to the screen. "Lay down your arms, Stig," he said. "I'm signing a formal resignation in favor of Andrew Grall."

· 9 ·

Ten minutes later there was a brief clamor outside the door. Pinchot's voice came over the talker.

"Open up, Andy! We're in complete possession."

Grall crossed the room and released the locking system. The door burst open. Hogan came through, grinning a wide fox grin. He saw Brill and jerked up the weapon in his hand.

Behind him a gun fired from six feet; Hogan shrieked as the gun flew from his hand in a spatter of blood. He went to his knees, gripping his wrist, his hand welling crimson, as other men crowded into the room. It was Halland who had fired. He came forward to stand beside Grall.

"Why'd the hell'd you do that?" Hogan keened. "That's the pig that had Fry and Len and Jeannie killed!"

"What did you expect him to do, give them safe conduct?" Grall said tightly.

"Here, what's going on?" Pinchot said, pushing forward. "You'd better give me the gun." He held out his hand, the other resting on the butt of the pistol at his hip.

"I thought the idea was to improve government, not to start a reign of terror," said Halland.

"There'll be no more killing," Grall said. "Get rid of the gun, Halland. You, too, Pinch."

Halland tossed the weapon aside. Pinchot failed to hear the command until Grall repeated it, firmly.

"Who are you to be giving orders?" Pinchot demanded of Grall, but he unbuckled his gun belt.

"I'm the only one here with admin training. I'll hold the office until we can stage elections—unless you want to start your new regime by killing me and maybe Halland and a few others. But I don't think a purge will convince BuDev that you're fit to run the continent."

Pinchot stared at Grall, eyes narrowed. Then he relaxed, thrust out a hand.

"Makes sense," he said. "Let's go, men."

"You took a terrible chance," Brill said after the others had withdrawn.

"I suppose that's part of any revolution, Mr. Administrator."

Brill sighed. "Call me Micky," he said. "There are a few things I ought to familiarize you with before I go."

· 10 ·

Four weeks later Andy Grall sat behind the big desk, frowning at the papers before him. He shuffled through them, then sighed. There was a perfunctory tap at the door, and Pinchot came in.

"Afternoon, Mr. Administrator," he said. "What are you looking so glum about? They elected you, didn't they?"

"I'll step down in your favor any time, Pinchot."

"No, thanks. I never did like paperwork." He eyed the stack on Grall's desk. "In any case, the CDT and BuDev have both recognized you as the people's choice. You're stuck with it. I'm quite happy as chief of operations." His genial expression faded a bit as he spoke. He swung a chair around and sat down.

"In that connection, Andy, what about the import program I outlined? You've had it three days now—"

"I know. Luxury goods. Official cars, cooler units, trideo programs."

"So? Don't we have the right to spend our money to suit ourselves? Isn't that what the takeover was all about?"

"Sure. What money?"

Pinchot's face went tight. "The price of the last shipment of ores, for example," he snapped.

"It all went toward our credit deficit with Outplanet."

"You expect me to believe that?"

"You can check the figures with Anderson if you like. No matter how many times we add them up, they still come out the same. We're running in the red—and what credit we still have has to go for necessities."

"I heard all that from Anderson. That's why I'm here. It's not good enough, Grall. This isn't why we threw out BuDev—just to carry on the same old swindle."

"You can take over any time, Pinchot." Grall slid a sheet of paper across to the other man. "My resignation, all ready for signature."

Pinchot stared at the document, pushed it away.

"I don't get it," he growled. "You're spouting Brill's line, the BuDev line—"

"It's nobody's line. It's just the facts, Pinchot. We're exporting X kilotons of minerals at Y creds per ton, and we're importing Z creds' worth of basic Terran products. And we're sliding a little deeper into the red every quarter."

"They're overcharging us, holding us up on prices—"

"Negative. They're selling to us at seven percent under market scale. BuDev policy."

"Then we can raise our prices—"

"Negative again. It's marginal now. If our prices plus haulage go above costs of local procurement and refining, we're out of business."

"Then, what in God's name can we do?"

Grall pushed another sheet of paper across the desk. Pinchot glanced at it, then stared at Grall.

"Are you out of your mind? This is Brill's Opening Order for Sector Twelve."

"Wrong. It's *my* Opening Order for Sector Twelve."

"You can't do it. The people won't accept it. What will Hogan and Williver—and Pyle and Tomkin and the others say? They —we—risked our necks fighting this same crazy scheme."

"We need more income, less dependence on imports. We have to extend our usable acreage and expand our mining operations. If you can think of another way to do it, I'll welcome the suggestion."

Pinchot's face looked slack and grayish. "Is this what we took over—the same old headaches, only worse?"

"Did we really take over, Pinchot?" Grall asked tiredly. "Or did they con us into standing on our own feet?"

Pinchot swore.

"I agree," Grall said. "Now let's get to work. I need five hundred names for Sector Twelve. Any suggestions?" [Extract from the journals of H.C. Andrew Grall, FOS, COO ends.]

Editors' Note: Omitting the passages in the Grall journals covering the decades of intensive economic development, the editors here include a later passage recorded during the time of social unrest which preceded the foundation of today's stable society.

· 11 ·

The crash of breaking glass was like an explosion in the darkness. Continental Administrator Andrew Grall came awake, rolled off the side of the bed, and hugged the floor. In the silence a final glass fragment fell from the window frame to the rug. Grall got to his feet, then saw the paper-wrapped bolt lying by the dresser.

END TYRANNY ON NORTH was lettered neatly in red on the back of a recently published ration application form. Grall grunted and tossed the paper away. It was nearly dawn, he saw. He dressed and went down to the kitchen. Freddy, his butler-valet-driver-bodyguard-secretary was there brewing coffee.

"You're up early, Mr. Administrator," he said formally.

"No protocol this early in the day, Freddy," Grall said as he sat down at the table. "A few of my admirers came by to give me a nice send-off for the day. Colmar's twentieth anniversary of Unification." Grall gave a snort that was not quite the laugh he had intended.

"Don't take it so hard, Andy," Freddy said. He poured coffee, put a cup before Grall, and sat down opposite him. "You've always done what was best in a tough situation."

Grall looked at him sardonically as he sipped the bitter brew. "Funny how you assume it wasn't flowers they threw, Freddy. Anybody would think I wasn't popular."

Freddy lifted his powerful shoulders. "You can't please 'em all," he said.

"It seems I'm not pleasing any of them."

"You're doing what you've got to do, Andy. The colony's still a marginal operation. It's not your fault that times are tough. These babies want it all now, that's all. They see too much interplan trideo, they've got ideas about how life ought to be fat and soft. They've got to face up to facts sometime. Colmar's still a poor world. We just can't afford a three-hour day and welfare caviar."

"Try telling that to some econ graduate doing his time in the labor pool."

"I know; so they gripe. What about it? If they'd been here back in the old days, they'd have had something to gripe about. Do they ever think about what the first scheduled colonists here on North had to face up to seventy years ago?"

"Of course not," Grall said. "Why should they? These aren't the old days. This is now. And they're young. They want to live today, not some time in the next century. I can't blame 'em."

"Sure . . . and so did your grandad want to live—and mine. That's why they came out here—to nothing. To make something of it—of an alien world—something that hadn't existed before. They had no guarantes, no route back. They had to whip Colmar or die—and plenty of them died."

"Ancient history, Freddy. Today they know there's something better than hard work and rationing. They want it. And Freddy, so do I—"

"But you're not whining for it. And one day it'll happen—because you're working for it like they did back then. It must've been a frightening thing, Andy, when they unloaded from the freighters and looked around and saw a barren continent, not even a tree. In seventy years we've turned it into a place where a man can live—but not without effort. Let 'em gripe, Andy—just so they put in their time like everybody else, like you did."

"Involuntary servitude. 'Tyranny' is what they call it."

Freddy snorted.

"So? What are you supposed to do, back down because they call you dirty names? You know what's got to be done, Andy. You're doing it. It takes guts. You got 'em. More coffee?"

"No, thanks. I might as well go on down to the office. Maybe we'll beat the rock throwers for a change."

"If it was me," Freddy said in the car, "I'd stay home and to hell with 'em. Let 'em see how things go after a few days with nobody making the decisions. They're complaining now: let 'em see how it'd be if you weren't on the job to untangle the knots—"

"Don't get carried away, Freddy. Any competent administrative type could do the same job."

"Maybe," Freddy said. "It's not seeing what you have to do that's tough; it's doing it when the mob is yelling for your head. You could be the most popular man on North tomorrow if you'd give in."

"And we'd be bankrupt the day after. Sure, Freddy. But those are just facts; they don't have any appeal to the emotions."

· 12 ·

A few early pickets gaped as the administrator's car swung in through the open gates.

In his office Grall attacked a stack of priority applications: fifty tons of fabricated steel sections for shaft #209 versus sixty tons of the same urgently needed for the extension to the loading docks—with precisely nine tons on hand for issue; four loads of feeder fuel in stock to be allocated among nine agencies, all yelling for immediate action; computer components on order for six months by Supply, demanded by Routing at once to prevent imminent shutdown of the entire NW range . . .

Grall looked up at a sharp rap at the door. Halland, the executive officer, poked his bald head in. Through the open door Grall could hear sounds of an altercation.

"Another delegation to see you," Halland said. Grall rose and went out into the corridor. From below came voices chanting slogans. Feet clattered on the stairs. A disheveled young man in maintenance grays appeared, Freddy close beside him, two perspiring guards at their heels.

"Hold it, Freddy," Grall said. The men stopped. "Let him come up."

"Chief, he might be armed—" Halland said quickly, but Grall brushed that aside.

"You want to see me?" he asked the intruder.

"That's right," the man in gray said defiantly. He brushed back his hair, straightened his jacket. "We're citizens; we've got a right to be heard."

"Who's we?"

"The Party." The young man said it flatly, as if inviting a challenge.

"Come along to the office," Grall said.

"Frisk them first," he heard Halland order the guards as he turned away.

There were five people in the delegation, three men, two women, ranging in age from eighteen to thirty-five, Grall estimated. He knew them by sight, two by name—not a difficult feat in a city population of thirty thousand. One of the women —a plump, pretty girl in nurse's green—stepped forward and offered Grall a folded paper. Halland read it over Grall's shoulder.

"The same old refrain," the exec said. "Improved public transport, more entertainment facilities, shorter hours. It's nonsense—"

"It's not nonsense to us," the girl said sharply.

"Or to me either, Miss Tey," Grall said. "I'd like to lead an easier life myself. Unfortunately we can't afford it—not yet."

"You've got yours," the man in gray said. "Official mansion, official car, the best of everything—"

"Look here," Halland started, but Grall waved a hand to silence him.

"Let's keep it factual—Jonas, isn't it? My official residence is a standard class-Vb unit; I get the same food, clothing, and energy ration as anyone else. As you know. As for the car, I used to walk—until the rock density got a bit high."

"If you were doing your job the way you ought to nobody would be throwing things," Jonas snapped.

"I've got an idea Freddy was at the point of bruising you a bit when I happened along. Does that mean you had it coming to you?"

"He's a hired goon—that's different."

"What is it you expect me to do, Jonas, Miss Tey?"

"Ease the restrictions on life," the girl said promptly. "Let people enjoy living while they can. Shorten the work day, give us some leisure-time activities and facilities, end rationing, increase consumer imports."

Grall nodded. "Anything else?"

"Plenty more," Jonas said. "End the labor draft. Raise pay, right across the board. Lift the off-world travel restrictions, bring in more outsystem entertainers."

"For what it costs to open this new sector," another of the delegation spoke up, a small, timid-looking man with a bad complexion, "we could've founded a program of concert artists that would've given us some contact with our Terran cultural heritage."

"Sector Eleven gives us a marine agricultural facility," Grall said mildly. "In twenty years it may be our biggest food producer. We may be able to shorten the time to self-support capability by three decades—"

"We know all the propaganda lines," Jonas said. "We heard all that before."

"Then what are you doing here?" Grall snapped.

"That's easy, Mr. Administrator," Jonas said with a sneer. "We don't believe the official line."

"The records are open to the public," Grall said.

"They can be faked too."

"Why?" Grall shot back. "Why would I want to delude the public?"

"For obvious reasons—"

"Name them," Grall snapped.

"All right. To justify your program of overwork and under-pay, long hours and no recreation, luxury for the few at the cost of slavery for the many—"

"What luxury?" Grall cut in sharply. "We've already covered that particular allegation. It's nonsense and you know it—and so does everybody in this room."

"Look, Chief, this has gone far enough," Halland started, but Grall cut him off.

"You're here charging me and the rest of the administration with a deep, dark plot—"

"You're depriving the people of their basic rights," Jonas shouted.

"You name one right you're being deprived of Jonas, and I'll personally see that you get a lifetime pension," Grall said.

"All right—the right to a reasonable amount of leisure time, for openers. The eight-hour day went out with coal-fired ground-cars."

"What would you call a reasonable amount of leisure time?"

"Time enough to do a few things. To have hobbies, play a musical instrument, visit your friends—"

"Wrong, Mr. Jonas. That's nice, maybe, but it's not reasonable. Reasonable means what's physically possible. We have just so much manpower," he went on, raising his voice as Jonas tried to cut in. "We have to allocate that manpower in such a way as to keep industrial operations going at the rate required to produce enough exportable output to keep the economy afloat. You want more imported trideos and traveling art shows? Fine. Then we'll have to work longer hours, not shorter."

"Official bullwash," Jonas spat out the words like a bite of wormy apple.

"As I said, the records are public. Look at them or not, suit yourself. But don't come bursting in here again with your proposals for instant Utopia until you've done your homework."

"That's what I thought we'd get," one of the women said in a shrill, nervous voice. "A brushoff. Excuses. We should've known better than to waste our time." She glared at Grall with eyes as sharp as stakes through a vampire's heart.

"I welcome constructive suggestions," Grall said, meeting

384 -

her gaze steadily. "Come back when you have one."

"We won't be back," Jonas said. "We're through talking." They departed, slamming doors.

· 13 ·

"Remind you of anything?" Grall asked Halland when silence had fallen again.

"Painfully. Except there were only fifty of us—"

"Forty-two," Grall corrected.

"—and this time half the population is agitating. No one tried to explain to us; if they had, we might even have listened."

"Don't count on it. We wanted change—any change. We got it."

"And all the grief that went with it. But these people today won't listen. They remember when we threw BuDev out; Pinchot and a few others were promising them the world. Twenty years later they're still on short rations. They're unhappy. And they mean business, Andy. This isn't just a little band of soreheads—"

"I know all that, Ben. Are you suggesting I should promise them pie in the sky? What happens when they discover it isn't there?"

Halland looked solemn. "Andy, for this generation—and for a lot of people who ought to know better—you symbolize everything that's wrong with life. By removing you, you see, they can remove their problems—they think."

"You're suggesting I quit while I'm ahead?"

"I'm suggesting you quit while you're alive, damn it!"

"And do what? Sit back and watch North Continent—maybe Colmar itself—die?"

"You've had offers—three in the last six months that I know of. I wrote the answers turning them down. You could still take that post at East U, lecturing on problems of the frontier economy—"

"And read in the fax about how the Omega Experiment failed. Ben, have you ever considered what would happen if we had to throw in the towel and invite BuDev back in? They'd have to close the colony down, try to evacuate us to Terra—to beehive housing, synthetic rations—"

"I know. It's unthinkable. And dammit, Colmar *can* make it! We have the minerals, the seas—a whole world to exploit!" Halland smacked his fist into his palm. "If they could just see it! Just give us time!"

"Bringing Terran life to an alien world is a big undertaking, Ben. Maybe too big. Maybe we haven't got what it takes. But I have to stay and do what I can—for as long as I can."

"And be a martyr," Halland said grimly.

"There's nothing noble about it," Grall said. "This is my homeworld. I couldn't survive on Terra. I'm fighting for my life —the only life I know."

"Then don't throw it away. Let me recruit an escort for you. I can get a dozen CSA regulars detailed from East—"

"Negative, Ben. Importing foreign gun-handlers to protect me from the people that voted me in would be the end."

"Then what in God's name are you going to do?"

"Play it by ear—and hope Sector Eleven starts paying off in time."

"Comes up with a miracle, you mean."

"I'd accept a miracle right now," Grall said wearily, "if it could be arranged."

· 14 ·

Two weeks later Halland laid a paper on Grall's desk. It had been a time of rising tensions and near-riots, broken glass—and at least one assassination attempt which had put Freddy in the hospital with third-degree laser burns.

"Weinberg, out at Eleven," Halland said. "I thought you ought to see it." The executive officer's face was haggard with lost sleep.

Grall scanned the paper. "Livestock? Chickens? What the devil's he doing out there, starting a zoo?"

"Experimental animals," Halland pointed out. "He wants to run some kind of tests on them."

Grall rubbed his eyes. "He knows we're on the shortest meat ration since colonization," he said wearily. "I'm surprised at Weinberg. Tell him no. Remind him he's out there to supplement our protein supply, not deplete it. And ask him what he's doing about the slime mould contamination problem he's been reporting on."

Halland nodded and turned to go. Grall stopped him before he reached the door.

"Wait a minute, Ben. Disregard that last outburst. I'm too damn tired to think straight. If Dick Weinberg thinks he needs a flock of goats, damn it, he probably needs a flock of goats. Set it up—triple A priority."

Halland nodded again, more brightly.

"And tell them to save a seat on the flier for me," Grall added. "I'm going out to see what he's up to."

Halland frowned. "That might not be a good idea, Andy. There was rioting at the port this afternoon and—"

"Set it up," Grall snapped, then grimaced. "I'm sorry, Ben. Nerves. Just get me on the flier. I'll ride out under a stack of old burlon bags if you say so."

"I'll set it up," Halland said tonelessly.

· 15 ·

The view from the cargo flier was a monotonous vista of eroded ridges, gullied plains, of rock, gravel, and sand, of gray, native desert turf stretching across the endless miles. After the narrow green belt of the capital had been passed—and its surrounding five-mile farm strip—forty miles of undeveloped desert intervened before the dull green of the bioadapted New Shenandoah valley appeared far off to the west. Another seventy miles of arid, treeless graylands unrolled beneath the flier; then ahead, the curve of the coast and the black-blue sea beyond.

They were within five miles of the Experimental Station before Grall could make out the fragile tracings of irrigation ditches, the patterns of agriformed fields, the vivid green specks that were transplanted trees shading a straggle of buildings. Offshore of the station, Grall noted, the lifeless sea was stained a dark amber. The flier landed on the scraped rectangle behind the sprawling, aluminum-and-white station. A chill wind blew sand across the open ground to ping against the flier's sides with a restless whispering.

Weinberg was there to meet Grall, a sturdily built, red-haired man with big solemn eyes and a wide, down-curving mouth that belied his brisk optimism of manner.

"Glad to see you, Mr. Administrator—you bring my goats and birds and stuff?" he said, pumping Grall's hand. "Come on out of this damned wind."

The marine biologist's office, laboratory, and living quarters comprised a single untidy room with stone countertops, a clutter of glassware, a desk heaped with papers, a cot, a table with a hotplate, and dirty dishes.

"Here, sit down, Andy. How about a cup of coffee and a slice of nut cake?"

"Dick, what's this about animal experiments? I understood you were going to add seafood to our diet—"

"Sure, sure. I'll tell you all about it. How're things in the city? I hear they're giving you a hard time, throwing rocks, the works."

"Things aren't good; but Ben Halland says all we need is a small miracle from you to solve everything. You don't happen to have one in stock, do you?"

"A small miracle, the man says," Weinberg said cheerfully, rattling cups. He poured, dumped things on a tray, brought it over. Grall took the cup and sipped, then accepted the small plate with the slice of yellow-brown cake.

"Where do you get coffee?" he barked. "I thought the last stocks of luxury imports went last New Year."

"Try the nut cake. It's not too sweet."

Grall took a bite; it tasted good. He hadn't realized how hungry he was, but then he hadn't eaten in—how many hours?

"Like it?" Weinberg looked as expectant as a new bride serving her first meal.

"It's fine, Dick. But—"

"A small miracle, the man says," Weinberg repeated, rubbing his hands together. "Come this way, Andy. I want to show you something." The biologist led the way through a long room where half a dozen green-smocked technicians working over complicated constructions of glass tubing and containers of bubbling liquids looked up—expectantly, Grall thought. A sharp, burnt-toast odor filled the air. At the rear of the station Grall and Weinberg emerged on a sloping shelf of beach that led down to the waterline. Masses of dull brown scum lay in long windrows there. The surface of the sea was a dark brown, oily-looking with sluggish swells.

"You remember the problem I reported I was having with the slime formation," Weinberg said.

"I see it hasn't improved any," Grall said. "I hope it's not interfering seriously with your work."

"Fact is, Andy, I've about dropped everything to work on it. I think I've identified it as a mutated *Fuligo septica*, probably introduced on some imperfectly sterilized glassware from Terra. We tried high-pressure steam first, but—"

"Just a minute, Dick. Dropped everything?" Grall's voice was harsh. "Maybe I haven't succeeded in making it clear that the mission of finding food supplements for the Omegan diet is absolute top priority—"

Weinberg looked reproachfully at Grall. "Mr. Administrator, may I make my presentation?" His wide mouth quivered, the corners turning upward in spite of his obvious effort to hold them down.

"What the devil are you grinning at?"

"How did you like the coffee?"

"Drinkable," Galt snapped. "What—"

"It's made from the sporangia phase; the stalks, you understand, desiccated, ground, and roasted."

"You made coffee out of—this?" Grall prodded a mass of crusted brown flakes with his toe.

"Uh-huh. The cake was made from the spores, with an admixture of plasmodium, plus a little sweetener."

"Slime cake?" Grall said.

"Of course all this required a certain amount of processing. We're running some ideas in glass, looking for shortcuts—for commercial quantity-production, you understand. But with a little drying and compressing, we get what, unless I flunked Chem 1, is the best all-around livestock feed going." He took from his pocket a hard, dull-shiny, purple-brown cake the size of a bar of soap. "Hence the goats," he said. "And the chickens."

Grall stood as if stricken. "But—if this is true—" He took a deep breath and became brisk. "Fine. One miracle to order—" His voice broke and he cackled in glee. "Dick, you sneaky bastard, you just saved a world, damn your hide!"

"All in a day's work, Mr. Administrator—" Weinberg, grinning, was gazing past Grall toward the open desert to the west. "Well, more visitors," he said. "Word must've leaked out—"

Grall turned; a dust cloud was boiling toward them, raised by a speeding vehicle. The car swung past the station, slid to a halt near the storage sheds and was immediately veiled by the dust of its own passage.

"That looks like one of my maintenance carts," Grall said. "What—" There was a shout. A man at the lab door was waving.

"Call for you, Mr. Administrator. Sounds urgent."

Grall started toward the building, Weinberg behind him. Three men emerged from the dust cloud now blowing away from the car; they broke into a run on a course that would intercept Grall. Something bright flashed in the hand of the leader; the flat sound of a gun cut the air. Grall threw himself down. The man in the doorway started out; there was a second shot and the technician halted, turned, fell sideways. Grall looked up to see the second of the new arrivals knock the gunner's arm aside as he fired a third time, the slug whining past Grall's face.

"—alive," he heard. "We can always kill him later if it works out that way."

Grall got to his feet. Weinberg went to the man who had been shot, squatted beside him, ignoring an angry command from the man with the gun. He looked up, his face pale and bleak.

"Pat's dead," he said to no one in particular.

The third man stood with his two fellows, all three looking dusty and windblown, a bit uncertain now. The wind whined restlessly.

"You, Grall, over here," the gunner said. "You—addressing Weinberg—"stay out of the way and you won't get hurt."

Grall walked over to the trio. "Proud of yourself, Jonas?"

Jonas swore and swung at Grall, who casually knocked him down.

"Any guns inside?" Jonas called to Weinberg, scrambling up. "No."

"If you're lying, I'll kill you. Get the stuff," he said to his companions. "I don't want a stick left of this place to salvage."

The two went to the car, brought out packages Grall recognized as standard melt charges. They hurried toward the entrance to the station, went past the corpse sprawled on the sand, disappeared inside. An instant later there were screams; steam boiled from the entrance. A man ran out, tatters of what looked like wet gauze flapping from his face. He stumbled and went down, lay thrashing.

Weinberg came up, stood by Grall, breathing hard. Jonas reached for him, and Weinberg stamped backward in a short, sharp kick that snapped the assassin's knee. He sank down on his face in the sand.

Weinberg picked up the gun dropped by Jonas. Men were coming out of the station, one still holding the live steam hose.

"There's bad trouble back in the city," one of the men told Grall. "It was Mr. Halland on the box. He said you'd better get back right away."

· 17 ·

The hour was near dusk when the copter dropped Grall directly on the grounds of Admin House, bypassing the noisy crowd surrounding the building. Halland met him, looking grim.

"This isn't just the usual unrest, Andy," he said, "it's a concerted uprising. Mobs at the port, the Power Complex—" he broke off. "What happened to you?"

"I've had a sample. A demolition team hit the Marine Experimental Station and killed Pat Rogan. Weinberg is holding our old acquaintance Jonas—and a couple of others—in the vault."

Halland swore with feeling. "They tried to fire the Com Center about an hour ago. We saved it by the skin of our teeth. There are enough citizens on our side to make a standoff, but killing a noncombatant—"

"Let's get inside, Ben; I want a complete status report."

Halland finished his account twenty minutes later.

"That's about it. The best estimate is three hundred activists; another ten thousand going along for the ride, ready to jump either way. That's damn near a third of the city population. Opposed to them, we've got a hundred old guard with compound bows and blunt arrows and maybe two thousand volunteers with axe-handles and chair legs."

"Get some cots set up, Ben. It's going to be a long night."

"What do you plan to do, Andy?"

"Wait. Maybe by morning they'll have cooled down enough to talk sense to. I have some news for them." He outlined the gist of Weinberg's discovery.

"But this is what we've been waiting for, even praying for at odd moments," Halland said, running his fingers through his remaining hair. "Good Lord, Andy—this is the best news you could have brought—"

"But nobody out there's listening tonight. Relax, Ben. So far we're holding our own. Maybe this will tip things our way."

All through the night there were reports of fires, quickly quenched, roaming bands of slogan-shouting looters, clashes between vigilantes and demonstrators which petered out indecisively. The hours passed. Grall dozed. Pale light was filtering through the windows when he was awakened by a man who burst into the office.

"They've fired the library," he said. "A crowd of them got inside the kindergarten, too. Shall we try to hold it?"

"Let it go," Halland snapped. "We've got to concentrate on essential installations." He broke off. "Sorry, Andy. It's your decision, of course."

"I agree. What are they really after, Ben? What's their prime target?"

"What do you think?" Halland snapped. "Admin House. If they get in here—"

· 18 ·

A muffled explosion in the near distance punctuated the remark. Objects rattled on the desk. Somewhere there was a sound of breaking glass. Grall whirled to the window. Smoke was billowing from a point near the main gate, which was twisted off its mountings. Men came streaming through the opening in a ragged spearhead.

"Where are our militiamen?" Halland yelled and left the room at a run. Shouts sounded from downstairs, accompanied by heavy thuddings. Grall arrived in the foyer to find a dozen volunteer defenders, all of them smoke-smudged and bleeding from small cuts and abrasions, grouped behind the massively barred doors.

"They're starting to get rough," one of the men called. "They've got guns—a dozen of them anyway. God only knows where they got them. Nobody killed yet, far as I know, but that explosion they set off—"

The pounding at the heavy doors ceased abruptly. Voices could be heard beyond the heavy panels, shouting over the rumble of crowd noises.

"We're in a hopeless position," a man said. "We've done all we could—these hoodlums mean business. I say let's get out while we can."

"Dammit, you can't run away now—" Halland began.

"Go ahead, Jacobs," Grall cut in. "Anybody who wants to leave now, make it fast. Thanks for your help."

All but two of the volunteers departed hastily, some silently, some with apologies. A chant had started up outside the doors.

"What the devil are they shouting?" Halland said.

"Give-us-Grall!" the chant came through clearly in a momentary lull in the background roar. "Give-us-Grall!"

"The damned murderous swine," Halland cried. "Andy,

we've got to get you out of here. They want a scapegoat, some-body to blame—and you're elected."

Grall shook his head; he went up the stairs to the landing. From the narrow window there he could see the drama spread out before him: the ruined gate; the ragged crowd of rebels fanning out from it, forming a loose arc fifty feet from the steps; the packed mob beyond the walls, craning for a better look.

"Like ghouls watching a beheading," Halland said beside him. "Don't the damn fools know if these anarchists get inside it's all over for Colmar?"

"Don't blame them; they're just ordinary citizens caught in something outside their scope. They're waiting for leadership —any leadership." Grall glanced at Halland. "And if we can't give it to them, somebody else will." He pointed to the tall man standing front and center, with a bandoleer of cartridges slung over his shoulder, a heavy power rifle gripped in a brawny fist.

"A malcontent named Brauer," Halland said. "By God, if I had a gun—" He looked at Grall, dropped his eyes to the dress pistol in Grall's belt. "Let me borrow that, Andy," he said in a low, intense voice. "I can drop him in one shot."

Grall shook his head. "You know better than that, Ben."

"If killing one man will stop this—I say it's justified."

"I'd probably agree with you—if one killing would stop it. The fact is, we'd be giving them a martyr—shot from ambush. I think I know which way the crowd would go then." He turned and went back down the stairs.

"Open it up," he said to the two men waiting beside the big doors.

"Mr. Administrator, you can't surrender to that mob," one of the men blurted. "They'll skin you alive. That's all they want."

"Who's surrendering? Get that door open."

Over the protests of Halland, the men withdrew the locking bars and swung the portals wide. A sound went up from the crowd as Grall stepped out on the portico; it faded quickly as the big man named Brauer stepped forward. He stood for a moment fingering the rifle in his hands; then he turned and called over his shoulder: "Let's go; the rats are throwing in their hand."

He started forward, walking with a defiant swagger, all eyes on him. Those directly behind him followed. The crowd edged forward, more rioters sliding quickly in through the gate, spreading out. Brauer came on.

When he was six feet away, Grall flipped back his jacket to expose the pistol thrust into his belt; he dropped his hand to the butt. Brauer stopped dead. A number of expressions crossed his face: surprise, anger, determination. His eyes narrowed. The rifle in his hands started to come up.

"Throw that gun down or I'll put a bullet between your eyes, Brauer," Grall said quietly.

Brauer froze. He glanced at Grall's face, at his chin, his belt buckle.

"You crazy, Grall?" he asked. "Get out of my way—"

"Five seconds," Grall said.

"You want to get killed?" Brauer burst out.

"Four," Grall said. "three, two—"

With an oath, Brauer threw down the gun. A murmur went up from the crowd. A man behind Brauer started forward.

"Get back in line," Grall snapped. The man halted.

"Drop the bandoleer, Brauer," Grall ordered. Brauer complied. He looked up at Grall, his face slowly turning red.

"Come inside," Grall said. "I want to talk to you." The big man stood fast. "Move, I told you!" Grall snapped.

Brauer attempted a cocky smile, but it became a sickly grimace. He went up the steps.

Grall followed him inside. When he glanced back from the door, the crowd was already melting away.

"You can't get away with this," Brauer was saying. "We don't have to stand for this—"

"I think you will," Grall said.

"We've got rights!" Brauer yelled. "The power belongs to the people!"

"That's right," Grall said. "I agree you're under no obligation to support the government just because it's there."

"Well, then—" Brauer started.

"Certainly you have a right to revolt," Grall went on. "But that doesn't mean I'm under any obligation to let you get away with it."

· 20 ·

"What I can't understand," Halland said an hour later, after the militia had reported all quiet in the city, "is why you let him get so close before you stopped him."

"Simple," Grall said. "There's no power-cell in the pistol; hasn't been since Jaxon's administration." He smiled. "Brauer made the same mistake in judgment Brill did—they both let me get too close. And when we started talking—I had the better argument. Brauer agreed he would've made a lousy administrator." He yawned. "Tomorrow we'll announce Weinberg's discovery—and a new plan for Colmar's economy."

Editors' Note: It is of course common knowledge that Independence was formally recognized by the Terran Council in the year following Colmar's unilateral Declaration. Thus ends the First Phase of Colmar's history.